A
SHADOW
BRIGHT
AND
BURNING

A
SHADOW
BRIGHT
AND
BURNING

KINGDOM ON FIRE BOOK ONE

JESSICA CLUESS

Random House 🏠 New York

Text copyright © 2016 by Jessica Cluess
Jacket art copyright © 2016 by Hilts

All rights reserved. Published in the United States by Random House Children's Books, a division of Penguin Random House LLC, New York.

Random House and the colophon are registered trademarks of Penguin Random House LLC.

Visit us on the Web! randomhouseteens.com

Educators and librarians, for a variety of teaching tools, visit us at RHTeachersLibrarians.com

Library of Congress Cataloging-in-Publication Data
Names: Cluess, Jessica.
Title: A shadow bright and burning / Jessica Cluess.
Description: First edition. | New York : Random House, [2016] | Series: Kingdom on fire; book 1 | Summary: "When her unusual powers mark her as the one destined to lead the war against the seven Ancients, Henrietta trains to become the first female sorcerer in centuries—though the true nature of her ability threatens to be revealed"—Provided by publisher.
Identifiers: LCCN 2015014593 | ISBN 978-0-553-53590-7 (hardcover) | ISBN 978-0-553-53591-4 (lib. bdg.) | ISBN 978-0-553-53592-1 (ebook)
Subjects: | CYAC: Fantasy. | Magic—Fiction.
Classification: LCC PZ7.1.C596 Sh 2016 | DDC [Fic]—dc23
LC record available at http://lccn.loc.gov/2015014593

Printed in the United States of America
10 9 8 7 6 5 4 3 2 1
First Edition

Random House Children's Books supports the
First Amendment and celebrates the right to read.

FOR ANGELO CLUESS,
WHO SHOWED ME WHAT DETERMINATION LOOKS LIKE

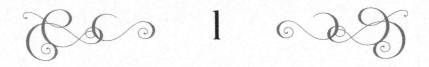

1

THE SORCERER ARRIVED ON A SATURDAY.

Sarah, barely six years old, squeezed my hand as we walked the school corridors toward the headmaster's parlor. I'd allowed her to wear her gray cloak indoors because the morning fires hadn't yet been laid. Fog pressed in against the high windows, darkening the stone hall. For Sarah's sake, I kept a smile on my face. My fear could not win today.

"Will he beat me, Henrietta? I mean, Miss Howel?" She often forgot to use my last name, but I'd only become a teacher two months before. Sometimes when I stood at the head of the classroom to give a lesson, I'd look at the empty place on the student bench where I used to sit, and feel like a fraud.

"A sorcerer would never harm children," I said, squeezing her hand in return. Granted, I'd never met a sorcerer, but Sarah didn't need to know that.

She smiled and sighed. How simple to reassure her. How difficult to reassure myself, for why would a royal sorcerer travel to Yorkshire for an audience with a child? Was the war against the Ancients going so poorly that he needed young girls, armed with sewing needles and a little French, for the front lines?

No. He had heard about the fires.

We entered the parlor to find two men seated before the hearth, sipping their tea. This was the only heated room in the entire school, and I rubbed my numb fingers in appreciation. Sarah raced past the men to warm her hands and, embarrassingly, her backside before the fireplace.

"Miss Howel!" our headmaster snapped, leaping up from his chair. "Control that child at once."

I motioned Sarah back to me, and we curtsied together.

"Good day, Mr. Colegrind," I murmured. Colegrind was a pale, hook-nosed gentleman with gray whiskers and a gray personality. When I was five, he'd terrified me. Now that I was sixteen, I found him repulsive.

He frowned. "Why does Sarah wear her cloak?"

"The fires haven't been lit, sir," I said, stating what should have been bloody obvious. Dreadful man. "I didn't want her shivering before our illustrious guest." Colegrind sniffed. I gave him my least sincere smile.

The other man, who had been surveying our scene with a cup of tea, rose to his feet.

"It's all right," the sorcerer said. "Little girls must keep warm." He knelt before Sarah. "How are you, my dear?"

This man couldn't be a sorcerer. I'd always pictured the royal Order as being filled with humorless men who wore simple robes and smelled of cabbage water. This gentleman was more like a grandfather from a storybook, with a shock of curling salt-and-pepper hair, dimpled cheeks, and warm brown eyes.

He swept off his cape, trimmed with sable fur, and wrapped it around Sarah. She hugged herself.

"There, now," he said. "Just the right fit." He nodded to me. "You're very good to take such care of her."

I lowered my eyes. "Thank you, sir," I mumbled. As he stood, I noticed something hanging in a sheath by his side. It was the length of a sword, but it had to be his sorcerer's stave, the great instrument of his power. I'd heard of such things but never glimpsed one. I gasped without thinking.

Agrippa patted the handle. "Would you like to see it?" he asked.

Bloody fool, I was supposed to be *unnoticeable* today. For once, I was grateful for Colegrind's interruption.

"Master Agrippa," Colegrind said, "shall we proceed?"

The sorcerer guided Sarah to a chair while I remained by the wall, invisible as always. Schoolteachers don't stand out naturally, and I was far too thin and dark-haired to make much of an impact. Granted, I didn't want to stand out to Agrippa today, not if he'd come about the fires. I exhaled, praying that my heartbeat would slow. Please say that he had come for some other reason. The scenery, the terrible April weather, *anything*.

The sorcerer produced a toffee from his coat and handed it to Sarah. While she munched, Agrippa took a lit candle and held it before her. The flame flickered. Grabbing a fistful of my skirt, I squeezed to distract myself. I wouldn't be afraid, because fear often summoned the . . .

I wouldn't be afraid.

"Think of the flame," Agrippa whispered. "Think of fire."

No. As if responding to the sorcerer's words, my body grew warm, desperately warm. I slipped my hands behind my back, knotted my fingers together, and prayed.

Sarah was clearly doing her best to be helpful, thinking so hard that her face turned bright red. The candle did nothing in response.

"Don't lie," Colegrind ordered Sarah. "If you hide anything, Master Agrippa will know. Do you want him to think you a bad girl?"

A bad girl. That was whom they hunted. Eleven years earlier, girls with magic would've been tolerated. Now, my God, only death awaited them. Awaited *me*. I curled my toes in my shoes, bit my tongue until my eyes watered. My fingers burned so badly. . . .

"Look at the flame!" Colegrind said.

I pressed my palms against the cold stone wall. I thought of freezing things, like snow and ice. Hold on. Hold on. . . .

Sarah burst into tears. Between Colegrind's cruelty and my own physical pain, I snapped. "There's no need to make her cry."

The men turned. Agrippa raised his eyebrows in surprise. Colegrind looked as if he'd like to strike me down where I stood. With a sorcerer present, he'd have to contain himself, though after Agrippa left, I suspected I'd feel the headmaster's birch cane. Beatings were his favorite form of exercise. But the burning eased somewhat, so my outburst had been worth it.

Agrippa said, "Miss Howel is right. There's no need to fret,

Sarah." He shushed her crying and waved his hand above the candle. He collected the fire into his palm, where it hovered mere inches above his skin. He then took his stave—it was a plain wooden staff, quite ordinary-looking—and pointed it at the flame. Concentrating, he made the fire dance and swirl into different shapes before extinguishing it with one deft movement. Mouth open in astonishment, Sarah applauded wildly, her tears forgotten.

"You're all done," Agrippa said, giving her another toffee. Sarah took it and ran from the room as fast as she could. Fortunate child.

"I apologize for the inexcusable outbursts, Master Agrippa," Colegrind said, glaring at me. "At the Brimthorn School for Girls, we try to curb female waywardness and insolence."

He could try to curb me all he liked. But right now that was the least of my worries. My hands were beginning to burn again.

"I find a dash of insolence to be quite enjoyable from time to time." Agrippa smiled at me. "Would you be so kind as to bring me the next girl, my dear? I will be testing every child at this school."

If he was testing all thirty-five of them, he *had* to be searching for a witch. I groaned inwardly.

"Of course. I'll return shortly." I left the room, breaking into a run. I had to get outside. Pushing through the front door, I raced out the yard and up the hill. Just a few more steps and I'd be hidden from sight.

I collapsed to my knees as the fire spilled from my hands.

Blue flames tickled my outstretched palms. I closed my eyes and sighed as I grabbed fistfuls of the damp grass.

Colegrind and Master Agrippa couldn't know, not ever. Female magic—witchcraft—was criminal, and the sentence, death. As the flames slowed and sparks glinted off my fingertips, I felt someone sit behind me.

"There's a sorcerer from the royal Order here to test the girls," I told Rook, without turning around. Only my dearest friend would react with nonchalance when my hands were burning. Smoke hissed out from between my fingers. "He's looking for the one starting the fires."

"This is why you should only unleash it out on the moor. I've told you," he said.

"I don't always have that luxury, you know." If my temper got the best of me, if something startled me, if Colegrind did something particularly loathsome, the fire would come upon me. I could never control it for long.

"The sorcerer won't test you, will he?" Rook leaned his back to mine.

"As a teacher I'm spared, thank heavens. Can anyone down there see us?" I was fairly safe here, but not as far away as I'd have liked. If someone came up the hill unexpectedly, it wouldn't end well.

"Not with me sitting around and ignoring my work." I could tell from his tone that he was smiling. "Whoever looks up here will only find me."

"Thank you," I whispered, nudging his arm. "I should get back. They've more girls to test."

"Think of the cold," Rook said as he rose and helped me to my feet. His left hand gripped mine tightly, and he winced.

"Do your scars hurt?" I asked, pressing a hand to his chest. I could imagine the older teachers clucking at my "forward" behavior, but we'd known each other since we were children. Granted, Rook *was* attractive, with sharp, elegant features and blue eyes. His hair was still the same flaxen down it had been when we were eight. He looked like a poet or a gentleman, I'd always thought, even if he was only a stable boy. But most people would turn away from Rook, for all his beauty, if they knew what he kept hidden beneath his shirt.

The scars were terrible. They weren't visible, as he took care to button himself up, but they were there. Most who suffer an Ancient's attack die. Rook had been one of the lucky few to survive, but he'd paid dearly for his life.

"Bit more painful than usual. You know how bad it gets in damp weather," he said. As if in response, thunder rumbled in the distance.

"Meet me after the girls are tested," I said. "I'll bring the paste."

"You know how to make a fellow happy, Nettie." He nodded, his eyes serious. "Be careful."

"Always," I said, and returned to the school.

Two hours later I knelt in the empty parlor. Tears filled my eyes as the cane landed across the back of my neck. *Fifteen, sixteen, seventeen,* I counted. Three to go. I pictured banks of snow in winter. Thankfully, I'd gotten through the rest of the students' tests with only an occasional flush of heat. *Twenty.* A warm trickle of blood ran down my neck and into my collar. I tried to rise to my feet, but Colegrind gripped my shoulder and kept me in place. Damn him.

"You were a wayward child, Henrietta. Do not allow your passions to lead you astray as a young woman." I stifled a shudder as Colegrind's hand trailed across my back. He'd taken to "noticing" me in such ways these past three years. Disgusting man.

"Yes, sir," I said automatically. It was the single acceptable answer to Colegrind's tirades. A slow heat prickled my palms. If only I could loose my anger and show him the response he deserved, but that was an insane thought. As I got to my feet, Agrippa entered the room.

"Beg pardon," he said, and stopped. His eyes flicked to Colegrind's cane, to me. I put a hand to the back of my neck to hide the marks, but I could tell he understood. His next words were cold and clipped. "Mr. Colegrind, there seems to be confusion with my carriage."

"The servants are useless," Colegrind said, as though we should pity him.

"Perhaps you might see to it yourself, then." That was an order dressed as a request. Colegrind tightened his jaw, on the verge of talking back, and then thought better of it. He left, grumbling to himself. Agrippa came toward me, concern written on his face.

"Are you all right?"

He spoke so kindly that I felt tears forming at the corners of my eyes. I nodded and began neatening the room.

"Mr. Colegrind's angry that we didn't find the one starting the fires," I said, placing a chair against the wall. "It's been a hard three years for him. He was certain the culprit would be discovered." I felt a twinge of pride; the old fool was disappointed again.

"Has it really been going on for three years?"

"Oh yes. Mostly it's been patches of fire around the stables, but several of the headmaster's favorite coats have met 'accidental' deaths." I worked to keep glee out of my voice. "I would give you a list of those who dislike Mr. Colegrind, but I fear that wouldn't narrow your search. I knew it was bold to speak this way, but Agrippa laughed. "How did you hear of us, sir?"

"My Order keeps its collective ear to the ground for cases like these," he said. I turned to look at him. He seemed to be choosing his words with care.

"Cases of witchcraft?" I nearly stumbled over the word.

"In a sense."

"What you did with the fire was brilliant," I said, straightening a corner of the rug. "I mean, putting on that show for Sarah."

Agrippa laughed. "I appreciate a good audience." The rain became a dim roar on the roof. I winced as I listened to it. "Really, are you all right?" Agrippa asked, noticing my reaction.

"They say that rain usually brings Familiars with it. Or, heaven forbid, one of the Ancients."

At this, Agrippa sobered and nodded. "There's nothing to fear. The only Ancient who favors this weather is Korozoth, and he's near London at present."

Korozoth, the great Shadow and Fog. They called him the fiercest warrior of all the Seven Ancients. "Have you ever fought him?" Thoughts of Agrippa rising into the air against a giant black cloud flashed through my mind, as thrilling a picture as I could create.

"On several occasions. This doesn't frighten you?" He said it with a laugh. I'd sat down in a chair, entranced.

"No. I always want news of how the war's progressing." I knew I should wish him a speedy departure, but my curiosity got the better of me. I'd spent countless childhood evenings awake in my bed, watching shadows and moonlight form images on the ceiling. I'd imagined them as monsters, pictured myself meeting them in battle. Miss Morris, the head teacher, had sniffed and informed me how *unfeminine* those dreams were.

"How old were you when the Ancients arrived?" Agrippa said as he took a seat opposite me.

"Five." I remembered hiding under the bed when the news first came, listening as my aunt shrieked orders to our maid. We had to pack only what we needed, she said, because we must travel by nightfall. Clutching my doll to my chest, I whispered that I would protect us. Now I nearly laughed to think of it. My doll, my aunt, my old life in Devon—all had vanished.

"You've never seen one of the Ancients, have you?" Agrippa asked, returning me to the present.

"No. I'm grateful, mind, but I've always wondered if it was normal. Perhaps the beasts have no interest in Yorkshire's natural splendor." I rolled my eyes. Outside, it sounded as if the rain were drowning the countryside. We'd have *such* delightful mud. Agrippa laughed.

"It's true, the Ancients focus their attention on cities. It costs them more effort, but the reward is greater. And, of course, Brimthorn falls under the protection of Sorrow-Fell lands, which makes it difficult for our enemies to access."

"Yes, indeed." Sorrow-Fell was a great magical estate and the seat of the Blackwood family, a line of powerful sorcerers. We kept Lord Blackwood in our daily prayers, though we'd never seen him. "Do you know the family?"

"The earl boards at my house, for his studies. He's about your age, actually." I started, surprised that a young man of sixteen could be so distinguished. Agrippa smiled. "Shall I tell you of London society? The balls and parties, the fashion and intrigue?"

"No, thank you. I'd rather hear more about the Ancients." Agrippa made an incredulous noise. I blushed. "Knowledge of them is useful. I want to be useful."

"You're a teacher. What's more useful than educating young minds?"

"I'm no good at a charity school. My strengths are history and mathematics." I sighed to recall my teachers' displeasure at my obvious gifts in those more practical areas. I was practical, indeed, but like a *man,* not a woman. My thoughts were orderly, but I was unyielding. I wanted to argue my opinions, not conciliate others. "Most of the girls here require only reading and sewing, while the more promising ones study French so they may become governesses. And when they're governesses, they teach girls to play other people's music and copy other people's sketches. It sometimes feels as though young women are trained from birth never to contribute anything original to a conversation." I flushed with embarrassment. My tongue had got the better of me, and Agrippa was regarding me with a look of some interest. "I shouldn't have bored you with my thoughts."

"They're not boring. You remind me of a young lady I used to know." He gave a sad smile.

Colegrind returned, soaked to the skin. "Your carriage is ready," he said with somber dignity, then turned and walked from the room, his shoes leaking with every step. Agrippa chuckled and shook his head.

I liked this man. I wished I didn't have to fear him.

THE RAIN HAD STOPPED BY THE time we walked outside. Agrippa and I waited by the doorway while the men brought the carriage forward, careful not to get its wheels trapped in the mud. As we stood there, I found myself humming a soft singsong tune.

"What is that?" Agrippa asked.

"An old schoolyard chant about the Ancients. I suppose our conversation brought it back to me." It took a moment to recall the words, and then I sang,

"Seven are the Ancients, seven are the days,
Monday for R'hlem, the Skinless Man,
On-Tez on Tuesday, the old Vulture Lady,
Callax is Wednesday, the Child Eater,
Zem the Great Serpent crisps Thursday with his breath,
On Friday fear Korozoth, the Shadow and Fog,
Never sail on Saturday says Nemneris the Water Spider,
And rain on Sunday brings Molochoron the Pale Destroyer."

When I'd finished, Agrippa applauded.

"Very nice," he said. "Not much of a rhyme, though."

"It was less about the song and more about chasing each other," I said. Agrippa laughed and was summoned to his coach. He kissed my hand.

"Farewell, Miss Howel. It was a pleasure."

Though I should've been glad to see him depart, a queer sort of sadness descended on me. I watched until his carriage vanished up the road into a bank of fog. Only then did I go down to the kitchen to prepare Rook's paste.

As I struggled to remember ingredients and mash herbs, I cursed my subpar potion making. Most witches were skilled herbalists. If I must live in fear for my life, why couldn't I have helpful magical powers? I wished I'd had a mother to teach me. Bother that, I wished I'd had a mother for anything. Finished, I ran outside and down the lane toward the moor.

Even weighted by my stays and heavy skirts, I loved racing through the pale purple-and-white heather. The hills rolled and crested around me, and I soon arrived at the meeting place, an outcropping of dark gray stone on the heath. Rook and I had discovered it years ago, during a failed attempt to run away.

Rook sat beneath an overhang of rock, rubbing his eyes. His left arm hung limp in his lap. Damn. His suffering must've been worse than he'd let on.

"I have the paste. How bad is it?" I knelt beside him.

"Oh, I'd call it bad," he said. His voice didn't break, but I could tell by the tense line of his jaw that he was in terrible pain. He attempted to slide off his jacket without upsetting his left arm.

"Let me help." After removing the jacket, shirt, and cotton vest beneath, I inspected a body that was lean and hardened from work.

A body covered in scars.

Rook was Unclean, wounded by one of the Ancients. Great circular scars like suction marks, still an angry and swollen red these many years later, covered the left side of his chest. They decorated his collarbone like some obscene necklace and ran down his back and left arm. Sometimes, when the pain was extreme, his hand would go rigid and his fingers would curl into his palm. Korozoth himself had mutilated my friend during an attack on a camp of brick makers. The soldiers who'd rescued Rook brought him to shelter at Brimthorn, thinking he'd be dead by morning. Eight years later, and that morning hadn't come.

I rubbed the paste into his palm, kneading the skin until his fingers loosened. I straightened them out, ignoring his hissed intakes of breath at the pain. Within a few minutes, his hand relaxed. Rook closed his eyes in relief.

"Thank you," he murmured, clasping my hand in his. Slowly, I twined our fingers together.

"Your grip is still strong," I said, smiling. When I reached to touch his chest, he flinched.

"You needn't help me more than necessary. I'm in your debt enough as it is." He often shied from my touch these days. It made me feel clumsy and perverse, as if I should be repulsed by his scars when I wasn't at all.

"Let's look at your back," I grumbled. Dabbing at the paste, I sat behind him and gasped.

Besides the scars, long red welts blazed on his skin. Someone had struck him with a birch cane.

"Bastard," I hissed as I tried to soothe the wounds.

"It was my own fault," Rook said. "I wasn't able to help with the horses. Colegrind had to come out and see to it himself."

"Of course you're slow when the scars flare up. He should know that by now."

"I don't want special treatment," Rook said, his voice firm. I held my tongue and worked quickly. Finished, I laid my hand on his back.

"Movement should be easier now," I said.

"Oh yes." He sighed, shifting beneath my hand. "God knows what I would do in this world without you, Nettie."

"Stop calling me Nettie, Rook." I smiled. This was an age-old battle. A terrible childhood nickname, Nettie made me sound like an old lady or a hen.

"Have to call you Nettie, Nettie." I felt him laugh. "You can't break with tradition, as Colegrind tells us." Rook leaned away from me and took up his vest. With a grunt, he began to pull it over his head. I held back, knowing he'd be cross if I tried to help now. "The sorcerer's gone?"

"Yes. That was far too close." Unladylike as it was, I flopped onto my back and stared up at the sky.

"Even if you are a witch, it's not as though you're Mary Willoughby herself." Rook sighed, lying down beside me. "She's dead and gone."

"Her legacy isn't, though." For thousands of years, witches had existed on the fringe of society. They were known as strange women, a bit dangerous if you weren't careful, but they'd mostly lived in peace. That all changed when a witch named Mary Willoughby opened up a portal between worlds and summoned the Ancients, starting this long, bloody war. I remembered a book I'd had when I was ten, *A Child's History of the Ancients*. In it, there was a picture of a lady with wild black hair and insane eyes, her hands raised to a stormy sky. *Mary Willoughby, the worst woman in the kingdom,* the caption read.

"She was burned," I said. "All witches are burned." If Agrippa had found me out . . . well, I actually couldn't be burned, could I? He would have to be creative with my death. Lord, what an unsettling thought.

"Seems un-Christian, don't it? Burning people alive."

"Especially when you consider she had help," I said.

"Yes, from the magician." Rook smiled as I sat up in surprise. "You taught me to read with that old Ancients book, remember? Howard Mickelmas. He helped open the gate. Never caught him, did they?"

"No, magicians are tricky by nature." Magicians were filthy beasts, full of deception. *Everyone* knew that. At least witches had an air of tragic nobility about them.

"Why d'you think they burn one kind and not the other?" Rook said. "Why aren't magicians killed, too?"

This conversation was doing nothing for my nerves. Brushing the whole topic aside, I stood and walked around the rock, clutching my shawl. Rook joined me.

"I don't want to worry about magic any longer," I said, standing in the road. All around us was silence, except the wind sighing through the heather. Awful as Brimthorn was, one could never match Yorkshire for moments of grand solitude. Rook and I were alone, save for a traveler on horseback in the distance. "I want to think about the shop we're going to open."

"It'll be in Manchester, or maybe Canterbury," Rook said, going along with the old game. "We should open a bookshop, with all the books bound in old leather."

"I think that's the most glorious smell, a library of old books," I said. Apart from Rook, my only good memories of Brimthorn consisted of hours reading in a favored window seat. Colegrind, bad as he was, had at least been generous with his personal library. One summer, I'd gone through *Le Morte d'Arthur* three times. My favorite moment had to be when Arthur pulled the sword from the stone, transforming from commoner to king in one instant.

Rook shook his head. "Granted, we can't move to Canterbury. The Vulture Lady lives on the cathedral." He was right. On-Tez, one of the Ancients, had ruled the city for the past three years. She was a large, hideous beast with the body of a filthy carrion bird and the head of an insane old woman. The name Vulture Lady suited her rather well.

"One day she'll be gone, and we'll sell books and anything else we want. Now, what shall we call our shop?" I asked. Rook didn't respond. I nudged him. "Don't say you can't think of anything." Rook moved away from me down the road, hands in his pockets. Surprised, I walked beside him. "What's wrong?"

"The shop is a story we told ourselves when we were younger," he said, looking at me. "You could have been a governess in a good house by now, with better food and pay. Why haven't you tried for a position yet?"

Lord, not this argument again. "I'll apply when I want to, but I don't want to right now."

"Why not?"

"Because I might set fire to the master's drapes," I said, rolling my eyes. "Besides, I can't just . . ." I bit my tongue, but Rook caught on.

"Can't what?" His jaw was set, his eyes hard.

"Leave you," I said, wincing as I waited for his reaction.

He stopped us in the road. "Nettie, I don't want you to ever keep yourself low because of me."

"You're being silly," I snapped, wrapping my shawl tight around my shoulders. "I'm going home." With that, I turned and walked off the road at a brisk pace, tramping across the moor. I waited to hear Rook's footsteps, but he didn't follow me. I stopped, exasperated. "Are you planning to live out here?"

Rook remained on the road. He faced the traveler on horseback, who was only about a half mile away now. Something about Rook's stillness was unsettling. I hurried back to him.

"Are you all right? Do the scars still hurt?" I asked, gripping his shoulder. Instantly, he crumpled to the ground, groaning in pain. When I touched him, he shuddered. Panicking, I hooked my arm with his and tried once, twice to get him back on his feet. I pulled so hard I lost my balance and fell beside him in the dirt.

Had the paste I'd given him been bad? There was no response when I shook him.

"Rook?" I whispered. The sound of hooves brought up my head. The traveler had arrived. Relieved, I started to ask for help.

When I glimpsed what had found us, the words died in my mouth. Terror made me mute.

The traveler didn't ride a horse at all. The creature was a black stag with thick, gnarled antlers and glowing red eyes. As it snorted, sparks flew from its snout. The stag opened its mouth in a hideous cry. Its teeth were jagged, designed for tearing flesh.

The rider wore a hooded, mistlike cloak that whispered about his body. He stank of the grave. Slowly, the hood peeled away from his face. I gasped and shrank back.

A young woman, not a man. She was scarce older than I. Her once-fair hair had thinned and gone nearly white, clinging to her scalp in filthy clumps. And her eyes—dear heaven, her eyes—had been sewn shut with a crude black thread. But even without sight, she appeared to know where I was. She stopped her stag right before us. Licking her lips with a thick, wolfish tongue, she leaned down toward me.

"Death," she croaked, scenting the wind like an animal. "Death tonight."

The air exploded with the sound of hooves.

2

THREE MORE SHRIEKING RIDERS ON BLACK STAGS plummeted from the sky, landing in a circle around us. The monsters closed in, unsheathing black daggers. Rook sat up straight, mercifully coming back to his senses. He shoved me behind him, away from the creatures.

The eyeless girl leaned toward him from her stag, yellowed teeth bared in a grimace.

"The Shadow's chosen," she whispered to her brethren. "He is ours."

The Shadow had to be Korozoth. These were Familiars, humans transformed into servants of the Seven Ancients.

Rook lifted his head so I could see his face. His eyes had gone pure black. When he opened his mouth to speak, all he emitted was a terrible screech. It was the sound a damned soul might make in the fires of hell. I covered my ears, shaking as I listened. When the shadowy Familiar reached to pull him onto her mount, my palms grew boiling hot.

I thrust my hands forward, and fire billowed out of me. The girl managed to pull away before I could scorch her. She growled and reached for Rook again.

"Don't touch him!" I cried. Panic set me in full, furious motion. They would *not* have us. Screaming, I thrust my hands out, blasting again and again. This time I caught one of the other riders as it tried to rise into the air. The rider and stag fell to the ground, hissing and screeching as they burned. Their screams died with them, and charred bits of the monsters floated away on the wind.

It was like opening a cage in my chest to free some wild creature. The power rushed out of me. The harder I pushed, the more it gave. I closed my eyes in one moment of pure joy.

I was so blissful that I forgot to protect my back. A Familiar gripped me by my hair. Rook grabbed my waist and tore me out of the creature's grip. I grunted in pain as Rook shielded me with his body, his arms raised to the sky. The eyeless girl hovered there like a phantom, snarling, with her long dagger poised to strike.

"We have to go." Rook pulled me to my feet.

We ran, and the monsters gave chase. They raced through the air, cackling as they spurred on their mounts in the hunt. When I felt them get too close, I risked a glance back and launched a volley of fire behind me. The flames did not come as quickly as before; sometimes there were only sparks. I'd used too much. My breath sounded ragged, and I tripped on my skirt. All we needed was to make it to Brimthorn. The men in the stables would be enough to hold the monsters while we got the children to safety.

We were almost there. One last hill and we'd be within sight of the school, but the riders were at our heels. As we neared the top, Rook lost his footing and slammed down, taking me with him. I howled as my shoulder caught the ground and pain knifed through me. When I rolled onto my back and summoned the fire, there was nothing.

I tried once, twice, but my hands were numb. I couldn't even draw breath for a scream as the Familiars leaped out of the sky, daggers prepared for a killing blow.

A cold wind blasted out of the west, scattering the riders. Master Agrippa stood at the crest of the hill, cape billowing in the breeze, his sorcerer's stave held out before him. He jerked his head, ordering us to move.

"You came back! How did you know?" I gasped as we staggered up the hill. I wanted to fall at his feet in relief.

Agrippa nodded toward the horizon. The dark clouds boiled in the air. "This is no ordinary storm. Get to the school. Now."

The riders regrouped and shot toward us, forcing Agrippa to attack. The sorcerer moved more quickly than I'd have thought possible for a man his age. He slashed toward the monsters, using his stave like a sword. Wind battered the creatures until he'd forced them down the hill. Agrippa made a fast, whipping motion and slammed his stave to the ground. The earth itself rose up, formed a wall several feet high, and sped toward the Familiars. They fell beneath the muddy onslaught and rolled to the bottom, lying so still that I prayed they'd died.

I watched, transfixed, as Agrippa advanced slowly. I'd always wanted to see a sorcerer fight. I looked over at Rook, who had his hands pressed tight to the sides of his head. His eyes remained a terrifying black. My stomach tightened, and I put my arm around him.

"We should get to shelter," I whispered.

Agrippa's yell made me look down the hill. He lay on his back, arm shielding his face. He'd dropped his stave, and one of the Familiars had kicked it out of his reach. The eyeless girl stood over him, cocking her head at different angles. Agrippa seemed frozen. He wasn't fighting. With a grunt, the Familiar lifted her dagger into the air while her two companions held back and bobbed around her. They were letting her have this kill.

I dug my hands into the earth. I could distract the Familiars with my ability, but if I did . . . if Agrippa survived and knew what I was . . .

Rook got to his feet and picked up a rock. Running down the hill, he threw it and struck the eyeless rider on the side of her head, knocking her down. Her monstrous friends rushed to tend to her. This gave Agrippa enough time to roll over and grab his stave. Rook shuddered and collapsed.

The eyeless rider leaped back to her feet, dagger still in hand. Agrippa wasn't her focus any longer. She turned toward Rook, now lying helpless. With a sneer, she sprang and caught him by the back of his shirt. He fought her, but his movements were slow. The blackness was overtaking him. Agrippa tried to get to them but was caught fighting off the other two monsters. The eyeless Familiar whistled for her stag.

She was going to take Rook away.

"No," I whispered, getting to my feet. Gritting my teeth, I ran forward, my skin hotter than ever before. Fury stoked something deep inside. Power flooded me.

"Miss Howel, wait!" Agrippa cried.

"No!" I screamed. My whole body ignited.

The fire engulfed me, rippling over my clothes, my face, shooting out from my hands. Every inch of my skin tingled, and the blood in my veins seemed to hum. The world fell away around me, until all I could see or feel was fire. The column of blue flame swirled above me while the Familiars wailed. Grass sizzled as I advanced on the eyeless girl, still struggling to pull Rook onto her stag. She bared her teeth and groaned low in her throat. If I touched her now, I somehow knew I'd kill Rook as well. But I'd sooner see him dead than let her take him to God knows where. He would do the same for me.

"Let him go," I said, "or I will kill you."

She ran a tongue over her cracked lips, deciding. Then, slowly, she released Rook. He dropped to the ground and lay there. The girl turned for one last look at Agrippa, then spurred her stag and took off into the sky. The others joined her. They galloped away, spitting and crying into the storm. When they'd vanished, I felt my whole body relax. The fire died at once. Dark spots danced before my vision. My hands felt numb. But I'd done it.

My joy was short-lived as Agrippa pointed at me.

"You," he said. "It's you." He didn't sound friendly.

I turned to run. But the moment I stepped forward, the last energy fled my body. I collapsed into the mud, where darkness took me.

I STOOD BEFORE A FIREPLACE, TRYING to warm my hands. It didn't work. With a sigh, I studied the pictures on the mantel. Small, exquisitely detailed portraits of a man and a woman. The man had hair and skin as dark as my own, so dark some would mistake him for a gypsy. The woman was soft and fair as a rose petal.

My father and mother. I never knew them. Father drowned in a boating accident before I was born. Mother perished in childbirth. My aunt Agnes took me into her home, this home. These were the pictures she wouldn't allow me to take to Brimthorn. Why couldn't I have them? They were my parents, after all.

My thin, hollow-eyed aunt appeared beside me. She looked the same now as she had eleven years before, when she'd first brought me to school. The last time I'd seen her.

"Henrietta, you overspent yourself. Your powers must be governed. Do you understand me?" Odd. She spoke with Master Agrippa's voice.

"Yes," I replied.

"Horrid child," she snapped. Now she sounded much more like my aunt. She leaned in. "You are a horrid child."

"No." I tried to leave. She grabbed me, pulled me close to her as I struggled. She opened her mouth wide, wider, then wider still. I screamed as I disappeared into the void of her mouth, and Agrippa's voice came out of the blackness to whisper:

"I've waited for you."

I WOKE IN A SMALL, DARK room. A candle burned on the table beside me. Head spinning, I found my feet and staggered to the door. Locked. There was a barred window at my eye level. Peering out, I glimpsed a dim stone corridor.

This was a prison cell, probably where condemned witches were housed before being taken out to be executed. Agrippa had seen my fire.

I was going to die. At that moment, with my wretched head throbbing, I took that thought as a comfort. I returned to the bed and closed my eyes.

Someone cleared his throat, and I bolted upright. Looking about in a panic, I glimpsed two pointed ear tips sticking slightly over the edge of the bed. With a wheezing sound, a tiny creature climbed up the mattress and stood beside me.

Perhaps I'd already died and been damned to hell; the demon before me was ugly as sin. Its long, twitching ears were rabbit-like, but the rest of the beast resembled a bat more than anything. It scratched its ears with two hands and then *brought two more hands out from behind its back* to rummage in its coat pockets.

Yes, the demon wore a coat, a purple coat with a blue silk cravat. It retrieved a glass vial filled with shining liquid from its pocket and tossed it to me. In my hands, it was no larger than a thimble.

"Now," it said in a high-pitched voice, "drink that."

"Have I died?" I closed a shaking hand around the vial.

The thing snorted. "Yes, of course. You died, and I'm giving you medicine to keep you dead." It folded its ears together and down its back in annoyance. "What does Cornelius think you can do for us?"

"Who is Cornelius?"

"Cornelius Agrippa. Who are you?"

"Henrietta Howel. *What* exactly are you?" Lord, if only my head weren't pounding.

"I'm a hobgoblin, cherub. My name is Fenswick." He bowed, his four arms outstretched in a showy display. "Her Majesty lent me to aid the Order in this war."

"Queen Victoria owns hobgoblins?"

"No one owns me, and certainly not any Victoria. I serve Queen Mab of the dark Faerie court, but doubtless you've never met her. Now, drink your potion."

Faerie queens. Hobgoblins. I'd gone absolutely mad.

"Where's Master Agrippa?" I rubbed my forehead and gasped. "Where's Rook?"

"See here," Fenswick snapped as I tossed the blankets onto his head. I threw the silver vial to smash on the floor, the world spinning before me. Falling to one knee, I caught myself, then stood and ran to bang on the door. My legs buckled.

"Rook! Help me! Rook!" I cried. Footsteps sounded in the corridor, and someone unlocked the door. I stepped back as Agrippa entered the room, one hand raised as if to calm me.

"All is well, Miss Howel. Please sit," he said.

"Where am I? What've you done with him?" I took a faulty

step backward and collapsed. The bundle that was Fenswick slid off the bed with a grunt. Agrippa took a chair. The door closed again, and I heard the lock turn. "It's not my fault." I was nearly in hysterics. "I didn't choose to be this way."

"Enough now." He sounded gentle, understanding. I didn't trust it.

"I'm no follower of Mary Willoughby!" I said. My head threatened to split in two. "I didn't choose to be a witch. I don't want to die!"

"I'm not going to kill you," he said, his tone soothing. I wouldn't believe him. I couldn't.

"Where is Rook?"

"He's all right. He's waiting below."

"Is he a prisoner, too?" I gripped the side of the bed. "He's not responsible for any of this."

"You're not prisoners, neither of you. And you're not a witch, either, Miss Howel," Agrippa said. He smiled, bemused and, as far as I could tell, delighted. "You're a sorcerer."

Whatever I had been about to say was lost. My mouth hung open, but no words escaped. I blinked. Agrippa might as well have said *You are a lost Babylonian princess* or *You are a rare species of cod*. Both made as much sense as my being . . . I couldn't even think the word. While I sat there, Fenswick extricated himself from the blankets and stomped over to Agrippa.

"You don't want this one," he said, waving his four arms at me. "I can't believe you had me travel all the way from London through the Undergrowth just to see to a dangerous psychotic.

As if it's easy getting to Yorkshire in no time flat. I hate traveling through Faerie. It's too easy to lose your way."

"Doctor, perhaps you'd grant Miss Howel and me some privacy? I've a feeling I'll need to answer some questions." Agrippa watched me, judging my reaction.

"Very well," Fenswick said with exaggerated dignity. He flicked a piece of lint from his sleeve, walked under the bed, and did not come out again.

"Where?" I asked. My voice sounded hoarse. Even though I'd been trained to always keep a straight back, I rested my elbows on my legs; I couldn't seem to get enough air.

"Faerie is located out of the corner of one's eye or on the edge of a shadow. It is wild, but a fast shortcut through England."

"Oh," I said, as if that were a natural explanation. Swallowing, I shook my head. "How on earth can I be a sorcerer?"

"I can explain that. The prophecy seemed to call for a female *child,* but how old are you?"

"Sixteen." *Prophecy?*

"I knew we needed a different translation, but you try persuading Palehook . . . I'm sorry," he said, noting my baffled expression. "This must be hard to take in."

"I'm sorry, a prophecy?" There was a faint ringing in my ears. None of this made sense.

"I shall explain more in due course, I promise you. Right now, what you need to know is that the prophecy calls for a girl to rise and fight in a time of great need. It mentions this girl's use of fire."

"But I thought all magical women were witches. There hasn't been a female sorcerer in hundreds of years." Not since Joan of Arc, in fact, and look where that got her.

"Not all magic is equal. Witches cannot control fire, water, earth, or air. They work with the life force of plants and animals. Only sorcerers control flame. And magicians are tricksters by nature. They deal in underhand spells and manipulations. The fact that you risked exposure to protect your friend, especially when you believed you would be killed as a result, proves you are not one of them."

My breath came in shallow gasps as I realized that I might not die tonight. I put my head in my hands.

"Now, listen, Miss Howel. I've never seen another girl who could do what you've done, and I've searched for four years. I've never met another sorcerer who could burn and walk away unscathed. As I say, sorcerers control flame." He took the lit candle from the table and collected the fire into his palm, as he had done before. "But we cannot create it."

Searched for four years. That was why he'd come to Brimthorn, why he'd tested the girls. "What does this mean?"

"That I will take you to London, if you're willing, to be commended by the queen. You will become a royal sorcerer, and when you're ready, you will fight alongside us. You'll join my household, live and train there. Not to worry, there'll be six others your age, all young men, of course."

"Young men?" What on earth would that be like? The only

boy I'd ever known was Rook. And there would be so many of them. . . .

"They are all gentlemen. One of them is your benefactor, Lord Blackwood. I know he'll be proud to meet an accomplished young lady from Brimthorn."

I would *meet* the Earl of Sorrow-Fell? Study with him as an *equal*? I nearly lay back onto the bed so that I could wake up from this dream.

Agrippa continued, "I can teach you to use a stave to control the fire and to master the other elements."

"Control?" I whispered. Was such a thing possible? For years I'd lived at the mercy of my power, praying it wouldn't come upon me at an inopportune moment. To think that I could be its master and not the other way around . . .

It all seemed too good to be believed.

"I would go to war with you?" I wished I hadn't smashed that vial of medicine. My head felt several sizes too small.

"Yes."

Though I'd never seen a Familiar until today, I knew what happened to the villages they plundered and the victims they left behind. I'd heard men tell horrific tales of families torn to pieces inside their homes, of entire towns burned to the ground. Hadn't I yearned to do something about it? My childhood games had been full of battling the Ancients, of destroying them. Could those dreams come true?

And as a sorcerer, I would belong in ways I'd never allowed myself to dream of before. I knew what life at Brimthorn would bring: years of hunger and cold, of teaching young girls how to do figures while my own life passed by in a blur, and one day I would be an old woman and still chained to the spot where my aunt had left me when I was a child. Now I had a chance to become something.

"Will you join us?" Agrippa asked.

"What about Rook?" Great destiny or not, I wouldn't leave him behind.

Speak of the devil. There were voices in the hallway. I got to my feet, still unsteady. Agrippa held my arm to support me.

Rook told the men who pursued him, "I'll see her if she's awake. Nettie? Where are you?"

"Rook, I'm in here!" I cried.

Agrippa banged on the door and called for it to be opened. A moment later, the constable entered, holding my friend by the shoulder. When released, Rook hurried toward me.

"Are you hurt?" he said, taking my face in his hands. His blue eyes blazed with concern. He looked human again, like his old self. Mud smeared his face and had dried in his hair.

"No. I'm a sorcerer." I didn't mean to laugh, but I couldn't help it. Rook's eyes widened.

"You can't be," he said, gripping my arm. "Are you sure?"

"You seem less surprised than I was." I laughed so hard I began to hiccup. He let me lean against him until I stopped.

"Well, after today I doubt anything could surprise me again. A sorcerer, of all things." He tilted my chin up and smiled.

"I know it's mad to say, but it's true. And I think I'm going to London."

Rook's smile faded somewhat. "Then I suppose this'll be goodbye." He took my hand and squeezed it. "I'm glad for you."

"No, I have even better news. You're coming with me." I knew it was daring, but I turned to Agrippa. "He is, isn't he?"

Agrippa looked as if he didn't know what to say. Rook turned me to face him again. "Nettie, you can't have me along. I don't belong in a sorcerer's world."

"Miss Howel," Agrippa finally said, "the situation's not as simple as you'd like."

"He has to come with us." I couldn't believe I was speaking this way to a sorcerer. But if he wanted me to leave Rook behind, he might as well ask me to cut off my own arm.

"Nettie, please don't," Rook said. He sounded on the verge of anger.

"Do you want us to be separated?" I grabbed his hand again. "If you don't care to stay with me any longer, say so." I waited, half fearing the answer.

Rook closed his eyes. "You know I'd hate to ever leave your side."

I breathed out in relief. "Then don't."

Agrippa cleared his throat. "London isn't a good place for the Unclean, especially one with Rook's scars." He gestured at Rook's shirt, ripped down the front from the battle. His wounds seemed even redder and angrier after the encounter.

"Why?" I asked.

"Because I know them well. Those are scars that Korozoth gives his victims, and Korozoth attacks London on a regular basis. Some believe that the Unclean are bound to the Ancients who mark them and call to them."

"But if Korozoth is already attacking the city, would Rook's presence make that much of a difference?"

"Well." Agrippa appeared stumped. "No, but—"

"Master Agrippa." I swallowed to keep my voice from breaking. Rook was not going to leave me, not today, not ever. "I want to help you, but I can't do so without Rook. You must take us both, or none at all." Agrippa studied me with interest. I raised my chin, hoping my expression was determined enough. Rook kept silent.

"Very well," the sorcerer said at last. "He'll have a place in my service. If that is what you want, Rook?"

Rook bowed his head. "I can do all manner of work, sir. You won't be disappointed."

"I'm sure I shan't. Well, Miss Howel?"

There was nothing left for me here. Nothing left for us.

"I'll come with you."

Agrippa smiled in satisfaction. Rook's hand found mine. We would go together.

THE NEXT MORNING, THE CARRIAGE PULLED up to Brimthorn so I could collect my things. I shook hands with all five teachers and smiled at the youngest two, Margaret Pritchett and Jane Lawrence. We'd grown up together, though we weren't as close as

I'd have liked. My friendship with an Unclean made them keep their distance.

I was walking away when a child's voice wailed, "She can't leave! Let me go." Sarah broke through the lines and flung herself at me, sobbing. I knelt and caught her, hugging her tight. She cried on my shoulder as I stroked her hair. "They say you'll never come back," she whimpered.

"I will someday." I thought of Colegrind's beatings, of his roving hands. I wouldn't let Sarah or the others remain at his mercy. I squeezed her and said, "I swear it."

Sarah let go reluctantly. Getting up, I walked to Colegrind for a few last words. He leaned on his birch cane, running his thumb along the handle lovingly. He'd find an excuse to use it on one of the girls before too long. He always did.

"Have you forgotten something, Miss Howel?"

"Remember me by this." I grasped his cane and set it on fire. With a curse, he dropped it to the ground and stamped the flames out, breaking the blasted thing in two. "I will be back." I stared into his eyes. "So take care how you treat the children."

Colegrind grunted as I turned and climbed into the carriage. Rook sat up in front with the coachman. We rumbled down the lane, waving. The girls raced after us, calling goodbye. I felt a pain in my chest as I watched them disappear. Much as I hated Brimthorn, it had been home and felt safe. Where I was going, nothing was certain, and everything was dangerous.

3

WE TRAVELED FOR THREE DAYS AND NIGHTS, BARELY stopping to rest. Agrippa sat with his stave in hand, always on alert for signs of Ancients or Familiars. Having discovered me, he seemed fearful that something catastrophic would occur.

I watched the countryside roll by our window, excitement and nervousness mounting with every passing day. I'd never set foot in London before. What would it be like? Sometimes for reassurance I would tap on the roof of the carriage three times, wait, and smile when Rook knocked back in answer.

Finally, it was the day of our arrival. I leaned out the window with a thrill of anticipation. As we neared the city proper, however, my excitement faded. I paled at the horror that lay before me.

All about me were buildings half-demolished, brick blackened by soot, and people living in the open streets. The sky was a metal gray, and the air tasted oily. Ragged, filthy men slept on doorsteps, and women and children huddled together for warmth. Young boys swept the road of horse manure. Little girls dressed all in black sat on street corners, selling strange wooden dolls.

They cried, "Totems, totems for sale. Korozoth. R'hlem. Molochoron. Protect yourself with the power of a totem."

"Is this truly London?" I whispered. Brimthorn had been oppressively gloomy, but not burned and ravaged.

"This is outside the warded territory." Agrippa sighed as he looked out the window. He didn't seem to like it any more than I.

The totem children noticed our elegant carriage and called to us, leaping up and down in excitement.

One of the girls, a tiny blond creature, ran toward us, calling, "Totems, totems! Take one home!" The horses reared up, and we jolted to a halt. There was a scream. I leaned out the window to discover the girl lying in the street.

Agrippa grabbed my arm. "Stay inside," he said.

As the child wailed in pain, an old man with the blackest skin I'd ever seen burst through the crowd, raced across the road, and fell beside her.

"My li'l Charley," the man wept, wrapping her in a shockingly bright cloak of purple, orange, and red. "My p-poor li'l girl."

"Shouldn't we do something?" I asked. Agrippa looked white and pinched with worry. He opened his door and leaned up to speak with the driver while I craned my neck out the window. The child's sobs tore at me. With a half-apologetic glance back at Agrippa, I climbed out of the carriage.

"Nettie, what are you doing?" Rook said, sliding to the ground.

"We can't just sit there." I knelt beside the girl.

The child was in a dreadful state, covered in blood. Sickened, I turned to the old man. "Sir, how may I help?"

"Oh good, miss, 'ow kind you is, 'ow k—" The man's smile melted from his face. The large, glittering tears in his eyes seemed to dry at once. He dropped the girl and snatched my wrist, squeezing tight. "It can't be. Not you," he murmured. "What's your name, girl?" He had been talking like a poor man of the streets; now he sounded like a cultured gentleman. "Who on God's earth are you?"

"Let go," I said, struggling against him. Rook pulled me away and wrapped his arm around me protectively. I glanced at the child and gasped. All the blood had vanished. She opened her eyes and sat up.

"Sorry," she said to the man. "I let the charm wear off."

"My fault, Charley. I lost my train of thought." The man swept the child into his arms again and nodded at me. "Thousand pardons. Mistook you for someone else." But his gaze was too intent for it to be a simple case of mistaken identity.

"How do you know me?" I asked, getting to my feet.

"Magician." Agrippa strode forward, glaring. "You are a thief and a swindler."

Magician? Instinctively, I wanted to wipe my wrist, to be rid of the memory of his touch. Rook tightened his grip on me.

"Swindler? Ridiculous," the man said, backing away. "And look, little Charley's well. Sometimes all you need is a wish and a prayer. It's a miracle!" The magician searched for an avenue of escape.

"You know the law," Agrippa said. People watched and murmured.

"Oh, you wouldn't harm an old conjurer, would you, sir? We're so very sorry for the disturbance. Here, have some flowers to make amends." The magician snatched a bouquet of red roses from his sleeves. "A peace offering?" He released white doves from his breast pocket.

"Call a constable!" Agrippa shouted.

"Oh, very well. Suppose I'll go quietl—" At this, the man sneezed and vanished in a burst of fire and smoke. I put my hand over my mouth. The crowd gasped in amazement.

Agrippa looked about, baffled, and then returned to me, signaling to get back into the coach. "Come, Miss Howel."

Rook jumped onto the driver's bench, and I climbed inside. We rode along while Agrippa seethed.

"I've never seen a magician before," I said, trying to calm him with conversation. Agrippa cleared his throat, mopping his forehead with a pocket square.

"I know it must seem harsh, cornering an old man like that," he said. "Apprehending a magician can be difficult alone. You never know what they'll do."

I kept silent. I knew that magicians had been royally pardoned for aiding Mary Willoughby, so long as they abided by the law, but they were all rogues and criminals. When I was a child, there was gossip that one of them had come through a nearby village, offering to tell fortunes. Three days later, he took off with six chickens, two sets of good candlesticks, and the miller's daughter. Still, I'd never thought magicians to be as dangerous as Agrippa implied.

"Do you hate them, sir?" I asked.

"They're selfish, dangerous men. They would rather tinker with obscene parlor tricks than lift a finger to aid the crown in a time of war. Considering it was their magic that helped the Ancients cross into our world, that attitude is even more intolerable." His cheeks tinged pink.

I decided not to mention how the magician had spoken to me, or that my appearance had stunned him. Truth be told, I preferred not to think about it myself. Surely it had been an attempt to trick me. Surely.

We continued onto a broad, bustling avenue. The street was a sea of activity, waves of humanity cresting and breaking.

"This is Ha'penny Row," Agrippa said, pointing out the window. "The trade hub of unwarded London. Anything you've ever wanted you can find here."

We passed women carrying baskets of loaves in their arms. People hauled trays of turtle, panes of glass, bags of flour. Voices called out wares of fruits and vegetables.

Agrippa sighed in exasperation as our carriage came to another abrupt halt. "What on earth is the matter today?"

He looked out the window for the source of trouble. He appeared to find it as, laughing merrily, he waved at someone. Curious, I leaned out to look for myself.

A young man on horseback trotted up to us. He rode a beautiful bay, and he removed his top hat by way of greeting. Reaching down, he drew out something that hung in a sheath by his side. He presented it with one hand to Agrippa, bowed at the waist, and then put away the stave and nodded. Here was another sorcerer. My stomach lurched as I gazed up at him. I hadn't expected to be so nervous.

"Now, you can't keep me away, Master Agrippa, you really cannot," he said. "There's five pounds riding on my seeing her first." The young man peered in the window and cocked an eyebrow. "Is this the lady in question?" This last was addressed to me. "Mr. Julian Magnus of Kensington, at your service." He bowed, a bit awkward, as he was still astride the horse. After nearly losing his seat, he said, "You're the prophecy girl, I'll be sworn. What's your name?"

Magnus had thick, wavy auburn hair and bright gray eyes. He was broad-shouldered and, I admitted to myself, almost absurdly handsome. His mouth was set in a grin, and he seemed to believe us old friends, not strangers who'd only just met.

"Henrietta Howel." I smiled in a way I hoped was friendly but not *too* encouraging. I didn't know this young man, after all. Magnus laughed.

"Well, now that the pleasantries have been exchanged, we must make certain you're the prophecy. A demonstration of your power at once!" He clapped his hands. "Come along, start burning. Nothing too grand—a small inferno will do."

"Perhaps when we get home. I should hate to startle the

horses," I said. Magnus seemed to like that response. "What was your name again, sir?"

He snorted. "'Sir,' is it? I told you, Mr. Julian Magnus of Kensington, at your service." Here he gave a bow again. "To be commended by Her Majesty. You're from Yorkshire, aren't you?"

"Yes," I said. I had to force myself not to tuck a stray curl behind my ear. The force of Magnus's attention was disconcerting.

"Northern girls have the ice and chill about them, but now that you've come south, you can thaw out as fast as you like." He kept smiling, as though this wasn't an insult.

"I'm sure I don't need any 'thawing out,' as you put it," I said, conscious of the edge in my voice. My irritation appeared to delight him.

"Cross with me, are you? That's the glorious thing about northerners. They're all Sturm und Drang."

"Oh, you have no idea," I muttered.

Magnus laughed, reached through the window, and shook Agrippa's hand.

"Thank you, Master. It's like Christmas. She's the funniest girl I ever met."

Agrippa struggled to contain a smile. "Mr. Magnus is one of my Incumbents. The son of a magical family spends ages fourteen to sixteen living under the supervision of an established practitioner."

"That would be our dear Master here," Magnus said. "It's his duty to make sure we don't fail our great test before the queen."

So I was to share a roof with Magnus. I prayed I wouldn't want to murder him every time we had breakfast.

"Allow me to escort you home." Magnus grinned as he rode alongside our carriage.

After a further ten minutes, Agrippa pointed out the window. "Here comes the ward."

There was nothing ahead but two men in crimson soldiers' uniforms standing in the center of the road. "What do you mean?" I asked.

"Wait a moment." He knocked on the roof of the carriage, which rumbled to a halt. The soldiers stood directly ahead of us, their hands out in a signal for us to stop. I thought them ordinary guards until they each unsheathed a sorcerer's stave.

"We request entrance," Magnus called.

There was no gate. "Can't we just ride past them?"

"Wait," Agrippa said.

The guards bent down, touched their staves to the ground, and traced them slowly upward. Floating into the air, they moved toward each other, one from the left and one from the right. The men met in the center, drew their staves together, and dropped to the ground. They'd sketched an invisible square, about ten feet long and ten feet high.

Satisfied, Agrippa knocked on the roof again, and the carriage lurched forward and through the square. I gasped; it felt as if some enormous pressure was squeezing the sides of my head. An instant later and it was done.

"What was that?" I asked, hands over my ears.

"The ward is designed to keep the Ancients from entering the area. Only sorcerers' staves can cut through the shield to create a brief entryway," Agrippa explained.

Magnus gestured to the streets before us. "Welcome to London proper," he said with a flourish.

If the unwarded area had been hell, this was paradise itself. Wrought-iron gates bordered parks and gardens. The sweet scent of fresh bread and cinnamon wafted from a bakery, and we passed a coffee shop where laughter and conversation bubbled out the doors.

"This is wonderful." I leaned from the window for a better look as elegant women passed by in an open-air barouche. "The Ancients have never attacked here?"

"Not even R'hlem has set foot in the heart of London." Pride tinged Agrippa's voice.

I knew that sorcerers had the power to create a shield around themselves to block an attack. But I'd never dreamed of a ward like this.

"What about the area outside? Can't you shield them?"

"No." Agrippa cleared his throat and shifted uncomfortably. "The sorcerers' power forms the ward, and one of our members specifically designs it. Master Palehook assures us that we have stretched our ability to its limit."

"Over there," Magnus called, pointing to the front of a beautiful building, "is the Theatre Royal. I should take you for a show sometime. Have you ever been to the theater, Miss Howel? Do they get much Shakespeare up in Yorkshire?" His smile was full of false innocence.

"No, but I can spot bad acting when it's right in front of me," I said. Magnus laughed so hard I feared he'd fall off his horse.

WE REACHED AGRIPPA'S HOME IN HYDE Park Corner as the last traces of daylight vanished. Magnus dismounted from his horse, and a servant came to take the reins. A footman in gray livery opened the carriage door. Agrippa climbed down, then helped me out. Rook leaped down beside me, and together we gaped at the magnificent structure.

We'd passed tall, elegant white town houses on our way through Kensington. I'd assumed Agrippa lived somewhere similar, but this was no small residence. It was several stories of cream-colored stone with a marble portico and fluted columns. Awed, I turned to speak to Rook, but he was walking away, following the footman.

"Rook! Where are you going?" I said.

"Below stairs, miss. He's a servant; he can't enter through the front door." The footman wore a pained expression.

"But . . ." I couldn't finish my thought. Hadn't Agrippa said that he would take Rook into his home *as a servant*? There was just something about the way the footman studied Rook, the formality of the whole thing. Rook, for his part, didn't seem to care.

"Don't worry about me, Nettie." He disappeared down a

flight of stairs near the front of the house. Agrippa came up beside me.

"He'll be well treated. I promise."

I believed him, but it was more than that. Rook and I had never been so separate before. We were from different classes, yes, but at Brimthorn it hadn't mattered. We'd played together, spoken to each other, and no one minded. Now Rook and I wouldn't be allowed to use the same door? Somehow I felt alone, even with Agrippa and Magnus waiting.

MY HEELS CLICKED ON THE TILE floor as another footman took my cloak and bonnet. I turned in a circle, unable to contain my astonishment. The hall was a work of art in itself, with a great staircase twisting up several floors. Here in the foyer, oil paintings of beautiful spring countryside hung on every wall, along with exotic collectibles such as elephant tusks, fans from the Orient, and a sword in a lacquered sheath.

"A girl could spend months simply exploring," I muttered.

"I hope you'll make yourself at home," Agrippa said. Could I ever really call a place this magnificent my home? The thought made me dizzy. "Now, before I take you to your room, perhaps you'd like to meet the rest of the household?"

With Magnus behind us, we walked upstairs. Housemaids in starched aprons bustled by, curtsying when they saw us. I curtsied in return, until Agrippa whispered that I didn't need to. On the second floor, we walked down a long hall and came to a door at the very end. Agrippa tried the handle, but it was locked.

A voice from within yelled, "Go away! We're busy."

"Open this door," Agrippa called.

Silence. The lock turned. We walked inside and found two young gentlemen with their staves pointed toward the ceiling. One of them, a large red-haired boy, put out a hand to stop us. "Careful, Master."

Twenty books floated in the air, hovering as if held by a current of strong wind. I watched the balancing act with interest. "All right," the boy said with a nod. "Now."

The books darted across the room, slamming into one another. I cried out as books began to rain from the sky. Magnus pulled me out of the way, but Agrippa was hit in the head and fell. The rest of the books collapsed to the earth.

"You could've killed him!" the red-haired boy cried, rushing to Agrippa and helping him to his feet. "I'm so sorry, sir. We never meant to hurt anyone. We did warn you, though, didn't we?" His green eyes widened when he saw me standing beside Magnus. "Oh, it's the girl!"

"The girl's here?" The other dueling-book boy turned to stare at me as well. His hair was wavy and black. "You idiot. You almost killed the lady sorcerer." He hit the other fellow in the shoulder after Agrippa had got himself safely to the couch.

"Don't be fools," Magnus said, stepping forward. "The important thing is I saw her first, so I won the bet. Both of you, pay up."

"That was five pounds together," the dark-haired boy said.

"Each."

"Liar!" Now they were all grappling, though they seemed to enjoy themselves. I pressed myself against the wall, taken aback. I came from a place where silence and order were strictly enforced. Waiting for them to stop, I looked about the room.

Two more young men sat by the window. They played a game of chess and paid no mind whatsoever to anything around them. One was so small and slight he seemed on the verge of fading from existence. His hair was pale and almost colorless. The other, by contrast, had black hair and shoulders so broad they stretched the material of his jacket.

The brief fight died. Sensing a cue, I stepped forward to introduce myself. "How good to meet you. My name is Henrietta Howel," I said, extending my hand. I hoped I didn't sound too nervous.

"I'm Arthur. Arthur Dee." The red-haired boy blushed as he respectfully bent his head over my hand, though he didn't kiss it. "Sorry about the books," he whispered.

"And this," Magnus said, straightening the dark-haired boy, "is Cavaliere Bartolomeo Cellini de Genoa. That's in Italy."

"I know where Genoa is." Magnus liked to speak for his friends, which didn't surprise me. Cellini bowed with a flourish.

"I speak veddy good-ah Een-glish," he said in a dreadful accent. "But my Italian is terrible," he added in a perfectly normal voice, which made me laugh. He winked at me.

I met the chess-playing fellows by the window as well. The

small, pale one was Clarence Lambe; the large one, Isaac Wolff. They seemed pleasant and polite, but immediately returned to their game. Not the most social of creatures.

"Where's George?" Agrippa said, glancing about the room. "I was expecting a full welcome."

Of course, Lord Blackwood. My heart sped up as I looked back at the door, waiting for his entrance. I smoothed and fluffed my skirt.

"He went out," Cellini said. "His Lordship said he had important matters to attend to." Cellini pursed his mouth and stuck his nose in the air. Magnus and Dee laughed.

Agrippa frowned. "I asked everyone to be home this evening."

"Oh, it's all right," I said, trying to hide my disappointment. I would meet him eventually, after all. And being an earl, he probably *did* have important matters.

"Well," Agrippa said, "it can wait until tomorrow. You look as if you could do with some rest, Miss Howel." He eased up from the sofa.

"Good night," I said, curtsying to the gentlemen. They bowed in return, Dee laughing a little. I suppose this was as strange to them as it was to me.

Agrippa and I climbed the stairs to the third floor and made a right down a long hallway. Agrippa gestured to a door at the end. "This is the Rose Room. I trust you'll be comfortable." He smiled, but his eyes kept nervously flickering toward the door.

"I shall have a maid come up and assist you. Good night." He bowed and left me to enter the room on my own.

Agrippa had struck me as an old bachelor, so I was surprised to find a room with pale pink walls and a dusky rose bedspread. A mirrored vanity sat to one side of the room, laden with glass bottles of scents and oils, a silver-backed brush, and an ivory comb. A china pitcher and bowl with delicate floral patterns waited on a table, along with a cut-glass vase of roses. The fire in the white marble hearth blazed. Having a fire laid only for me was such a luxury that I nearly began to cry. At Brimthorn, I'd gone to bed shivering more often than not.

"Beg pardon, miss." I turned to find a maid in a cap and apron. She opened the wardrobe and laid out a white cotton nightgown. I sat on the bed, not knowing what to do. How did one go about having a maid? Was I supposed to talk to her, or was that not allowed? I smiled at her, shy, and was grateful when she smiled back.

Moments later, I lay beneath the pink silk coverlet and basked in the quiet of the room. Only a few nights before, I'd been in the attic, sharing a bed with Jane Lawrence. The teachers and children all slept together in one long dormitory, and there was never any peace, with everyone's wheezing and snoring. The silence here was almost disconcerting. But I'd never been this comfortable before in my life, and it had been such a long day. I closed my eyes, and sleep carried me away.

THE NEXT DAY, I WOKE FIRMLY tangled in blankets. My neck was stiff, and I groaned as I sat up. My hair hung in my face. How long had I been asleep? Someone pushed the bed's drapes aside. It was the maid from the previous night.

"Good afternoon, then, miss!" she said, smiling. I blinked stupidly at her. "Almost evening, really. Nice to see you awake. Not that you can't have a lie-in, but Master did want you up soon. An hour more and I'd have had to shake you myself. Wouldn't have liked to, of course. After the journey you've had, I think you should be allowed to sleep until next year." She couldn't have been more than fifteen, a girl with a heart-shaped face and strawberry-blond hair.

"I'm sorry," I croaked, rubbing my eyes. "What's your name?"

"I'm Lilly. I'm to be your maid till Master sees fit to hire a lady's maid." She never stopped beaming. "You're from Yorkshire, they say. Is it pleasant there? Seems dangerous nowadays, but I always wanted to go. 'Course, can't just up and leave on holiday when you're in service, can you? And not when there's a war on, at any rate. Maybe one day it'll end, though I can't see how. Still, suppose it's not for me to wonder. Master says I'm to have you cleaned and ready by half past seven. My, but you're dark. Not that it's bad—I think dark women look mysterious—but Miss Gwen's colors may not suit you, but we can try nonetheless."

I'd never known a girl to talk so much. "Thank you," I said as Lilly opened the wardrobe and pulled out several beautiful dresses, laying them on the bed beside me. "Are you certain

Miss Gwen won't be irritated with my taking her gowns? Or her room, for that matter?"

Lilly startled. "Miss Gwen was the Master's daughter. She's been gone these last four years."

"Oh." My hand flew to my mouth in embarrassment. Poor Agrippa. "I'm so sorry. How did she die?"

"Scarlet fever. I never knew her, as I came to work here afterward, but all the servants loved her."

"I hate to think of Master Agrippa disturbing this room for me." I got out of the bed, feeling almost guilty for sleeping there.

"No, it was no trouble. This room's turned down regular as clockwork. Just as when she was alive." Lilly shook her head. "Anyway, I've hot water and lavender soap for your wash. Afterward, we'll dress you for the gentlemen."

"What gentlemen?"

"Oh, it's quite an occasion. The Imperator's coming, you know, along with another from the Order. Master says they're to evaluate you." Lilly smiled and helped me prepare my toilette. She'd brought up tea and sandwiches, but I felt too nervous to eat.

The Imperator was the bloody prime minister of English magic. What if I failed their test? What if I truly were no sorcerer? And if I disappointed them . . . what exactly would become of me?

4

LILLY HELPED ME INTO A SKY-BLUE DRESS, SAT ME BE-
fore the vanity mirror, and arranged my hair. "Sorry if it's awful,
miss. Haven't had much time for learning hair." She pinned it
up, but left two loose curling sections by my cheeks. With a final flourish, she sprayed a citrus eau de cologne and clapped her
hands. "Oh, miss. Maybe the dress is no great color for you, but
you do look lovely."

The girl in the mirror couldn't be me. At Brimthorn, I'd
dressed in a shapeless gray uniform that aged me by at least ten
years, but I'd never given great thought to my appearance. Now
my shoulders were bare, and the sleeves belled out at my elbows
so that my hands seemed small and dainty in the folds of cloth.

"Lilly, you're a miracle worker," I breathed, admiring the fit
of the dress. The maid blushed. I pulled my shoulders back and
nodded at my reflection. "I think it's time." Stomach lurching,
I left the room and went down the stairs, praying I didn't trip
over my skirt. Once on the second floor, I paused and clutched
the banister. I was utterly lost. There were ten doors, all closed.
Which way was the bloody parlor? I looked up and down the hall.
Perhaps I should just start wandering until I found someone.

To my left, I heard voices. One of the doors was open a crack. Relieved, I went to it and was about to knock when I heard my name. I stopped and peered inside. The room seemed to be a small study with a desk and several bookshelves taking up much of the space. Two gentlemen were discussing me before the fireplace.

One of them was Agrippa. With his back to me, he said, "I've no business ordering you about, George, especially as you're nearly commended. But when I ask you to receive someone, you will be home to do so. Is that understood?"

The fellow who stood before Agrippa was a handsome sort, with a triangular face and black hair. Agrippa had called him George. Heavens, this was Lord Blackwood at last. He was so *young*.

Colegrind and the teachers had spoken of Lord Blackwood with such reverence. My whole childhood, I'd been reminded how blessed I was to live under an earl's protection. And here I was, about to meet him. I gripped the doorknob, trying to steady my nerves, and was about to go in when Blackwood said, "All due respect, sir, there's no need to wait eagerly on a simple country girl. She will keep." He sounded bored as he rested one elbow on the mantelpiece.

I bit my tongue.

"I never thought you a rude fellow," Agrippa said in a huff. "While you live here, you will be respectful of her position."

With a shrug, Blackwood continued, "I'm sure she is intelligent and charming, just as you wrote to us. But I don't know what you think to do with her."

"Train her for commendation, obviously," Agrippa said. He sounded angry.

Blackwood shook his head. His expression was cold. "We'll do our best, but with her background, I doubt she'll be capable."

My face felt flaming hot. I had to dig my fingers into the palms of my hands, lest the fire come upon me suddenly.

Agrippa said, "You had better keep these thoughts to yourself when you meet the young lady."

Taking the opportunity provided, I knocked and entered the room. Lord Blackwood casually looked me up and down. Judging everything he saw, no doubt.

Agrippa made the smallest, softest noise and glanced away. I winced, remembering that I was wearing his dead child's dress. Oh God. Still, it wasn't as though I could take it off—not now.

"Good evening," I said. My voice didn't waver. Excellent.

"You must be Miss Howel." Blackwood sounded disinterested.

The bloody cheek of it all. I forced a smile onto my face. "And you must be Lord Blackwood. A pleasure." I curtsied, very prettily, if I may say so. "How nice to finally meet my benefactor. I grew up at the Brimthorn School for Girls, you know. On Sorrow-Fell lands."

"Yes, I know where the school is." He looked at me. His eyes were green and tilted up at the corners, almost like a cat's.

"I only mention it because I can't remember ever seeing you before. So many Brimthorn girls always wanted a glimpse of our benefactor. To think I had to come all the way to London to find you." My voice was bright, my smile easy. I wasn't going to let him see me rattled.

Blackwood sniffed. "I'm sorry to have been absent. Sadly, only the most pressing matters can command my attention in wartime."

A spark glinted in my hand. I managed to quash it, but Blackwood noticed.

Agrippa extended his arm to me. "Shall we go to the parlor?" he said. We walked out at a leisurely pace, Blackwood behind us. I clenched my jaw. The Earl of Sorrow-Fell was nothing like I'd hoped he would be.

I DOUBT SHE'LL BE CAPABLE, BLACKWOOD had said. As though it were already decided. My frayed nerves felt stretched to the breaking point when we entered the parlor to find the rest of the boys waiting. The hair on my neck prickled as I watched them appreciate my newly glamorous appearance. Cellini raised an eyebrow. Dee nudged Magnus, grinning.

Agrippa guided me over to the sofa to meet the two gentlemen from the Order.

One of them stood and introduced himself as Augustus Palehook, master warder of the city. "Aren't you a pretty sight, my dear," he said, bending over my hand. "Such loveliness is a relief to tired old eyes." His voice was soft but not gentle. He turned to Agrippa. "And Cornelius. Always a pleasure. What a suit," he said, eyes flickering over Agrippa's coat. "Mmm, what a cravat. Is this Egyptian blue? You are always clever in your dress."

"As are you, of course," Agrippa said, bowing. On the surface, Palehook didn't appear the intimidating sort. No one would cower before a thin fellow with receding red hair in battle. But the way Agrippa seemed uneasy around him, the way Palehook smiled as if he had garnered a point in some private game, indicated he wasn't a man to be trifled with.

My head buzzed as Agrippa then turned and presented me to Horace Whitechurch, the Imperator himself. He did not rise, did not reach to kiss my hand. I'm not sure what I'd expected from the head of English magic. Some giant, perhaps, with the power of nature coursing through his veins. Instead I found an elderly man with wet black eyes. I curtsied to him. He didn't smile.

"Shall we begin?" he said.

Impressing him was of the utmost importance. Palehook grasped my hand. His touch was soft and dry. "Are you ready, my dear?"

"Yes," I said, though it was a lie.

"Come, then." He led me to a circle of seven stones arranged on the rug before the hearth. The stones were smooth and black, and each bore a different symbol: a dagger, a circle with a cross on top, a triangle, a curl of flame, an eye, a rectangle, and a five-pointed star. How strange to see these odd items lying on an Oriental rug before a fireplace in a proper London home. Palehook gestured to the circle. "Step inside."

My heartbeat quickening, I did as he asked.

Agrippa knelt before the two sorcerers. "Masters, I offer Henrietta Howel for evaluation, to receive instruction in our most learned arts and to take up arms against the enemies of the Order and the kingdom." Whitechurch gestured for him to rise.

They placed a bowl of water to my left and a plain brown rock to my right. Before me, they put one white feather. A candle was lit behind me. Once these preparations were done, they drew together and watched.

"Clear your mind," Agrippa said. "Make yourself a vessel for the magic."

My heart beat faster. "What am I supposed to do?"

"You do nothing. In a circle of the seven stones, the elements will recognize a true sorcerer." This was a baptism, a rite of passage every sorcerer boy went through when he was six months old. They all fell silent, and the ceremony began.

Nothing happened.

A full minute ticked by as they stared at me. Whitechurch coughed. Palehook narrowed his eyes. Even Agrippa began to twitch, oh so subtly.

The boys frowned, whispered to one another. Magnus at least smiled at me. Blackwood, of course, wasn't watching. He stared into the fireplace.

They would cast me out in another minute. I could picture Agrippa wincing, ringing for a carriage to take me back to Yorkshire.

My hands began to prickle with heat. An image jumped into my mind, unbidden: the water, rising in a ball. Agrippa had told me to leave my mind blank, but I focused on that image, clung to it. An instant later, the room gasped as one. I glimpsed the water out of the corner of my eye. It hovered in the air, a perfect, round orb. I lost my concentration, and it splashed back into the bowl.

Everyone murmured in excitement. This was what they wanted. I looked at the feather and imagined it lifting up, up into the air on a current of wind. . . .

My skirt rustled as a breeze swept through the room. The feather danced on the current. The boys applauded, even whooped with joy. My stomach turned. I knew that I wasn't doing this the way they'd wanted me to. My hands grew even hotter.

I imagined the rock beside me leaping up and down three times. It did just that. The boys stomped their feet. Agrippa laughed. Whitechurch even raised the corners of his mouth in a thin smile. Only Palehook did not rejoice. He watched me through lidded eyes, as though he was trying to decide on something.

I knew they wanted something from the candle, but the fire under my skin demanded its own way. For the first time since I'd discovered my ability, I could use it without fear. I exploded into flame, a wash of warmth over my whole body. Everyone gasped. It felt glorious, but it was dangerous. Quickly, I tightened my control and the fire disappeared. The carpet was a bit singed, though. Magnus ran over and smothered the dying flames with his coat, laughing.

"You know how to put on a show, Miss Howel," he said with a wink when I helped him to his feet. The boys cheered for me. I'd done it, somehow.

"I should like to see one more thing," Palehook said, standing. Everyone fell silent. "Mr. Magnus, I should like to see her with a stave. A simple maneuver, of course. Merely have her split the rock in half." Palehook reached into his pocket and pulled out a needle.

Before I could ask, Magnus took the needle and pricked his finger, so that a drop of blood welled on the tip. He reached for my face. "What are you doing?" I said, backing away.

"You haven't a stave of your own yet," Magnus said, his voice soothing. "It's all right." I stilled and let him put his blood on my lips, though I flushed with the strangeness of it. He touched my forehead, tracing a few lines on my skin.

Magnus handed me his stave. It was almost two feet long, with odd images decorating it. It wasn't as heavy as I'd thought it would be. I twirled it about a few times, entranced. Cradling it to my chest, I inspected the line of stars that someone had carved with great delicacy.

Taking up the plain brown rock, Magnus held it toward me and said, "Swing the stave in one fast arc, as though you're chopping wood. It should split the rock down the center."

I'd never swung an ax before, and at first I felt like I was trying to smack him with the stave and not doing an especially good job. I focused. I wouldn't fail when I was so close. When I next brought the stave up to swing, I pictured the rock shattering in my frustration.

Magnus covered his eyes as the stone exploded into dusty fragments. There were gasps throughout the room, but a smattering of applause as well.

"It worked. Well, in a way," Magnus said, laughing while he dusted his hands. "You must have a great deal of power." He gave me a handkerchief to wipe off his blood. "Congratulations, Miss Howel."

"Congratulations indeed," Agrippa said, coming forward. His eyes seemed to glow. "I believe you have the makings of a true sorcerer."

The boys rushed in on me, gripping my hand and shaking my arm as if they'd wrench it free. Magnus caught me about the waist and whirled me in a circle.

"Julian! Put that young lady down," Agrippa said, laughing.

Blackwood was the only one who didn't join the merriment. He watched me from the fireplace, his great green eyes narrowed. I turned from him, cool as could be. Let him glare.

The Imperator stood and stepped forward. The room quieted.

"Yes," he said. His voice was almost a whisper. He turned his watery eyes to Agrippa. "Yes," he said again with a nod.

With that, he shuffled out the door and into the hall. I heard him collect his hat and coat, and call for his carriage. Agrippa said nothing; apparently the Imperator was allowed to be rude.

Palehook took my hand in his. His eyes searched mine, a small smile playing on his lips. "My dear girl," he said. "Happy day, is it not? The queen shall commend you. Yes, Cornelius," he said, nodding. "The Imperator has spoken. You may train her. The Order grants permission."

WE WENT TO DINNER, WHERE THE aromas overwhelmed me. There was buttery oyster soup, roast duck with cherries, a succulent leg of mutton, a rib of beef, marrow and potatoes, three types of vegetables, and a plum pudding. Sorcerers ate better than kings, I decided. I'd been too nervous to eat before, but I wanted to make up for that. I yearned to tuck in with the most unladylike relish possible, but I managed to contain myself. Brimthorn had schooled its girls in nice table manners.

"A toast," Agrippa said, raising a glass, "to our lady sorcerer."

The gentlemen joined him. Looking down the candlelit table, seeing all these men toasting *me*, I felt as if I'd entered some bizarre dream world. Nervous, I tried some wine, coughing at the taste.

"Once you've received Her Majesty's commendation," Palehook said, sawing at his duck, "you'll be the most admired woman in all of London. We shall host a ball in your honor, Mrs. Palehook and I. Of course, there's certain to be an undercurrent of nasty gossip. The masses are always ready to condemn a young lady of such independence. But you needn't worry, Miss Howel. I've seven daughters, did you know? They should be glad to meet such a charming and unusual girl. To get on well in society, why, the Misses Palehook might be instrumental." His tone indicated I must force myself to become chummy with his daughters. He was apparently used to getting his way.

"I suppose they might." While Palehook intimidated me more than I cared to admit, I bristled at his veiled order. I would choose my own friends. Taking a sip of water, I said nothing else. Magnus elbowed Cellini. This exchange had captured his attention.

"Mmm." Palehook took a bite of potato. "Cornelius tells me you've an Unclean friend who's joined this household as a servant. We typically send the Unclean away, you know. To a colony near Brighton, where they might live peacefully."

"I'm sure Rook will be peaceful here," I said, keeping my tone pleasant. "You have nothing to worry about."

Palehook nodded. "We shall see." Before I could respond, he turned to Blackwood. "Your father designed that system, did he not, Blackwood?"

"He did," Blackwood said without looking at Palehook. I got the feeling he didn't much like the sorcerer. Well, that was at least one thing we had in common.

"*He* was a great man. You must be careful not to let down the family name. You work hard, but you haven't your father's charm. Well, children cannot inherit everything."

Blackwood nodded, his eyes fixed on his plate. "Yes, sir. How right you are."

I couldn't think of any response to this shocking display of rudeness.

"Cornelius also tells me the boy's scars probably came from Korozoth," Palehook said, turning back to me as if nothing had happened. "And as you know, Korozoth often attacks London. This puts all of us in a precarious position. But for you, we will make an exception and allow this boy to live behind the ward."

"Rook is the best person I know," I said, clenching my fist. This was not the time for going up in accidental flames. "The Order is so wise and kind to show him mercy." I swirled the wine in my glass, watching it catch the candlelight and make a beautiful, glowing pattern of red on the tablecloth.

Palehook nodded. "Of course. No matter what the cost to us, Miss Howel, we will do most anything to please you." His words didn't feel as nice as they sounded. "For women, as we all know, are the most simple and tenderhearted of God's creatures."

My temper rose. I gripped my glass as the fire practically danced under my skin. Palehook seemed the sort to subtly draw out another person's anger. Everyone had their eyes fixed on us, looking back and forth as if we were characters in a play.

"Women are tender, of course," Cellini said, lifting his eyebrows. "Much more tender than men. But women can also be wise. Don't you find, sir?"

"Oh, certainly," Palehook said with a nonchalant wave of his hand.

"Many sorcerers choose an area in which to become an expert," Agrippa said, desperate to steer the conversation to a safer shore. "Isaac wants to be a warder, as successful as our dear Master here." Palehook nodded at the compliment. "And Julian seems to think going into the navy would be a good option."

"What's wrong with the navy? Pounding Nemneris the old Water Spider herself into submission? I think it's brilliant of me," Magnus said, humble as ever.

"What about you?" I asked Lambe, seated beside me. He had barely touched his dinner, preferring to arrange and rearrange the vegetables and meat on his plate into odd shapes.

"I'll become a Speaker, a soothsayer," he whispered. I knew

that prophetic ability was rare in the sorcerer community. Lambe was probably the only boy here who'd tested positive for those skills. Honestly, I should have guessed it before. He seemed a bit detached from everything going on around him. He spoke to people as if he were half asleep.

"Mr. Lambe has quite a talent," Palehook said.

"Speakers live in a monastery in Northumberland, on the border of Scotland," Lambe said. "It will be a quiet life."

"There's no need to go all the way up north," Wolff said. He frowned. "There's plenty of work to be done in the Order's service down here, you know." It sounded like an argument they'd had several times before. I noticed that whenever Wolff spoke, Lambe lost that dreamy, unfocused look.

"I must go where I'm needed," he said. Wolff began cutting into his food with a vengeance, as though his chop had done him some serious wrong.

"Would nothing compel you to remain in our society?" Palehook asked. Lambe considered this.

"If the slab of obsidian breaks," he said slowly, "I will remain."

What an odd thing to say.

"Another toast," Magnus said, lifting his glass. "To lady sorcerers, and the spirit of change."

At the word *change*, Palehook nearly spit his wine. Magnus winked. Apparently, he had chosen my side. I hoped he'd chosen rightly.

GENTLEMEN AND LADIES SPENT TIME APART AFTER supper. Being the only lady, I was forced to wait in the drawing room for fifteen minutes by myself. I paced and stared at portraits. One young woman's image caught my attention. She was a lovely yellow-haired girl in a blue gown. A placard at the bottom of the frame read GWENDOLYN AGRIPPA.

There was something familiar about her, though I couldn't place it. Then I realized that the gown in the painting was the same one I wore now. I flinched and looked away. Poor Agrippa.

"Sublime, wasn't she?" a voice behind me said. Palehook helped himself to a glass of brandy. I didn't like his watchful gaze, and hoped the others would arrive soon. "I always thought Miss Agrippa to be among the brightest lights in our society. Her death was an incalculable loss." He sipped. "You have much to live up to."

"I'm not here to replace Miss Agrippa," I said, a bit stiffly. "I'm here to become a sorcerer."

"Mmm," he said. "Of course." He moved away as the others entered the room. I turned back to the portrait, glad to have Palehook's attention off me. I kept thinking about what he'd said regarding Rook and the colony in Brighton. They wouldn't send him away, would they? I tried my best to appear at ease, but I doubt I succeeded.

Twenty minutes later, Palehook mercifully left. We bid farewell at the front door, and I had to let him kiss my hand. He smiled. "Until we meet again, my dear," he said, taking his hat and coat and walking out. At last.

Magnus stood beside me. "What's wrong?" he whispered. Damn. I wasn't hiding my feelings as well as I'd hoped.

"I'm worried about Rook."

"Well, we can't have that. I'll take you below stairs this instant." He smiled.

"Is that really proper?" It wasn't that I thought the downstairs an unseemly place, more that going anywhere privately with a young man could be bad for my reputation. I had to worry about reputations now. London was not Brimthorn.

"We might cause a scandal, a young lady and a gentleman going to the kitchen without an escort. We should shock them by baking something together."

We slipped down to the servants' dining area and found them almost through with their supper, the butler and housekeeper at each end of the table, the footmen and the housemaids and Lilly along the sides. They got to their feet as we entered, Lilly with a napkin before her mouth to disguise her chewing.

"At ease," Magnus said. He looked about. "Where's the new boy?"

"In the kitchen, sir," the housekeeper said. She was an older woman with a lined and unsmiling face.

"What's he doing there?" Magnus asked.

"Eating his supper, sir."

"Why isn't he eating with the rest of you?" I asked, looking from one face to the next. Lilly twisted her napkin.

"We thought it'd be more comfortable, miss," the house-keeper said.

"Comfortable for whom?" I snapped.

The housekeeper gave a thin smile. "Comfortable for him, miss. Considering his infirmities, we didn't want him to feel shame before us. His scars are most unappetizing, but of course he knows that. He shouldn't be forced to put himself on display as if he were normal." Her face was cold and blank. If she didn't watch out, she'd wake up with her blankets on fire one night.

"Now, see here — "

"Thank you," Magnus interrupted, placing a firm hand on my arm. "We'll let you return to your supper." He guided me off. Once out of earshot, I pulled away.

"I suppose you think it's fine for them to treat Rook this way?" I whispered.

"Not in the least. I was trying to save him before you made his life even more difficult." He frowned. "Draw attention to him down here, and they'll torment him further."

"They're frightened sheep," I said, though I knew he was right. At least at Brimthorn, Rook had been allowed to eat at the table with the other servants.

"Give them time. Most people aren't accustomed to sharing living space with the Unclean."

We went into the kitchen and found Rook standing by the window, looking out onto the stables. He was dressed as usual, with no visible scars. Unappetizing indeed. A bowl of stew lay by the fire, untouched.

When he saw me, his mouth fell open. "Nettie. You're, well, quite lovely," he said, looking me up and down. My face warmed at the compliment.

"Thank you," I said. Magnus snorted. "Are you getting on all right?"

"Certainly better than Brimthorn, isn't it?" He hadn't answered the question. "What's happened upstairs?"

"The Imperator agreed to my training. Master Agrippa wants to take me to the queen for commendation. Can you believe it?" My smile stretched wider with every word I spoke.

"You'll be the greatest sorcerer of the age." Rook didn't sound nearly as excited as I'd hoped he would be.

"Oh, will she?" Magnus said, studying his fingernails. "Where does that leave me? Handsomest sorcerer of the age? I'm more than just a pretty face, you know."

"I meant no offense, sir," Rook said.

I didn't like him calling Magnus "sir." "Why don't you stand by the door outside, Mr. Magnus? I'll be finished soon," I said firmly.

"Ah, I only meant to tease. If there's one thing Miss Howel loves, it's a bit of teasing." He clapped Rook hard on the shoulder. "I've noticed that already, upon such a short acquaintance. But you knew that, surely? You being so close." Rook gently but firmly took himself out of the other fellow's grip.

"I've noticed much, sir," he said. There was a coldness in his look that I hadn't seen before.

"So have I. Well, I shall wait to escort you back upstairs, Miss Howel." He left with a bow. What a tiresome young man.

Rook nodded toward the door after Magnus had gone. "He seems to like you."

"Sadly, that feeling is not mutual." I spoke a bit louder than necessary. Around the corner, I heard a laugh.

"It's good to see you with others of your rank," he said. Lord, not this again. Don't argue——you know it's true. Magic sorts, Nettie. You belong in their world now."

"You make it all sound so formal," I said, letting my irritation show.

Before we could continue this discussion, Lilly appeared and cleared her throat in the doorway. She fidgeted with her apron.

"What is it?" I smiled.

"Rook, you must help. There's trouble outside with Master Palehook's carriage," she said, sounding rather breathless. Rook nodded by way of thanks. Lilly made a strange sound and accidentally banged against the doorframe on the way out. Apparently Rook had an admirer. I shifted uncomfortably.

"I'm glad he's going," Rook said. "He asked the most peculiar questions."

"Who? Master Palehook?" A chill walked down my spine.

"That thin one, yes. He was very interested in me."

"What did he ask you?" I murmured, deep in thought.

"Where'd I come by my scars, did they hurt, did I ever feel urges to run away or do things I couldn't control." Rook frowned. "I don't like him, Nettie."

"I don't like him, either."

"Don't let him near you more than necessary."

"I can't exactly order him about, can I?"

"Oh, I don't know. You handled the young gentleman nicely," he said, mimicking Magnus with an exaggerated bow. I laughed. Once Rook had gone, I turned the corner to find Magnus leaning against the wall, waiting for me.

"I am here to spirit you back upstairs. Don't swoon," he said.

"I'll try not to." I rolled my eyes and brushed past him. Emerging into the foyer, we found servants dimming the lamps. Everyone else had gone to bed.

"Well," he said as we climbed the stairs, "congratulations. You've survived your first dinner with bloody Master Palehook. An Incumbent rite of passage. This calls for celebrations. I'd compose a sonnet on the occasion, but all I can think of that rhymes with *Palehook* is *bailbook*."

"It can wait till morning," I said. "Thank you for your help."

I turned to walk down the hall but stopped when Magnus said, "By the by, I hope you won't set me on fire for asking this." He leaned against the banister. "But I have to know: How long has that boy been in love with you?"

All the air left my lungs. When I managed to speak again, I

said, "Rook is *not* in love with me. He's been my friend since we were children."

"All right, all right." Magnus tried to hush me.

"No." I gripped the railing. Between Palehook's veiled threats during dinner and Magnus's behavior downstairs, I could no longer contain myself. "You shouldn't make comments like that. And you shouldn't tease him like you did in the kitchen."

"Steady on," Magnus said. He frowned.

"He's a servant. He's not allowed to answer back to you. It's easy to poke fun at the world and think yourself clever, but it's much harder to stand silent and endure." With that, I turned for my room. Magnus stepped in front of me, blocking my exit.

"You're right," he said, bowing his head. "I behaved badly. The problem with being the adored only son of a widow is that everything I do is made out to be clever, even when it isn't. Please accept my apology."

I wasn't sure how to respond. "Well . . . you should apologize to Rook as well."

He nodded. "I shall."

I hadn't expected to win the argument this easily. "Then thank you."

"Of course. Actually, I like when women yell at me. It makes a nice change from all those adoring love letters." He posed tragically. I laughed; I couldn't help myself. "In all seriousness, I never meant to insult your friend. It's wonderful, you two being thick as thieves." He tilted his head. "You must have had an unusual upbringing."

"To say the least." I wasn't sure why I should say this to Magnus of all people, but there was something genuine in his interest. "Rook was the one steady part of my childhood."

"In that case, he's a lucky young man," Magnus said. "Anyone who could be so indispensible to you would be fortunate indeed. Forgive me?"

I felt strangely hot. Were young men allowed to give such compliments? "Of course."

"Anyway, I don't mean to push in where I'm unwelcome. It's just that I haven't been this excited since the Christmas when I was eight years old."

"Why?" I found myself smiling.

"Because our cook made *two* plum puddings at my request. I was sick for days, but, oh, it was worth it."

"No," I said, rolling my eyes. "I mean, why are you excited now?"

"Because you're going to be a lady sorcerer. I think the idea of women doing proper magic is brilliant. Those stuffy Order meetings and congregations will liven up considerably with a few petticoats thrown into the mix." We walked slowly down the hall toward my door.

"Well, it sounds as if you take the concept of female sorcery *quite* seriously."

"I never take anything seriously, but I am delighted by the thought of ladies working magic. Women raised me, you know. My mother and my grandmother, God rest her soul. I had a governess, Miss Watkins, whom I simply adored. Ladies are so

- 74 -

much cleverer than gentlemen. They enjoy good conversation and great fun, two things without which I cannot live."

"Life truly is just a game to you, isn't it?" I said, almost impressed.

"I'm always on the lookout for a worthy opponent." He laughed as we stopped outside my room. "Look, I believe we got off on the wrong foot. Let's reintroduce ourselves, eh?" He bowed low before me. "I am Mr. Julian Magnus, your obedient, humble, and ever-loyal servant, Miss . . . ?"

"Henrietta Howel." I was *not* going to laugh.

"An honor, Miss Howel. Please, you may address me as Mr. Magnus, or just The Great. That's the Latin for *Magnus*."

"I knew that."

"You are brilliant. Now I take my leave. *Adieu. Bonsoir.* Good evening." He kissed my hand, his lips soft against my skin. Then he was gone.

I would remember how exasperating he could be the minute I finally stopped smiling.

6

GWENDOLYN AGRIPPA SAT BEFORE THE MIRROR, CRYING *and running an ivory comb through her fine hair. I reached out to touch her shoulder, but she pulled away, her face twisted in fury.*

Tap, tap, tap.

The old magician with the dark skin and the multicolored coat sat at the foot of my bed.

"I knew it," he said.

This was clearly a dream. Everything in the room lay faded in mist, except for my visitor.

The magician wagged his finger at me. "I knew."

"Knew what?" I asked.

"Go to Ha'penny Row. Buy a totem for the answer."

Tap, tap, tap.

"Stop tapping on my bedpost."

The magician shrugged. "I'm not. Perhaps someone's at the door."

I WOKE TO SUNLIGHT STREAMING THROUGH the window. Rubbing my eyes, I sat up and froze when I heard tapping.

"Hello?" I called, but no one answered. It sounded like something hitting my bedpost. Turning my head, I found a stick of polished wood lying on the pillow next to me, utterly still. I pulled the blankets to my chin. "Hello?" I said again, like a fool. But what else does one say to a mysterious object?

The stave was perhaps two feet long . . . a stave . . .

"Are you mine?" I whispered, taking it in hand. I swore I felt the briefest flicker of a pulse, as if it were some living creature. At my touch, the wood stretched and squeezed, like taking a damp cloth by both ends and wringing it. When the wood relaxed, it no longer appeared smooth and polished. An unseen hand had etched the sorcerer sigils for fire, water, earth, and air into the wood. A five-pointed star appeared at the handle. A tendril of carved ivy leaves wound along the stave's length.

My hands trembled as I traced the images. It was mine. God, it was *mine*.

I threw the blankets back and leaped to the floor, twirling the stave around and around in my hands.

Lilly entered with a tea tray and gasped.

I bowed it toward her, and a gust of wind erupted through the room, blowing her skirts above her knees. She jumped and a cup fell off the tray and smashed to pieces.

"I'm so sorry!" I threw the stave onto the bed and went to help her.

"Quite all right, miss." She bent to pick up the pieces, joining me crouched on the floor. When our eyes met, we burst out laughing. I had a magic stave. What was a broken cup compared to that?

LILLY FOUND ME AN APPLE-GREEN DAY dress that suited my complexion a bit better than the blue. After she'd made me presentable, I took the stave and went downstairs to the breakfast room. Blackwood, Dee, and Magnus were already there. Blackwood stood by the window, sipping a cup of tea. He wasn't wearing a jacket; it was shocking, seeing him in only his shirtsleeves. Dee ate his eggs in silence. Magnus was slumped over in another chair, asleep.

Blackwood turned from the window and saw me. "Miss Howel," he said, rushing to get his coat off a chair. "Forgive me. I forgot we have a woman in the house now. I only just got in from my training." Fully dressed, he nodded at the others. Dee stood, and Magnus blinked awake. "Did you sleep well?" Blackwood asked.

"Very, thank you," I said. It took only a second for Dee to spot what I held in my hands.

"She's got a stave!" he cried. An instant later, he and Magnus were crowded around me. I held it out, feeling rather proud. "Look, the carvings," Dee said, gleeful.

"She's a true sorcerer." Magnus yawned and clapped a hand on my back. Blackwood seated himself and gazed at me over the rim of his cup.

"I'm glad this is so excellent," I said, taking my seat. "I was worried when I woke to find the stave on my pillow. Who put it there?"

"Master Agrippa left it outside your room last night, but the stave placed itself beside you. It chose," Blackwood said. "That is yours for the rest of your life." He watched me with a curious intensity. "I hope it pleases you. It was cut from a magical grove of white birches on Sorrow-Fell grounds."

"I shall endeavor not to break it," I said lightly.

"Don't break it. You will never have another." Blackwood widened his eyes.

"Yes, I understand. It was only a joke," I murmured.

"Your bond with that stave comes at a heavy price. Most of your power has been placed into it. If the stave breaks, you will die."

"I do know that," I said. I didn't need to be talked down to. "I may not have been raised a sorcerer, but every English child knows the rule about staves."

He took up a newspaper. "Pardon. It was arrogant of me to presume to instruct the chosen one." There was no point speaking with Blackwood.

We focused on breakfast. Sausages, smoked haddock, bacon, and soft-boiled eggs waited in steaming silver dishes; toast stood in racks beside glass bowls of butter and jam, and porridge bubbled in a china tureen. After the rich meal the previous night, I needed something simple. I helped myself to the porridge and some tea.

"Is that all you're eating?" Dee asked, horrified. "No one eats that."

"I do. Plain food is good for the morning." I took a spoonful and found it rather delicious. Magnus sat across from me, buttering a piece of toast.

"Spoken like a proper teacher," he said. "You must have loved your old school's diet."

"Not really. At Brimthorn, the porridge was always burned. So was the coffee." I didn't tell them how the portions had been too small, how I'd gone to bed with a cramping stomach more often than not. I doubted anyone else in this room had much experience with hunger. I didn't want to set myself apart even more.

"You were a teacher, Miss Howel?" Dee said. "What did you teach?"

"History and mathematics, mainly."

"No French or music?" Magnus said.

"I didn't excel at those subjects. I don't enjoy literature or poetry, either, really."

"What? Those are some of life's chief pleasures." I didn't think Magnus was trying to bait me. He seemed curious.

"I'm not interested in what's pleasant. I'm interested in what's useful," I said. Blackwood lowered his paper and looked at me. Something about his gaze was unsettling.

"Are you a good judge of what's useful?" he said. By his expression, he clearly disagreed.

"I like to think so. Yes," I said, pulling my shoulders back. "Do you doubt it?"

"I think that you feel things very strongly." He returned to his paper. "And emotions often cloud better judgment."

I wanted to rip his paper away, but I knew that would be proving the point. Instead, I aggressively drank my tea. Two months of this would feel like a lifetime.

"Anyway," Magnus said slowly with an annoyed glance at Blackwood, "is that why you never went for a governess position? Your love of what's useful?"

"That, and the other thing." I looked into my porridge, toyed with it.

"Setting fires?"

"No. Well, not only that. Rook. Taking a position would mean leaving him behind."

"I doubt he'd have wanted you at Brimthorn forever on his account," Magnus said.

"No. He did not." There was silence. When I looked up again, I found Magnus staring at me across the table, wearing a troubled look.

"What on earth is wrong with you?" I asked.

Magnus started, then glowered at me. "I have to imitate you, Miss Howel, until you give us a smile." He replicated my expression so exactly that I clamped a hand over my mouth to stop the laughter. He winked.

Blackwood folded his paper. "Magnus, if you're finished, perhaps you can report to Master Agrippa in the obsidian room. The day's lesson should begin after breakfast."

Magnus put his hand to his heart. "Dear God. Has Lord Blackwood deigned to speak with me? Is anyone paying attention to this historic moment? Will there be commemorative dishware?"

Blackwood closed his eyes and sighed. "Please get ready for Miss Howel's lesson."

Magnus pushed back from the table and whistled as he left the room. Blackwood took a final sip from his cup. "Shall we, Miss Howel?"

As I rose, Dee said, "You really should name your stave, you know. Names give one a bit more control over something."

Bemused, I picked up my stave as I put my spoon back in my empty bowl. "Perhaps Porridge?" I said, grinning.

To my surprise, the carvings glowed with blue light.

"Oh no!" Dee said. "You should've given it a grand name. What'll it say in the history books? Miss Henrietta Howel, the savior of England, and her stave, Porridge?"

I felt the pulse again, almost like a heartbeat. Somehow I knew the stave was pleased. "I think it'll look quite nice in the books, actually. Porridge it is," I said, and left with Blackwood for my first lesson.

We walked down the stairs, past curtsying maids and bowing footmen. I kept half curtsying in return, still not sure how to behave. Blackwood acknowledged everyone with ease. He kept his chin up, elegant with his smooth black hair and those strange green catlike eyes. I was sure he thought me graceless. I hoped my training wouldn't require us to spend too much time together.

"Miss Howel." He stopped. "I would like to ask something."

"Oh?" Damn, I really didn't fancy a private conversation with him.

"May I see your stave? I wondered at a certain design."

I gave Porridge to him, a bit reluctantly. He twirled it in his hands, a frown creasing his forehead.

"What's wrong?" I asked.

"I would have thought the decoration would be a flame, given your obvious gifts in that area. Instead, it's tendrils of ivy. That's a—" He paused.

"A what?"

"A rare insignia." He handed Porridge to me. I was relieved when it was back in my hands. I didn't know another person touching one's weapon could feel so uncomfortably intimate. We continued toward the training area. He kept his hand on his own stave in its sheath, protecting it, as though I might reach over and snatch it without warning.

My heels clicked as I entered the training room, and the catch of breath in my throat echoed throughout the space. I knew that sorcerers called their training areas obsidian rooms, but I'd never dreamed of this.

The room was eight-sided, each wall a shining, polished obsidian. Within the walls, strange glowing symbols appeared and disappeared. The floor was jet black as well, save for a great five-pointed star carved with that queer, glowing firelight.

Agrippa stepped forward. He wore black robes with pooling sleeves that draped to the floor. The silken fabric spilled over the obsidian like black moving within black. "These are the official robes of a commended sorcerer," he said. "It's not necessary to wear them for training, but I like to, for tradition's sake." Hopefully, I would receive robes just like these.

"We do so many things for tradition's sake," Magnus said,

circling me, "that few of us can remember why we really did them in the first place."

"Perhaps we should begin," Blackwood said, removing his stave from the sheath on his hip.

"Did Joan of Arc have a sheath for her stave?" I asked, wanting one of my own. The Maid of Orleans had been the last recorded female sorcerer. I knew our English Order hated that she was so very French.

"I don't think so," Agrippa said.

"It's difficult," I said, looking down at Porridge, "when your last point of reference died over four hundred years ago."

I felt a strange charge in the air, as if Magnus and Blackwood and Agrippa all shared some private glance. But when I looked up at the three of them, they were each focused on some separate task. The moment, if there had even been one, was gone.

"There are other sorcerer women in history you might admire," Agrippa said. "Hypatia of Alexandria, the teacher. Much like you." He smiled. "Hatshepsut, deemed by many as the greatest pharaoh in Egypt's long history."

It struck me as odd that most sorcerer women belonged solely to antiquity, as if the glory of female magic were some crumbling myth to be debated by scholars.

"Now, no more talk," Agrippa said. "It's time for the lesson." He bid me to remain where I was, at the center of the star. They formed a triangle around me. "Sorcerers are strongest in numbers, working best in groups of three. We're forming this triangle and allowing you to stay in the center so that you don't have to work as hard in the beginning." Agrippa took out his stave. "You haven't named yours by any chance, have you?" He looked pleased when I nodded. "Excellent. Do as I do and say its name." He brought his stave to the floor, crouched down, and whispered, "Tiberius."

I copied him and whispered, "Porridge." Magnus snorted in pleasure. The blue light crept back into the carvings.

"You call power when you do that." Agrippa noticed my timid handling of the stave. "Do you understand its purpose?"

"Er, it's a magical piece of wood?" I realized that my book knowledge would take me only so far in this course.

He smiled. "In concert halls, a conductor takes his baton to command the music. It's the same principle here. Your stave directs the elements of the earth as a baton directs instruments." He circled me and continued. "You're at somewhat of a disadvantage. There are six required maneuvers for commendation, all of them enormously tricky. Four demonstrate your mastery of the elements, one shows warding proficiency, and one highlights a specific skill. The young gentlemen have been training since they arrived in my home two years ago. We'll have to work hard to have you ready by late June." Sorcerers were always commended on Midsummer Eve, so that gave us nine weeks. Not much time at all. "George, if you would please demonstrate water?"

Blackwood went to a small table, on which sat objects to help with the training. He picked up a bowl of water, brought it over, and set it down in front of me.

"Allow me, Master," Magnus said, sliding past Blackwood.

"George is more skilled at water play, Julian."

"But Howel should get an idea of sorcerer form, and I'm the best example of that." He winked at me. I pretended not to notice. He really was a shameless flirt.

Magnus readied himself. With a whispered word, he swung his stave like a sword. The water before him began to spin, rising into the air from its bowl. He turned and, with a sweep of his arm, brought the water to circle around him.

With one decisive whip of his stave, Magnus raised his arms, and the water flew up over his head, re-forming into a flurry of snow. He struck into the air, and the snow grew into a storm that chilled the room with its power. With another fast movement, Magnus morphed the snow into jagged-looking shards of ice. He sent them flying but stopped them before any of us came to harm. Finally, he summoned the ice back and melted it into a threatening black cloud. He punctured the cloud, and the water rained down into the silver bowl. Not a drop was spilled.

When he'd finished, Magnus slammed the end of his stave to the floor. His breathing was heavy, and sweat beaded on his forehead. He looked enormously pleased with himself.

"What do you think?" Agrippa asked.

I could feel the raw energy buzzing over my skin. It was both exhilarating and terrifying. "I'll have to do that?" I swallowed.

"First you must learn to channel the element," Agrippa said. He picked up the bowl and emptied it in front of me. The water grew into a perfect round circle, stopping inches from the toes of my slippers.

"What should I do?" I breathed deeply and prepared.

"Try to get it into the air, in an orb," Agrippa said. "With your stave activated, take it in hand and touch the carved symbol for water."

I did as he asked, pressing my fingers against the triangle. It glowed briefly.

"Now," Agrippa said, "touch your stave to the floor, your left knee bent. Yes, your left knee specifically. Bring the stave up slowly. Clear your mind."

"How do I shape the water if I can't think about it?"

The sorcerers' reactions were interesting. They looked as if I'd said something both amusing and grotesque. "You don't shape it so much as you let it be shaped through you. Sorcerers ask permission; they don't take control." Sensing I'd made a colossal blunder, I blushed. "Again, bring the stave up. Feel it in your marrow, the water floating up from the floor."

I felt like I was only standing there, moving my arm in a silly way. Every time an image entered my head, I quashed it.

The water didn't move, not even a ripple.

"Try again." Agrippa frowned. My stomach gave a painful lurch. I did as he asked. After three more tries, I huffed in frustration.

"I'm sorry. Shouldn't I be able?" How hard could this be, with three sorcerers aiding me? How incompetent was I? I searched Agrippa's face for the smallest signs of disappointment.

Agrippa didn't respond.

"You've enough power to make something happen, Miss Howel," Blackwood said. "That it doesn't is mystifying."

"Don't scare her, Blacky," Magnus said.

"Enough," Agrippa snapped. "Miss Howel, you mustn't worry."

"Should it be this hard?"

He clearly debated with himself for a moment. "No, I don't believe it should."

What kind of prophetic savior can't even complete the easiest task?

"You mustn't worry. Keeping a clear mind isn't easy, especially for someone who's never trained as a sorcerer before. I'll give you some breathing exercises to help control your thoughts. Now. Try again," Agrippa said. He crossed his arms and watched. I did as he'd asked.

My anxiety rendered my mind blank, just like he wanted. But whenever I touched Porridge to the water, nothing happened. Two hours ago, I'd created a wind current. Why was it so difficult now?

My powers, whatever they were, seemed to work only when I was actively thinking. But that was *wrong*.

Suppose the queen would not commend me? Suppose I was a failure? They would put me on the street for certain, and Rook would go with me. No. He wouldn't lose his security because of me.

"Miss Howel, stop. You'll hurt yourself." There it was, that tinge of disappointment in his voice. The water would not move.

I thought of Gwen, beautiful Gwen in her beautiful room.

Had she felt like this? That if she didn't please him, she would die a little inside? Or had she always been secure in his love, as a daughter should be? I felt like a changeling, a peevish, whining, solemn creature stealing beautiful Gwen's place and lingering in Agrippa's house, to feed off him and give nothing in return.

There was no trace of a smile on Agrippa's face. Beside him, Blackwood watched with interest. Frustration sparked something inside me. Bright light appeared at the edges of my vision.

Magnus said, "Well, perhaps the Ancients aren't fond of crossing puddles."

A great sweep of flame covered me, not blue this time, but orange and blood-red at the heart. Agrippa and the boys threw up wards to protect themselves as the fire reflected in the walls and ceiling. As quickly as it had appeared, the fire died.

"Why did I do that?" I put a hand over my chest; my heart was pounding.

"I've no idea," Agrippa said.

I had been so frustrated, so furious. Instinctively, I decided not to mention this to the others. They'd responded to my question about control in such an odd way; perhaps it would only cause trouble. "What's wrong with me?" I asked.

"Nothing's wrong," Agrippa said. "It's odd, of course. Usually, when supported by three others, when in a triangle . . . But this is helping no one." He scratched his head and sighed. "Perhaps we've begun a bit too soon and fast. Miss Howel, why don't you rest this afternoon? We'll speak more at dinner."

I did not want to rest. I wanted to fight on until I'd conquered the lesson, but I sensed Agrippa needed time to think. To reflect on my failure.

"Of course," I said, praying that no one heard my voice waver. I left, pretending that I didn't feel how heavy their gazes were on me.

THERE WAS NO TALK OF THE training at dinner, but afterward the butler asked me to follow him to the library on Agrippa's orders. Feeling ill, I walked down the corridor to two large oak doors. Inside, the room took my breath away.

The shelves rose high above my head, with a ladder that stretched to the uppermost volumes. Huge bay windows looked out onto the garden. Several green velvet armchairs clustered before the hearth. The firelight flickered on the walls and the carpet, with the occasional snap of wood the only noise. I padded into the room and admired the shelves bursting with books and the portraits hung on the walls. I recognized Agrippa's image, but examined the others more closely. Some had been painted recently, judging by the style of clothing, and some dated back hundreds of years.

One particular image drew my attention: the painting of a great house on an emerald lawn, fringed on all sides by a dark wood. The house glowed in the sunlight. I couldn't tell if the dark, foreboding woods lent the place its air of grandeur and beauty or if the house's splendor caused the woods to appear more threatening by contrast. Something about it stirred my imagination, like a scene from a fairy tale. I felt in some way that I'd been there before.

"Do you like it?" Agrippa said, startling me. He stood behind me, smiling at my curiosity.

"It's exquisite. Are these all books on magic?" I glanced around.

"No. Sorcery doesn't require much literary knowledge. Only scholars or magicians write anything. But my father was a great reader, and so am I. I've the most extensive collection of magical theory and history in London, I'm proud to say."

The thought of devouring centuries of sorcerer history excited me. "I should love to read one or two, if I may?"

"We'll set up a little desk for you by the fire. I'll have my personal librarian make recommendations." That was generosity itself. I wanted to hug him, but of course refrained. He motioned for me to follow. On either side of the great bay windows hung a tapestry, and Agrippa bid me to stand before the one on the left. "This is a special creation. It was fashioned by the Speakers in the Dombrey Priory." I'd heard of it. Dombrey—*d'ombre,* French for "of shadow"—was one of the great jewels of English sorcery. But I hadn't known how the Speakers communicated until now.

"They're weavers?"

"The Speakers drink the juice of the Etheria flower, a night-blooming plant that increases psychic ability. It leaves them in too much of a haze to have a proper conversation, but they see their visions and weave them."

I took in the details. A great white hand reached into the

sky from a tangle of black trees. Tongues of fire bloomed from the tips of the five fingers. In the center of the palm, two lions flanked a shield: Agrippa's own seal.

"They created this sixteen years ago," Agrippa said, reaching out and stroking the fabric with two fingertips. "So many of the tapestries the Speakers make seem confusing, and no one had a clue what this one meant. The words, especially, seemed like nonsense."

"Words?" I looked closer, and, woven along the tapestry's edges, I could make out:

> *A girl-child of sorcerer stock rises from the ashes of a life.*
> *You shall glimpse her when Shadow burns*
> *in the Fog above a bright city.*
> *You shall know her when Poison drowns*
> *beneath the dark Waters of the cliffs.*
> *You shall obey her when Sorrow falls*
> *unto the fierce army of the Blooded Man.*
> *She will burn in the heart of a black forest;*
> *her fire will light the path.*
> *She is two, the girl and the woman,*
> *and one must destroy the other.*
> *For only then may three become one,*
> *and triumph reign in England.*

I wasn't too keen on being told I must destroy one part of myself, but seeing Agrippa's obvious pride, I chose not to mention that. "Even after the Ancients attacked, no one thought of it," Agrippa said. "But six years ago, on an inspection of the priory, they found the tapestry again. 'Shadow' and 'fog' are obviously an allusion to Korozoth. 'Poison beneath dark water' has to mean Nemneris, the Water Spider. 'Sorrow falls unto the army of the Blooded Man'—that *must* mean R'hlem. The tapestry seemed to identify the Ancients, and to give us the key to their demise."

"I can't possibly best all the Ancients by myself."

He laughed. "No, we wouldn't expect that. It seems obvious, though, that a girl-child, a sorcerer, one presumably with some aptitude for fire, is needed."

I looked to the other tapestry on the right side of the window. "Is that from the Speakers as well?"

"No, an Agrippa family heirloom."

This tapestry displayed a hunt for a white stag, with medieval ladies in pointed hats and long-sleeved gowns watching as sorcerers burst into the fray, wielding staves. One fallen sorcerer touched the lips of a young boy who knelt by his side.

I pointed at them. "What's he doing?"

"It's a way to share power. Magnus did it yesterday, when he marked you with his blood. He gave you the temporary ability to use his stave, as this man is allowing his human servant to wield magic for a time. Sorcerers in battle would often do that if they were too weak to continue."

The young boy's forehead bore the image of a star, presumably drawn in blood. So that was what Magnus had painted on my head. Extraordinary. "Can you teach me how to do something like that?"

"I can and will teach you everything," Agrippa said, leading me out of the library. "When I've finished, you'll be commended, and all will be well."

"Then you don't doubt?" I asked. I couldn't bear to look at him. "After my failure this morning?"

Agrippa placed his hand on my shoulder. "I wanted you to see the tapestry because I believe you're destined to help us. That was no failure. It was our first try."

His kindness was almost overwhelming. "I can never thank you enough for all you've done," I murmured, bowing my head.

"In time, I believe I will say those exact words to you. And I'll have every cause to mean them."

7

THE NEXT MORNING, I WAS HEADING TOWARD THE training room when Magnus stopped me. "You're to rest today. Master's orders. I've been instructed to escort you about the town." He put my arm in his and wheeled me toward the front door.

"I've no wish to see the inside of your five favorite taverns," I said, biting back disappointment at missing a lesson.

"Don't be absurd. I've *eight* favorite taverns, thank you very much. Besides, Blackwood's coming along." He laughed at my pained expression. "My thoughts exactly. You should have heard him grumble. I actually found him in the training room after breakfast, running through his maneuvers. Just for extra practice, he said."

"I suppose you have plans that Lord Blackwood won't like at all."

"On the contrary, I've designed an educational outing." He grinned with excitement but said no more.

WE RUMBLED ALONG IN AGRIPPA'S CARRIAGE, Blackwood and Magnus seated opposite me. As we drove, people on the street smiled and bowed to us.

"The carriage has Agrippa's seal on the door," Magnus said. He waved through the window. "They love Master Agrippa. They'll love you as well."

"Unless I fail." I was still focused on yesterday's lesson. "What happens if I don't receive the queen's commendation in June?" I asked Blackwood, certain he of all people would answer with honesty.

"You won't be a sorcerer, Miss Howel." He stated it matter-of-factly, as if I'd inquired about the weather. "On the rare occasion that an Incumbent cannot complete the assigned maneuvers, his stave is taken from him and he's removed from the family record in disgrace."

"So I'd receive the same punishment as someone who's trained these past two years?" The panic of my botched lesson came thundering back, but I held it inside.

"They need to know you're the one named in the prophecy. If you're not what Her Majesty seeks, you won't be encouraged to develop those abilities," Blackwood said, his tone effortlessly cool. *I doubt she'll be capable,* he'd said to Agrippa. "Most feel that women should not learn magic."

"Do you?" I raised my eyebrows.

"I support whatever the Order thinks is right," he said after a moment of careful consideration. How very *generous.*

"Blacky, much as I adore your conversational contributions, I really think we should focus on enjoying the day," Magnus said. He knocked Blackwood's hat off his head for emphasis.

They took me to St. Paul's Cathedral, at Blackwood's suggestion. Magnus stifled a groan as we walked up the church steps. We passed along the nave, and I marveled at the marble floors and golden ceilings decorated with angels. Down in the crypt, we visited Christopher Wren's tomb, surrounded by an iron gate. The grave was topped with a slab of obsidian.

"Wren came from a fine sorcerer family," Magnus said. "That's why the obsidian. All sorcerers try to be buried with some piece of it on them." He whistled, listening to the echo play off the walls. "Nice place for eternal rest, but I prefer Poets' Corner in Westminster Abbey. You wouldn't like it, probably. You're not one for poets or playwrights, are you, Miss Howel?" Magnus paused before a collection of prayer candles. With a sweep of his stave he lit them. Their glow highlighted his hair and played on his cheekbones. If he wanted me to notice how handsome he was, perhaps he was succeeding.

"I didn't say I hated them, only that I had no time for them."

He responded in a low, powerful tone, speaking the words, "'What a piece of work is man, how noble in reason, how infinite in faculty, in form and moving how express and admirable, in action how like an angel.'" His voice reverberated in the great space, soft yet clear. "That's *Hamlet*."

"You should've been an actor." I was impressed.

"Do you think?" He seemed pleased. "Sometimes I imagine I'd give up sorcery and duty just for the opportunity to tour the countryside with a small troupe. Mother always said I had a knack for voices."

Blackwood came by and hushed us.

After my tour, we stopped at an inn for lunch, complete with chops and potatoes and ale. A few more months eating this way, and I might attain some feminine curves. Magnus entertained us with stories and jokes, but I tried bringing Blackwood into the conversation. Despite how badly our relationship had begun, I wanted us to be civil. It would make training easier.

"How old were you when you became the Earl of Sorrow-Fell, my lord?" I asked.

"I was eight when my father died," Blackwood replied, studying his half-drunk ale. "The youngest seal bearer in the history of my family. They thought that was terribly exciting."

"I'm so sorry," I said, and meant it. To be that young and head of a family was one thing, but seal bearers were responsible for their entire magical line. The pressure would've been tremendous.

"Father died battling R'hlem in his country's service. It was a noble end," Blackwood said, as emotionless as if he were reading the words out of a book. "What of your family?"

"Father died before I was born, mother soon after." I felt uncomfortable, as I always did when talking about my parents. I'd no memories, no connections. I wished I could feel something more than curiosity and longing when I thought about them.

He nodded. "So you truly grew up at Brimthorn?"

"Well, I lived in Devon until I was five." There. There was a real memory, a real flash of pain. Blackwood noticed.

"Why did you leave?"

I thought of my aunt walking away from me, back to her carriage. And me, hanging on to her skirt, begging her to take me home. She hadn't listened. She hadn't cared.

"Several reasons," I said quickly. "The war, for one. I'm sorry that training in London left you so little time on your estate. As I've said, the girls at Brimthorn would have loved to meet their great benefactor."

"I've visited Brimthorn before. I might have seen you. We just would not have been formally introduced." Of course not. He was an earl's son, and I, a charity girl. Very little chance of meeting. "Before the war, Sorrow-Fell used to host events for the Brimthorn children. I'd have continued the tradition, but I couldn't arrange it from London. It's better to be present for those sorts of things."

"Yes, one of the wretched girls might make off with the silver tucked under her bonnet," I said. Magnus snickered.

"I don't like strangers on the estate when I'm not there," he said defensively, as if this were an old argument.

"Perhaps it's for the best. 'Sorrow-Fell' sounds like a gloomy place for a picnic."

"No. It's beautiful." Blackwood's expression cleared. "The founding earl received it as a gift from a faerie lord. The land is steeped in magic. Some find it rather melancholy." No wonder he loved it. "But the forests and grounds are deep and lush. White stags live on the property. My father always forbade a stag hunt, as he said it would be wrong to kill any magical creature. My father . . ." The light vanished from his face in an instant, and he said no more.

"Do you see Sorrow-Fell often?" I asked, feeling a small flash of sympathy.

"No. My studies keep me in London." He withdrew into himself; I couldn't get another word.

A pretty serving girl arrived with more ale. Magnus winked at her, sending her into a giggling frenzy.

After lunch, Magnus hustled me toward the carriage. "We have to move fast or all the best spots will be taken," he said.

"For what?" I asked as we drove down the street.

"Have you ever seen a ship launch before?"

The docks were outside the protected area. Living in Agrippa's fine house only made the devastation I witnessed beyond the ward more terrible. Magnus talked, but I didn't pay much attention. I watched the burned houses and debris-strewn streets roll past the window. Just sitting in a fine carriage made me feel guilty.

We got out at the docks, elbowing our way through crowds as they waved handkerchiefs and flags. Squeezing between them, we strained to catch a glimpse above the throng of cheering humanity. A massive sailing ship moved down the river, toward the sea. It was a great square man-of-war with billowing white sails and an unfurled blue flag. The launch had the air of a national celebration. A small brass band played as men selling apples and meat pies moved through the crowd.

"Isn't it wonderful?" Magnus cried. He seemed to glow with excitement.

"You want to go with them when you're commended?" I

was impressed despite myself. With Nemneris the Water Spider attacking the coast, the navy was about the most dangerous place for a sorcerer.

"Yes. I don't want to stay here and uphold the ward. Put me in the midst of the battle. I'm ready!" He whooped and threw his hat into the air. The people around us applauded his enthusiasm.

"I never thought so many would turn up for a ship launch," I said. Some poor woman sobbed beside me as she waved her handkerchief toward the departing vessel. Then again, perhaps seeing *any* boat leave the harbor was cause for celebration. Even if a ship got past the Water Spider, the English were persona non grata on the continent. Europe did not want to invoke R'hlem's wrath by aiding refugees. "Do ships never come in?" I asked. Magnus easily followed my train of thought.

"Well, naturally there's been some contact. How else would Cellini have arrived? Italy's the only nation that will offer assistance. Other than that, dear Miss Howel, we are on our own. Here. Cling to me for comfort." When I didn't fall into his arms, he continued. "You hear of smugglers taking men and women out of England, heading for America. They'll charge a fellow a king's ransom for the chance to escape to a new life. Just between us, if I'm to choose between Korozoth and a Yankee tavern brawl, I'll take my chances with old Shadow and Fog any day."

Blackwood came over to us, jostled by a drunkard and his chums. "We should escort Miss Howel home. The people are getting rowdy." As we walked through the crowd, I studied the faces about me. Many looked pinched and worn with hunger, with tiredness. I knew these people, how they felt. I certainly understood them better than I did the sorcerers.

Rushing back behind the safety of the ward didn't appeal to me.

"Wait," I said as we walked toward the carriage. "We're here anyway. What's to stop us from looking about?"

"You want to see the slums?" Magnus sounded puzzled.

"I don't think it's the safest idea," Blackwood said.

"If I'm going to fight for London, I should see how *all* of its people live."

"Perhaps one day, but not now," Blackwood said, taking my arm. He spoke with beleaguered patience, as if I were an errant child. I shook myself firmly out of his grasp.

"Don't you ever make charity calls? Look." I held up my reticule. Inside, I had the three shillings I'd saved from my time at Brimthorn. A poor savings after eleven years, but it would do. "I'd rather give this to someone who needs it than spend it on myself, especially now that I have so much. Come on, just through Ha'penny Row. It's not too dangerous there."

Blackwood set his jaw. "I said no."

"Let's put it to a vote," I said, ignoring his order. I raised my hand into the air. "I vote yes."

"No," he said again.

"I say yes as well." Magnus winked at me. "I want to stretch my legs." He extended his arm, and I took it like a proper lady.

"Thank you, sir. That suits me perfectly." Together, we strolled past a scowling Blackwood.

"A short visit," he muttered, stalking after us.

"Here's an idea," Magnus said as we followed the surging crowds away from the docks. "Since you're to be a sorcerer, Miss Howel, perhaps we should address you as one. We all use our plain surnames with one another. So, may I call you Howel?"

I wanted to be one of them, didn't I? "All right. Shall I call you Magnus?"

"Perfection. What do you say, Blackwood? Is she Howel the sorcerer?"

"Miss Howel is a lady. One must always address ladies with proper respect." Blackwood nodded to me, the image of politeness, but I understood. He would not acknowledge me as his equal. He did not consider me a sorcerer.

IN THE ROW, THE PEOPLE PRESSED so close I wondered if we mightn't all congeal together into a quivering slab. We passed the little girls in black dresses holding trays of totems, each trying to outshout the others. I stopped before one of them, a tiny blond creature with a clean face but the dirtiest hands I'd ever seen. She offered a figure with tentacles erupting from its center.

"Please you, miss, here's Korozoth, great Shadow and Fog, for protectin'. Save yourself and your family. Tuppence only, miss." With a start, I recognized her from the street the day before, when she had been "crushed" by our carriage.

She gasped, remembering me as well. "There you are, miss. He told me you'd be by."

"What? Who?" The hair along my neck prickled.

- 103 -

"The magician Jenkins Hargrove. Says you have to come with me to meet him, miss. He'd love to talk to you, would Mr. Hargrove."

"How did he know where I'd be?"

"He told you to come." She said it as though I were very silly for not understanding. "While you were sleeping."

Yesterday, Jenkins Hargrove had spoken to me in a dream. I shook my head slowly. "That's impossible."

"Nothing's impossible with Mr. Hargrove. Come on, then," she said, grabbing my hand. "We'll go together."

"I can't," I whispered, looking over my shoulder. "There are two others with me."

Magnus caught up with us. The girl pretended we hadn't been having a serious conversation.

"Buy a totem for tuppence, sir," she said to Magnus. "Ward your home and fam'ly." Magnus handed the child two shiny pennies, which she snatched away and hid within her clothes.

"What's your name?" he asked.

"Charley," the girl said, a bit wary.

"Don't be afraid, Charley." Magnus crouched to see eye to eye with her. "We're sorcerers." He made the totem in his palm rise and wobble on a current of air. Charley clapped with delight. Magnus's ease with her was rather sweet. I knelt beside them.

"I was just telling Charley that we came to see what life is like for her."

"Life is very good, sir," the child said.

"Where do you live?" Magnus asked.

"With the magician, Mr. Jenkins Hargrove. We sell totems for him, and he gives us a place to sleep at night," Charley said. Blackwood pushed through the crowd and came up to us. When Charley saw him, she jumped. "Oh, m'lord. Didn't think to see you again till next week." She curtsied to him. I looked up in surprise.

Blackwood stayed perfectly still, as if a sudden movement would set off a trap. What was all this?

"How do you know little Charley?" I asked, standing.

"My family performs charity work." He took care not to look at me.

"I thought you weren't so keen on charity." I raised my eyebrow.

"I never said that," he muttered.

"He comes to see us every Friday." Charley beamed.

"Pretty regular charity to hand over to some old conjurer," Magnus said, studying Blackwood as if memorizing his uncomfortable expression.

"Jenkins Hargrove is the greatest magician of the age." Charley held tight to her little wooden tray.

"What say we pay a visit to the greatest magician of the age right now?" Magnus said. I flinched. I didn't want to meet this man with Magnus and Blackwood in tow. "Take us home to meet your master, Charley, and you'll have a bright new guinea."

Blackwood looked up and down the avenue for some method of escape. My stomach cramped.

"Perhaps another day," I said to Magnus.

"Er, maybe not today, sir," Charley muttered, though she looked tempted.

"What if I make it two guineas?" He took the gleaming coins from his pocket and showed them to the girl. That did the trick.

"Follow me." Charley spun about and ran.

"I think it's getting late," I said to Magnus, trying to hide my desperation.

"You want to rob a poor little girl?" he asked with mock innocence, and walked after her, wearing a mischievous grin. Blackwood appeared to have frozen in place.

"Do you want to leave?" I said.

"No. Let's get this over with." He led us after the others.

Charley guided us onto quieter, more cramped avenues. On the way, we passed wreckage of burned houses and hovels, scorched buildings with broken windows and smoke-blackened walls. The smell of damp and rot permeated the air.

"Korozoth mostly attacks at night," Charley said, happily playing tour guide. "Lot of people lost their homes."

On the corner opposite us, a bare-knuckle boxing match was in full swing. Two shirtless fellows circled each other, punching and jabbing as the smell of sweat and blood and ale filled the air. Drunken men jeered and shouted as they watched.

"They're animals," Blackwood said, shielding me from view.

"They're desperate," I said sadly. "They feel cheap, so that's how they behave."

To our left, women in pancake makeup and rouge slid shawls from their shoulders to reveal pushed-up breasts and bare arms. They smiled at Magnus and Blackwood, who looked away.

Charley took us down an alleyway, past two dirty and ragged men begging with tin cups. I gave them each a coin. As we rounded the corner, I gasped.

An Unclean man huddled against the brick wall, gazing blankly at the world ahead. There was no question that he'd been touched. His right arm had ballooned to a grotesque degree, the flesh white and pale green and patched with rot. The entire right side of the man's head had swollen to three times its normal size, so that he had to lean it against the wall in an effort not to tip over. A few wisps of hair dotted his scalp. Shiny, clear fluid dribbled out of his eyes, so foul-smelling as to make one sick. It was clear which Ancient was responsible. Molochoron, a great festering ball of mold and filth, had touched this man— touched but not killed him. I knelt before him, a handkerchief to my nose.

"Is there anything I can do?" I asked. The man didn't respond. His breathing sounded raspy and soft.

"He can't hear you," Charley said. "He's dead to the world." I took the last coin I had and pressed it into his hand. Magnus gently urged me to follow the group.

We moved along a flight of rickety wooden stairs that led up the side of a brick building. There was a door at the top, which bore the painted words:

Charley knocked. A little boy with a dirty face opened the door, and inside we found five other children working in a corner. A stove kept the room quite warm. The children were carving pieces of dark wood to make more totems. "This is my home," Charley said.

Besides the mattress and the stove, the only other furnishings were a wooden table and four chairs. The table was covered with glass bottles and tin cups. Though outside it was a bright afternoon, grime caked the windows so completely that we remained shuttered in twilight. The walls were exposed brick and chunks of broken plaster. Walking around the bare space, I noticed a patchwork curtain separating a corner of the hovel into its own private area.

Charley hugged two of the children and introduced them to Magnus as her sister and brother. They pecked her with questions. Had she brought them anything to eat? Did she sell any totems?

"Where are your parents?" I said.

"Dead and gone, miss," Charley replied. Magnus gave her two guineas. The children rejoiced, and I felt ill.

"And your master?" There was a banging noise. The man from my dream stepped out from the curtained private area. He bowed to us and hobbled over to the table, moving like an arthritic crab, all sideways-stepping and gnarled limbs. Easing into a seat before us, he spread a deck of cards on the table.

"Come in, dear lady and gents, an' 'ave a look upon your future. We are but 'umble folk, dear miss, an' think—" Here Hargrove stopped and looked at us, his eyebrow raised. He recognized me. "Miss. How pleasant to make your acquaintance." For one terrifying moment, I thought he'd mention the dream. "And your companions. How charming." He nodded to the boys. Blackwood nodded back.

The magician changed upon the instant. He stretched and popped his joints into place, so that his legs straightened and his head settled right on his shoulders. "A thousand pardons, dear gentlefolk. I mistook you for easy marks that might be swayed by pity to donate a few coppers. How may I assist you?"

"We wanted to join His Lordship on a charity visit," I said, glancing at Blackwood. "I know it's not his usual day of the week."

Hargrove took a glass bottle of something from his collection on the table, poured a little liquid into a tin cup, and handed it down to Charley. The smell was frightful.

"Drink your gin, that's a good girl." She took it with glee.

"You know, I'm not sure that's appropriate for a growing child," I said, watching her guzzle it.

"Well, I try to keep her in ale, but it's an expensive habit." He laid out three cards. They showed a woman with a wand, a man with a sword, and a grinning skeleton that capered down a road. This was unlike any game I had ever played. "I'm the magician

Jenkins Hargrove, purveyor of the finest arcane artifacts and occult odds and ends. I read tarot, tell your fortune, traffic with spirits, and raise the dead, but only on a full or new moon, and never on church holidays." He looked up, his dark eyes dancing. "You're sorcerers, come down from your lofty perch to gawk at the little people. How refreshing." He turned the cards facedown, and when he flipped them up again their pictures were different. They showed a boy and girl kissing, seven coins falling through the air, and a man with a cloak and a pointed hat making a toy soldier dance. Hargrove narrowed his eyes at me. "I've never seen a female sorcerer before," he said.

"I'm not commended yet."

"Mmm. Magic is a dangerous business, girl, especially for one so young and lovely as yourself." He snapped his fingers, and a gold coin dropped out of thin air and into his hand. He bit it in two, spit one half onto the table, and waved his hand over the piece. It transformed into a bright golden beetle that opened its shell and beat its thin wings. I leaned in, stunned by the display.

"Real magic," Hargrove said, waving his hand again and returning the beetle to half a gold piece, "is about pushing the limits of what can and cannot be imagined. But I expect you're all still content with starting fires and making it rain." He swept the cards back into the pack and slid it into his purple-orange-red coat.

"At least our magic is perfectly natural," I muttered, stung by his rudeness.

"I won't have the Order insulted," Blackwood said. Magnus put on his glove and poked at the gold piece, mystified.

"Of course not," Hargrove said, steepling his fingers. His nails were uncommonly long. "We mustn't insult our faithful friend Lord Blackwood, must we, children?" Charley hugged the magician, making it clear where her loyalties lay. He grinned, his mouth full of surprisingly white teeth, and stroked her hair. "My Lord Blackwood, can you accept my apology?"

"Of course I forgive you," Blackwood said, in a tone that indicated he wanted to get out of here and would say anything to make that happen.

"The Blackwood family is generous with its charity. Did you know that?" Hargrove said to me and Magnus. "Yes, I've been on the receiving end of their charity many times in my life." It didn't sound as nice as the words implied.

"We are always happy to help in any way we can," Blackwood said, staring at the door like it was the closed gate of paradise. I'd never imagined he could look so unsettled. I honestly, I found it a little enjoyable.

"And you are so helpful, my lord. Especially seeing as I can only make so much money by way of charms and totems. Your Order, my young friends, is not generous with what it will allow magicians to do."

"Why would the Order have any say in your affairs?" I said. Granted, I could understand why sorcerers would want to keep magicians under control.

"We must blame the accursed Howard Mickelmas, my dear girl. He's the one who thought it such fun to rip a hole in time and space, to summon those evil Ancients from some far, distant world. He's to blame, along with that witch, that Mary Willoughby. They ruined it for the rest of us." He sighed. "Did you know that magicians flourished back in the Golden Age, when good Queen Elizabeth was alive? We were the most learned, the most ambitious. We were the future." He took the half piece of gold off the table, gripped it tightly in his fist, and presented the piece whole and intact. When I touched it, it turned into a brown cockroach and leaped at me.

I cried out, and Hargrove stamped on the bug, squashing it into the floorboards. "That, my dear girl, is exactly what happened to my kind. We were stamped by the Order's boot. But never fear, for a roach is impressively difficult to eradicate." He removed his foot, and the unhurt insect dipped its antennae and scampered away. The children tried to catch it. "The Order only flattened us, didn't kill us. Sorcerers are nothing if not compassionate."

The feeling in the room had turned bad. Even Magnus looked uncomfortable.

"Perhaps we should go," I said.

"Without your fortune told, my dear?" Hargrove took out his cards again and shuffled them. "Care to learn your future? Care to know the identity of your admirers?" He looked at Blackwood and Magnus. "Or do you have the names already?" He leaned back in his chair and rested his boots on the table.

Any desire I had to speak with this man, to learn how he'd crept into my dreams, had vanished. I couldn't stand to be here another second. Blackwood placed a few coins on the table, and we walked quickly for the door.

"Return anytime, young miss. I'm sure we'd have much to talk about," Hargrove called as we hurried down the steps and back to the carriage. The ward was a most welcome sight. Blackwood removed his hat and rubbed his eyes. Magnus stared at the floor, the muscles in his jaw working.

"What exactly were the terms of the royal pardon for magicians?" I asked.

"In exchange for their lives, they would take no apprentices and perform no public magic," Blackwood replied. "When this generation of magicians dies, their magic will end in England forever. To break the pardon is to forfeit your life."

"That's cruel," I said. "Mickelmas was only one man. Why punish the rest so harshly?"

"Because you cannot trust a magician's work."

"Why not?"

"Because they are evil." Blackwood turned from me, the conversation ended.

"Thank you for escorting me," I whispered, my voice dull.

We were silent all the way home.

8

MY LESSONS THE NEXT DAY WERE ANOTHER DISAS-
ter. I set fires when I was meant to form ice and drowned flames
under torrents of water. I tried the breathing exercises to clear
my mind, but they only made me more anxious. Magnus encouraged my skills, while Blackwood silently judged the lack of them.
Afterward, while we were filing out of the room, he approached
me. I tried to excuse myself before he could tell me what a failure
I was, but he surprised me by saying, "It would be my privilege to
escort you to Madame Voltiana's. She is my sister's favorite dressmaker, and would be happy to service you with compliments of
my family." He stood with his hands behind his back and spoke
as though conducting a business transaction. It took a moment
for me to understand that he wanted to pay for my new clothes.

"Thank you, but I couldn't possibly. It's too generous." And I
really didn't want to be in any special debt to Blackwood.

"Nonsense. You must be suitably dressed for the queen's
commendation in June."

"I couldn't repay you. Besides, I have clothes—"

"Miss Howel," he whispered, "you haven't considered Master Agrippa. I know he meant his daughter's wardrobe for you,

but I've seen his face these last few days. Perhaps a change would do him good."

How stupid could I be? I would do anything to save Agrippa pain. "In that case, my lord, I accept your offer. You're very kind."

"It's merely a responsibility. Someone must think of these things," he said with a wave of his hand, as though he were going over the monthly accounts. Only Blackwood could make someone feel like an oaf for thanking him.

Madame Voltiana's was a fashionable establishment on a bustling street in Mayfair, with gold lettering over the door. I'd never been in a dress shop before, and I gazed around in wonder. Swatches of expensive silk and satin lay in folds; gowns of frothy lace sat on dressmaker dummies. Women in white caps sewed, barely looking up from their work. A young lady, too richly dressed to be employed in a shop, sat on a sofa with a cup of tea. When she saw us, she rushed over.

"George, you're late. Mamma wasn't about to let me go without a chaperone, but I convinced her." The girl kissed Blackwood's cheek. I assumed this had to be his sister. Otherwise, she was *very* forward.

"You had better do as you're told in the future," he said, but there was no harshness in his tone. He actually smiled.

"How dull life would be if I only did *that*." She was bold; I found I rather liked her. Blackwood turned her to me.

"May I present my sister, Lady Elizabeth Blackwood."

"You must never call me Elizabeth, as it sounds practically ancient. Eliza will do," she said, beaming. Eliza had the same coloring as her brother, the pale skin and black hair and green eyes, but that was the extent of the similarity. Her whole person vibrated with energy. She wore a deep purple day gown, one that beautifully set off her hair and eyes, but was too extravagant for a simple outing. She kissed my cheek before I could say hello.

"We're going to be friends," she announced. "George wrote and said you seemed clever, which is a sight more than other girls in my circle. I daresay they've taken to staying quiet so as to better catch a husband. I don't need to be modest, of course— who wouldn't want a Blackwood? Arrogant, perhaps, but true."

At that moment, Madame Voltiana swept through a pair of gold curtains. She was a faerie, half a head taller than Blackwood and thin as a reed, with purple skin and a snarl of moss-green hair.

"My lord, you do me too much honor." She took his hands, to his embarrassment. "And Lady Eliza, always your servant." She curtsied to the girl. "My lady, are you in need of anything in particular?" Madame Voltiana smiled, revealing a mouth filled with sharp black teeth.

Eliza pushed me forward. "This is my dear friend Henrietta Howel, and she must be properly equipped."

Voltiana stood back, clapping her hands as she studied me. She wore a great gold monstrosity of a gown, with enough frills and flounces to drown a normal woman. I was growing more and more nervous at the thought of being dressed by this faerie.

"I see." With that, Madame Voltiana burst into violent tears, turned, and fled through the curtains. Blackwood and Eliza looked at each other, clearly surprised.

"I'm sure she'll be back," Eliza said, attempting a smile.

Sure enough, after a stunned moment, Voltiana returned, composed.

"Forgive me," she said, flicking away a tear from her thin cheek, "the challenge was almost too great. But I shall triumph." She pointed at me and nodded. "Yes, girl. You will be my masterpiece."

Perhaps I should run.

It took her fifteen seconds to pop me up on a stool in front of three mirrors. While she grunted and sighed and measured and pinched me, turning me this way and that, Eliza chattered, discussing different cuts and colors. Almost as soon as I was up on the stool, I was dragged down again and seated on a sofa. Eliza sat beside me, explaining certain fashions with the air of an expert. Lovely shopgirls in different-colored frocks and gowns paraded choices before me, in and out of the curtains so fast I hardly had time to see what the faerie had in mind.

I looked around for Blackwood and found him talking with one of the seamstresses, a pretty blond girl. He smiled at her, obviously enjoying their conversation. She laughed at something he said. Interesting.

Perhaps my wardrobe wasn't the only reason for this visit.

"You'll need red," Eliza said, snapping her fingers at a shop girl. "Your complexion is positively designed for red, as you're so dark. No pinks. Pink will be the death of you, and green will turn you sallow. Yellow might work, but only the right shade. Ivory! It's the only thing. What do you think?"

I had no idea what to say, so Eliza started another conversation.

"Julian Magnus is one of your fellow Incumbents, isn't he? To be frank, I rather hoped he'd come with you today." She turned toward the doorway as if to check whether he'd appeared. "Mamma would be horrified at my saying so, but he's so good-looking it could drive anyone to distraction. And he makes me laugh. Of course, he hasn't a penny. Therefore he's totally unsuitable."

"Oh?" It was all I could think to say. I liked Eliza's spirit, but I didn't like her being so mercenary about Magnus. If a man talked about a woman that way, I'd have called him a cad.

"He's not the Magnus seal bearer; his cousin is. And his cousin is fat and married. Shame." She sighed. "One never thinks of handsome boys as being without wealth. Beautiful women who live in poverty are an everyday tale." Eliza clapped her hands, and the shopgirls departed. "You'll have three day dresses and three for the evening, along with gloves and accessories and such. Not your commendation gown, though; I'm going to dream up something special."

It occurred to me that Eliza was used to having her way over every living creature.

"Perhaps we might discuss it together," I said.

"Nonsense. My taste is bound to be better than yours," she said, waving her hand as if to dismiss me.

The remark stung. "There's no need to be rude."

Eliza gasped, putting a gloved hand to her cheek. "You're cross with me."

"No, I'm not," I said, but to my surprise she shrieked with glee.

"No one's ever cross with me! No one ever calls me rude! Listen, that settles it. I know it's almost two months off, but you simply must be our special guest for the Court Players' annual *Dream*."

I had no idea what any of that meant. "Pardon?"

"*A Midsummer Night's Dream*. You know, the play? It's a social obligation every year, and it would be tedious except that the Court Players are the only troupe with actual faeries as actors, so it's marvelous. You'll be in our box. Say yes. Right now."

I'd never been to the theater before. The closest I'd come was the Christmas play we performed each year at Brimthorn, so this was massively exciting. "Thank you, yes," I said, feeling overwhelmed.

"Not at all. This is wonderful. I'm ever so glad they found a lady sorcerer I could be of an age with. When the last one was alive, I was too young."

That was a baffling thing to say. "The last one was four hundred years ago. We were *all* a bit too young to be her friend."

Eliza looked at me as if I were an adorable fool. "No, dear, *four* years ago. Remember? Gwendolyn Agrippa?"

"What are you talking about?" I felt as if I'd missed an important conversation.

Eliza gasped again. "They never told you? Oh, they're positive fiends, all of them. Keeping you ignorant of something like that, well."

"What are you talking about?" I couldn't help speaking harshly. Eliza rolled her eyes.

"Gwendolyn Agrippa was a sorcerer. Or at least she was going to be. She tested positive for powers at her baptism when she was a baby—don't look shocked, they baptize girls as well as boys for tradition's sake—and you can imagine everyone's reaction when she was found to have an active ability. The first girl in four hundred years! She received a stave, was an Incumbent in her father's house. Good Lord, did they think you'd never find out? They thought *she* was the prophesied one, you know. Then she died of that piddling little fever, and they had to find another. So I'm ever so glad you're here." She beamed.

I thought I would be sick. Palehook had said I'd much to live up to.

I always thought Miss Agrippa to be among the brightest lights in our society. Some had clearly believed Gwen to be the prophesied one. Which meant that some would search for reasons to despise me. After my recent efforts in the obsidian room . . .

"You look ill," Eliza said. "What's wrong?"

"This is a great deal to take in," I murmured.

"Don't tell George I told you. Dear boy, he's positively the most wonderful brother, but he does tend to think his word is law. Back in a tick," she said, and bounced off to drag Blackwood out of his conversation with the seamstress.

Watching them, I wondered what Blackwood thought of Gwendolyn Agrippa's status as the prophesied one.

We were soon back out on the street. Eliza drove off in her family carriage, leaning out the window to wave to me.

"Come next week for tea!" she called.

"She likes you. Eliza doesn't like most girls," Blackwood said, sounding rather impressed. He absently twined a pink silk ribbon around his hand. I was certain the pretty seamstress had given it to him.

I smiled wanly at his comment; my mind was preoccupied.

"A SURPRISE, MISS," LILLY SAID WHEN I entered my room that evening. Seven parcels lay on the bed. "Your clothes from Madame Voltiana."

"That was just hours ago!" Incredulous, I opened a bundle and uncovered a gorgeous wine-red evening gown with gold embroidery. "How is it possible?"

"Madame Voltiana's special. Works like magic. I suppose it is magic, isn't it?" Lilly giggled as she laid out my clothes. "These'll suit you ever so much better. How about the red for tonight, miss? We'll do your hair lovely again."

Besides the gowns, there were stockings, a chemise, even knickers trimmed with lace. Everything was pure white; in my old life, such delicate things would have been impossible to keep spotless. There were soft goatskin gloves in fawn and cream. I petted one against my cheek and sighed. Every Christmas Eve, I'd listened to Jane Lawrence whisper about how she longed for kid gloves. Perhaps I could send her a pair this year.

There were flannel and cotton petticoats, and also a black velvet hip sheath, perfect for carrying a stave. Madame Voltiana had thought of everything.

I sat on the bed, unable to truly enjoy the presents. What Eliza had said about Gwendolyn Agrippa kept gnawing at me. And besides that, the images of yesterday's slums kept repeating themselves as I admired the gowns. Who was I to wear such fine things when so many were suffering? "Lilly, where do you come from?"

"Miss?"

"Where's your family now?"

The girl's smile disappeared. "My family's all gone, miss. Callax the Child Eater carried off my folks and sisters. Gram felt the only safe place for me'd be behind the ward, so she got me a position in this house. I'm grateful, mind. It's safe here." She played with the sleeve of a yellow tea dress.

"I'm sorry," I murmured.

"The past's the past, miss," Lilly said, bustling to organize my vanity table. "Shall I help you dress for dinner?"

We chose the wine-red gown, and the color did flatter me, bringing out the darker tones of my skin. Lilly pinned up my hair so elegantly that it appeared almost beautiful. While Lilly arranged the ringlets by the sides of my face, she clucked her tongue. "You're lovely, miss. Just as he said."

"Who?"

"Rook. He's ever so nice." Lilly flushed a deep pink. "The others don't like to be around him, but he's beautiful. Even with the scars." Her open admiration for Rook surprised me, but why should it? Rook was my dearest friend, and I should be happy she could look past his scars to see the person underneath. I really should.

"Do you like him, Lilly?" My tone was surprisingly clipped; I felt a kind of low anger. I forced myself to stop. What right did I have to be angry at Lilly? None.

"Suppose I do," she said, lowering her eyes shyly. For some reason, my stomach began to hurt.

"Yes," I said. "Do you know where Rook is, by any chance?"

I FOUND HIM SWEEPING THE STABLES, humming as he worked. The horses blustered, the happy sound they made when all was well. Rook went to Magnus's mare and rubbed her nose.

"Hello, tricky beauty," he said, laughing as she nuzzled at his shoulder. "Nothing for you tonight. Can't have you growing fat, can we?"

"Hello," I said, feeling strangely shy.

"Nettie?" Within the stalls, horses whinnied and stomped. Clearly I had disturbed them. Rook gazed at me, his mouth open. "You're a vision."

I'd never felt more bizarre, standing there in an elegant evening dress while Rook cleaned out the stalls.

"I missed you today," I said.

"I missed you, too." He moved to collect a bucket of water.

"Are they treating you well?"

"Compared to Brimthorn, what isn't good treatment? Mostly I see to the horses, which I like. I've taken on a few extra tasks, just to see they get bedded down properly." He reached out and stroked one of the carriage horses. "I give them hot water and oats at night, instead of hay. Master Agrippa's pleased with how much better they seem. You are better, aren't you?" he murmured, laughing as the horse whickered in response. Rook was a genius with animals.

"Don't let them work you too hard."

"Work keeps me sane. Always has." Of course. It was a distraction from the pain.

"The servants are kind?"

"They aren't rude," he said. "Lilly's quite nice." He lit up. "Funny, too. Knows a million jokes and twenty card games." The cold, angry feeling flared up again inside me for one instant. I quashed it.

"She's the sweetest girl." More silence. Rook's expression when he looked at me seemed pitched somewhere between admiration and sadness. He picked up the bucket, wincing a little. When we were children, he would carry water up the long hill from the well. To help with his stiff hand, I would grab one end and he the other. Sometimes we'd play games to see who could slosh the least. "May I help?" I asked, desperately grabbing for the handle.

"No, of course not!" He pulled back. "You can't ruin your new clothes."

"I can carry a bucket." The fluttering lace at my elbow tickled me. All right, perhaps this outfit was not entirely appropriate for manual labor.

Rook agreed with my thoughts. "Not as you're dressed now."

"These clothes are just a part I need to play for the sorcerers." Every word seemed to widen the breach. "Nothing's changed."

Rook frowned. "Everything's changed."

The sorcerers were different from everyone else, irretrievably different. They dined lavishly while, less than a mile away, people starved; they took trips outside the ward to walk for a few hours among the impoverished, only to come straight back again. My path led me away from people like Lilly and Charley and Rook, the kind of people I'd grown up with. The kind of person I'd been. My throat tightened.

"How are your scars? Do they hurt?"

"That's not something you should trouble yourself with now." He dropped his eyes from mine.

"Will you at least take care of them and not go mad with the pain?" I said stiffly.

"Of course," he replied. The silence grew between us.

"Well. I have to go back. They'll be starting soon." We paused for a moment, Rook with his bucket, me with my damned fine dress. I turned and rushed away, my long skirt whispering over the ground.

"Wait." He sounded worried. "My scars do hurt."

"Oh?" I almost tripped over myself in my haste to turn around.

"They hurt this way before the attack at Brimthorn. So tell Master Agrippa and the rest of them." He looked off toward the darkening evening sky, with the clouds rolling in. "Tell them something bad might be coming tonight."

9

"ARE YOU CERTAIN?" AGRIPPA ASKED, HIS GLASS OF claret half raised to his lips. We were seated at dinner, where I toyed with my roast beef.

"Rook isn't the type to invent things."

"I hope the old Shadow and Fog does show himself tonight," Magnus said, spearing a Yorkshire pudding and spooning gravy on top of it. "I'd a new coat made especial for the occasion, and Korozoth should see it while it's still in fashion."

"Don't be too eager," Blackwood said. "For all we know, it might be R'hlem."

That silenced everyone. R'hlem the Skinless Man was the most threatening of the Ancients. Beasts like Molochoron and Korozoth were just that, beasts with great talent for mindless destruction. R'hlem showed superior intelligence. Some whispered that he had once been human, twisted by the darkness into a monster. Of course, no one really believed such nonsense.

"Master Agrippa," I said, "can nothing be done to better protect the unwarded areas? If we cannot shield our own citizens, why should the rest of England have faith in us?"

"Us?" Blackwood said. He kept doing that, dividing me from

the rest of the boys with a word or a look. Every time Magnus or the others addressed me as "Howel," he cleared his throat or made an exasperated noise. I'd thought my getting along with his sister had softened him somewhat. Apparently I was wrong.

"I know you don't yet consider me one of you, my lord," I said, struggling to maintain a polite tone, "but I'm only trying to help."

"I agree with Howel," Wolff said. "It's an outrage, and I'm glad someone else is saying it. Clarence agrees with us, don't you?"

Lambe nodded, his pale hair falling into his eyes. "It's a shame when families are separated."

Everyone stopped talking. Uncomfortable looks were passed around the table. I was confused until Wolff explained. "Only sorcerers who favor the Church of England may remain inside warded London. My family follows an older religion, so my parents had to leave for the country." He pushed his knife and fork aside; evidently his appetite had vanished. "Once I'm commended, I'll have to live outside the ward as well."

What a hideous practice. "Surely it's important to protect *everyone*," I said to Agrippa.

Agrippa nodded. "We can discuss this further after you're commended."

Blackwood coughed. Really, I was worried about the failure in today's lesson enough as it was. My breaking point had been reached. "Do you have a cold, my lord?" I said, rounding on him.

"No, Miss Howel."

"Do you dislike the idea of a lady sorcerer?"

"As I told you yesterday, that would mean my going against the Order." That was another clear attempt to *not* answer the question. I didn't care if I was wearing the bloody gown he had purchased.

"*Are* you against the Order?" I asked.

His eyes widened in surprise. "I stand with the Order entirely."

That answer was sincere. "I'm sorry, I'm just upset."

"It's all right. Compassion for the poor is admirable." That tone. I would've gladly given the topic up but for that condescending tone. I rapped my fork against the side of my plate, to calm and focus myself.

"Admirable, but not practical?"

"In this case, no. The ward protects Her Majesty, and, of course, the high sorcerer families. If we fall, England falls." He sounded almost as if he regretted it, but what could he do? "The most exceptional individuals are also the most necessary."

"Have you ever considered that you were lucky to be born into circumstances that made you such an exceptional individual?" I breathed slowly to keep myself from yelling. "Rook, for instance. He might have done as well as you if he'd been born to a wealthy family, sent to the best schools, educated by the best people. But he's the orphaned son of a brick maker, and Unclean, so whatever he might have been is unimportant."

"I don't think this is very good dinner conversation," Cellini said, sounding irritated. I got the feeling it would be more comfortable for everyone if I gave up the topic. But we were in this argument now, Blackwood and I.

"Of course Rook matters," Blackwood said, as if explaining to a child. "I don't believe it's fair that some receive everything and others nothing, merely by the luck of being born. But it is the reality."

"So the reality is that the poor should be sacrificed to protect you?" This was what the Earl of Sorrow-Fell truly believed?

"You're twisting my words, Miss Howel." He was right; I *was* twisting his words, but his manner infuriated me. He'd lived behind the ward all his life. How could he presume to know how other people suffered?

"Have you seen a village destroyed by Familiars? Have you ever met children with their limbs torn off, their bodies covered with scars just like Rook's? Do you know what it's like, as part of your school charity, to travel to the site of a battle and nurse the wounded and dying? Have you ever been attacked with nothing to protect you? The first time I glimpsed a sorcerer, in eleven years of war, was when Master Agrippa came to my school hunting for the prophesied one. Eleven years. What were you all doing in that time?" I stared right into Blackwood's eyes. "What were *you* doing, my lord? Riding and playing country sports on your estate?"

Agrippa cleared his throat. "That will do, both of you," he said.

"In fact, I was preoccupied with my studies. I wanted to be *useful*. Isn't usefulness your chief interest?" Blackwood's voice was silken coldness. "I did not see much use in a girls' school."

Magnus set his glass down, eyes flashing. "We found our prophesied one at that girls' school, didn't we?"

I had to put my hands in my lap; they were beginning to spark. "It's good to know how little your responsibilities at home matter to you. It explains why Brimthorn has been open to violence for so long!"

"Sorrow-Fell protects your school, Miss Howel. You said yourself, in eleven years you had never seen an attack."

"Some monsters wear human faces. You kept out the Ancients, but you allowed a cruel, violent man who should never be put in charge of another living soul to run Brimthorn. Where was your protection then?" The whole table stopped eating. Magnus's eyes widened. Blackwood grew still, but I could see the fury flickering inside him.

"You said that if only Rook had been born into my position, we would be exactly alike," he snapped. "Well, you're wrong. We are fundamentally different."

"If you're so certain," I said, my voice rocky and low, "that the poor are born inferior, then all the shame in the world on you for *not* protecting them. If people are born generation after generation into poverty and deprivation, it is your duty to look after them, not sacrifice their lives to save your own!"

I threw down my napkin and fled from the table. I raced up the stairs and into my bedroom, where I struggled to tear myself out of my dress. My fingers burned so badly that I had to stop to perform the calming exercises that Agrippa had taught me. I breathed in and out to the count of four, imagining a cool stream of water running down my hands. Slowly, the fiery pain left, but I still trembled with rage.

There was a knock at the door. "Who is it?" I asked.

"Lilly, miss." She entered and surveyed my crumpled state with a sad eye. "They said you'd gone to bed. Let me help you." She moved to unlace me, when there was another knock.

"May I speak with you?" a familiar voice asked. Lilly opened the door. Agrippa stood upon the threshold. He cast a quick, miserable glance around his daughter's old room. How often, if ever, did he come inside? "Are you all right?" he asked.

"I'm sorry." Agrippa didn't deserve people screaming at his table. I kept my eyes on the floor. "I can't believe I said those things."

"Don't apologize. When you're commended, you'll also be the founder of the Howel line. Part of your responsibility as a seal bearer will be speaking up in Order assemblies. Besides, I was pleased." Surprised, I looked up. He made as if to enter but stopped. "What you witnessed tonight was sorcery's ugliest face. Many believe that common men and women are inferior. I hope," he said, lowering his voice, "that you can do more for this country than help destroy the Ancients. There are minds that need changing."

"I can't imagine that's something Lord Blackwood will like."

"Nonetheless, it's what I believe. Don't fret, and don't think too harshly of George. He dwells on his responsibilities to a punishing degree. I'm sure he'll brood on what you said for the next few days." Agrippa glanced about the room once more. My stomach lurched at his obvious sadness.

"Do you wish me to change rooms? I can't stand how much pain my being here seems to cause you."

"No, this is as it should be." Agrippa closed his eyes. "I've gotten to avoiding this wing of the house. This room needed a new occupant, and I'm happy to find a lovely young lady living here again. Now get to sleep." With that, he was gone.

Lilly took my dress off, put it away, and unlaced my corset. I pulled the pins from my hair, cursing Blackwood under my breath. I got into my nightdress and stared at my reflection in the mirror, feeling bone-weary.

"I don't know how I can face them again."

"I think the gentlemen are more with you than not," Lilly said. "'Least that's what Jimmy told me, the first footman. Says Mr. Magnus in particular is on your side. Apparently he had some strong words for His Lordship after you left."

"That's good to know." The thought of Magnus berating Blackwood was pleasing. I was sure he'd done an excellent job.

"You should rest now, miss. Gram used to say it looks better in the morning."

"Thank you, Lilly."

She stopped at the door. "Miss, Jimmy told us downstairs what you said to Lord Blackwood." Her eyes glistened with tears. "I come from Potter's Borough, south of the ward. Thank you."

She left before I could respond.

I woke from a dream of Gwendolyn lying beside me, silent and rotting in death. I didn't think I could go back to sleep after that image. Outside, it was pitch black. I lit a candle and stepped, shivering, onto the thin rug beside my bed. I hastily threw on my wrap and headed downstairs. Candle in hand, I retraced my steps to the library. The fastest way to calm down after a nightmare was by reading history.

When I crept into the room, the fire was, surprisingly, still lit. My hands were cold, so I moved before the hearth. I craned my neck and looked at Agrippa's portrait. He'd been younger when it was painted, his hair black. What must it have been like to have Agrippa for a father? For a moment, I selfishly wished my own father hadn't been William Howel, a faceless phantom I'd never met.

There was the picture of that great estate again, the gleaming white one hidden in a dark valley. I turned to it, entranced by its serene and somehow terrifying beauty.

Someone coughed, startling me. Blackwood was seated with a book open on his lap. He appeared as bewildered as I.

"What on earth are you doing here?" He stood hastily. He had not been to bed, never taken his jacket off.

"I wanted something to read." I didn't know where to look. Just seeing him again made my stomach cramp.

"Ah. Anything in particular?" Even his voice irritated me. His eyes brushed the length of my body, and then he looked away.

"I hadn't given it much thought." I pulled my wrap even closer around me.

"Might I make a recommendation? This is a basic introduction to the Ancients. It's been instrumental in drawing up plans to attack them." He offered me the book in his hand, *The Seven Ancients: Theories and Observations* by Mr. Christopher Drummidge. The book was slim but handsomely bound. I opened to a sketch of R'hlem the Skinless Man. His exposed muscles almost glistened on the page; whoever had painted this had done an excellent job.

The first chapter was titled "Origins." "Do they know where the Ancients came from? I've only read one book on the war. It said the Ancients were demons from hell, but I don't know that I believe it."

"Drummidge makes a case that perhaps they are monsters summoned from the planet's core." He sounded amused. "I like his work, but I don't agree with all of his ideas."

"Thank you." I pressed the book to my chest and stood there, silent, while a log crackled in the fireplace. The clock struck three.

I was about to make a hushed exit when he said, "What did you mean about the headmaster?"

"Pardon?"

"That he was cruel and violent. What did he do?" God, how could one go about describing Colegrind in any decent way? I flushed, and that was all the answer Blackwood required. "I see." His eyes widened. He looked younger, almost sad. "I'm sorry that happened to you. I wish . . ." He turned away so I could not see his face. He straightened his shoulders. "I'm sorry I didn't do more for you, but it couldn't be helped. That's the one thing you refused to understand at dinner." That condescending tone had returned. He didn't look at me, though.

"It's nice to know it's all down to my lack of understanding."

"You have a right to be upset, but you don't comprehend my situation." He turned, took my candle, and led me to the other side of the room. Portraits gazed down on us from above. Blackwood gathered the candle flame in his hand, rolled it into a ball, and tossed it to float up, up to a portrait that hung several feet above our heads. The fire held there, and the light revealed the image of a man, young and handsome and just like Blackwood. No, not just like. There were subtle differences in the face; the eyes crinkled at the corners in some secret merriment, and the full mouth rested in a comfortable smile.

"That's my father, Charles Blackwood, eighth earl of Sorrow-Fell." His voice was soft, somehow bitter. "He was one of the most tireless workers in the war against the Ancients. That's why his picture hangs in this room."

"Of course." Why was he telling me this?

"My father was a great sorcerer," Blackwood said, running a hand through his hair. "He believed that we, the Blackwood family, had a responsibility to rid England of these monsters."

"Why your family?"

"We are the most powerful members of our society, Miss Howel." He paused, as if struggling with what to say. "We have been the most blessed, and therefore, we must be the most cursed." He stepped closer. I could feel a need for understanding coiling off him. "You must realize how seriously I take this war.

From the moment my father died, the only duty I had on earth was to destroy these creatures. I neglected my other obligations, Brimthorn included. I have no time for games, or sports, or love. My whole being belongs to this cause," he said. "Sorcerers should be bent entirely to the task of saving this land, not attending parties and taking carriage rides through the park." His face twisted in anger. I finally understood his resentment of Magnus. "How much do you know of the rest of the country's struggles?"

"I know very little." I racked my brain. "The Ancients have Canterbury?"

"They have held Canterbury for three years. Three years! Manchester and Liverpool are on the verge of collapse as well. Up north, the textile works and the coal mines are attacked on a regular basis, to keep us from having fuel and goods. The workers, many of them children, are slaughtered." There was real fury in his voice now. "Some sorcerers have gone to aid them, but most of our energy is spent keeping up the ward. We're not fighting. We're hiding.

"Yes, we must protect the ones most capable of doing something, but only so long as the strong prove themselves worthy of that protection. And I don't believe the powerless should be left entirely to their own devices. One of the greatest legacies my father left was the creation of that colony for the Unclean in Brighton. It allows those unfortunate people to live with peace and dignity.

"I wanted you to understand how deeply I care," he said.

"And I wanted you to understand why I won't address you or bow to you the way the others do. Until you are proved to be a sorcerer, beyond any doubt, I can't address you as such. I need certainty." His eyes seemed to gleam in the firelight. "Do you understand?"

I thought about what I'd seen of Blackwood so far. He rarely smiled or laughed. And he trained by himself every morning before even coming in to breakfast. He assisted in every one of my lessons, unlike Cellini or even Wolff and Lambe. Here he was, reading long into the night.

Yes, he took his responsibilities seriously.

Everything he had said he meant—I could see it in his eyes. Perhaps we could finally be honest.

"So you've no objection to a woman fighting?"

"The prophecy declares that a woman will rise to fight the Ancients, and I will give my allegiance to that woman." The way he said it forced me to speak her name.

"Gwendolyn Agrippa. You believe that *she* was the prophesied one." Blackwood blinked in surprise. "Lady Eliza told me this afternoon. Did you all think you could keep something like that a secret?"

"The Order doesn't want complications," Blackwood said. "When they found the Speakers' tapestry, Gwendolyn had just become an Incumbent. There was no doubt in anyone's mind that she was chosen, and so all of Agrippa's efforts went into training her. She was fantastic." His eyes softened. "Nothing was a challenge, not for her. Her commendation would have been a triumph the likes none has ever seen." His expression twisted in bitterness. "And she died of a fever three weeks before the commendation ball."

"She wasn't the prophesied one, though," I said, checking his reaction. "According to Agrippa."

He winced as though I'd struck him. "Don't you dare say that of her."

"You made up your mind before you ever laid eyes on me, didn't you?" I stepped toward him. "I was an impostor. And if Gwendolyn was truly the chosen one, she's dead, and all your hopes died with her. You would choose that certain doom over the possibility that I might be the one. Why?"

"Who are you exactly?" He nearly spit the words. "Gwendolyn was from one of our oldest and finest families; glory was her birthright. I don't hate you for your low birth," he said as I opened my mouth to give him the greatest hell he'd ever know. "But tradition is all that our society stands upon. You are an outsider, and you cannot change that."

It was as if a door had slammed shut in my face. I almost dropped the book. "It's a wonder you've helped me at all, hating me as you do."

"I don't hate you."

"You *do* hate me, because you hate how I was born." His profile in the firelight was beautiful, marred only by the cold expression he wore. It is amazing how, under any other circumstance, I would have thought him beguilingly handsome. He was beautiful in the way a Roman marble is, hard and inhuman. "Your stupidity is terrifying."

"This is what I believe." He narrowed his eyes. "Is that too truthful for you, Miss Howel?"

"I respect truthfulness. It's always good to know who isn't your friend."

"I said I don't hate you." Then, with a strange air of weariness, he said, "I fear you, perhaps."

"Why?"

He nodded toward the painting of the house I'd admired. "You said you never took trips to Sorrow-Fell when you were a child?"

"I've never seen the place."

"You have now. That painting is an exact likeness." Surprised, I turned back to the beautiful image on the wall. Blackwood continued. "You seem drawn to it, which is why the carvings on your stave perplex me."

"What's Porridge to do with any of this?" I said. Blackwood unsheathed his stave—he had not taken even that off—and handed it to me. A twining strand of ivy, identical to mine, was carved on his weapon.

"The Blackwood family crest is a pair of clasped hands with tendrils of ivy binding them together. In the entirety of sorcerer history, only Blackwoods have ever borne the image of ivy." His brows knitted together. "Until you."

I felt nauseated as I handed his stave back. "Does that mean we're bound in some way?"

"I don't know." He crossed his arms. "I fear we may be."

"Believe me," I said with a shudder, "my feelings are exactly the same."

THE BLACKWOOD HOUSE LAY AHEAD, SHROUDED in mist. The hedge-lined path guided me up toward the front. When I broke through the mist, I found the sky clear and the sun warm. The circle of black forest all around was no more frightening than a make-believe monster in a children's story. This was home, the surest sensation I'd ever had in my life. The great house was even more beautiful than it had been in its picture. With tears of joy, I ran up the steps to be welcomed inside.

Someone grabbed my sleeve. Gwendolyn Agrippa pulled me away, shaking her head and shouting. I struggled against her, but it was no use. She was fearfully strong. No. This was where I was supposed to be. This was where I belonged.

The church bells tolled.

I stood alone in the center of a circle of standing stones. Gwendolyn had vanished. I walked about, inspecting my surroundings. The stones were twice as tall as I was. There were twelve of them, each spaced several feet apart. Odd symbols had been carved into the granite faces, symbols that I had never seen before. A strange noise made me stop and press my ear against one of the rocks. There was a buzzing coming from inside. It was almost music. Like the stone was singing.

I stood there as the Seven Ancients arrived, filling in the gaps of the circle. There was no way out for me now.

The church bells tolled.

There was Molochoron, a perfect blob of filth and disease. It leaked rancid water, bristling all over with dark, sharp hairs. Black shapes moved and darted within it, like eels trapped in jelly.

How odd to see Nemneris the Water Spider here. She lived in the sea. She was beautiful, with long, delicate legs and a slender green-and-purple body. Her eyes were three shining obsidian orbs. If only she weren't fifty feet long and absurdly venomous . . .

The church bells tolled.

Callax and Zem came next, the ogre and the serpent. Callax was twenty feet tall with a flat skull, an extended jaw, and arms that dragged to the ground. Those arms were very good for smashing through buildings. Zem, with his long lizard body and fiery gullet, would burn whatever stood in his way.

On-Tez perched on the stone above me and cawed loudly. Flapping her vulture wings, she bared her teeth. She was the size of a horse, and deadlier than a pack of wolves.

The church bells tolled.

R'hlem the Skinless Man stood across from me. Even though he was the smallest and most human-looking of the Ancients, he was terrifying. Perhaps it was because of the intelligence in his gaze.

And then there was Korozoth.

The church bells . . .

I WOKE TO A CACOPHONY OUTSIDE my window. Every church tower in London was ringing out a warning.

An attack.

I grabbed my wrap and ran out into the hall. Doors down the corridor burst wide, boys spilling out in different states of undress. Dee staggered half blind, putting on a top hat while still in his dressing gown. Only Magnus was ready. He threw on his coat as he raced toward me.

"They should have listened to you, Howel," he said, nodding at the sleepy, unprepared young men. "If you and Rook thought there'd be an attack, I saw no reason not to be alert. It's probably old Zothy himself. Won't he love this coat?" Magnus took the steps at a rush, whooping with joy. I was stunned by how quickly everything had happened.

"Miss Howel!" Agrippa came up the stairs, his hair sticking wildly in every direction. "Stay in your room. You'll be quite safe." He tried to sweep me down the hallway toward my door.

"Is it Korozoth?" I suppressed my fear. After all, this was my destiny, or at least I hoped it was. "Let me help." Below us, I watched Blackwood call for the Incumbents, organizing them as they arrived.

"Not yet. Stay here. We'll be back soon."

"Where are you going?"

"Trafalgar Square. That's where the Order always meets. Stay here," he said again, and took off after the boys. There was a flurry of activity, with servants in nightdress rushing about below, lighting the lamps and calling to one another. I didn't see Rook among them.

"Rook." I remembered his black eyes, how that hideous Familiar girl had called him "the Shadow's chosen." If Korozoth's riders had such an effect upon him, this Ancient might call to him especially and irresistibly. . . .

I ran down the stairs and past the servants, who paid me no mind. I fled to the kitchen, calling for Rook, but didn't find him. Lilly sped past me in her nightcap. I grabbed her. "Lilly, have you seen Rook?"

"No, miss. What is it?"

"I need to find him."

We ran upstairs to the servants' corridor. He was nowhere to be found. We went back down to my room, just in case he should be there. He wasn't, and I kicked the bed in frustration. "Where is he?" Lilly looked terrified.

"I need you to help me dress." I threw open the wardrobe doors.

"Why?"

"I'm going to find him," I said.

"Outside? The master wouldn't like that, miss."

"I know where he might go." Sighing, Lilly pulled out my simplest dress. I wished I had a pair of trousers all my own. Corsets were not designed for battling monsters.

10

PEOPLE RUSHED PAST ME AS BELLS TOLLED AND FLAME and smoke lit the night sky. I clutched Porridge and stopped to beg for directions to Trafalgar Square.

I found the sorcerers before the National Gallery. There might have been over one hundred of them with their staves pointed upward. A great glow appeared in the sky, reflected as a glint of light on the underside of a glass bowl. Apparently London's ward was a dome of energy. Thunder sounded in the distance, and there, somewhere beneath that rumble, came the horrible scream of a beast.

I pushed through the crowd until I stumbled upon Blackwood, his brow knit in concentration.

"What on earth are you doing here?" he shouted.

"Are there any breaches in the ward?"

"Of course not. Why should there be?"

"It's Howel!" Arthur Dee pushed through to us. "He said you'd come."

"Who did?"

"Magnus. He said you'd inspired him."

"What are you talking about?" I asked.

"What are you doing here?" Blackwood shouted at me again. Older gentlemen turned to glare at us.

"Rook might have gone to the creature," I said.

"He can't get through the ward."

"But if somebody saw an Unclean wandering the streets, who's to say they wouldn't kill him?" That frightened me almost as much as Rook actually making it through to Korozoth.

Blackwood shook his head. "I can't worry about that now."

Bother this. "What were you saying about Magnus?" I asked Dee.

"He went to fight Korozoth."

Blackwood gripped the poor fellow by his shirtfront. "What?" he snapped.

"He and Cellini said they were going to the Row. They planned to break through and fight—"

Blackwood threw the enormous boy away and took me by the arm. "Those fools," he said, his face twisted in anger. "Where's Master Agrippa?"

"We have to go after them."

"You're not going anywhere. I'm putting you in a carriage."

"I am coming with you," I said in my best classroom tone. "I'm going to find Rook if he's there, and you are going to release me." Blackwood did just that.

"I'll take you if you can fly," he said.

"I beg your pardon?"

He brandished his stave. "Touch Porridge to the ground at north, south, east, and west, then raise it high into the air. This will summon the four winds. If you can't do it, I shall send you home." He sounded indulgent, certain I would fail.

Blackwood placed his stave in four points and raised his arm. A great torrent of wind swirled about him, and he hovered in the air with a natural ease.

I copied him and lifted Porridge, willing myself to fly. A cold funnel of wind swirled my skirts and nearly dragged me down the square. Blackwood looked surprised.

"Hold it straight!" he cried.

The thought of Rook strengthened my arm, focused me. I lifted from the ground, my feet unsteady upon a cushion of wind.

"Move your arm down," Blackwood said. He leaned forward onto his stomach, supported by the air. I copied him, feeling as though invisible hands upheld me. "Well done."

"Don't sound so shocked."

"Please go home," he said.

"Just take me to the ward. I only want to find him if he's there." My bargain worked. Blackwood took my free hand in his, and we moved forward, the sound of wild winds in my ears.

I was flying! I'd never felt so light, nor so aware of my physical body. For the first few minutes, I kept waiting to fall. When the wind didn't die or shake me off, I couldn't help but laugh. Blackwood guided me when I had to move the stave left or right or shift to make a turn. We shot over the heads of men and women, two black wraiths on their way to battle. Blackwood's hand was cool in mine, and he tightened his grip the faster we flew.

Soon we pointed our staves toward the heavens again and lowered our feet to the ground. I stumbled but wasn't hurt. We stood at the edge of the ward.

The streets beyond were alive with hundreds of people running. It was a crush of humanity. "I'm going to find the others. Please, for God's sake, stay here," Blackwood said. He nodded. "You did well, Miss Howel." With that unexpected compliment, he put his stave to the ward, sliced downward, and walked through. I touched the place where he'd gone, but it had closed.

I pressed my hand against the ward and peered into the crowd beyond, searching for Rook. It was impossible, of course, for him to be on the other side. How could he have gotten through? The idea had only been a panicked imagining, impossible to be real.

But then, through the crowd, I caught a glimpse of pale yellow hair. The brightness flashed in the dark mass of humanity and disappeared.

"Rook!" I thrust Porridge into the ward but met an invisible force. "Do it, do it," I snarled, jaw clenched tight. I dragged Porridge, looking for any tear. "Open up!" I shouted, teeming with frustration. Porridge sliced into the ward like a knife through a piece of paper. I fell forward and landed on my hands and knees on the other side of the barrier.

I checked; the opening was gone. Racing into the crowd, I called, "Rook, come back!"

Screaming faces rose up before me. Elbows struck me in the stomach. Feet tripped me. I fought against the current, half insane with desperation. A small body collided with mine, arms wrapped tight around my middle. I pulled the little person away and found myself staring down at Charley. She wailed and sobbed, "I can't find 'em! They're not at home!"

"Who?"

"Mr. Hargrove and the others. Ellie and Billy! They're all gone." She wept, laying her head on my stomach. I gathered her into my arms and carried her. Rook's fair hair was nowhere to be seen.

"We'll find them," I murmured over and over. The crowd thinned as a bright mass of fire spread ahead of me.

I heard Blackwood: "Magnus, you idiot, you'll get yourselves killed!" My heart raced as I ran to them.

As I struggled through the last of the people and into an open street, the beast screamed above me. I gazed up and up into the blackness upon blackness, the Shadow and Fog.

Korozoth.

A great black funnel cloud, so dark that it stood out against the night sky. The beast towered fifty, sixty feet, and every time he roared, houses creaked and groaned. When the lightning flashed, I saw a great horned creature's head perched atop the cloud with fiendish, slit red eyes. Tentacles, like those belonging to some undersea monstrosity, waved wildly from the center. One crashed into a window and sent half a brick wall tumbling down. Those tentacles had given Rook his scars.

Rook. I still didn't see him, and I was glad of that. I set Charley down and turned her toward the fleeing crowd.

"Go with them."

"But where'd they go?" she sobbed as I pushed her, begged her to run and hide. When she finally did as I asked, I strode toward the others. My palms were so sweaty I nearly dropped Porridge.

Their figures were dark blurs, brightened with the occasional burst of fire. I caught sight of Cellini as he went into a deep crouch and rapidly spun his stave in a circle over his head. He sent a cyclone roaring toward the beast, powerful enough to knock Korozoth backward.

Blackwood stood weaving a net of fire as quickly as possible, his face illuminated in the flame's glow. Korozoth roared and twisted, filling the air with debris and dust. I ran to Blackwood and leveled my stave alongside his.

"What are you doing here?" he screamed, so furious that a vein stuck out in the middle of his forehead.

"How do I help?" I pretended not to hear him. He looked ready to throw me to the Ancient, but I said, "This will go better with another person."

With an angry sigh, Blackwood showed me how to dip Porridge into the growing cloud, how to move my wrist to make the fire grow. I was slow and awkward, but not totally inept. On his command we willed it up and out. My aim wasn't as good as Blackwood's, but it worked. Korozoth wailed as our attack struck home, covering the mountain of Shadow and Fog with light.

Overhead, a figure flitted back and forth through the air, shooting bursts of flame. With a scream, the Ancient launched a tentacle in the figure's direction, but received a blast across the mouth for his trouble. While Korozoth bellowed in pain, Magnus dropped out of the sky, landing gracefully beside us.

"Give us a light, then, Howel," he said.

I built up flame in the palm of my hand. He swirled the fire into the air, waved in thanks, and raced toward the creature. Hovering at eye level with the beast for an instant, Magnus brought his arms down in a mighty swing and delivered another shot across the monster's face. Korozoth, blinded, lashed out with all of his tentacles. Magnus floated back fast and landed beside us with a victorious cry. With his windswept hair and his coat flapping free, he looked like a hero from a storybook.

"I'm ready to see the lady sorcerer in action. What do you say?" he called.

"Yes!" I yelled back.

Magnus's laughter was joyous. It didn't take me long to realize that, for him, battle was a gift. Cellini ran to join us, talking excitedly at Magnus. When he saw me, he frowned.

"She shouldn't be here," he said.

"My thoughts exactly," Blackwood snapped. "But right now, we can use the help."

"Trust me, you'll need it," I shouted.

Cellini took his place near me, but leaned in and said, "You shouldn't be here."

As if he weren't *also* here against Agrippa's orders. We

formed a diamond with me in front, Blackwood behind, Cellini and Magnus to the left and right. After all my difficulties in the obsidian room, I prayed I didn't falter. My legs trembled; there was no running now. I gave us a small light, and we began. Cellini prayed in Latin as we wove another net of fire.

"Pater noster, qui es in caelis, sanctificetur nomen tuum," he called, and kissed a crucifix that hung about his neck.

"Italian sorcerers," Magnus muttered as the net swelled. "They take war so seriously."

Korozoth roared and unleashed a tentacle, the fat black thing striking the ground ten feet from where we stood. A voice inside me was screaming, but I couldn't be afraid. Fear equaled death. It was time to respond.

"Get ready," Blackwood yelled. We reached back and, as a unit, threw the fire toward the creature. It blanketed the shadow beast, slowing him down. Giving us time for another attack.

"Let's do it again," I cried.

Then I saw him. He appeared before Korozoth out of thin air and darkness.

Rook stretched a hand out toward me. His shirt was torn down the front, putting his pulsing scars on display. I could tell that his eyes were black, even from this distance.

"Rook!" I broke the pattern and ran for him. Blackwood seized me by the waist. "Let me go!"

Rook raised his arms and issued that high, unearthly scream. The fog swallowed him whole.

"No!" I beat at Blackwood. Porridge tumbled to the ground.

"It's not real. He wasn't there," Blackwood shouted in my ear as Magnus grabbed my stave. "He tries to lure you in. It's an illusion."

An illusion. Not real. Rook wasn't there. And then I heard her voice, her little voice as she raced toward the blackness, screaming, "Ellie! Billy! There you are!"

Charley ran to Korozoth, ran for the little brother and sister who she thought had appeared. Magnus and Cellini shouted for her to get back, but she was too far away. The child tried to put her arms around the two phantoms, mystified when they vanished. She looked up as the roaring blackness overwhelmed her, and disappeared beneath the folds of smoke and fog. Her high, thin scream sounded for an instant, then faded away. When the shadow moved back, Charley was gone.

Magnus attempted to assemble us into the diamond pattern, but I couldn't join him. Fire heated me, and anger fed the flames. Head pounding, I wrenched away from Blackwood and rushed toward the towering black cloud.

The creature's roar reverberated through my bones as I lifted my arms to welcome him. I was shaking. *Come for me, you bastard,* I thought. *If you enjoyed the taste of that little girl, just see what I'll do for you.*

"Come on," I said through my teeth. The tentacle appeared above me, poised to strike.

"Howel!" Magnus shouted.

Every inch of my body, from the roots of my hair to the

bottoms of my feet, hummed with energy. I let the power have its way.

The world exploded in flame, the heat glowing blue and then scarlet. I looked up and up as my column of fire rose twenty, thirty, forty feet. A shattering, beastly cry erupted in the air above. I smelled sulfur. Something struck me hard and sent my body rolling along the ground. A million stars exploded in my vision. I felt horribly cold and fell into blackness.

I WOKE IN BED, A DAMP cloth on my cheek. Fenswick stood beside my pillow, his mouth pursed in a sour expression as he twitched his ears.

"So you're awake at last." He didn't sound pleased.

When I sat up, the room swirled before me. I sank back down onto the pillow. A candle burned on a table beside my bed, and I focused on the orange flame. I was alive, somehow. Was I whole? My arms and legs worked, and I studied my hands, forearms, chest, but found no scars.

"You're not marked," Fenswick said as he pulled on a silk bell cord. "He struck you with the wrong side of his tentacle. Or the right side, from your perspective."

"How did I get here?"

"Magnus carried you back through the ward." My face warmed a bit.

"What happened to Korozoth?" The door opened, and Agrippa entered, followed by all the Incumbents. Magnus and Cellini perched at the foot of my bed; Dee, Wolff, and Lambe remained nearer the door. Blackwood stood with his back to the wall, apart from all of us. As usual.

Fenswick took my face in his paw and snapped his fingers before my eyes.

"She's fine. I've no earthly idea how," the little creature grumbled.

Agrippa clasped the bedpost and came to my side. "You have violated every directive the Order could ever give!" He grabbed my hand and kissed it. "And you are everything I hoped you'd be." His eyes shone with tears. "Everything."

"What happened to Korozoth?"

"He retreated." Magnus knelt beside Agrippa. "You sent him packing. Should've heard the old boy roar and scream. He disappeared in the air, vanished like the shadow and bloody fog he is. He's never run like that before."

The boys came closer, all except Blackwood. He didn't even smile. He was probably just angry because I'd disobeyed him and gone through the ward for . . .

"Rook." My throat was dry. Wolff poured water from my china pitcher and handed me a glass. "Is Rook all right?"

"He never left," Magnus said. "They found him outside, in one of the horses' stalls. He'd tied himself to a post."

"What?"

"He said he'd felt the urge to run to the damn beast, so he went down to the stables. Said he knew we'd keep you safe, but he didn't want to go and get himself killed and have you worry.

We found him a few hours ago. Looked as if he'd had a rough night, poor devil. He was soaked in sweat."

Rook had been secure the entire time. I collapsed onto the pillow again and closed my eyes. The relief was sweet. But then, with a pang, I remembered Charley.

"If Korozoth comes back . . ."

"You will not fight him again until you're commended," Agrippa said sternly. "You were brilliant, but you were also lucky. The Order was only just able to forgive what happened. That goes for the rest of you," he said, specifically to Magnus. "From now on, you do as you're told or face being excommunicated." The boys grumbled their agreement.

Magnus pointed his stave toward the ceiling. "To Henrietta Howel!" The boys cheered, all except Blackwood. Fenswick spooned some powder into my glass of water. Drinking it down, I discovered I couldn't keep my eyes open. Everyone's faces blurred. Sighing, I relaxed into my pillow and watched the candle flame burning beside me. It grew smaller and flickered feebly. In my drugged state, I imagined that the darkness itself cupped a hand around the light. I giggled at the absurdity of that idea and slept.

ROOK BRUSHED A STRAND OF HAIR *from my face. "Nettie?" he whispered. He was robed in blackness. It hung from his shoulders and moved along his skin like folds of drapery.*

"You were safe," I sighed, reaching up to touch him. He grabbed my fingers, kissed them. The ease with which he did it thrilled me.

"Better than that. I'm free now. Can you see it?"

The shadows buoyed me up, and I floated on a dark, depthless sea. Rook hung suspended above me, his solid black eyes gleaming. We were two small objects spinning in a void. Exhausted, I fell back onto my bed.

"Rest now," Rook whispered. "But come to me tomorrow. You will come, won't you?"

"Of course," I said, rolling over and gazing at the last dying spark of the candle. The rich, velvet darkness extinguished it, and the dream vanished with the light.

HARGROVE SAT ON THE EDGE OF my vanity table, still wearing that ridiculous red-and-purple-and-orange coat. "So," he said. "You're a little fireball. I should have known." He took a bite out of the crisp red apple he held in his hand. "You really should come and see me. It's about to get much harder for you." He picked up a glass bottle of scent, sprayed some, and made a face.

"Go away and let me sleep," I grumbled, sitting up in bed. My room filled with that dream mist again. Everything appeared cloudy, except the magician. He slid down and stood by my bedpost, eating the apple to the core.

"Stupid thing, you can't even imagine what you're in for. Come to me tomorrow, and I'll help you. It'll be your reward for trying to save little Charley." His smug expression vanished. He sighed. "Yes. It was my own fault. I never remember to count heads."

"Leave me alone."

"You must come. The information I have is delicate. You'll want it."

"*Go away and let me sleep, Jenkins Hargrove,*" *I grumbled, fluffing my pillow.*

"*All right. Here.*" *He threw the apple core at me, and I leaned up to catch it.*

AN INSTANT LATER, I WOKE. THE room was empty, both of mist and of magicians. I sat up with a groan.

I didn't scream when I discovered the apple core in my hand. But I certainly wanted to.

11

I SHOULDN'T BE HERE, I THOUGHT AS I RETURNED TO Jenkins Hargrove's home the next day. Part of me wanted to turn around, to ignore the magician's *visitation* the night before. But this was twice now he had come to me in a dream, twice he had spoken to me. And that trick with the apple—how had he done it?

He'd said he had delicate information. Fine. I would listen, and then I would tell him never to come to me again.

I'd been given the morning off to rest, and it had taken a great deal of work to be allowed outside to walk about the neighborhood, to take in the air. They would miss me before too long. I knew I must hurry.

Rounding the corner, I looked about for the poor Unclean man. I'd brought a coin and a piece of bread to give to him, but he was no longer at the wall. Perhaps he'd moved on. Perhaps something had happened. What a horrible thought. I prayed someone had taken pity on him.

Steeling myself, I swept up the wooden stairs and knocked at the magician's door. A chorus of small voices told me to enter.

As before, Hargrove burst through the curtains, bent over in his old-man act.

"Come in, dear lady, and 'ave a look upon your future. We are but 'umble— Oh, it's you." He popped and cracked his bones back into place. "You might inform me when you're planning on a visit. It takes me a minute to get my spine all out of order for that entrance." He sat at the table, fluffing his coat.

I spotted Charley's little brother and sister, their faces swollen from crying. "I'd like to speak to you privately."

"Shall I send the children to the parlor or the library?" he drawled, looking about the cramped single room. Noting my lack of amusement, he clapped his hands and said, "Take what totems you've finished and go out onto the street. Go, hawk the wares." They gathered their pieces and trundled outside. Once they'd gone, Hargrove beckoned me to join him. "How may I serve you? A tarot read? A fortune told? Would you like me to fix your overlarge front teeth?"

He said nothing about the apple. I thought of three different ways to start the conversation. None of them came out of my mouth.

"Well?" Hargrove said.

"I . . . I'm here to see if there's anything I can do for the children," I said lamely. My lie was part cowardice, part hope. Perhaps there was a logical explanation for the apple. Perhaps my vision of him really *had* been a dream, like my dream of Rook. Nightmares brought on by too much stress.

He leaned back in his chair. "More charity?"

"Yes." I fiddled with the strings of my reticule.

"You're the sorcerers' long-awaited prophesied one, aren't you? I should think vanquishing the Ancients will be a great help to my children."

I started. "How did you know?"

"Please don't insult my intelligence," he snapped. "I'm aware of the sorcerers' absurd antics. Why they should get a nice, juicy prophecy is simply beyond me. Sorcerers are stunted, timid children without the stomach to go beyond the boundaries of the possible." He laid his hand on the table, then took it away, revealing the card of the woman holding a wand, her hair flying behind her in a great breeze. The card read, *The Queen of Wands*. "You want to help my children? Let me tell your fortune. Tuppence a pop."

"All right." I sat down heavily in relief. He wasn't going to talk about the dream.

He snapped his fingers and produced two more cards out of thin air. The first one showed a happy boy with one foot hanging off a cliff, a little dog at his heels.

"The Fool, my dear, signifies the beginning of an adventure or journey of some kind. The Fool is you." He smiled at this veiled insult. "After that, we have the Queen of Wands. You might think this obvious, you being a lady sorcerer and all. But really, the Queen signifies reaching a new stage in your development, able to understand your past and look to your future."

"That's nice." My voice sounded dull.

"Yes, roses and hugs and puppies. But look," he said, and threw down the third card to reveal that grim, capering skeleton dancing down the road, its skull mouth open in a great cackle. "Death. Don't misunderstand," he said when I flinched. "The Death card means a great change approaches. Your life will forever alter." He pulled at his graying beard and winked one dark eye. "Her Majesty will commend you, and you'll be the most revered and beautiful sorcerer ever to have all her dreams come true, huzzah, hurrah, biscuits and cocoa." He produced another card from his great purple sleeves and placed it atop the other three. The card showed a boy and a girl locked in an embrace. "Ah, the Lovers. An inner struggle between two things. And now, one more." Down came the picture of the little man in the pointed hat making a toy soldier dance. "The Magician. It can signify taking control of your life. Or, in this case, it can be quite astoundingly literal." The cards vanished into the folds of his sleeves.

"Is that it?" I asked, wary.

He shrugged. "Those are the cards that spoke to me. Is there something else you wanted?"

I couldn't do it. Perhaps it was cowardly, but if he wasn't going to bring it up, then I wasn't going to tempt fate. I'd write the whole dream off as a peculiar occurrence and leave it at that.

"Thank you for my fortune," I said, opening my reticule and placing the pennies on the tabletop.

"Your hands are trembling," he observed.

"Last night was quite an ordeal," I muttered.

Hargrove flipped the pennies into the air, and they disappeared. "Yes. Korozoth makes for a rather destructive guest. But they're saying you sent him away, with those unique fire abilities." He pulled at his beard. "Such a talent. Where did you come by it? I wonder."

"Goodbye," I said, turning for the door.

I was almost out when he said, "Thank you for your interest in the lives of little people, Miss Henrietta Howel."

Part of me screamed to leave, but it was too late for that. I released the doorknob. Slowly, I turned back to him. "How did you know my name?"

"Oh, Lord Blackwood said it when you were last here, didn't he?" he asked in mock innocence.

"No. He never used it." That sick, knotted feeling settled in the pit of my stomach. There was no avoiding it. "And I didn't tell it to you in my room last night. In the fog."

Hargrove hummed. "I wondered when we'd come to that topic of conversation."

The room seemed to spin about me. "How were you able to do it? How could I have caught that apple core while in a dream?"

"My dear, you may not like the answers to those questions."

"I knew you recognized me the first time I met you on the street. You tried to hide it, but I saw." I came toward him, my heart hammering.

"Oh, my little blossom, we're at the start of such a slippery journey." He picked up the foul-smelling gin and took a swig.

"I didn't want to do this," he said, wiping the back of his hand across his mouth, "but I owe him that much."

"What are you talking about?"

"Yes, I recognized you, but not from a previous encounter. No, it was *who* you looked like—that was the killer." He took another swig, wincing as it burned on the way down.

"Who do I look like?"

"Your father, obviously."

I sat down heavily in a chair. How on earth could this dirty London magician have known my father? "That's a lie."

"William Howel. A Welsh solicitor living in Devon with his lovely young wife, Helena, née Murray, and his widowed sister—let me think, what was her name? Anne, Amelia, Agnes. Yes, Agnes. He looked just like you, dark complexion, dark eyes and hair. Drowned. What was the story, in a boating accident? Almost seventeen years ago. What a tragedy." He looked at me with cold, laughing eyes. "Have I hit the mark?"

My hands felt numb. "How could you have known him?"

"Your father was a magician, Henrietta Howel. As are you."

I was on my feet before I could think. Gripping the edge of the table for balance, I said, "He couldn't have been. He practiced the law, not magic."

"The magical arts don't pay much, as you see," he said, gesturing to his squalid living conditions, "but they're a fine place for a talented dabbler. Your father was exactly that; your aunt Agnes as well. You're shocked. Didn't know women could be magicians? It's rare, but the potential is there. It all boils down to blood. And you should never try boiling blood, incidentally, for it's a disgusting mess." He offered me the bottle of gin. I refused, though I craved a drink. "It's even rarer that a girl from a sorcerer family inherits her father's ability. You've no sorcerer parent, so how would you explain your newfound status? A prophecy?" He blew a loud, wet, and rude noise. "You're a magician living a most magnificent lie. Which is why," he said, leaning in closer, "I feel a stupid urge to help you."

I was a magician. A low, dirty, common magician. Not a sorcerer. Not the prophecy. The thoughts appeared and disappeared in my mind like ripples of water. I couldn't hold on to them.

"How did you know my father?" I could hear my voice rising.

"We met when he came to London to see about joining our Guild. Magicians are disorganized creatures, but for a time we did discuss having another go at a Guild, much like the sorcerers' Order. Never worked, though. Most people didn't remember to show up for meetings. Or they'd turned themselves into a teacup and couldn't make it. That was when the illustrious magician Howard Mickelmas presided." He sloshed the gin bottle back and forth, lost in thought. "I must say, it was nice meeting you upon the astral plane. I haven't conversed with a fellow magician in that way since before the ban on apprenticeships."

My head swam. "Astral plane?"

"Another magician trick. Our souls may leave our bodies and wander the spirit dimension. Sorcerers can't do that. That's how I got into your room and gave you that delicious apple. Anyway, we're getting off topic. Suffice it to say I knew your father, and after his death, Agnes told me that Helena had given birth to a daughter and that the poor widow had died from complications in the delivery. We fell out of contact after that, and I thought no more of it. Until all this happened." He leaned over the table. "Which is why I'm trying to help you. You're in a dangerous position."

"Yes, because of the Ancients," I croaked.

"No, because of monsters closer and more cunning than old R'hlem could ever be. If they discover that you're really a magician . . ."

"Don't threaten me," I snapped.

"Threaten? Why should you feel threatened? After all, no one's ever tortured you. No one's forced you into giving the locations and names of other magicians, so they can be added to the sorcerers' files on magic-born." He rolled up his long sleeves and extended his dark, wiry arms toward me. White and gray scars lined his skin, along with old, cauterized wounds that looked suspiciously like burn marks. My hand flew to my mouth. "No one's told you, have they, that magicians are demented versions of sorcerers? Or even worse, that we're the descendants of the devil himself? But I'm certain you'll never face that. After all, *you* can perform their magic."

Blackwood had said that magicians were evil, his face twisted in disgust. Agrippa had spoken freely about how horrid they were. Magicians were obscene, deceitful, dirty. . . .

"I can't be one of you! I'm a sorcerer!" I knocked the chair over as I backed away. My legs were so weak I almost stumbled. "This is a trick. You're trying to get money, like you did on the street. Liar!"

"I can hear your terror," Hargrove said, sneering as he rose. Perhaps I'd wounded his pride. "You're right to be afraid. Do you know what they'll do when they find out you're a magician?" His voice turned cold. "They'll toss you out of that nice house and onto the street. They'll drag you before the queen and have you put your name down as a potential threat. And if you so much as breathe in a manner they don't like, they'll cut all your pretty hair from your pretty head and bind you in chains. And they'll take you out on a cold gray morning and sweep a shining ax through the air and straight into your pretty little—"

"Shut up!" I screamed. A burst of flame shot out of my body. Hargrove collapsed to the floor as the fireball exploded in the air. He laughed.

"So temperamental. The magic reacts to that very nicely." Hargrove rolled his sleeves down. "Come back when you can't perform their spells and your Master gets truly nervous. Come back if you ever want to know a little bit more about your own father." He dusted himself off and returned to the table. Seated, he tipped the gin bottle to his lips and recovered only a few drops. "And when you come back, bring food and drink, will you?"

ONCE BACK INSIDE AGRIPPA'S HOUSE, I collapsed at the end of the foyer, shaking so hard I couldn't take my gloves off. It couldn't be. It couldn't. It felt as if a hand were squeezing my heart. What was I going to do? What on earth could I do?

A girl-child of sorcerer stock rises from the ashes of a life. Sorcerer. Not magician. Not me. But I couldn't be a magician.

"Miss, there you are! Where were you?" Lilly said, dragging me to my feet. Her blue eyes were huge. "The master wants to see you in the library at once, with all the young gentlemen." For a terrifying moment, I thought he'd discovered where I'd gone. But then I recalled we were to have a class in the library this afternoon and—murder it all, I was late.

I found them seated near the windows. The fellows all turned as one when I entered. Agrippa had rolled up his sleeves and was dipping his hands into a silver bowl of water.

"Miss Howel," Agrippa said as I sat down beside Dee. "I was about to send out a search party. Where in God's name were you?" He looked simultaneously relieved and irritated.

"I'm sorry. I lost track of time walking around the neighborhood." The words sounded distant, as if someone else were speaking. "I needed the air."

Agrippa sighed. "I understand that last night was an ordeal, but that is no excuse for missing lessons. All right?"

"I'm sorry." Even I could hear how shallow my breathing was. Blackwood, seated on my other side, regarded me with interest.

Agrippa dipped his hands into the bowl of water again and said, "Now, let's start with easy questions for Miss Howel's benefit. What is the difference between hydromancy and traditional water play?"

Dee's hand shot up. Blackwood said, "Water play controls the element of water itself, such as parting the seas. Hydromancy uses water as a magical tool, often as a mirror to another location."

"Well put. Hydromancy, along with pyromancy, geomancy, and aeromancy, is one of the few sorcerer skills that magicians tried to relearn after the Great Magic Schism of 1526. If they wanted our abilities so much, they shouldn't have struck out on their own." The boys chuckled.

I coughed violently. Dee thumped me on the back.

"Get her a glass of water," Magnus said. He'd draped himself along a chair, his arm flung dramatically over his eyes. "Poor Howel. I'm so bored I could choke to death as well."

Agrippa used his stave to swirl the water into the air, spreading it until it resembled a large pane of glass. He instructed on how to project a specific location on the hydromancy mirror. I listened, but Agrippa's voice kept morphing into Hargrove's. In my imagination, Hargrove's smile became sinister as he dealt the cards on the table. He showed me the Queen of Wands, frowned, and tore it up. Then he dealt the Magician card and laughed. *There you are,* he said, stroking his bearded chin. *You're a magician, Miss Howel. Miss Howel.*

"Miss Howel!" Agrippa said. I nearly fell out of my seat. "Are you listening?"

"I'm sorry. What?" I dug my fingers into the chair's arm to steady myself.

"Where does Cornwall stand in the war?" All eyes were fixed on me. Agrippa seemed concerned. "Are you sure you're well?"

On the pane of water glass, the cliffs of Cornwall appeared in perfect likeness. "Um, yes." My tongue felt heavy, and I swallowed. Sweat beaded at my temples. "Cornwall sustains a great deal of attacks, second only to London in frequency. The west in particular has long been under siege. No one is sure why, as it's not heavily populated. Nemneris the Water Spider is the Ancient most often tasked with plaguing the area."

"Good. What are we doing to counter these attacks?"

Dee waved his hand back and forth. As Wolff discussed the ward we were trying to design to shield the cliffs, Blackwood leaned to my ear and whispered, "Where were you?"

"Out." I snatched pen and paper and tried to take notes. Mercifully, he said no more.

We addressed the situation in Lancashire, where Her Majesty had dispatched additional forces to protect the cotton manufacturers. "There've been calls to evacuate," Wolff said, shaking his head sadly. "But the workers have nowhere else to go. They'd die sooner than lose their livelihood."

We glimpsed Yorkshire. "Nothing much to report up that way," Agrippa said as the moorland appeared. "Besides warded London, Yorkshire is the safest place to be in this war."

We discussed why the north remained relatively untouched

(fewer tempting resources, coupled with difficult terrain), while London and the coast received the greatest amount of abuse (R'hlem wanted to destroy the government, capture the queen, and decimate the Royal Navy). Much of it was lost to me; my blood was so loud in my ears. Agrippa turned us again toward Cornwall. "Admiral Ethermane leads the fleet against Nemneris. What is his new plan with regard to combating the Water Spider?"

Dee raised his hand for the tenth time, wiggling his fingers in the air for extra attention. Magnus sat up and answered, finally interested.

"Admiral Ethermane believes we must freeze the creature in its web. Ice magic on such a massive scale is difficult, but they're attempting it. The goal's to keep Nemneris from taking the war to the rest of Europe. Not that the rest of Europe cares what happens to England, of course." He swatted his papers against the back of Cellini's head.

"How can you say that, you bastard?" Cellini laughed. "I'll return to Rome to complete my education and let you all rot."

Agrippa cleared his throat. "Very good, Julian. Now, who can—steady on, Arthur, don't wave your arm like that—who can tell me what . . ."

His voice trailed away. We gazed in horror at a new section of the Cornwall coast. Several ships lay wrecked and impaled along the rocky shore. Their masts had been snapped in half, their hulls ripped apart. Webs covered them like a ghostly shroud. Nemneris's lice, her Familiars, scuttled along the smashed hulls.

We got to our feet and crowded toward the water glass. "Look," Magnus said, pointing to a ship with a blue flag still raised in the air. I recognized that ship. It was the one we'd watched sail out of the docks while the crowd cheered. But it couldn't be the same vessel. Those sails had been white, and these sails were a pure . . .

"Why are the sails red?" I asked. Agrippa put his stave to the water glass and stirred in a queer little figure eight. The ship grew larger and more detailed.

Hanging from the masts like ghastly ornaments were the bodies of the men. They were masses of dark, mottled crimson. I wanted to turn away, but if I were to be a sorcerer and not a magician—not a magician—I would have to take in grisly scenes just like this one. The bodies had been stripped of all skin, the sails stained with their blood. We realized what we were looking at before Agrippa spoke the words:

"That's R'hlem's handiwork."

12

"YOU'RE NOT FOCUSING," AGRIPPA SAID AS I LISTED OFF to the side of the obsidian room. He clapped his hands. "You have to pay attention."

"Yes," I said, staring at the wall. In the shining reflection, I could just make out the dark circles under my eyes. I didn't sleep anymore. All I could hear in my dreams were the frantic cries of Charley and the other unfortunates dragged into Korozoth, of those sailors as R'hlem flayed them alive. I was supposed to help them.

I had been *chosen* to help them. Hadn't I?

You are a magician. It had been one week since I'd gone to see Hargrove, and his voice wouldn't leave me. We'd reached the end of April and made no progress. Agrippa was now officially worried.

"Now then. We start at the beginning of the earth maneuver. Prepare," Agrippa said, pointing at the large rock in the center of the room. He was right to sound irritated. We were massively behind on the day's lesson. I was supposed to be breaking the rock and putting it back together, and I hadn't even begun.

I turned, bent my knees, and burst into flame by accident.

"Watch out!" Agrippa cried as I nearly scorched his jacket. He beat at his sleeve. I stopped burning and cringed with embarrassment. "What is the matter with you today?"

"I don't feel well," I murmured.

"That's no excuse." His voice was firm. "You have to fight through pain. There will be times in battle where you will feel *decidedly* unwell."

I centered myself and prepared again for the maneuver. I lunged forward, spinning the stave above my head. The rock should have split apart into ten different pieces. Instead, it rolled once, twice, and then stopped. Nothing I did worked properly.

Nothing would ever work properly, not if I wasn't the girl in the prophecy.

"Something's wrong," Agrippa said. He came up behind me. "You've been scattered this entire week."

"I just don't sleep well." I bit the inside of my cheek.

Agrippa's voice grew soft. "You can say it if something's troubling you."

I turned to him, to tell him about my visit to Hargrove . . . and kept silent.

I couldn't lose my position. Not for anything.

Not even for the sake of the truth.

AFTER LESSONS THAT DAY, I WENT to the drawing room and curled up in the window seat, the book on the Seven Ancients open in my lap. I studied the picture of R'hlem, his muscles and veins disturbingly exposed to the world. He'd one hideous yellow eye positioned at the center of his forehead. Even in the drawing, I felt that gaze cut to the heart of me. Shuddering, I turned the page to the chapter regarding Korozoth.

Light and flame are the only known deterrent, I read, *for what is a greater ally against the unstoppable force of shadow and darkness? There is, however, still no example of light or fire strong enough to eradicate the beast.* That massive black cloud glared up at me.

I shut that book and picked up another, very slowly. It was titled *Heresy: The Great Magic Schism of 1526.* Inside, I read of battles between sorcerers and magicians. There were pictures of the two armies: the sorcerer side was armed with staves and accompanied by a choir of heavenly angels; the magicians rode into battle on herds of swine, the devil himself at their backs. I didn't think it was historically accurate, but the picture was memorable. I read descriptions of how one murdered a magician so that his soul might grow closer to God in its final moments. The procedure involved cutting off the magician's arms, legs, and tongue while he was still alive. I read until I could read no more, until my heart was thundering in my chest.

Closing my eyes, I shut the book and leaned against the sun-warmed window. I didn't hear him enter, and I jumped when Magnus knelt before me.

"Did I startle you?" he said, smirking in that devilish way of his.

I fluffed my skirt out over the copy of *Heresy,* hoping he hadn't noticed. "What do you want?"

"To give you this." He offered another book. *Henry V,* Shakespeare. "I thought, since you're so fond of history and I'm so fond of theater, we might bring them together." He took a seat beside me, the sunlight catching in his hair. "I always wanted to play Henry."

"You wanted to wear armor and make grand speeches with thousands of men hanging on your every word."

He gave a dramatic sigh. "My one childhood dream." He took the book and opened to a page near the end. " 'Fair Katharine, and most fair,' " he said, his voice deep and soft and almost pleading, " 'will you vouchsafe to teach a soldier terms such as will enter at a lady's ear and plead his love-suit to her gentle heart?' " He closed the book and looked at me with an appraising eye. "On second thought, you wouldn't make much of a Katharine."

"No? Too sullen? Too dark?"

"Too bold. You're more of a Henry. You've the name, sort of. What if I called you Henry from now on?"

"What if it rained in your bedchamber throughout the night?"

"You're finally learning how to be a true sorcerer!" He gave me *Henry V* again. "You should read it and tell me what you think."

" 'Your Majesty shall mock at me,' " I said in a bad French accent. " 'I cannot speak your England.' " Stunned, Magnus grabbed the play and found that I had spoken the next line perfectly. I rather liked seeing him surprised.

"You've read it before?"

"Mr. Colegrind had a copy of Shakespeare's histories."

"Well, they're nothing to his tragedies. We'll have to start you on a strict diet."

"Don't I have enough work already?"

"It won't be work. It'll be fun." We opened the play back to the scene, and continued. "'O fair Katharine, if you will love me soundly with your French heart, I will be glad to hear you confess it brokenly with your English tongue. Do you like me, Kate?'"

"'*Pardonnez-moi,* I cannot tell what is *like me.*'"

"Oh go on, do the French accent. I've never heard anything so funny. Ow! Why did you hit me?" We spent the next hour or so reading through the play, and I never laughed so much in my life as I did for that one hour. For a little while, the stress of the last few days evaporated. The supper gong sounded, and we rose. "Howel, would you go with me to a party in Hanover Square this evening?"

"A party?" I grew uneasy at the thought. I didn't want to go into public until I had my lessons under control.

Which might be never, at this rate.

"It will only be a few other Incumbents. Dee and Cellini are coming, too."

"What if people stare?" I pushed open the door, and we walked into the hall.

"You'd have me at your side all evening. No one will pay you any mind when they could be looking at me." He winked.

"I'm not much use at a party. I don't know how to flirt, I can't dance, and I'm not funny."

"What do you mean? I think you're hilarious." I stopped walking and struck him lightly on the arm. "That's the funniest slap I've ever received. Just don't drink so much punch that you wind up sleeping under the stairs." When I didn't answer, he spoke more softly. "You're going to be commended. These people will be your allies. It's not a bad idea to make them like you."

Was I going to be commended? These people wouldn't be my allies if they knew what I was. What Hargrove had said I was.

"That's easy for you, isn't it?" I blushed. "Being liked."

"It's what my music master always told me. Practice. Listen to me now!" He belted out some lines from an Italian opera in a voice so off-key and wretched I ran down the stairs to be away from it. He raced after, singing louder and louder.

"I'll go to the party if you'll never sing again," I cried.

"Done!"

Perhaps gaining a few more allies was exactly what I needed right now. And for all I knew, with Magnus about, it might be fun.

"I DON'T KNOW WHAT TO SAY at these things," Dee said, staring into his empty glass of punch. "All the girls want to dance, and I'm no good at dancing. Then they giggle and walk away."

"I can't think of anything to say, either." We stood guard by the punch table and watched the whirl of activity. Couples danced while members of a string quartet played by the side of the room and sweated in the close glow of candlelight. Old-lady chaperones in black crepe and lace dozed upon straight-backed chairs.

The music was wonderful. The dancing looked a great deal of fun. Magnus took to the floor with a beautiful red-haired girl.

"Is she from a sorcerer family?" I said, trying not to pay much attention to Magnus's new partner. It didn't matter to me anyway.

"That's Eugenia Whitechurch, the Imperator's daughter. Her magic lines go all the way back to the Conqueror." Magnus and Eugenia danced a quadrille, laughing as they turned around and about each other.

"I wish I could dance," I muttered.

"I'll teach you," Dee said, grinning shyly. "I'm no good, but I at least know how."

"Oh, would you? I feel stupid just standing here."

"See, it's easy." He took my hand in his and made a couple of paces forward and back. Unfortunately, he took too great a step and trod on my toe. "I'm sorry," he said while I bit my lip and bobbed up and down to manage the pain. "I'm better when it's not crowded."

"I'm sure. So long as my slipper's all right. Lilly will kill me otherwise."

"Oh, she wouldn't. She's the kindest girl in the world. And the prettiest," he murmured. So he liked Lilly, did he?

"Does she know you admire her?" My voice held a slight

edge. Servant girls who caught a master's eye could be pressured into things they did not want to do.

"Oh no." Dee blushed. "I wouldn't want to make her uncomfortable." He was utterly sincere.

"You're a true gentleman," I said, slipping my arm through his. Dee smiled.

Cellini appeared out of the crowd and waved at me. Two boys stood beside him, one dark-haired and one fair. They whispered to each other and followed Cellini as he came over to us.

"Howel, you are beautiful this evening." Cellini kissed my hand with a grand gesture. He swayed on his feet and smelled strongly of punch. A slow, contented smile stretched across his face. "Beautiful. *Bella ragazza.*" He muttered some more Italian, impossible to follow. I patted his arm, and Dee helped him stand. "These are my friends," he said with a flip of the wrist. "Lovett"—the fair-haired one smiled—"and Hemphill." The black-haired boy nodded as well. "Very fine fellows, these two. They're Master Palehook's Incumbents, but we mustn't hold it against them." He said this very slowly, waving a finger in Dee's face as if he were making a point. "They always lose at cards. That's so helpful."

Lovett and Hemphill bowed to me.

"So you are the prophesied one, Miss Howel? Charmed to make your acquaintance," Lovett said. He was a handsome young man, but there was something off about his smile.

"Thank you," I said, hoping I sounded confident.

"Perhaps we'll be inspired to fight in petticoats and bonnets from now on." Hemphill laughed. "Won't it surprise old R'hlem to see an army of sorcerers charging uphill in women's clothing?"

"Perhaps it won't shock him so much, then, to see a woman leading the charge," I said.

"You're going to lead us, Miss Howel?" Hemphill grinned. "That's quite an ambition."

"Well, not immediately, of course." I took a small step away from them, pressing my back into the wall.

"Ah yes, take it one step at a time. How wise." Lovett said. "How are you, Dee?" he asked, changing the topic. "Have you danced tonight? There've been no screams of pain from the ladies, so I'd assume you haven't." He laughed. I didn't find it amusing.

Dee said nothing, though his face flushed.

"I'm grateful there've been no more attacks the last few nights," Hemphill said. "It must all be down to you, Miss Howel. You walloped the old Shadow and Fog, they say. Some might think that display of strength unbecomingly masculine."

"Some might consider what you did unnatural," Lovett said, hastening to add, "but we don't think that."

Cellini looked drunkenly puzzled. "You boys aren't being friendly." He squinted at Dee. "Are they? I can't tell; it's all fuzzy."

"They're *not* being friendly," Dee muttered. Cellini left our group and staggered away, back into the crowd.

"They also tell us," Lovett said, stepping closer, "that you've brought an Unclean boy with you into the city. Is that true?"

I bristled. "Who's told you that?"

"Master Palehook, of course. Everyone's wanted to know all about you, and you've strangely kept so silent."

"So kind of you to look after anything so damaged," Hemphill said. "I imagine the sight of it turns the stomach."

"See here," Dee said, turning crimson, "why don't you leave us in peace?" The two young men paid him no mind.

Yelling at these fools would do nothing for me. I tried to push my way past them, but they blocked my path.

"You're lucky to be our chosen one, Miss Howel." Lovett leaned close to whisper in my ear. "Otherwise, there'd be no power on earth that might persuade us to allow such a freak to live within the safety of our ward."

I reached out my hand, perhaps to push him, perhaps to burn him, for at that moment I felt the flames nearly on my skin. Magnus prevented it by stepping in and grabbing the two boys by their shoulders. Cellini had brought him just in time. The cretins cowered before Magnus. However jovial his nature, he could be fierce when he wanted.

"Get out of here," he said, his voice menacing and low. He released them, but they lingered for a moment.

"It's got to be such a treat for you, Magnus," Hemphill said, shrinking back. "We all know you like the ladies. Having *her* down the hall must make it so much easier. You don't need to go prowling the streets looking for it."

I couldn't breathe. Magnus grabbed Hemphill by his collar.

"Be careful how you meant that," Magnus whispered. In that moment, he might have given Blackwood a lesson in icy intimidation. "Or I'd have to challenge you to a duel."

"Sorcerers may not duel one another," Hemphill said. He sounded a bit shaky, though.

"We're not commended yet. We'll fight with warded blades, and I'll slit you down the middle. Spill your entrails along the hall and see if there's any real blood in your veins. Now leave." He stood aside, and the two boys slipped into the crowd.

"They don't like you," Cellini said to me, yawning. "Can't accept a lady as one of us." He then closed his eyes and began to snore.

I put a hand to my cheek and discovered it was still hot. Making a hushed excuse, I escaped into the foyer. Music and laughter bled through the walls as I walked toward the front door.

I stopped at the stairs and leaned against the banister to steady myself. If that was how people behaved when they thought I was the prophesied one, what on earth would happen if they found out that I was a magician?

No one could ever know. Ever. God, if only my lessons would improve . . .

"Howel, wait." Magnus caught up with me. "I'm so sorry. They've always been hideous."

"Do you think they're spreading those kinds of tales about us?" I knew the value of a woman's good name. Though the rumor was blatantly untrue, the fact that it existed could be enough to damage my reputation. And right now, my reputation was all that kept me safe.

"I'll tell Master Agrippa to look into it."

"Why did I come here? I should've stayed home." I sank down onto the stairs.

"Not all sorcerers are like them. I'm not. Dee's not. Even Blackwood's a better sort, and he's as much fun as a wet hen." Magnus glanced about to make sure we were alone, then sat beside me. "I wanted you to feel at home."

"I can't feel at home here." *Because you're a magician, and you're lying to everyone.* The voice in my head was ugly. Tears were very close now. I turned from Magnus and put a hand to my mouth.

"What is it?" His voice was gentle. He put a comforting arm around my waist and took my chin in his hand. Turning my face to him, he said, "You can't let them frighten you."

"I'm not frightened of *them.*" I began to shake. He leaned in close, speaking softly.

"Something's been wrong since the night Korozoth attacked. It's eating away at you." His voice was soothing. "I know watching that little girl die was horrible."

Part of me wanted to bury my face against him, to tell him everything. The sane part of me knew that such a thing was impossible. Why did I have to lie to people who were so good to me? What type of person did that make me?

Breathing deeply, I told as much of the truth as I could. "I'm afraid I'm not what everyone needs."

Magnus took my hand. "You are. You will be."

His touch was warm. His gray eyes glowed in the dim candlelight of the hall. He had a confident smile, the kind that indicated he had never known defeat. The kind that promised he could protect me from whatever dangers lay ahead.

I felt the faintest charge, like the air before a lightning strike. Magnus tightened his grip on my hand.

Dimly, I remembered that there was a rumor going on about me. Even though we were alone, it was risky to sit with Magnus's hand in mine. I pulled away from him gently.

"I suppose my nerves got the better of me. Go back to the dancing. I'm sure Miss Whitechurch is looking for you," I said.

"Are you certain you're all right?"

"I could use a moment to catch my breath." I stood up and patted my hair. Magnus rose with me.

"Your problem is you've had one cup of punch all evening. Life's so much better when your head is fuzzy. Aristotle said that."

"No, he didn't." I laughed. Magnus left. Alone, I closed my eyes to compose myself. I had to put a smile on my face and return to the room, or people might talk.

A sigh turned my head. Palehook came down the stairs, a punch glass in his hand. He eyed me over a pair of spectacles.

"Miss Howel. Are you distressed?"

More than he could imagine. But I could have at least one frank conversation with him.

"I would prefer you not talk to people about Rook." I wanted to snap at him, but I must be polite.

"You are a topic of great conversation. Cornelius made a grave error in keeping you locked up. In the absence of anything factual, gossip is unavoidable." He traced a slender finger around the rim of the punch glass. It made a faint ringing sound. "Were you my Incumbent, the situation should have been handled differently."

"Regardless, please don't discuss me, Master Palehook. Not with your Incumbents or anyone else. I spoke with two of your boys just now, and they were exceptionally rude. People might think you don't want me to be commended." I turned to walk away, but he stepped before me.

"That is an unfair accusation, Miss Howel. I stand with you in the service of my country." He seemed to be telling the truth. I heard the firmness in his voice. "My only desire is to send the Ancients back to whatever hell they came from."

"That's good to hear. I was afraid you'd pledged your loyalty to the memory of Gwendolyn Agrippa."

Palehook smirked. "I must acknowledge you as the chosen one. But I do still revere Miss Agrippa. She was a steadfast servant of the Order. She knew our ways." He bowed to me. "She knew her place."

He walked away, his coded threat lingering in the air, leaving me chilled.

13

THE NEXT DAY, PALEHOOK ARRIVED TO OBSERVE A lesson. The butler announced him into the garden, where we'd all gathered to work. Agrippa believed that time out of the obsidian room would calm me, but it wasn't playing out as he'd hoped. All my attempts to create a maneuver ended with me dumping a bowl of water onto somebody's head. Poor Dee, still dripping, pretended he didn't mind.

"What's he doing here?" I whispered as Magnus fetched another seat. Palehook chatted with Agrippa over by the roses, swatting at some unseen insect.

"Just don't set fire to anything you're not supposed to," Magnus whispered back. We stood in a line while Palehook eased himself into a garden chair and shielded his face from the sun with a paper fan.

"It's a hot day," he said as he helped himself to a cup of tea. "Why are you outside?"

"Some require the extra space," Blackwood said. He didn't mention my name, but Palehook instantly looked to me. Damn.

"Really?"

"Just polishing a few details," Agrippa said with a concerned glance.

"Proceed," Palehook said.

"I think we've had enough commendation practice," Agrippa said. "Time for some dueling. We'll be using water. Howel, Blackwood, you're up first."

I knew his plan was to get me out of the way as fast as possible, so Palehook wouldn't sit there in anticipation. Blackwood and I took our places in the center and bowed to each other.

"Give me a moment to start," I whispered. We stepped apart and bent our knees. The beginning was always difficult, like mentally lifting a sack of bricks, but after that—

A blast of water struck my chest. I cried out as Blackwood called the water back and then sent it toward me again in a rocketing mass. Shielding myself with a thought, I fell to a knee. The attack sprayed over my ward. I stood, anger spurring me on.

The water in my bowl splashed into the air, and shards of jagged ice formed. I'd actually done it. With a triumphant cry, I slashed over and over. The ice shot forward.

Blackwood crouched, spinning his stave. My attack slowed and the ice liquefied back into water. He'd taken control of my weapon. Panicked, I tried to regain the element.

Blackwood leaped into the air and swirled the water into a six-foot-tall spout. I screamed as the funnel bowled me over. For a moment, I struggled beneath it. I felt like I was drowning.

Blackwood released the spell, and I lay on the paving stones, soaked to the skin and coughing. He offered a hand to help me up. I almost bit him.

"Excellent, Lord Blackwood. That was . . . original stavework, Miss Howel," Palehook said. He turned to Agrippa. "You've such unorthodox ways of training."

"I'm not certain I agree," Agrippa said. I could hear his embarrassment.

If Death had come for me at that moment, I'd have hugged him in relief.

While Wolff and Lambe fought the next duel, I pulled Blackwood to the edge of the lawn and hissed, "What was that?"

"I won the duel."

"You made me look foolish in front of the Masters." I wrung out my sleeves as best I could.

"You accomplished that on your own," he snapped. He applauded as Wolff struck the winning blow and said, "The Masters have a right to see your inconsistencies. You go from transforming water to ice in midair, one of the most difficult spells, to not knowing how to shield yourself from the simplest attack." He scratched his chin. "It's so strange."

"So I'm not allowed a mistake?" I shifted nervously. Did he suspect the reason for my uneven performance?

"I'd allow a thousand if you improved, but if anything you've gotten worse."

"Perhaps if you helped instead of flinging insults, we'd find a way to prepare me in time to be commended," I whispered. Blackwood crossed his arms and regarded me with a look of smug satisfaction. "Have I said something amusing?"

"All you care about is securing your own position," he said. "The responsibility means nothing to you."

How could I argue? What he said was painfully true. Though that didn't keep me from stepping behind a rosebush and cursing his name.

As Palehook was leaving, he bid me to speak with him. "Your performance is original," he said, unsmiling.

"We're working to steady my powers. I think we're making great progress," I said, a lie.

"Indeed. Master Agrippa continues to have hopes for your improvement." He nodded. "I must admit, my confidence begins to wane."

When he had gone, I went alone into the obsidian room and summoned my flames. I stared at my burning reflection in all eight walls. The fire whispered over my skin, its touch comforting as I stretched out my arms and tilted back my head. This was all that my power was good for.

Sometimes I wished that I could actually burn.

THE NEXT DAY, I WAS HEADED down the stairs toward the library when I heard them talking. The voices echoed out of the dining room, and I would have moved on had I not heard Agrippa say, "She might not be the prophecy."

It's a miracle I didn't tumble down the last few steps. I went to the door, open just a sliver, and listened to Agrippa rage at an unseen person.

"He didn't come out and say it, but it was implied. I don't know what Palehook means to accomplish." There was the sound of a fist striking a table.

"Perhaps he's simply stating his mind?" That was Fenswick's voice. I peered inside. The hobgoblin stood on the table, four arms crossed over his chest. "Perhaps it's true. How bad is she?" He twitched his left ear.

I wanted to run away. Agrippa shook his head as he stepped into view. "She's trying. God help her, I've never seen anyone try harder."

"That's all well and good, but trying's not the same as succeeding."

"If she isn't training, she reads in the library. Last week I found her slumped in a chair, asleep with a book in her lap. She's a wonderful student." Agrippa paced back and forth, in and out of my line of sight.

"I'm sure she can outread the best of us, but that's not the point. She's not good." Trust Fenswick to be blunt.

"No," Agrippa whispered. My corset pinched me. I couldn't breathe. He sat down at the table. "I don't know why this is happening. After Korozoth, I was so certain."

"Were you overhasty?" Fenswick sounded gentle. "Perhaps she's not the one you need after all."

I didn't wait to hear the reply. In my hurry to get away, I

stumbled against the door, pushing it open. Agrippa caught my eye and called my name as I fled.

Porridge in hand, I threw open the training room doors and faced my reflection in the black glass walls. I would perform the maneuver for fire right now, and perfectly. Lighting my hand, I swirled the flame into the air, where it formed a floating orb. Good. Now to transform it into a vortex.

I swung and spun myself around the room, getting every movement and gesture exact. But I couldn't make the fire transform, even a little. I hacked away at the air until my arms tired and I broke into a sweat, cursing under my breath. I caught sight of myself in the glass. I didn't look like a sorcerer. With my hair coming undone, I looked like a madwoman.

Cursing, I threw Porridge into the air and the fire exploded. Embers and ashes rained to the floor.

There was a knock. Agrippa entered, a sad expression on his face. I couldn't bear the sight of it.

"I'm sorry I've disgraced you," I whispered. "I didn't mean to fail in front of Master Palehook."

"You have nothing to apologize for." His voice was warm with anger, but not at me. "Palehook should never have said such things."

"He wants the prophecy to be realized. He must believe we've made a mistake." *And we have made a mistake,* I thought. *Haven't we?*

"Augustus doesn't like to share power. This is my fault."

"Yours?"

"Palehook applied to the Order immediately after we came to town. He wanted to train you himself."

"What?" I was nearly sick at the idea. Living with that man? "They'd have had to drag me into his house."

Agrippa smiled. "He may have seven daughters, but I don't think Augustus is an ideal teacher for a young woman, which you most certainly are. Are you all right?" He sounded alarmed. I'd begun shivering hard enough to make my teeth chatter.

"Perhaps it's a chill."

"Nonsense, you're terrified." He took my hand.

Here he was comforting me, and all I did was lie.

"I'm not what you need." My voice sounded so small. I was on the verge of admission, pushing to speak the words . . . but the cowardice in me was too strong.

"Of course you are. We knew this training would have its own challenges," Agrippa said, voice soft. "We will unlock a key to steadier powers—I promise."

I looked into his eyes. "Do you believe Miss Agrippa was the one prophesied?"

"What?" Agrippa released me.

"I know she would have been a sorcerer if not for the fever. It would make so much more sense, her being chosen." I discreetly grabbed my handkerchief and wiped at my eyes.

"I was proud of Gwendolyn. Words fail to express how proud. But she wasn't the prophesied one," Agrippa said firmly.

"But she was your daughter. You of all people should be the first to condemn me as a fake."

Perhaps I wanted him to.

"Gwendolyn possessed strength and grace, but she left us before her commendation," Agrippa said. "I refuse to accept that our one hope was carried off before she'd done anything at all. Frankly, if I reject my own daughter's candidacy, I would appreciate it if Master Palehook would fall in line." Annoyance crept into his voice. "I admit, it's unheard of for a girl with no sorcerer family to display your talents, but in my opinion that only makes your candidacy stronger. It's a miracle."

A miracle. Or magicianship.

My time was running out. I knew it. Hargrove had told me to come back when I accepted that I couldn't perform sorcerer spells. When I began to make Master Agrippa nervous.

But I couldn't give up. Not completely. Not yet.

14

I SAT BEFORE THE MIRROR, BRUSHING MY HAIR WITH LONG, smooth strokes. Lilly had gone to bed hours ago, and the slumbering house creaked and settled. I paused and set the brush down. *Why was I awake?*

Mist filled the room. I sighed and rubbed my eyes. Another dream from Hargrove, the last person I wanted to see. The bedroom door swung open.

"You can leave right now," I said as a figure moved into the light.

R'hlem the Skinless Man stepped toward me, the candle's glow a sheen on his wet, bloodied muscle. That one yellow eye, perched in the center of his forehead, widened.

I hastened to my feet, knocking over half the bottles on my table. A glass vial of scent fell to the floor and shattered, and instantly the whole room smelled of lavender. I ran to the window, intending to fling it open and plunge to the street below. The window wouldn't budge, though my muscles burned with the effort. I pressed myself against the glass as R'hlem approached.

Scream. I must scream, but when I opened my mouth, the faintest whimper escaped. I slid to the floor. The Skinless Man's presence filled my room. The air around him hummed with dread. He didn't roar or

*wave a fan of tentacles like Korozoth, but the fiendish intelligence in his
eye frightened me beyond all else.*

Leaning down, he whispered, "Perhaps."

*He reached for me, but I rolled aside and ran for my bed. I found
myself fast asleep. That image did the trick.*

I WOKE GASPING, MY NIGHTDRESS PLASTERED to my body with
sweat. Looking about, I assured myself that R'hlem was nowhere in sight. I smelled smoke and tasted blood. . . . I smelled
smoke!

Fire bloomed in the center of the bed. Beads of blue flame
dotted my palms. I fell to the floor, grabbed the china pitcher
from my table, and poured water onto the bedspread. The fire
died with a hiss, and thick gray smoke filled the air. I coughed and
went to open a window. Ducking my head outside, I breathed
deeply. I was all right.

No, I wasn't.

I collapsed to my knees. That had been no dream. It was the
bloody astral plane, just as it had been with Hargrove. How had
R'hlem found me? Had *I* found *him*? Perhaps my magician powers had granted him a way inside my mind.

Magician. The word still made me sick.

Lilly looked dismayed when she came in, hours later, to find
a scorch mark on the bed and me curled up asleep beneath an
open window. Always one to find the bright side, she offered
happy possibilities as she stripped the sheets. "Maybe it's a sign
that your powers are healthy." She sniffed the air and looked

dismayed when she found the broken bottle of scent on the floor. "Heaven knows how that happened," she said.

I knew.

Sitting at my vanity as Lilly brought me tea, I rubbed my head and thought. If I was not the sorcerers' prophecy, didn't I have a responsibility to step down and allow them to find the right person? But if I told them, the best scenario would be that I was put out on the street, along with Rook. After everything I'd done to keep us here, I couldn't face that.

I would work hard for the Order. I would be England's most faithful servant, chosen one or not. If only I could control my bloody powers.

Glancing in the mirror, I noted how awful I looked. My reflection was hollow-cheeked and sallow. The sleepless nights had taken their toll.

And after the dream of R'hlem, I doubted I'd ever sleep easy again.

"Was it a nightmare, miss?" Lilly said, handing me a cup of tea.

"Yes. A bad one."

She clucked her tongue. "We've all been havin' our share of nightmares."

"You've had them?"

"No, not me." She winced as if she regretted bringing it up. I guessed quickly and set my cup down.

"Rook? Is he all right?"

"He's been sleeping badly. Keeps crying out with his headaches, ever since the night you fought Korozoth. You can hear it all the way in the women's quarters."

Why hadn't Rook told me about his pain? Then again, when was our last proper conversation?

These past two weeks I'd seen him a few times out in the stables, but it had never been for long. He was busy with work, and I was always thinking about my next lesson. I couldn't recall anything we'd said to each other that went deeper than a few pleasantries. Wrapped up tightly in my own problems, I'd forgotten my friend.

"Lilly, you should have told me," I said, ashamed.

"He asked me not to. Said you had enough to deal with without worrying about him."

THAT AFTERNOON, I SLIPPED DOWNSTAIRS TO the kitchen to see if I might find Rook. I thought perhaps he was in the yard when I heard the music, a violin and cello, sonorous and sad, and, above it all, Rook's high, clear voice.

> *"She hears me not, she cares not,*
> *Nor will she listen to me;*
> *And here I lie, in misery,*
> *Beneath the willow tree."*

It was a song we had learned from the villagers near Brimthorn when we were children. In the morning we'd sneak out and watch the men on their way to work, singing it.

"My love has wealth and beauty,
The rich attend her door;
My love has wealth and beauty,
But I, alas! am poor."

Why did those words make me cringe? I peered around the corner and found them, Rook seated and singing, Lambe with a violin beneath his small chin, Wolff at the cello. As they finished the song, Lilly applauded and rushed forward.

"Oh, I've never heard anything so beautiful. You've a heavenly voice," she said, seating herself beside Rook.

"That's kind, Lilly, but I'm not that good." He laughed.

"Oh no. I think it's the most wonderful—"

Pretending I'd not been eavesdropping, I entered the room. Rook rose at once. "Miss Howel," he said.

He would never need to call Lilly *miss*. The thought made me ill. Lambe and Wolff stood and clapped Rook on the shoulder.

"You've a true voice," Wolff said. "Thank you for accompanying us. We needed the practice."

"It's a pleasure," Rook said. The boys nodded to me as they left.

"I sensed he required some cheering up," Lambe whispered. In that moment I loved him, and hated myself.

"Can I help you with anything, miss?" Lilly asked.

"I was hoping to speak with Rook privately."

"Of course." She beamed at him. "Meet you in the stables later? Jimmy's teaching the girls the waltz."

"Yes." Rook's smile faded as soon as Lilly had gone. "How are you, Nettie?" He took a sudden interest in a broom and would not look at me. Well, why should he be pleased with my visit? Now that I thought about it, this was the first time in two weeks I'd bothered to see him alone.

"Lessons are going along. How are you?" I sat down on the bench and waved him to come beside me. He sat as far away as possible, and folded his arms together so as not to touch me even by accident. He acted as though I were diseased.

"I'm well," he said, voice tight.

"Lilly told me you've had headaches, so I know that's not true," I muttered.

"It's just headaches. Nothing I've not had before." A moment passed in silence. I couldn't understand our awkwardness. Perhaps I'd ignored him, but from the way Rook was behaving, one would think I'd been gone two years, not two weeks.

"She says she can hear your cries all the way in her bedroom. Are you making the paste?"

"I don't take it anymore," he said. "It interferes too much."

"Are you mad? Don't you want to control this?"

Rook grimaced. "I know how much it repulses you," he said.

Perhaps I was losing what little I'd left of my mind. "You know it doesn't repulse me. I just hate to see you this way."

"I won't give it up." His bad hand tightened into a fist. "It's all I have."

"That's not true. You mustn't let it hold you down." To my surprise, Rook stood and faced me, trembling.

- 199 -

"I don't see it as holding me down. That's the way *you* see it," he said.

"Why on earth should I begin hating your scars after eight years? What's changed so drastically?"

"What's changed?" he cried. Then, his expression clearing, he sat beside me on the bench again. His quick shift in temperament scared me. "What's changed?" he repeated softly. "You don't know what we're talking about, do you?"

"What *are* we talking about?" I leaned away from him.

"Wait," he said. He placed his palms together and closed his eyes. Taking three deep, slow breaths, he raised his hands.

The shadows in the corner of the room moved.

At first I thought I was going mad, watching the inky blackness spread. The daylight that stretched across the kitchen floor seemed to shrivel and die as the shadow overtook it. The darkness was moving, growing. It congealed around Rook's feet like an oily pool. He leaned down and traced his fingertips along the mass. It shifted and swirled in response, a living thing.

"What in God's name are you doing?" I breathed.

The shadow dispersed, returning to the walls as if nothing had ever happened. Rook's pupils were wide and dark. "I've shown you before. The night Korozoth attacked, I came to your room when they'd all gone." I thought and thought . . . and recalled the dream where Rook floated above me, cloaked in darkness. Oh Lord. "Watch."

He closed his eyes and held his breath. The light in the

kitchen faded rapidly as shadows billowed out from the crevices and corners. The room around me swirled into blackness. With a startled cry, I created a ball of fire in my hand. Rook and I sat in the pure dark, my flame the only source of light. He leaned close to me, our foreheads touching.

"Fenswick gave me a potion. I thought your visit was a dream." I brought my ball of light closer to Rook's face. His eyes had gone solid black.

"It all happened when I felt Korozoth's attack. The closer it drew, the worse the agony became. And then, suddenly, I found I could call the night toward me. It was as if every bit of my body had been lit up, except that the light was darkness. I scared the horses a bit. Had to apologize to them with an extra handful of oats." He laughed. "Used to be that I couldn't understand why I'd been so cursed. I didn't realize it was a gift all along."

"You're happy, aren't you?" I whispered.

"Happier than ever, now I realize you thought I was a dream. When you stayed away, I assumed my power repulsed you."

"You could never repulse me."

"I'm sorry I doubted you." He reached out and touched a loose tendril of my hair. Despite my fear, I let him bring his hand to my cheek. His touch was wonderfully cool. "Ever since we were children, I've known that we were set apart from each other. Because of this." He waved his fingertips above the fire in my hand. The darkness over it warped for an instant. "But if we're both different, doesn't that bind us? I know you've been struggling with the sorcerers. What if we're the only ones of our kind?" He leaned toward me, the firelight playing on his cheeks and the now-total blackness of his eyes. "We belong together, don't we?"

Resting my cheek against his, I felt warm as Rook sighed against me. The fire in my palm began to die, smothered by a hand of darkness. It was as if the shadows were reaching out to touch and embrace me. It wasn't that something lived in the dark; it was more that the darkness itself was alive.

"No," I cried, drawing away. Instantly, the shadows dissipated. We sat once again in the sunlit kitchen. Rook looked shaken. "I don't mean 'no' like that. I mean that we can't give up on this path. To commendation, I mean." I was babbling and couldn't decide how to finish that thought. Rook did it for me.

"There's only one path." He said it like he didn't quite agree.

"We have to be careful. One misstep and they can be rid of us."

"I understand." He took my hand. "Tell me the truth. Does it disgust you, what I am?"

The shadows scared me; I wouldn't lie about that. It all felt too closely tied to Korozoth, and unnatural. But the shadows were a part of Rook. "No," I said. "But you must take care of yourself. Manage your pain. I'll do whatever I can to help you."

"It's not your help that I want," he said as he drew me closer to him. Every part of me felt warm.

I touched his cheek. "Didn't we want to get away from Brimthorn and stay together?"

"Yes," he whispered.

"The commendation will secure both our futures. You won't have to be a servant anymore."

"I could join the battle," Rook said. He brightened with the idea. "We could fight side by side."

"Why not?" Perhaps, if the Order saw what an Unclean could do, they'd regard the less fortunate with greater respect. Perhaps they could help Rook control his gifts. "We can keep each other safe, just as we always have."

"Always," Rook said. The air felt electric the closer we grew to each other. Rook laced his fingers through mine. His eyes, clear blue and beautiful again, widened. "Nettie?" he whispered.

"Yes?" I felt light-headed, leaning closer.

Someone cleared his throat. We almost flew apart from each other. Blackwood stood in the doorway, watching us with interest.

"I beg your pardon," he said. "Did I startle you?"

"No." How much had he seen? I stood, smoothed my skirt, and smiled at Rook. "I'll come back and see you again, if I've the time." The words sounded so dismissive I yearned to grab them and shove them back into my mouth.

"Of course." Rook's face was flushed as he picked up a broom and left for the stable yard. I pushed past Blackwood and up the stairs.

"Wait." He came after me. I stopped. "There's no need to leave in a huff."

"I don't take kindly to being spied upon." My hands balled into fists.

"I merely came down to speak with you. Rook is a frightfully interesting subject, though—"

I whirled about so fast I almost lost my balance. At least I would have taken Blackwood with me down the stairs. "Rook isn't an object for you to study. Do you hear?" I snatched up my skirts and ran, hoping he wouldn't follow.

When I heard the library door open, I knew I wouldn't have my wish. Cursing, I held my book before my face as though it would act as a soundproof wall. Naturally, it was to no avail. "I didn't mean to eavesdrop," Blackwood said as he sat beside me.

"You simply forgot how to announce your presence?"

"That was my first glimpse of Rook. I've never seen an Unclean that coherent."

"So you enjoy gaping at the less fortunate? You should really find better hobbies." I read the same paragraph in my book over and over, praying he'd leave. Had he seen Rook with the shadows?

"My family owns that colony for the Unclean, so I take an interest. Most of the patients are catatonic. Rook doesn't know how special he is. Have you considered sending him away?" He spoke in the casual manner of one conducting a business transaction. I slammed the book shut.

"You should ask Rook and not me what he wants done with himself. Since he's so coherent, he might like a say in his own future."

"It was only a suggestion," he said, putting up his hands. "We'll speak no more about it. Downstairs, you mentioned he suffered from pain?"

"Did you listen to my entire conversation?" My stomach turned at the thought.

"I came down when you were arguing over what path to take, or something of the like. You mentioned pain." He paused. "Again, I *am* sorry for eavesdropping."

He hadn't seen the shadows, then. In my relief, I answered his question. "He's having terrible headaches at night. I know it's because he doesn't take care of his scars properly."

"Has he tried laudanum?"

"The headmaster at Brimthorn wouldn't allow it on the premises. He claimed it destroyed people's minds." On that one thing, Colegrind and I had agreed.

"Bad pain is common among the Unclean. The physicians at my father's colony use a special balm of linseed oil and verbena, which they rub on the patient's chest. If you'd like, I'll have Fenswick concoct something similar. That might help with his headaches."

"Thank you. We'd be grateful," I muttered, lowering my gaze. I didn't want him to see how much I liked the idea.

"It's the least I can do for you both." He reclined into a wedge of shadow. "I've been thinking about your life at Brimthorn since the night we argued at dinner. I'd like to help you now, if I can."

Wonder of wonders, was Lord Blackwood apologizing? I felt myself softening a bit.

"It's not as if you were off enjoying yourself. You've many responsibilities." Complimenting Blackwood felt incredibly odd.

"So do you," Blackwood said. "Since seeing you with Rook,

I understand that. You look after each other." He cleared his throat and shifted several times in his seat, as if humility were a new set of uncomfortable clothes.

"When you aren't parading as the Earl of Sorrow-Fell, you can be fine company," I mused. Blackwood made a choking sound that sounded a bit like laughter.

As if making a small confession, he said, "I don't have a talent for speaking with people my own age."

"Surely you had friends growing up?" I frowned.

"I'd my tutor and governess." That told me a great deal. Sometimes when I joined Magnus and the other fellows in conversation, I would notice Blackwood stealing glances at us from across the room, almost longingly. He always returned to his book if he caught me staring. "Mother didn't believe association with other young gentlemen would improve me. It was . . . a bit lonely."

"She probably wanted to protect you," I said. Blackwood made a disdainful noise.

"In her own way, I suppose. She is not the most affectionate of women."

I was shocked by his openness. Perhaps his mother was like my aunt Agnes. Perhaps we *did* have much in common. "I know what loneliness is like, at any rate. Apart from Rook, I only had one real friend at school. But Judith went to live with her uncle in Glasgow when we were ten. Most girls kept their distance because of my friendship with an Unclean."

"Yes, we're quite the same." He choke-laughed again. I felt

almost tender toward him. I had to remember how irritating he could be, or this would become a habit.

"For what it's worth, you aren't despised. Dee told me he wishes he could be more like you."

"No, he doesn't." He leaned forward. "Does he?"

"He finds you intimidating, but that's an easy hurdle to overcome."

"He'd do better to take someone like Magnus as a role model." That bitter dislike crept into his voice again. "That's why I came to find you. The others are playing charades upstairs. I know how you enjoy being on his team."

Ah, there was that irritating tone. "I don't live to be on Magnus's team, thank you. He was merely the first person to make me feel welcome, and he never looked down on me for my low birth." I meant it half-jokingly, so I was surprised when Blackwood flinched.

"Forgive me for that. I should never have said such things," he said.

This *was* an interesting conversation. "What's brought all this on?"

He picked up my book and turned the pages in a clear attempt not to meet my gaze. "I've never seen anyone as close with one of the Unclean as you are with Rook, and I like that. I thought you wanted to be our savior to cover yourself in glory, but this is for his sake as much as yours. Isn't it?"

"Shouldn't that confirm your bad opinion of me? I care more about my friend than I do about your prophecy."

"I know what it is to love someone so much that you would move the world only to see them smile." He went from his chair to the fire, to hang on the mantel and gaze into the flames. I'd never imagined that Blackwood could speak so passionately. "I can't despise you for that, and I respect your choice of friend. Most people don't bother with the lowest among us."

Affection pulsed through me. "If there's one thing I took from those Sundays in church, it's that we're called to love the lowest."

"And the sinner? Should we love him, too?" His voice was rough and low.

"No one's ever beyond redemption," I said, surprised by his tone.

He shivered, bowing his head. Concerned, I went to him and laid my hand on his shoulder.

"Are you all right?"

"I lied," he whispered. He faced me. His gaze was cold; the smiling, vulnerable young man had vanished. "I didn't come to find you for parlor games. I wanted to gauge your reaction when I asked about taking Rook away."

"What? Why?"

"Master Agrippa thinks my Unclean colony might be the best place for him."

My whole body went numb. "No. He promised me they wouldn't send him away."

"He believes that Rook may be a distraction to you."

"How? I barely visit him as it is. Today was the first real conversation we've had in weeks!"

"No one wants to do this," Blackwood murmured, ignoring what I'd said. I pushed away from the hearth, away from him. "With Rook's bad headaches keeping the servants up and your sporadic performance, Master Agrippa doesn't want any problems."

"How could no one mention this?" I gripped the back of the chair. Would I simply have woken one morning to find Rook gone? "When will they separate us?"

Blackwood sighed. "Master Agrippa agreed to one more week."

"Agreed? Is someone forcing this?" I stepped toward him.

Blackwood shook his head. "I can't talk about it."

"This is Palehook's doing, isn't it?" Blackwood's silence only confirmed my suspicions. My hands began to spark. "They can't have him, do you understand? I'll leave this house first, which I'm sure delights you."

"I can't promise we'll win, but I'll fight to keep him with you," Blackwood said. He offered to shake on it. "On that, you have my word."

"I think I know what everyone's word is worth," I said, and ran from the library.

BACK IN MY ROOM, I LIT my bedside candle. I tried once, twice, to get the flame into the air, but each time the fire licked across my stave harmlessly. "Please," I whispered, leaning closer. "Please work."

The little flame became a fireball, then died.

"Why?" My voice choked with tears, I shook Porridge as one might a wayward child. "Why won't you do what I ask?" Furious, I flung my stave at the wall. It flashed blue for an instant.

It was as if someone had knocked my head against a stone. I collapsed, the ceiling spinning above me. My skull throbbed. Rolling onto my side was like a symphony of agony.

I had handled my stave badly. If the stave breaks, the sorcerer breaks with it. "I'm sorry, Porridge," I whispered.

"Miss!" Lilly swam into view above me. "What is it?"

"Hurts," I grunted. Lilly slipped my arm around her shoulder and helped me to my feet. The floor tilted at such a mad angle I was sure I'd be sick. I muttered something even I couldn't understand. Lilly laid me on my bed, and after a moment, her footsteps disappeared out of the room.

I closed my eyes and waited for the darkness to stop spinning. I might have stayed like this for moments or hours, until I heard his voice: "Nettie?"

When I opened my eyes, Rook sat beside me. "Lilly said you needed me."

"She did?" I sat up slowly. A dull ache had replaced the sharp pain in my head.

Lilly parked herself by my vanity and watched. "Thought you'd need Mr. Fenswick, miss, but you said all you wanted was Rook."

Rook squeezed my hand. "Do you need anything?"

I swallowed the tightness out of my throat. My chin wobbled, which meant tears were imminent. "We're in trouble. I've failed. I can't even attempt what Master Agrippa wants, and the queen won't commend me."

Lilly gasped, but Rook squeezed my hand tighter. "You can cry if you like."

"I don't like," I muttered. "They're going to separate us. Unless I improve my lessons and you control your pain, they'll send you away to Brighton. Lord Blackwood told me."

Rook's expression hardened. "They could do it?"

"Until I'm commended, they control everything."

"Very well," Rook said, and nodded to Lilly. "Start packing Miss Howel's things. We're leaving."

"What?" Lilly gasped.

"No." I grabbed his arm. "We're not leaving. This is the only way—"

"It isn't the only way." Rook brushed a strand of hair from my forehead. "You don't have to be a sorcerer. We'll leave for Sussex or Kent. They need teachers there, as well as servants. Or we can fight, head for the army on our own terms now that we know we've both got power." He whispered that last part to avoid Lilly's hearing. "We'll start again. Together."

"You know there isn't anything I wouldn't do to keep you safe." I gasped, the tears coming now whether I wanted them or not.

"I can keep you safe, too," he whispered. "We keep each other safe."

"Yes." I wiped my eyes with my handkerchief. "Bournemouth could be beautiful this time of year."

"Exactly! We can leave at first light tomorrow, all this in the past. We could be by the seaside."

Wouldn't that be heavenly? I imagined some stretch of pebbled beach with waves breaking on it. I could feel the water lapping against my bare feet, my ankles grainy with sand. Perhaps we'd head to Devon, where Aunt Agnes still lived in her little cottage. She'd see how I'd grown up and resolve to forget all the ugliness of the past. I imagined her embracing us and ushering us inside with tea already laid out before a hot fire.

What a silly fantasy. We both knew what life awaited us outside the ward. Starvation and scorn beckoned, accusations of witchcraft and hatred for the Unclean. If we weren't killed for our abilities, we would more than likely open ourselves to the Ancients' attack. Now when I envisioned that stretch of beach, I saw Nemneris the Water Spider lunging out of the waves.

"No. The only chance we have is for me to be commended. I need to improve my lessons, and you try to keep from screaming too loudly in the night. Even if that means using the paste." I was asking him to suppress his power for my sake. What a hypocrite I was. "Lord Blackwood has a good remedy for the pain," I said lamely.

"We can't trust them, Nettie." He was firm. "We shouldn't have to play a part to gain their acceptance."

He was right. In a perfect world, we would be able to declare our abilities openly. Then again, in a perfect world there would be no war against seven vicious monsters. "We must work to-gether."

"So you can be commended?" His voice sounded hollow. The connection we'd shared in the kitchen snapped, and I felt him drifting out of my reach again. "Perhaps it would be best for all if I went to Lord Blackwood's colony."

"No!" Lilly cried. She blushed.

"No," I said, taking his hand. "I've done this so the pair of us can have a better chance at life."

"Yes. The pair of us." After a moment of silence, he said, "It was selfish of me to ask you to run."

"Once I'm commended, we can show Agrippa your talents," I whispered.

"No. Right now they need the light, not more darkness." He leaned forward, fast, and planted a kiss on the top of my head. "You should rest." He got off the bed and left. Lilly promised to return with some tea before rushing after him. Alone, I lay down and thought. Whatever Rook believed of my intentions, all I wanted was for us both to be safe. Between his secret and mine, everything now relied on my commendation.

And I knew where I would have to go, and whom I would have to see, in order to succeed.

15

TWO DAYS LATER, I WALKED TOWARD HA'PENNY ROW during my free afternoon. I clutched a bundle of bread and cheese to my chest. I'd have taken wine as well, but the butler counted the bottles and I didn't want any of the servants to get in trouble.

A thin layer of yellow grime covered the ward. This time, slicing through was slightly harder than cutting a cobweb. Palehook wasn't doing his job well.

"'Scuse me, miss," a young man with a gruff voice said as he stumbled into me.

"It's all right," I replied. He shoved past and strode away.

I continued to Hargrove's, nearly treading on a black crow that pecked for grain in the road. I marveled at its wingspan as it soared upward to land on a rooftop. The bird joined a small cluster of other crows and ravens. By the time I'd turned off the street, I counted ten, all singing above us.

"I TOLD YOU TO BRING ME drink," Hargrove said as I handed the food to the children. I couldn't give the bundle to him, as he was slitting open a long spool of bloodied intestine that lay on the table. The smell was hideous. One of the children thrust open a window in a bid for fresh air.

"What *are* you doing?" I wrinkled my nose.

"These are the innards of a white sow. I bought them off a fellow in Shoreditch, a steal at a tuppence. He says he fed her a penny with the queen's face on both sides. Numismatomancy is divination through money. That coin will reveal wonders to me."

"Such as why you spent two pennies to purchase one?"

"Hilarious." He sliced away, brow furrowed as he inspected the bloody entrails. "This is your magical heritage, my little weasel. Show some respect." Sure I'd be sick, I removed my hood. Hargrove's eyebrows shot up. "You look terrible. When's the last time you slept?"

"I don't look that awful."

Hargrove gestured to one of the children. "Get the family mirror."

The child handed me a cracked looking glass before I could object. Even if my reflection hadn't been fractured, the damage was plain enough. My eyes were dark and sunken, my complexion pallid. I'd lost weight.

The dreams of R'hlem had kept me up again. That was three nights in a row. I feared it was becoming a pattern. "I don't sleep."

"Why not?"

My patience at an end, I made a wincing face. "Guess."

"I know you didn't want to come back here." He kicked a chair toward me, an invitation to sit. "You're a prideful little creature, eh?"

I doubted a smart remark would make him want to help me. "Teach me to be a magician."

"But I thought you were a sorcerer. Last time you were here you shouted it through the streets." He wagged a bloody finger at me.

"I can't work with their magic. You said you'd help me." My nerves were frayed enough as it was. My head started to pound.

"Why should I?"

"For my father's sake."

"Yes, but now that I've thought about it, I've realized that is a spectacularly good way to die. I like myself alive," he sniffed. I slammed Porridge onto the table, careful to avoid the entrails.

"If I'm commended, I could try getting the ban on magician apprentices lifted."

He considered this. "I can't imagine that would be an easy fight."

"Nevertheless, I'll do it if you help me."

"Yes, but I also want money. Twelve pounds, specifically. I've a project in mind that requires a certain sum."

Twelve bloody pounds? Where was I supposed to get that? "What do you need it for?"

"Rule number one: as my apprentice, you don't ask nosy questions."

If he got me commended, I'd commit highway robbery. I would find a way. "You'll have to take it in bits. I can't manage it all at once."

He nodded. "That and a bottle of wine next time you come will seal the deal."

Relieved, I tried to hand Porridge to him. "Show me what to do."

"I can't use that," he said, wiping his hands on a cloth. "Magicians can't handle staves, darling girl."

"I thought you said I was a magician." Pain throbbed in my temple. Why was everything so bloody complicated?

"Well, you might have an outmoded ability. Magicians are descended from sorcerers, after all. Your father was always vocal about uniting our two societies once again. Pity he drowned when he did."

"What was he like?" Despite my exhaustion, my heart sped up. No one had ever spoken to me about my father before. Aunt Agnes told me that he was a good solicitor and a poor sailor, and not to ask questions.

"Friendly, witty, always ready with a joke. That was the Welsh in him. Intelligent, to be sure, though a bit quick-tempered. Like father, like daughter. Can you really do that whole set-yourself-on-fire thing?"

"Yes." My skin tingled at the mention of it.

"Magicians have many unique and strange talents, my girl, and several of them can be passed down in families. Some magicians take the form of animals, some allow the souls of the dead to enter their bodies and speak through them." His face brightened. "Care to see mine? Haven't got a hankie on you, eh?"

I handed him my linen handkerchief, disgusted as he took it with bloody fingers. Hargrove examined it, murmuring and pursing his lips. Exasperated, I began to feel he was toying with me. Shaking my head, I reached out to reclaim it. "Now, what on earth did you do?" I said, looking up.

He'd vanished. I checked the corner of the room, underneath the table, even outside. The children giggled as they watched my confusion. Finally, one of them piped up and said, "He's in your hankie."

"What?" It was impossible. I unfolded the smallest crease and found a great black eye winking up at me. With a scream, I dropped the handkerchief, and Hargrove spilled out of it and onto the floor. "How?" I gasped.

"Magicians violate *all natural order.* Of course you're one of us. Your father could burst into flame and never harm himself. It's no wonder you've got the ability, too." So that was the secret. I was a magician's daughter with an abnormal talent. I sank into my chair.

"Aren't magicians descended from sorcerers?" The prophecy had called for a girl-child of sorcerer stock. He recognized my real question.

"Sorcerers like to pretend they've no connection with us. The Speakers might be a druggy bunch of fools, but they'd never be so vague about an important detail. If the prophecy calls for someone of 'sorcerer stock,' they mean a sorcerer parent." There was my last hope, gone. I closed my eyes. "That prophecy is a lot of blather." Hargrove's voice softened. "Dictating who can and can't be important is a waste of good brainpower. Give any-one the juice of the night-blooming Etheria, and they'll tell you hedgehogs are coming out of the woodwork and there are clouds of grapes hovering on the horizon. Now, wake the stave." I did as he asked. "The sorcerers want you to add your power to theirs, like pouring a bucket of water into a pond. Differences between sorcerers and magicians, chapter one, section one: our instincts are opposite. What do I mean by this? Let me answer with a question. What is the difference between a bird and a fish?"

"One flies and one swims?"

"No, the correct answer is: *everything*. Sorcerers *conduct* the earth's energy from one place to the next. We magicians are cre-ators. Do you understand?" He tapped a finger to his forehead in emphasis. "We generate, we don't manipulate. Your Master Agrippa surrenders himself to the power of the elements; he's a mere conduit for them. Meanwhile, your feelings, thoughts, dreams, ambitions, all build your magic. How do you feel now?"

Fearful. Angry. My throat was tight, and my head pounded. The blue flames ignited and swirled about me.

Hargrove cried out, "You'll burn us all! Calm down."

The anger released itself, and the fire died, until it was only a thin shell that clung to my body. With a thought, I stopped burn-ing. "What does it mean?"

"It means, cherub, that what you think and feel directs your ability."

I took a chair and placed it in the center of the room. Facing the chair, I used both arms to lift my stave, employing the earth's magnetic force. I didn't clear my mind. I imagined lifting it. Above all, I *wanted* to lift it. I felt something build inside me, a kind of pressure. After a few wobbly tries, the chair rose three feet and hovered without the slightest waver. I lowered it to the floor, giddy with relief.

"Can I work with sorcerers?" I asked, tension draining out of my body.

"Yes, as long as you focus on yourself. They can feed on your power, but never tell them what you really are." He returned to cutting open the intestines, inspecting them carefully. "You're a cuckoo in the nest. If they learn the truth, they'll push you out and break your neck."

"Master Agrippa wouldn't do that."

"Everyone has a limit. Aha!" He held up a coin, covered in blood. He wiped it and flipped it into the air. "Two-faced, just as the man said. How nice to know there are still trustworthy people on the black market."

"What else can you teach me?"

Hargrove shook his head. "I don't think I should show you any actual tricks. The less you know, the less you can slip up and reveal to the sorcerers."

"Mr. Hargrove," Billy said, standing on his tiptoes and gazing out the window, "come look at the birds!"

"Yes, nice birdies," Hargrove said absently.

"How much do magicians know about magic?" I asked.

He puffed himself up. "We've forgotten more than Master Agrippa could learn in a lifetime."

"Mr. Hargrove, the birds!" Billy called again. I peered through the window to where the little boy pointed. A ring of ten ravens sat on the street below. The passersby skirted around them.

"Why are sorcerers so afraid of magicians?" I said.

"Because of our potential for power. We could wipe out the sorcerer Order with little effort." He gathered up the rest of the intestines and dumped them out the open window. Below us, someone gave a disgusted cry.

"If we're so powerful, why haven't we done that already?"

"Because magicians don't like order. We enjoy our freedom." He shuffled to a bowl of water and washed his hands. "We make our own mistakes."

I was about to ask what he meant when screams started outside.

The ten ravens began to swell and change shape, like a child's balloon in the hands of a carnival worker. They hopped into the center of the circle and melded together into a fat, feathery mound. The blob grew, and a moment later one large black shape remained. It rose in the center of the street, a tall humanesque figure with dark robes and a cowl covering its face. Ebony feathers coated its long, vaguely winglike arms.

It was one of the ravens, the Familiars of On-Tez the Vulture Lady. With one swift, terrible motion, the monster swung out a claw-tipped hand and sliced off a man's head.

16

CHAOS ERUPTED BELOW AS PEOPLE TRAMPLED ONE another to get out of the way. The bird creature flapped its arms and struck a woman, knocking her to the ground.

"Why would On-Tez send one of her ravens? She stays in Canterbury," I said, horrified.

"Attacks don't only happen at night, my ducky. Old R'hlem's fighting a war, and he means to win it."

"Why don't the sorcerers do something?"

He glared at me. "Because the Familiars don't attack the ward, dear heart, and that's all the Order cares about." He grunted as he looked out the window. "This is the fourth time in two months. I should move. It's not fair to the area."

"Why should *you* move?"

"The magic," he said, as though it were obvious. "The Ancients and their Familiars are drawn to the scent of it like ants to a sticky bun."

London was filled with sorcerers. Was the city under constant attack because of us?

"Come," Hargrove said. "I'll show you a way out."

"If our power called these creatures, we should be the ones to put a stop to it." I grabbed his coat sleeve as he brushed past me.

"I don't have to do anything. If it's between them or me, I choose me." He yanked himself from my grip. I looked back out the window.

The Familiar sliced its way through a man's chest, leaving him to bleed out on the ground. The street turned a roiling crimson as the thing threw back its head and screamed in triumph, arm-wings bristling. My hands felt hot. When I pulled open the front door, Hargrove slammed it shut. "You'll get yourself killed!" he snapped.

"Help me. I know I can't fight it on my own." I grabbed Porridge from its sheath.

"You want to throw a little wind and rain at it? It'll take more than weather play, you stupid thing."

"Help me!" I pointed at the door. "Or I'll go down there and die in the attempt, and you'll have to live with the guilt of failing my father."

"I think you're overestimating how much I liked him," Hargrove muttered, "but all right. Wait." He ran to the back of the room and thrust the curtain aside, dispersing the children while he dragged out a wooden chest. He banged on the lid twice, and it swung open. One by one, the children stepped into the chest and disappeared, making little noises of excitement or terror as they did so. Once the last child had vanished, Hargrove closed the lid, tapped upon it three times, and reopened it. The trunk now contained a collection of odds and ends, bits of string and candles and toys, tarnished copper bells and golden rings in the shape of dragons, lace handkerchiefs, and glass vials of thick, odd-colored liquid. An aroma of moths and rose petals wafted out.

"Where did the children go?"

"Er, storage. This is what we need." He selected something, shut the box, and went to the window, covering it with what appeared to be a large and durable spiderweb.

"What are you doing?"

"I'll need extra power for this. Use your stave." He put his hands to the web and said, *"Weave it with your malice, woven with your gall, grow to catch a spider, strength to see it fall."* My nose crinkled in distaste. "Well, it works for me. Activate Toast or Marmalade or whatever that stave's name is, and use it as best you can. Only remember to envision something big enough to catch that creature."

I put Porridge to the web, closed my eyes, and imagined a great net strong enough to hold a bird. Nothing happened. "I thought you said I was a magician."

"Stop whining and think of exactly what you want to do." Intentions—I had to be specific in my intentions. The screams below spurred me on. I envisioned the web catching that raven, saw the bird squawk and collapse as I snared it. First, I had to weave the web, make it grow. I spun my stave in a gradual spiral, beginning at the center and spreading outward. I imagined it growing larger, big enough to catch the bastard. Catch it. Catch it. Catch—

"It worked!" Hargrove yelled. I opened my eyes and stared out the window. The Familiar lay pinned to the earth in the center of the street, trapped beneath an enormous spiderweb. I opened the front door against Hargrove's protests, pulling my cloak on and my hood around my face. The creature began to rip free.

Running down the steps, I sliced my stave through the air three times, using my anger as fuel. The wind rushed out of the east and pounded the thing. When the Familiar raised its winged arms to shield itself, the gale ushered it into the sky. I slipped back into an alleyway and hugged the wall, watching the Familiar struggle in the wind.

Out of nowhere, a great red-and-purple-and-orange cloak appeared, flapping in the breeze. The garment swept upward and wrapped itself around the raven. It looked as if the two were wrestling. With a wave of my hand, I stopped the wind. The raven plummeted to earth. When it landed, the coat rose up and flew away quickly, as if attempting to sneak off.

The Familiar lay still. Slowly, people began to approach. I kept my head down and inched forward in the crowd, stopping above the collapsed pile of rags and feathers to stare at the now-dead thing. I glimpsed the less-than-human face beneath the cowl. Its teeth were pointed and black, skin whiter than chalk, except where bits of crimson blood and gore had splashed onto its chin. Black feathers covered the top of the monster's head, so that I could not see the eyes, and a once-human nose had sharpened into a pointed beak. Brackish liquid oozed from a stab wound in the raven's sunken chest.

Someone grabbed me by the shoulder and, placing a hand over my mouth, spun me into a whirlwind. A moment later, hands released me. I stumbled around to face my attacker, Hargrove, who smiled and nodded behind me.

"Don't step back; it's quite a fall." He grabbed me when I didn't listen and almost tumbled into space. We stood atop a roof. Below us, the crowd's confusion was a persistent murmur. Balanced on the roof's slope, Hargrove cleaned blood off a silver blade. "Another great defect of the sorcerers is they don't get creative with their weaponry. Magic is fine, but a knife works marvelously well. Ravens tend to die best with a blade of silver. I wrote all about it in my journal, *The Life and Times of a Really Fantastic Magician, His Thoughts and Theories, Volume Seven*." He studied his reflection in the blade's surface and licked his thumb, rubbing it over a patch of black blood on his forehead.

"How did you fly without wind? How on earth did you disappear? How did you get us up here?" My voice was high and breathless. It was *impossible*. It was *brilliant*.

"Those," he said, slipping the knife into the folds of his coat, "are the sorts of questions you can't ask."

"You don't have to teach me how to do what you do. Just teach me—"

"How I do what I do, but not how to do what I do? What if what I do has to do with my knowledge of what to do, and doing requires only the knowledge of doing? What would you do then?"

I blinked. "I believe you hurt my brain."

"It's a good brain, all things considered. Listen, my adorable bonfire, I cannot teach you much. Our safety requires it. But I suppose a little magic never did a body a great deal of harm. Unless it was the magical art of rearranging bones. Or turning flesh inside out. Or—never mind. Really, I'd forgotten how much I missed being collegial with my own kind. A magician without an apprentice is like a dog without a bark."

"Will you teach me how to fight them?" I waved my hand over the Familiar's corpse, far below. "How to kill them?"

"Bloodthirsty, are we? You don't want to go and get yourself slaughtered before your big commendation."

"I can't let these people suffer. If the Order won't do anything, I will."

Hargrove sighed. "Very well. Next lesson, we'll discuss battle techniques."

"I may not be able to come often."

"Whatever time you can spare." He looked at me with something like sadness. "You did well today. You used a bit of magician trickery yourself, you know, even with the stave. I'm sure some of that will bleed into our lessons. Now, speaking of blood, I must seek out a bath." He wrapped the cloak around us and, instantly, we stood in the alleyway again.

"Thank you. I'm glad to know my father had such a good friend."

"No, don't think that." His expression darkened. "If there's one thing your father was unlucky in, it was his friends." Before I could ask what he meant, he folded himself tight within his cloak and vanished.

THE FAMILIAR APPROACHED ME FROM ACROSS the room. She licked her dry lips with a thick black tongue and hummed deep in her throat. This was the rider I had met, the one with the eyes sewn shut with coarse black thread. "Little lady sorcerer," she hissed. Her thin white-blond hair lay stringy against her face, down her back.

She was even more hideous than I remembered. I sank down onto the sofa, trying to keep my wits about me. This was a dream. We were seated in the mist-shrouded library. I looked across the room to my sleeping body collapsed over my desk. This would teach me to study when I was so tired.

Would these visitations happen every time I went to sleep?

I tried not to panic. If R'hlem could kill me in a dream, I felt certain he would have done so already. These last three nights, he'd followed me about the room wherever I went. He'd watched me struggle to wake up, an amused smile on his face. But he had never touched me. Perhaps he couldn't.

And there he was. R'hlem appeared beside the rider, a pleased expression on his skinned face. "Do you like her?" he said to me. The girl knelt at his feet, as if she'd twine about his legs like a pet cat.

"No," I replied.

R'hlem laughed at my sullen response. He chucked the Familiar under her chin. With a wave of his hand, she vanished.

"No fear this time. You did well."

Did well? "What does that mean? How are you doing this? What do you want from me?" He didn't respond, only came to offer me his hand. I rose without it and backed toward the fire. Wherever I went in the room, he moved after me at a leisurely gait. He seemed to take enormous pleasure in my confusion. I tried a different tack. "Are the Ancients attacking London because of the scent of magic?" There. That finally stopped him. "You're attacking us because so many magic users live inside the ward, aren't you?"

R'hlem sneered. "Ask your great men what sins they've committed." Sins? Now he regarded me with real interest. "Who told you this?"

I wouldn't give Hargrove away. "I want to wake up now."

R'hlem strode toward me. Before I could dodge him, he grabbed me by the wrist. His touch was slippery and cold. Bloody. I screamed and struggled. His grip tightened. He was squeezing hard enough to break my—

"HOWEL?" MAGNUS SHOOK ME AWAKE. I swung about blindly, sending paper flying all across the desk. "Sorry. I didn't realize you were so determined to sleep."

"I must have nodded off," I muttered, rubbing my eyes. Magnus grabbed my wrist.

"Did you cut yourself?" Looking down, I discovered fingerprints shining wet with blood. I pulled away and wiped off the marks with my handkerchief.

"I scratched myself when I was out in the garden. It must've bled more than I thought," I said lamely. What would have happened had Magnus not woken me? Perhaps he would've discovered my mangled corpse at this desk. Trying to appear preoccupied, I grasped my pen and looked over a piece of paper. Magnus watched me with his back against the hearth. After a minute, I gave in. "Yes?"

"I was just wondering," he said, arms crossed over his chest, "why you were outside the ward today."

I dropped the pen. "I wasn't."

"You were, and you clobbered that raven with a blast of wind. I planned to join in the fray myself, but it was over before I could do anything. Why were you there?"

I stood and turned away from him. "I didn't see you follow me."

"You spoke to me."

"I didn't." I looked back at him, confused. "When?"

He hunched himself and shouldered past. " 'Scuse me, miss," he said in a gruff, familiar tone.

"You were the fellow who bumped into me? How did you know where I was going?"

"I saw you sneaking down to the kitchen for food, so I followed. Why did you go?"

"I wanted to bring something to that horrible magician Hargrove's children. Please don't tell Master Agrippa." I realized I'd given Magnus power over me. Damn.

"How did you have such control over the wind? You couldn't even lift a feather during lessons this morning."

"Sometimes when you have to do something, you find you can." Would he accept that and say no more?

Magnus nodded. "I suppose that makes sense. You did well, actually, battling that thing. Hideous beasts, aren't they?"

"Yes. Were you aware that Familiars sometimes attack the unwarded area during the day?" I felt ill recalling the carnage I'd witnessed.

He looked uncomfortable. "No. The Order likes to keep secrets from us, don't you think?" He spun a globe that sat atop the desk, skimming his fingers across the Pacific Ocean.

"We should do something about it."

"We will. Once we're commended, we can change things." He leaned against the desk, the image of confidence.

"You believe that, don't you?"

"I never have any trouble believing in myself." He smiled, but there was no cockiness in his expression. "And I was right to believe in you. In time, you'll be a great sorcerer."

"Do you think?"

"Yes." He said it without doubt or hesitation.

"Why?" I asked, without thinking.

"Why what?"

"Why are you so kind to me?" I lowered my eyes. Somehow I felt very exposed.

"Because I'm wonderful. Hadn't you noticed?"

"No," I said. "Why have you never doubted my place as a sorcerer?"

His smile faded a bit. "Because I've seen how a woman is treated when she dares to step outside her domain." He went to stand before the fire. There was pain in his eyes, something I'd never seen before. "After Father died, my uncle thought I needed to be raised by men. I was a Magnus, after all. We're warriors, have been since before Rome fell. He wanted to raise me himself, but Mother fought to keep me. She endured many great men bullying her, telling her what a little fool she was, that I'd grow up weak. Weak like a woman." He winced. "Mother never yielded. Have I turned out so very bad?" He looked up as I came beside him.

"No." I smiled.

"So. When I see a lady go up against a group of men who claim to know better than she does, I find I want her to succeed. You *will* succeed, Howel."

My cheeks grew hot.

"I'll have a better chance of success once I get my blasted lessons down. There's still so much I don't know." I moved to the desk to straighten my papers. "Reading only takes me so far."

Magnus came up beside me. "I'm the very soul of experience. Let me tutor you."

"In what?"

"Whatever you wish." He raised an eyebrow. "Name anything."

I thought for a moment. "How did you bespell me into not recognizing you on the street?"

"Who said it was magic?" He laughed and clapped his hands. "That's what an actor does, my dear Howel. He shows you what you want to see."

"I'll remember that."

"Another question, my intrepid lady?"

I recalled Hargrove sheathing his silver blade. "Why don't sorcerers employ more human weapons? Maybe it would be useful against some Familiars, if not the Ancients themselves."

"Well, we *do* train in sabers and pistols," Magnus said. Lord, didn't I know it. The first time I fired a gun, I'd been thrown to the ground.

"But do we use them much in battle?"

Magnus gave a surprised laugh. "I suppose that's a topic to discuss with the Imperator. Anyway, we use some blades more than others." His eyes lit up. "How's this for helpful? I'll instruct you in another class of weaponry, one you haven't yet learned. You should handle it a bit better than the pistols."

Magnus was the finest warrior in our house, without question. Anything he had to teach would be massively helpful. "Thank you, yes."

"They're called warded blades. Master Agrippa wanted to wait until you'd a few more maneuvers in hand, but I see no reason to hold off. You take the ward you draw up around yourself, slide it down your arm to your stave, and fashion it with your thoughts into a weapon. Like this." He took his stave and activated it with the name Excalibur. "What?" he said when I laughed. "I loved the Arthur legend when I was fourteen. That was right before I noticed how exciting girls were. Good thing I didn't get my stave later, or I might have named it Louisa. Or Marianne. Or Emily."

"Perhaps we should start before you name every girl in London," I said.

He showed me how to put the ward up about myself, how to imagine that protective bubble shrinking on my body and gathering in my arm, and then how to slide it off my arm and onto my stave. "With enough practice, you'll be able to create the blade with a simple thought. Now you see it, faint yellow and pointed. This will cut better than a human sword."

Indeed, the outline was scarcely visible, but when I put my thumb to the blade it sliced me. Magnus showed me how to hold the stave, my index and middle fingers on top for balance. "Now your movement stays central. Always keep the torso firm," he said, placing a hand on my stomach. "As the weapon is light, you'll want more control. Movement comes from your shoulder, not your elbow." With Magnus lined up behind me, I created a few elegant sweeps. After that, he taught me some simple parries. We bumped into chairs and knocked over the desk globe.

"You won't have many great battles with these." I laughed, lunging at him. He easily blocked me.

"No, but this is tremendous fun if you want to see the fear in your enemy's eyes." With that, he knocked Porridge from my hand and grabbed me about the waist. "Voilà. I've captured you." His arm stayed firm about me. "Perhaps I won't allow you to escape," he said, his cheek against mine.

"Oh?" My pulse quickened as he pulled back just enough to meet my gaze. Magnus stroked the side of my face, his fingertips trailing warmth.

"*Mmm.* Has anyone ever mentioned that you have a little freckle at the corner of your eye?"

"Ah, no." I knew I should look away, but I couldn't. This wasn't Magnus with his normal, silly flirtations. "I suppose it's unattractive."

"Hardly. It draws attention to your eyes, which are brilliant." He leaned in. "I think you have the loveliest eyes I've ever seen, come to think of it. They're so dark they're almost black, which gives you a very fierce expression in battle. But if I draw closer"—and he did, gently—"I see warm brown. When your gaze is soft, there are flecks of gold. Nothing about you is ever quite how it appears."

"I look tired. I know I do," I murmured. His arm tightened around me.

"That's nothing a good night's sleep won't cure." He cupped my cheek in his hand for one brief moment. "You've a beautiful face, Howel," he whispered. He stroked my chin with this thumb. I closed my eyes.

What about Rook?

"Thank you. That is, for teaching me," I said, pulling away from him. I gathered Porridge, fumbling a bit.

"You did well for a first-timer. You'll play the game in the end, though not as well as I." He bowed. The softness of his look and voice disappeared, but we both knew what had happened. I felt as if the portraits, the books, even the fire, bore witness.

"You can win the games, and I'll win the battles," I said, exiting at a brisk pace. I took the stairs at a run.

Back in my room, I sat by the window, my breath fogging the glass. I closed my eyes. Magnus thought I was beautiful. The way he'd looked at me and touched me. What would have happened if I hadn't pulled away?

He's a flirt. I knew that, and I'd never taken his teasing seriously before. But this had felt like more.

Did I *want* more?

What was I talking about, after what had nearly happened with Rook in the kitchen? What was I doing, entertaining these ridiculous ideas of Magnus?

But Rook was still being distant with me. His disappointment in my refusal to run away was evident, no matter what he said. His disappointment in *me* was evident.

What was I doing considering *any* of this? Rook was my friend; Magnus, my ally. That was all they were, all they could be. There was commendation, and if I got that far, there would be war afterward. Life was complicated enough. I resolved to stop thinking about the pair of them immediately.

It took an hour of tracing patterns on the fogged window before I finally did.

17

HARGROVE PLACED THE TEAPOT ON THE TABLE AND rolled up his sleeves. "Your training begins. Turn this into a mouse, and be quick about it. I want it back into its regular form in time for tea."

This was far more than I'd expected from my first proper lesson. It was the following day, Sunday, where all that was required of Agrippa's Incumbents was to attend church. I had used my freedom to rush right back to Hargrove's.

"Do I just poke at it?" I murmured, gesturing with my stave. Hargrove's five children circled us, seated on the floor with their faces cupped in their hands.

With an impatient huff, Hargrove knocked four times on the lid of his wooden chest. It sprang open in an explosion of paper and parchment. He burrowed his way through scrolls and letters and scraps of notepaper, until, with a cry of triumph, he held up a leather-bound book. Dusting it, he threw it onto the table and riffled through the pages until he alighted on the desired one. "Here," he said. I squinted and stared at the watery, handwritten text.

"I can't read it."

"Must I do everything myself? It clearly says, *'Whisker from a steaming spout, handle to a tail, china cracks to beating heart, fur and tooth and nail.'*"

I pointed my stave at the teapot and repeated the words. Hargrove wailed in exasperation. "Well, what am I supposed to do?"

"No two magicians are the same. We're like delicate snowflakes, or ears. That line was originally written in Latin—something *muris fumo*, something—well, I knew a magician once, Peg Bottleshanks, who used some Latin and some English and some musical notes from her nose whistle. You see? Total madness!"

"Master Agrippa says a system is needed."

Hargrove blew a rude noise that thrilled the children. "We don't bother with rules."

"But how will I know what's correct?"

"Far as you're concerned, the word *correct* no longer exists. For instance, what say I walk on the ceiling?"

"Gravity doesn't work that way," I snapped.

Hargrove billowed his multicolored cloak about him, mumbled *"Flibberty bop, to the top, allons-y, charge,"* and to my surprise fell upward. Upside down, he danced a jig along the rafters, shaking free dust and a few cobwebs. The children applauded and cried with joy. After a moment, he returned in triumph. "You were saying, young upstart?"

"How do I do that?"

"I don't know if you can. Play around with it; see what you find."

"I don't like this," I said, shaking my head. "The sorcerers have traditions."

"You like traditions?"

I moved around the table to the wooden chest and rummaged through piles of crumpled rubbish. I winced at the mess. "I don't enjoy this much disorder."

"You're more of a sorcerer than I thought," he mused. "Which is as it should be, if we want you to pass. What say we focus on controlling your gifts? You made progress last time, when you lifted that chair."

Leave a lesson unfinished? Never. "I'll turn that teapot into a mouse, to show I can." With that, I waved my hands and said the words exactly as Hargrove had spoken them to me. Nothing happened. I repeated the words while pointing Porridge. Still nothing.

It went on like this for several minutes. Hargrove uncorked a bottle of gin with his teeth and sat, gulping it down. He drank too much. I attempted the entire thing in French ("And you've a fine accent, my cherub. I could listen to you say *souris* all day long"), and when that didn't work, I said a few unladylike words and sat down to stare at the little teapot. It was white and chipped at the spout, with tiny roses painted on it. I'd no idea what to do.

I took Porridge in hand again . . . and I could feel it warm in my grasp, almost like a living thing. It was impatient. I could picture myself *drawing forth* a mouse from the chiseled confines of a teapot. And in drawing forth, I imagined the sorcerer maneuver that called water from the earth, to be used in cases of dire thirst.

I spun my stave clockwise and counterclockwise, and swept it through the air in an arc. The teapot moved slightly. Hargrove stood.

I could feel the words he had taught me on my tongue. *Whisker from spout . . . handle to tail.* I completed the maneuver again, and this time, as the sweep of my arm came up, I imagined the teapot tipping over and a little brown mouse squeezing out, and whispered, *"Spout to a tail."*

The teapot bulged, then crumpled in on itself. It poured out a great blob of hair and ears, and a moment later, a bright-eyed little mouse with brown fur and bristling whiskers stood on its hind legs and wiggled its nose at us. It pounced from the tabletop and scurried across the floor. The children dove to catch it, but it slipped through a crack in the wall and vanished.

"I did it!" I cried, tossing Porridge into the air in triumphant glee. Hargrove bellowed with laughter, dancing across the room to snatch paper and pen.

"Write it down, exactly what you did. I've never seen anything like it." His wide grin fell as he stared at the wall. "That was my only teapot. Well. Can't be helped!" And then we returned to singing and twirling around the room. The children rejoiced, jumping to clutch my skirts.

"I want to do another," I said, breathless.

"Excellent, I've just the thing." Hargrove handed me an empty bottle. "Turn that into a teapot."

SOON AFTER, HARGROVE WAS POURING US cups of gin-flavored tea. "Little magic mule, that's what I'll call you. A delicate hybrid of both races."

"Do you think I'm the only one?"

Hargrove grunted. "Don't imagine yourself so special. I know for a fact you're not alone. There've been sorcerer children born as you are, and magician children as well. You're simply in a unique position to realize both halves of your talents."

"How many did you know like me? I mean, back when, well . . ."

"Back when it was legal to be a public magician? One or two. They're dead now, of course. Caught training apprentices."

I shuddered to think of it. "Bloody Howard Mickelmas. It's his fault we have to live like this," I said. Hargrove merely shrugged and poured himself some gin. "What was he like?"

"Mickelmas? Why?"

"You're the first person I ever knew who met him. Was it always clear he was evil?" I asked. Hargrove made a face.

"He was just a proper magical bloke. Bit stupid, of course, but if we executed for stupidity, there'd be no one left to walk the planet."

"What did he look like?"

"Don't know. We never saw his face at Guild meetings. He'd send a raven or a cat. It would sit in the center of the room, and he'd talk through it. Great party trick. Used to consider him daft, but now no one knows what he looks like.

Probably how he's survived all these years." He gulped more tea. "I don't like talking about him, if it's all the same to you. Irritates me."

I understood his feelings. "Could my father speak through animals?"

"Nope, just the old set-yourself-on-fire routine."

"But he could play with fire. Isn't that a sorcerer trait? Don't you think it odd that a mixture of the abilities can exist in one person?"

He snorted. "Lord, it's as if William Howel rose from the dead and returned to lecture me in a dress. That's a dreadful image."

"My father asked the same questions?" I leaned forward.

"Yes, and arrived at the staggering conclusion of nothing." He sighed. "William had such hopes for magic in England, insane, irrational hopes. He wanted a consortium." He put his thumbs and index fingers together to fashion a triangle. "Witches, sorcerers, and magicians, all on the same level. All in service of the crown. All equal."

"Why?" I was eager. Before our lessons, all I'd had of my father was a half-remembered picture on my aunt's fireplace.

"Because of his belief that all magic comes down in a straight line. Witches, sorcerers, magicians."

"Witches are first?" I frowned.

"Enough questions." Hargrove startled me with his brusqueness. "I used to tell your father this, when he got off on a ridiculous tangent. Knowledge is as powerful as fire. The brighter it burns, the more it devours. Now we must pay for our lessons, little one." He extended his hand, fingers wiggling.

I gave him a sovereign, wincing as I did so. "I sold three silk hair ribbons. I'll have to tell Lilly I lost them, or she'll be out of her mind with worry." Scowling at him, I said, "You've made me a thief."

"I notice you'd no qualms stealing that bread and cheese," he answered, pocketing his money. The church bells struck six. I leaped to my feet. How had I let time slip by like this? "Blast. I'll never get through the ward at this hour."

"Leave it to me." Hargrove guided me to the curtained-off area that contained his cot and magic trunk. Pulling the bed aside, he revealed twelve odd little squiggly symbols that had been carved into the floorboards, forming a circle about three feet wide. "Get in. This will take you home."

"What is it?" I stepped inside.

"A porter's circle. Old magician's trick. It will take you wherever you wish. But you must think clearly of the place, or it might become confused and drop you in northern Africa."

"What are those lines?" I inspected the squiggles around my feet. Something about them looked rather familiar.

My dream of the Seven Ancients, the night of Korozoth's attack. I'd stood in a circle of stones whose carvings were very similar to these. A chill slid down my spine. I'd learned not to take dreams for granted.

"These are letters borrowed from summoning circles, re-configured for our purposes," Hargrove said.

Summoning circles. These markings felt wrong. "Can't I be like you and disappear on my own?"

"Oh, I'm not that special, chickling. My cloak, you see, has porter runes sewn into the fabric." He swirled his coat, and I caught the glint of golden thread at the edges by his feet. There was nothing else for it but to use the circle.

"What do I say? Some magic words?"

"No, say 'please take me home.' It's only polite."

I did as he asked, thinking of the house near Hyde Park. With the loud rushing of wind in my ears, the room vanished.

"WHERE ON EARTH DID YOU COME from?" a startled Agrippa said. I realized with horror that I had appeared beside him on the street. Thankfully, there was no one else nearby. I tried for a nonchalant attitude.

"I was walking up the other way."

Agrippa shook his head. "Goodness, I need to be more attentive. Can't have Ancients popping up beside me, can I?" My heart sank to realize how he trusted me.

"May we do a lesson in the obsidian room?" I asked. Even if I was a magician, I could at least make him proud. Agrippa sighed and looked as if he wanted most to change into his evening clothes and have dinner. "I think I've made progress. It's all the reading Lord Blackwood's had me do."

"Very well. A little lesson won't hurt us."

———◇◈◇———

AGRIPPA FIDGETED IN HIS TAILS AND nodded at me, the image of patience. He wanted to eat. I wanted to prove myself.

Pouring a bowl of water before my feet, he said, "Lift it into the air and fashion it into an orb." He yawned, understandably expecting little from this. For whatever reason, water was my trickiest element.

This time, I could feel the power like a second skin. I bent my left knee, and the image formed perfectly in my mind. I concentrated on it, wished for it. I didn't speak, for I didn't have to. The water formed, then lowered itself to puddle on the ground.

Agrippa looked surprised. "Erm. That was good."

"Then let me try something more difficult." I prepared myself for the fire maneuver.

In an instant, I had a swirling vortex of yellow-and-red flame spinning toward the ceiling. It burned so hot that Agrippa shielded his eyes and dabbed at his forehead with a pocket square. Even in my gown, I found it easy to manage everything. I fell into a sorcerer's crouch with my left leg stretched outward, and spun the vortex faster and faster. When I flung both my arms wide, it exploded in a flash of bright light.

My powers responded beautifully to my every thought and wish. After so many years living at the mercy of my ability, I'd never imagined that control could feel so wonderful.

Agrippa coughed, swiping at flakes of ash that rained down on his coat.

"What on earth have you been doing?" he said.

"Studying, sir."

Agrippa began to laugh. "My girl! My dearest girl!" He took my hands in his own. We swung about the obsidian room, much in the way I had celebrated with Hargrove that afternoon. He pulled me close and kissed me warmly upon both cheeks. Pride was written all over his face. I was giddy with happiness, almost drunk with it.

"I knew you could do this," Agrippa said. Joyful tears glinted in his eyes. "You'll knock the Whitechurches and Palehooks down a peg."

"I'm sorry it took me so long."

"Oh, bother that. We got there in the end, didn't we?" He lit up with some new thought. "There are advanced techniques we can try. I've been teaching a couple of the fellows Russian stave movements. I was going to teach them to Gwendolyn, before she—" He stopped, that old sadness settling on him again.

"I'm so sorry."

Agrippa shook his head, and the gloom vanished. "Don't be. Now I'm going to train *you*, Henrietta. My dear girl."

I was Henrietta to him at last. I wanted to drum my hands against the blasted obsidian walls, to scream and shout my triumph. He led us out of the room, calling for everyone. When they appeared on the stairs, they looked at us as though we were mad.

"It's not dinner?" Magnus said, his disappointment evident.

"What's Howel done now? Set fire to the library by mistake?" Cellini said, heading downstairs. Well, a rude comment deserved a proper response. The spell to channel a gust of wind was quick upon my stave. I blew Cellini down the last three steps, leaving him sprawled and amazed.

Magnus burst out laughing and clapped his hands. "Brilliant! Show us something more!"

I turned to find Blackwood, blank with surprise. I bowed, as one does before a duel. His eyebrows lifted with understanding.

Are you ready? I mouthed. He bowed to me in turn, accepting my challenge. In a flash, we each had a stave in hand. "Use the wind," I said.

With a perfect movement, he cast a gust of air out like a fishing line, high above my head. It curved downward and struck me in the back, almost toppling me. I'd been purposefully slow to set him at ease. Before he could prepare his second attack, I swirled my stave, moving forward quickly. The wind swept his feet out from under him, and he landed with a grunt on the carpet. He sat up, looking baffled.

"Do you yield?"

Blackwood dusted his sleeves and extended his long, pale hand for mine. "Help me up, Miss Howel." He smiled faintly.

Everyone started talking at once. Dee was offering himself as the next dueler when Cellini said, "How did you manage it?" He frowned. "You can't have got that much better that fast."

"It all suddenly made sense," I said, keeping my tone light. I'd expected someone would bring this up. Really, my biggest surprise was that it wasn't Blackwood pointing it out.

Cellini kept at it. "But what happened?"

"Stop complaining," Magnus muttered, shoving him. "What are you, English all of a sudden?" Everyone chuckled at that, and began talking again. No one was interested in questioning this, to my relief. Feeling playful, I shot a small tongue of fire at Cellini. It exploded in smoke and embers right before his face. He coughed and glared at me. I shrugged. There was no use getting cross with me tonight. I planned on enjoying myself.

Magnus held his stave in the air and cried, "To Howel the sorcerer!" The others joined him, cheering away. Well, all except Blackwood. But he *was* smiling. As the boys rejoiced, Magnus put his lips to my ear and whispered, "You're one of us now."

THAT NIGHT, WHILE THE UPSTAIRS RESOUNDED with laughter and song, I snuck away from the celebration and ran down to the stables to find Rook. Perhaps it was the high of victory, but even the stables appeared transformed in some strange way. The world around me was reborn.

He was in the middle of rubbing down a horse when I knocked on the stall door. The animal nosed my hair, attempting a graze. Giggling, I waved my friend out and flung my arms around him.

"We're saved," I whispered. All the awkwardness between us melted away. It was as if our last argument had never occurred.

"I wish I'd seen it," he said, twirling me about in a circle. "Can you tell me how you managed it?"

"One day, when this is all over, I swear I'll give you every detail. It may surprise you." Rook set me down. He looked wonderful. His eyes were bright, and I'd never seen him wear such a carefree smile.

"What?" He laughed, noticing my stare.

"Forgive me, but . . . you look so happy."

"Then I look as I feel," he said, picking me up by the waist. I mock-shrieked as he set me atop a saddle and returned to his work. "When a night's sweet like this, how could I do otherwise? You'll be commended, the greatest sorcerer of the age."

"Second-greatest, to hear Magnus talk of himself," I said, rolling my eyes.

"Well, you'll fight him for it. And to top it all off, my pain's gone."

"No!" I jumped off the saddle. "Gone completely?"

"Haven't felt a twinge in days. Do unmarked people always feel this good? If so, how do they ever find the time to be angry?"

"This is the most wonderful news! It's the medicine Lord Blackwood described, isn't it? He'll never let me forget this great favor of his."

"Have no fear," Rook said with a grin. "You owe him nothing. I've stopped taking the medicine."

"What?" My smile faded. "Then how do you suppress the shadows?"

"Oh, I don't," he said. "See?" He waved behind himself as illustration, and I understood.

Upon my arrival, I'd thought that the stables' different appearance was due to my excitement. Now I realized that half the yard lay cloaked in deep shadow. Not even the strong light of the moon could penetrate it. The horses were more silent than usual, standing watchful in their stalls.

"Don't worry," Rook said, his voice soothing. "I do it when no one's about. It keeps me in good practice."

"But I thought the shadows came only when the scars hurt."

"So did I, but the most extraordinary thing happened. Just as I was going to ask Mr. Fenswick for the new potion, the pain stopped. For the first time since I can remember, the suffering left. Do you see? I hurt because I couldn't use my power."

Rook was no longer living in the prison of his own body. Tears blurred my vision as I wrapped my arms about him.

"Why are you crying?" he whispered.

"I'm so happy," I sobbed, pressing my cheek to his chest. His heartbeat was loud and steady in my ear.

"Now I have everything," he muttered into my hair. The air between us seemed to crackle with energy. It occurred to me that all I had to do was raise my head, and something would happen. I felt that he was waiting for me to grant permission. And though I'd promised myself no complications, I found I was slowly tilting my chin. . . .

But the darkness was behind me. It was touching my skirt. It was reaching for me. It was *wrong*—

"I need to go back upstairs." I broke from him so suddenly that he nearly tipped over. Part of me was screaming to stay; most of me had the uncontrollable urge to run. "The boys and Master Agrippa will wonder where I've gone."

"Of course." He didn't sound put out in the slightest. "There's time for talk later, after you're commended." Rook smiled at me.

His eyes were pure black.

You must get used to it. It's his power, the same way fire is yours, I thought. *For the first time, he's free.*

"I'll come see you later," I said, forcing a smile. Rook turned back to his work, whistling as he did so. Going inside the kitchen, I sat on a bench and passed my hand before my eyes. Honestly, I was acting like a child. Today I'd been given everything I could have ever asked for, and here I was, worrying. If Rook's pain was finally gone for good, then that was worth everything.

Yet I couldn't help but shudder as I returned to stand in the doorway and watch him at work, singing while the shadows ebbed and flowed about his feet.

18

THE MIDNIGHT BELLS CHIMED AS MAGNUS AND I skirted the edge of the ward, scanning the dark streets beyond the protective shield. "So you don't believe," Magnus said, "that the Ancients are demons from hell?"

"No. Medieval mystics described a fifth element, ether, that they claimed was kept from our eyes only by the thin skin of reality. Many held to those beliefs until they were declared heresy. Perhaps Howard Mickelmas and Mary Willoughby opened a portal into that fifth element."

"Never thought so practical a lady would accept such mystical theories."

I obviously couldn't tell him I'd discussed said theories with Hargrove. "Then where do you suppose such huge carnivorous beasts came from? Portugal?"

"I suppose your theory is better than the archbishop's belief that our Ancients are the seven deadly sins made flesh." He shuddered. "Is that great blob Molochoron the embodiment of Lust? Truly, nothing makes me more excited than the sight of moldy jelly."

I laughed. "I read an article by Blackwood's father, actually,

about that seven-deadly-sins idea. He called those beliefs hog-
wash. Did you know he was the first to name them Ancients in
print?"

"Yes, Blackwood's father was a great sort. Pity the son's
such a grim sort." Magnus swiped at the ward, creating a line
of sparks. I frowned, pressing my hand to the surface. It gave,
almost like rubber. For a while it had been firm again, but now it
was getting worse, and fast. Agrippa had brushed it off when I'd
mentioned it, but I continued to worry.

"We shouldn't be so harsh. I think he has a great deal on his
mind." Since our discussion in the library, my relationship with
Blackwood had improved. The angry, hateful thoughts I'd had
about him now made me uncomfortable.

"There's his brooding lesson at dawn, followed by instruc-
tional despair at teatime." Magnus walked backward to look me
in the face. "I didn't imagine you'd be so masochiotic as to like
someone who dismissed your lowly birth."

"Don't say it out loud!" Really, I told Magnus too much these
days. He looked about dramatically.

"No one nearby. Though perhaps we should turn back. Our
shift is near done." We turned and started walking the way we'd
come. All Incumbents took turns patrolling the ward as part of
the training. It had been three weeks since my triumph before
Agrippa, and I was now allowed to participate in all areas of Incumbent life. Before, it would have been unthinkable for me to
go about with Magnus unchaperoned in the middle of the night.
That no one objected proved that people had begun to take my

abilities seriously. Perhaps I was finally stepping out of Gwendolyn Agrippa's shadow. "I wouldn't blame you for getting a bit soft, of course. Blackwood *is* the Earl of Sorrow-Fell. Most girls would give their eyeteeth to claim that prize."

I groaned, the only appropriate response to such an idea. "Don't be ridiculous. I'm here to be commended, not to catch a husband."

"But it would be so nice to check both off your list at once, wouldn't it?"

"First of all, I wouldn't marry Lord Blackwood if he were the prince of plenty. I don't dislike him anymore, but that's hardly a love written in the stars."

"Very nice. What's the second-of-all?"

"I'll never marry. No man could want me in battle, and I wouldn't want anyone who might keep me away from my duty."

"Don't be so hasty to rule out gentlemen's understanding," Magnus said. "There are some who admire a capable girl. One of them might be closer than you think, if you'd take the time to notice what's before you." He leaned closer. For a second, I didn't dare breathe. Since our moment in the library, Magnus had returned to his old, harmless flirtation. I'd half hoped it would stay that way. He sighed gently and said, "Can't you see the way Palehook looks at you?"

He laughed. I was so relieved that I joined him.

"So who should I marry?"

"Someone confident, charming, insanely handsome, brilliant, who dances well and who can order the correct wine with any dish. Also, make sure he owns a horse. There's no use marrying if you don't have a horse. You'll have to travel to your honeymoon on the back of a turnip cart." He sheathed his stave. "Enough marriage talk. What say we pop round the coffee stalls at Covent Garden?"

Before I could respond, a scream pierced the darkness.

We pressed our hands against the invisible wall to peer into the streets. After a minute, the scream came again, high and wailing. It sounded like a little girl.

Magnus sliced through the barrier without a moment's pause. I grabbed his shoulder. "We need to wait for the others."

"It could be too late if we do." He stepped through and ran in the direction of the cry. Idiot. Well, he was going nowhere without me. I shot three streams of fire into the air and waited until I heard the watch bell toll. Someone would come. Satisfied, I followed Magnus.

He'd disappeared. My echoing footsteps were a lonely sound as I ran along the empty street. I began to think this was a bad plan, then the child screamed again. Down an alley to the left, I found the little girl, pale, thin, ragged, and all alone. I crouched beside her.

"Are you all right? Where's your mother?"

She shook her head. I noticed that her right fist was clenched. When I opened it, I found myself staring at a bright new guinea. How on earth did she have so much money?

"Sorry 'bout this," the little girl whispered. With that, she turned and ran.

Something struck me on the back of the head. Porridge rolled away from me as I fell forward and skinned my palms on the ground. Hands grabbed me by the hair, pulling me to my feet. Black figures loomed. Someone kicked me in the stomach. My breath left me in a rush, the pain so intense I crumpled into a ball. Struggling pathetically to breathe, I heard them mutter to one another.

"Make it quick."

"Not yet. Bloody her up a bit first."

The voices. They were horribly familiar.

As I unfolded myself, a boot struck me in the side. Sparks and stars danced on the edges of my sight. Bile flooded the back of my throat. I swung wildly, blindly, trying to fend them off.

"Where's the knife?"

A startled third voice: "What? We're not going to kill her, are we?"

I *knew* that voice. Hands reached for me.

Flames rippled over my body. A boy screamed as I crawled forward on my stomach, still burning, daring someone to touch me again. There was a cacophony of footsteps, racing toward and running from me. In my confusion, it seemed that footsteps pounded along the walls. Somewhere, Magnus shouted, "You filthy bastard!"

Now I caught the sounds of struggle, of men at each other's throats. My vision seesawed from one bizarre angle to the next as Magnus threw someone to the ground. Sitting up, I found an unconscious Lovett sprawled beside me. There was a cut across his forehead, bleeding fresh.

"Bastard," I gasped, my voice a strange wheeze. I clawed at him, shook him, but he didn't wake up. Above, Magnus struggled with someone else. I expected to see Hemphill as I turned my head.

Cellini hung in Magnus's grasp, a smear of blood beneath his nose. Something fell out of his hand and clattered across the ground. A knife.

My stomach rippling, I fell to my hands, heaved, and vomited. My head throbbed. Cellini couldn't be here. He couldn't have attacked me. He was my friend. He was one of *us*.

"Why?" I moaned. Cellini breathed heavily while Magnus held him by the collar, dumbfounded.

"I don't understand." Magnus's voice was small.

Cellini began to cry. "It had to be done. Don't you see?"

"Give me some excuse." Magnus's voice was pleading. "You don't really want to hurt her. They forced you."

Cellini's normally handsome face twisted in rage. "You choose her over us. Over your own kind. Can't you see how freakish she is? Or are you always this soppy once you get them on their backs?"

It was like he'd kicked me again.

Magnus punched him. There was a gurgling cry, and Cellini spit blood onto the ground. One white tooth lay gleaming in the gore. Undeterred, Magnus continued the vicious beating, all traces of his humor gone. I hadn't thought him capable of such fury. Cellini's face began to resemble a slab of bloody meat.

Crawling to my knees, I grabbed Magnus's arm. "Stop," I gasped. "Let the Order deal with him."

"Where's the other one?" Magnus cried. "There were three of you. It was Hemphill, wasn't it?" Cellini couldn't answer. He'd been knocked unconscious. When Magnus released him, he collapsed to the ground. "Do you know what he was going to do?" Magnus growled. He picked up the knife, blade gleaming in the moonlight, and tossed it away with a hiss of disgust. "Are you all right?" He helped me up off the ground and held me close.

"I'm fine." I leaned into his embrace and felt him trembling.

WE PACED OUTSIDE THE LIBRARY, LISTENING to the muffled voices within. Once or twice, someone shouted, and then the murmuring returned. Magnus glared at the door, as if he could bore a hole through it with the strength of his will alone.

"Thank you," I said. "I'm not sure I could have kept them off on my own."

"If it were up to me, they'd hang the pair of them." Magnus hadn't changed out of his bloody, torn clothes. His hair stuck wildly in the air, and part of me wanted to pat it down. "I can't believe they let Hemphill go."

"I can't be certain he was there. What will happen now?"

"Excommunication. They'll bind Lovett's stave, and he'll lose his position as heir to his father's estate. Cellini will be shipped back to Rome to face their brand of justice."

"Bind his stave?" I knew that excommunicates were sorcerer outcasts but didn't know the details.

"They dip the stave in molten lead to bind its power and sever its connection. Sometimes the sorcerer doesn't survive." He looked pale. "There are those who consider execution a more humane punishment."

The idea wrenched my heart. I touched Porridge in its sheath for comfort. "Even if Cellini hated me, why risk so much?"

Magnus shook his head. "I don't know."

I looked at my hands. "I know he was your friend. This can't be easy."

"It's easier than you think, Howel. I could never let anyone hurt you."

My hands prickled with energy. There was no time to discuss it further. Palehook opened the door, a rumpled, tearstained Lovett by his side.

"Miss Howel. I shall endeavor to see that every bit of justice is done. You've my word on that." I noticed that Palehook didn't quite look me in the eye while speaking, and he pulled Lovett away as soon as he was able. Agrippa exited next, his face pale. He took my chin in his hand.

"Are you all right, my poor, brave girl?" He looked me over, tilting my head this way and that. "You'll have a few bruises, but I think that's the worst of it. Go upstairs and let Fenswick look at you."

"I want to see him." I gazed toward the library door.

"No, I can't allow that."

"If you stay, Master, and I'm beside her, he won't try any-thing," Magnus said. He looked as if he'd adore one small excuse for another beating.

"Please. I won't feel well unless I've seen him." I didn't need more opportunities for nightmares.

The door creaked open, and Cellini slunk into the hall. His face was swollen, both from the bruises and from crying.

"Why did you do it?" I said.

"I didn't think they planned murder. We just wanted you to leave." When he spoke, I saw the hole where his front tooth had been. He wept. No sight had ever made me sicker.

"You should have wanted to help me. Since I'm the prophesied—"

"Oh, enough of that *stupid* tapestry!" His tears vanished; his anger startled me. "I held my tongue because English ways are not our ways. If you believed you could find salvation in a girl sor-cerer, who was I to disagree?" He sniffed and wiped his nose. "At first you were all right, Miss Howel, but now you're dreadful."

When Magnus started for Cellini, I put my hand on his arm to hold him back. Cellini noticed, and his fury grew. "Look at that! Ordering men about. The trouble is English sorcerers don't study their Bible. Paul's first Epistle to Timothy: 'Let a woman learn quietly with all submissiveness. I do not permit a woman to teach or to exercise authority over a man.' In Rome, women aren't even allowed inside an obsidian room." He looked to Agrippa and Magnus. "She's not one of us. She'll destroy every-

one if you let her, and it's only lucky I won't be here to see it!"
Magnus grabbed Cellini and lifted him off the ground by his collar. Agrippa stepped in at once to separate them.

She's not one of us. Cellini and I had always gotten along, or
so I'd thought. We played charades on the same team together,
laughed over breakfast. How could I not have seen this anger?
I had I really done something to deserve it?

Or had I simply been proud? I remembered his anger when
I'd flicked that little bit of fire at him, laughed at him. Perhaps
arrogance in a woman was unbearable. I tried to find some apology in his eyes. There was only fury.

"Give me your stave," Agrippa said.

As if it were torture, Cellini undid his hip sheath and handed
it over. Part of me hurt for him. But the colder, angrier part
won out.

"I will be commended," I said, my voice shaking despite my
best efforts. "You can do nothing about that."

"Someone will," he muttered.

I had to wonder, as they escorted Cellini off and I wiped my
eyes, if someone else *would* attack. Even with my progress, I
knew he was right. In a woman, pride was unforgivable.

"Take three drops of this in a glass of water," Fenswick grumped,
handing me a vial of bubbling golden liquid that changed to pink
when I turned it upside down. He flapped his ears as I helped
him off the bed. "Anything else troubling you?"

"I still have nightmares." The R'hlem dreams hadn't come to me as much since I'd gained control of my powers, but they did return.

"Well, keep chewing willow bark." He waddled to the door, when a housemaid entered with a tray for me. She wrinkled her nose at Fenswick and walked straight into him, bowling him over. He got to his feet, dusting himself off.

"Be more careful," he snapped. She set down the tray and swatted at him with a napkin.

"Disgusting little thing. Shoo," she said, driving a hissing Fenswick from the room. I sat up.

"Don't you dare treat him like that," I cried.

The maid scowled. Why was tonight Lilly's evening off? "Beg your pardon, miss, but it don't hurt him none. They don't feel things as we do."

"He's a person," I said.

"No, he ain't, miss, if you'll pardon me." She sniffed. "He's a beast."

Once, I might have agreed with her. Now, as she handed me my tray, all I could hear were Cellini's hissed words: *She's not one of us.*

AFTER LESSONS THE NEXT DAY, I took to the library to read about hobgoblins. We didn't have many volumes, but I found one passage in *A Compendium of Faerie* (Laurence Puchner, 1798) that said: *A Mandrake Root or moldy Onion can be most instrumental in welcoming a subject of the Dark Fae Queen into a home.*

Agrippa's kitchen didn't contain a single mandrake root. However, I found an old onion with green bits sprouting on it. This would have to do. I took myself to Fenswick's corner of the house. He lived inside a chest of drawers in an empty servant's room.

I found him relaxed in the bottommost drawer, his ears tucked behind him as he attempted a doze. "What is it?" he said. "Can't you let me rest?" He rubbed his eyes with two of his four paws.

"I wanted to give you this." I handed over the onion. He took it like he'd never seen one before in his life. "I thought it might make you feel more at home?"

For a moment, his expression didn't change. This had been a grave mistake. Then his ears parted to the side. His black eyes glistened. He hugged the onion to his chest, sniffled, and said, "I've been in this house six months, and no one's . . . welcomed me yet."

I'd no idea how a sprouty onion made one feel wanted, but there were many things I didn't understand. "I'm glad to have been the first."

"Why do you care?" His ears perked up.

"I suppose I know what it's like to not quite belong."

"You're a lady sorcerer."

"With the marks to prove it." Touching a finger to a purplish bruise on my cheek, I made to leave.

"Er, wait. The willow bark doesn't help with your bad dreams, does it?" Fenswick's ears slid down his back.

"Not much."

Later that night, I found a packet in a velvet pouch outside my door. It smelled of herbs and rose hips. A note, in a chubby, childish hand, read: *For nightmares. Place under pillow.*

From that night forward, I didn't see R'hlem. He wasn't missed.

19

MY NEW BOYS' CLOTHES WERE A TERRIBLE FIT. I HAD
to roll the sleeves three times and tie a rope around my waist to
hoist up the trousers, but racing across London rooftops was a
job unsuitable for frocks. I lay on my belly and crawled forward.
Hargrove pointed to the roof opposite us.

"Let's see if you can place it . . . there," he said, indicating the
chimney stack. Careful to avoid tumbling, I pointed Porridge
at my heart, twisted the stave while muttering a few key nonsense words, and then flung my arm toward the other rooftop. It
worked. A vision of myself, a complete copy of my current trou-
sered state, gazed back at me from the chimney's base.

It was startling to see myself outside a mirror. My copy's
mouth hung wide open, like mine. I lost my balance and slipped
toward the roof's edge. Hargrove pulled me back by the collar of
my coat, and the vision opposite us disappeared.

"Don't be a bloody fool, girl. No need to go tipping your
balance over a good reflection. Now I want to see you fly. Due
south, aim for the edge of the ward. By the docks, where we
had that pork pie last time." With that, Hargrove swept his cloak
around his body and floated into the sky. I'd be damned if he

beat me. The last time I lost a race, I had to buy him a bottle of gin and massage his temples.

Summoning the wind, I took off across the rooftops and above the labyrinthine alleyways of London. How marvelous it was, to have a bird's-eye view of the evening goings-on and lamp-lightings. I was glad to be able to stay this long. Agrippa had gone to Surrey overnight on business for the Order, and no one else felt the need to check on my whereabouts. I arrived at the meeting place and dropped gracefully to the ground.

I heard a rush of wind and turned to welcome Hargrove down from the sky, but it wasn't his face that greeted me. It was *hers*.

She fell to the earth, lacking the company of her terrifying friends. The shadow rider dismounted from her monstrous black stag, and even before she unrolled her smoke hood, I knew she would be the one with sewn-up eyes. She was no dream or illusion this time. The girl unsheathed her dagger and swung toward the screaming crowd. Men dropped their wares and ran; women scuttled inside their houses and slammed the doors. I prepared to open fire when she whirled away from the people. Sniffing the air, she turned to face me.

"Not dressed properly," she muttered to herself. Tilting her head, she sniffed again, deeply. "But the same smell. And a stave." Her face scrunched up, a momentary flash of pain. "Little lady sorcerer."

"What are you doing here?" I readied myself for an attack. The rider threw her head back and laughed.

- 266 -

"Follow your scent. The bloody king wants to know how you fight." R'hlem. She swung her dagger in the air twice, testing. "He wants to see if you'll die." Leaping, she brought her blade in an arc toward me. I struck her with a gust of wind and rolled to the ground. I stood with my back against the ward as she drew herself up and hissed. This time, I fell aside as she attacked, and her dagger dug into the pale yellow outline of the barrier itself. The place of impact glowed bright green for an instant, then began to fade. She turned for me, nostrils flaring. "Good, good. Not afraid. He likes those with courage."

"What does he want?" I said.

She struck again, and I met her with my warded blade. She was good, but Magnus's training had helped. We crossed swords a few times, and then I leaned back and kicked her in the stomach. You could accomplish so much in trousers and boots! Men didn't know how lucky they were.

Before she could regain control, I blasted her with a tunnel of wind and twirled a spell that sent the earth up around her like a hand, to catch and drag her down. She was chest-deep next to the ward when Hargrove alighted beside me.

"I've never seen that before," he said, eyeing the trapped rider.

"A blend of the two styles," I muttered as the girl shrieked and thrust her hands upward. It was as if she *became* smoke and bled through the earth to free herself.

Hargrove and I unleashed a volley of magic. I called down the wind to dissipate the still-smoke Familiar, and he shrank her demonic steed to the size of a small dog. She re-formed into her solid state and fell to the earth with a piercing screech. The rider stared stupidly at her dwarfed mount, which bleated like an angry lamb. Grabbing the stag under her arm, she held up a hand in a signal of surrender.

"Leave." I pointed Porridge with more confidence than I felt. "Or I'll fire."

Hissing, she reached out and touched the ward. "Soon," she croaked, giving a small, hideous giggle as she slid her fingertips down the glowing surface.

The stag ballooned back to its normal size, and she climbed atop it. They galloped into the sky and vanished before we could attack again.

"We should go," I whispered, tipping my cap over my eyes.

"Indeed. After a hard day of protecting the city, I should think we'd earned a meat pie." Hargrove didn't seem as carefree as his words implied. We looked to where the Familiar had sliced the ward. When I put my fingers to it, I found the smallest cut in the surface.

"Well," he said as we landed on a rooftop to catch our breath, "now you see the challenges of defeating one of the Shadow's pets. They always were the trickiest to destroy. The best Familiars to kill, of course, are Molochoron's slugs. You remember that fat, slimy fellow last week in Hoxton? The one we exploded?"

"What's happening to the ward?" I whispered. "It feels like rubber on the inside, and fragile glass without."

"The ward usually wears down the closer we get to the sol-stice," Hargrove said, cracking his back and wincing. "It's at its strongest around Christmas."

"Why?"

"Some believe the Ancients are tied to the pagan calendar, so Midsummer Eve is a particularly wonderful time for them. I think there's truth to it. Of course, the sorcerers used this con-cept to attack the witches." He sounded bitter.

"Did you know any witches?"

"Before the burnings, you mean? Yes, one or two." He snorted and spit off the roof. "A bunch of ladies with flowers and rye in their hair, farming and making potions to help with a toothache. Truly the most fearsome magical practitioners of all."

"If they're so innocent, why were they outlawed?"

"Many believe that magical women are difficult to control," Hargrove said. "As you are well aware." The memory of Cellini and the knife returned in vivid color. "While we're talking, have you payment for another evening's lesson?" He snapped his fin-gers. Groaning, I dug into my pocket and produced two sover-eigns. Handing them over, I muttered, "Try to spend it sensibly."

"This makes ten pounds and four shillings. Almost there. And the rest?"

"Next time." Agrippa now gave me two pounds a week for spending money, so he unwittingly paid for my lessons. That made approximately five weeks of sneaking off to visit Hargrove when I could. I swung my legs over the roof and looked to the ward, a glowing bubble in the night. "What happens if the barriers don't hold?"

"What do you think? Total pandemonium. Hopefully when that happens, I'll be an ocean away."

"What? Where are you going?" Surprisingly, the thought of losing him hurt. Hargrove had never been exactly warm, but he knew my secrets. That was something.

"Where you're sending me with that twelve pounds. Or to be more exact, ten pounds and four shillings. The rest of Europe won't take in a refugee from England, but America might."

"You'll never get out to sea."

"I know the right person," Hargrove said.

"Who?" Then I recalled Magnus's mention of smuggler ships that charged money for a clandestine voyage.

"Better if you're not privy to the whereabouts and who-is-its. All I need is the money, which I'm about to have in full."

"You'll leave me? What of the children?"

"The commendation's in less than two weeks. You won't need me anymore. I didn't say I wouldn't take the children, just that I'd only need one ticket." Of course, he'd store them inside the magical trunk. "I'm not a total bastard, you know."

"I thought you wanted to see magicians come back into power."

His face lost all traces of joviality. "I've sacrificed enough for this bloody cause. Let the young fight, if they've the will."

"Did you train me to feel like you'd done your share?" I asked quietly.

"Perhaps. I believed there was a debt I needed to acknowledge."

"To whom?" I scooted back from the roof's edge and stood, dusting my trousers.

"Not to anyone in particular," he said. "Now I consider it paid, because of you." He smiled. "You're my last laugh. The sorcerers will honor an upstart magician's daughter as the answer to their precious prophecy." He spit once again.

"CINDERELLA'S WICKED STEPSISTERS HAD TO WALK behind the wedding party, sulking. The birds, who had seen all the cruelty in their hearts, flew out of the sky and plucked the sisters' eyes from their heads." I hissed at the children, bundled up for bed, and they gasped. "But Cinderella, who had been good and true, ruled with her prince for many years." They sighed at this revelation. Charley's little sister clung to my skirt and wouldn't let go. Gently, I took her into my arms and went to sit at the table with Hargrove. He looked pleased and drunk.

"Taste of the spoils?" he said, offering me the bottle. I declined. "Where was I, before you had to change your clothes and tend to these ragamuffins?"

The little girl had already fallen asleep on my lap. I hugged her close. "You were telling me of the magical schism." Magician history was one topic I'd been interested to learn, and he to share.

"Ah, yes. You'll recall Henry the Eighth, great hairy king, who liked having things his own way. His first wife, Catherine, couldn't give him a son. So he went to his Order of royal sorcerers and said, 'Find a way to let the queen conceive.' No one knew how, of course, and told him he was being a crazy git. One of them, Ralph Strangewayes, dreaming of fortune and fame, decided to see what he could do.

"For two months, Strangewayes locked himself in his room. He ordered books of all sorts, alchemical, medical, biblical. One day, he summoned the king to his chambers and presented a woman. Some say he fashioned her hair from ribbons, her skin from candlelight, her body from the west wind, and her tongue from three notes of birdsong, but she was the most beautiful and the strangest woman anyone had ever seen. The king fell in love upon the instant. Strangewayes said, 'Here is the woman who will birth your new sovereign.'"

"Anne Boleyn?" I said, certain he was playing me for a fool.

"Indeed. So the king divorced Catherine and married this magical creation. For a while, Strangewayes and magicians eclipsed sorcerers in every way. Of course, as history tells us, Boleyn got her head lopped off, and Strangewayes fell out of favor. Ended up in the tower waiting to see if anyone would have him executed. But when Queen Elizabeth came to power, that child of magic and royalty, she commended Strangewayes. Magicians became, for her reign at least, the preferred magical practitioners. Elizabeth was a mule. Did you know that? Born not of human woman, but seeded by human man. Many believe the reason she was the virgin queen was because she had no means to procreate." He giggled until his dark skin flushed darker still. "You know? Down there? Smooth as the wickless end of a candle."

I shushed him, nodding at the child asleep on my knee. "I think these are all lies."

He made a rude noise and drank some more. "You're a good apprentice."

"Thank you."

"Granted, you're as much fun as pig slop dressed up for a Friday night, but you can't have everything." He wheezed with laughter. "Y-you're so sour that if Molochoron swallowed you, the whole mass of him would pucker!" He drummed his feet upon the ground and laughed like he'd die.

"I know," I said. "Tell me more of magician history."

"No, you tell me *your* history, my little kipper. Why are you such a grim-faced melon?"

"Because I know what I am." I stared at my hands.

"Which is?"

"As you've said yourself. Unlovable." To my annoyance, Hargrove stuck out his tongue at me.

"You young girls are all the same. 'Oh, my life is so impossible. No boy will ever desire me, and I'll live alone in a hovel with sixteen cats. Such is my woe.'" He said it all in a piercing, effeminate voice.

"I don't pity myself. I simply know that I'm not easily loved."

He stopped his mimicry. "What's so awful about you?"

I'd never told this story to anyone before, not even Rook. Unsure as to why I should relate this to Hargrove of all people,

I said, "When I was five years old, my aunt Agnes brought me to my Yorkshire school." I could recall her vividly after all this time, a tall, proud woman in black clothes who wouldn't look at me as I clung to her skirt. "I cried as she walked back toward her carriage. I yelled, 'Please, Auntie, don't leave me here. I want to go with you. I love you.' That was when she turned to me and said—" I stopped when a hitch formed in my throat.

"What did she say?" Hargrove lost his smirk.

"'You are a horrid child. If only you could be pleasant, I would love you. But how could anyone care for a peevish, whining, solemn little thing like you?'" The words were exact. I'd run them through my mind at least once every day since they were uttered. "And there you have it," I said, my voice artificially bright, forcing a smile. "Nothing to be done." I turned my face away as a tear crept down my cheek.

"Poor child," he said, his voice soft. He reached across the table, and I gave him my hand. "Poor, poor child." In that moment, he sounded as tender as Agrippa. "You have a good heart. It wasn't your fault." Then he said, so quiet I nearly missed it, "It wasn't hers, either."

"What?"

Hargrove released me. Placing his head in his hand, he said, "Please use the porter's circle. I'm tired."

"Did I offend you?"

"It's not enough that I have several little mouths to feed and you to teach. Now I have to be bogged down by these depressing stories."

Stung, I laid the little girl to sleep and went to the carved porter's circle. "I didn't mean to ruin your night. Goodbye." I lifted my skirt to step inside.

"Henrietta." He rarely used my name. "You've suffered a great deal. Remember that you're not the only one." He laid his head on the table, as though he was exhausted.

"It was selfish of me to burden you," I muttered, and vanished toward home.

THE NEXT NIGHT, I SAT BEFORE the parlor fire with Blackwood. He used cards to test my memory on the Ancients. "Zem," he said. The firelight danced on his features, shadowing his eyes.

"A fire-breathing serpent, as long as a small ship. He's seen frequently in Hertfordshire and has leveled, at present, two entire villages." I squeezed my eyes shut in concentration.

"Good. What's being done in Hertfordshire to defend the citizenry?"

"All sorcerer families with estates in the area have sent at least one son as protection. They're also creating a series of canals in each village to bring in water as a natural deterrent to Zem. It's a slow process."

"Excellent." He laid down the cards. "How have you been these last two weeks?" There was concern in his eyes. Ever since Cellini's attack, Blackwood and the others had taken extra care of me. Lambe and Wolff showed me new strategies for chess. Dee tried especially hard not to step on my feet during dance practice.

"I'm all right."

"Do you still need to be alone on your afternoons off?" Something about the way he said it took my attention. "You've become so skilled. Surely the entire afternoon's no longer necessary."

"Is there something you'd like to ask?"

"Some are sure to be interested in what you do. I advise you to be careful." His tone and look suggested this was serious.

"Who's interested?"

"Only try not to draw too much attention to yourself." He sank deeper into his armchair and shuffled his cards. I knew that look he wore. Try as I might, I would get nothing else out of him on the subject. "Now, then. Tell me about R'hlem, and be sure to focus on his campaign in Scotland."

20

OVER THE NEXT NINE DAYS, I AVOIDED GOING TO SEE
Hargrove. I played games in the parlor, attended lessons, and
took chaperoned cart rides with Magnus. I tried to convince myself that I didn't care if I ever saw the magician again. But I woke
the morning of June 19 feeling guilty. The commendation ball
was in a mere two days, and I doubted I'd get a chance to visit after I became a sorcerer. Besides, he needed the last of the money.
He'd earned it.

One final lesson before we both moved on with our lives.

When I arrived, we didn't speak for the first few minutes. I
laid out a sack of oranges for the children, which they joyfully
snatched up. He sat with his face cupped in his hand, drumming
his fingers on the table. I gave him the last of the money and
spent a great deal of time folding and refolding my gloves.

"You seem distant today," Hargrove said at last.

"If I am, I don't want to concern you," I replied. "It's rude to
ask you to share my troubles."

"I'm sorry about the other night." He ran a copper penny
along his fingers, over and over again. "Responding to such a
story in such a way was the height of bad manners." His apology

shocked me. Surely the real magician had been kidnapped by faeries, and this polite copy left in his place. "I have always been uncomfortable with fragile things, like feelings and confessions. Butterflies, too."

"I forgive you," I said, studying an orange. "Shall we have a lesson?"

"There's nothing more I can teach you. No, I thought today we might talk." The penny glided over his fingers at a faster pace. Hargrove wanted to talk? Why did he seem so nervous? "Are you ready to be commended?"

"As I'll ever be," I said. Hargrove didn't respond, only watched the children devour the oranges. "What is it?"

"When you first came here, I thought you'd be just like your father. I was wrong." He slammed the coin down on the table and rubbed his chin. He looked like someone preparing to dive into an icy river.

"In what way? You think I'm not as good a magician as he was?"

"Hardly. I think with more time you could be a better one. William was a talented sort, but he had no real discipline. At least, not when I knew him." He leaned back in his chair.

"Is my being a sorcerer what's concerning you? I won't forget what you've taught me about where I come from. Maybe before you leave for America, I can return one last time—"

"No. Once you're commended, you cannot return." So this would be our final meeting. Sadness lumped in my stomach, even though Hargrove could be gruff and smelled of cabbages and alcohol.

"Thank you for everything," I said. "I'll do what I can to help the magician cause. I swear."

Wincing, he stood and turned his back to me.

"No, you're not like William. You have his same impulsive rashness, but you can be reasonable when you try. I think," he said, pausing as he turned to face me, "that you could bear it."

"Bear what?"

"Sometimes I believe that our lives are lived in an endless cycle," he said. "That our error becomes our children's burden, and eventually that burden becomes their error, and so on. The only way out of it is to break the cycle. Do you understand?"

"No. I don't think I do."

He sat down and grasped my hand. "There's something I need to tell you about your father. You see, he wasn't—"

There was a knock at the door, and Blackwood opened it without waiting for a reply. When he saw me, the color drained from his face.

"What are you doing here?" he said. He half attempted to hide a small velvet pouch behind his back. Cheeks flushed and breathing deep, he looked as if he'd been running. "Well?"

What on earth was *he* doing here? It wasn't Friday, his regular charity day. I wouldn't have come if it were. To add to my surprise, Rook appeared in the doorway with a parcel in his arms.

"Nettie?" he said, shocked as Blackwood and I. We made a sort of trinity of bewilderment.

Before I could speak, Blackwood took my arm. "What are you doing?" I said, stunned by his boldness.

"We're leaving," he snapped, tossing the velvet pouch to Hargrove. It landed with a jingle of coins. "Charity," Blackwood mumbled.

"It's always appreciated," Hargrove said drily, spilling the money onto the tabletop. "Come back anytime, miss. Tuppence for another tarot, ha'penny to read your tea leaves. Though you must bring your own kettle."

"I will walk on my own, thank you," I said, wrenching my arm out of Blackwood's grip. We tromped out of the room, Rook and me walking ahead of him. I was deliberately slow, just to be irritating.

"What are you doing here?" Rook whispered.

"Paying a call." I stumbled over the words; I still wasn't comfortable with lying to him. "Has he had you rushing about all day?"

"Don't worry about me." He jerked his head in Blackwood's direction. "I won't let him be rough with you."

"There's more danger of me being rough with him." Once below, I turned to Blackwood. "You can't treat me that way in front of people."

"Why are you here?" He sounded furious.

"I brought something for the children. Weren't you doing the same?"

"Why would you visit a magician? If Master Agrippa knew—"

"I'd be so grateful if you wouldn't tell him," I said, trying to sound as gentle and conciliatory as possible. He set off down the street, and I hurried to catch up.

"Perhaps I should," he said.

Well, bother gentle and conciliatory. "Master Agrippa's certain I'll be commended. Are you looking for an excuse to sabotage that?" It was a childish thing to say, but I wanted to lob *something* at him.

"Do you really believe that?" he shouted, stopping dead in the road. The crowd flowed around us. "After I've told you about my responsibility toward the Order? After I've spent hours helping to train you? Haven't I warned you that people are curious about where you go?"

"Yes, but you never told me who exactly was so curious."

He huffed. "I'm attempting to protect you."

"Because I'm a fragile lady?"

"Because you're going to be a sorcerer!" he yelled. "I can't believe you'd come here alone, after what happened with Cellini." He had a point. "And visiting a magician is dangerous to your reputation. Magicians cannot be trusted."

"Why not?" The urge to hit him increased tenfold.

"What do you mean, why not? No good can come from associating with—"

"Where's Rook?" I'd turned around to speak to him, but he was gone.

"He's fine." There was a wild, haunted look in Blackwood's

eyes. He froze, and stared with such intensity at the brick wall behind me that I wondered if he could see *through* it.

"What is it?" I touched his arm. "Are you well?"

"Something's wrong. Please stay here." He turned and, without another word, pushed through the crowd. Mystified, I called his name as I ran after him. We returned to the alley just outside Hargrove's. That was when I saw them.

Rook was locked in a struggle with two men dressed all in black. One of them had an arm around Rook's throat. He kicked out at the other attacker, striking him hard in the chest.

In an instant, I'd readied a blade. Blackwood followed my example, and together we ran toward the fight. Rook's face twisted in terror.

"Nettie!" he cried. At first I thought it was a call for help, but he put up his hand, a gesture intended to stop me. "No!"

The darkness rushed in from the walls and the crevices. Rook and the two men disappeared behind a veil of shadow. Blackwood and I stood helpless before the void. I could see nothing, but I heard the men's terrified cries.

"What the devil?" Blackwood breathed. I panicked. He couldn't know about Rook's powers, not yet. Hating myself, I collected my ward's invisible force and threw it at Blackwood. A great blast of energy knocked him against a wall, and he slid to the ground. Checking quickly, I found him unconscious but breathing. I prayed I hadn't truly hurt him, then ran toward the attackers.

The covering of darkness pulsed before me. Inside, the men's voices began to fade. I reached out a hand to pierce the shadow but drew back in fear. Something was different and awful about this blackness.

"Let them go!" I cried. "Can you hear me? Rook!" I flung a layer of fire over the writhing mass. The shadow patch dissolved, revealing the three men lying on the ground. None of them moved. Rook was curled on his side.

"Rook, are you all right?" Terrified, I knelt next to him.

Rook lunged at me. His eyes gleamed black. There was nothing human in that look. He gripped my arms and threw me to the ground. My head struck the earth, and I grasped for Porridge. If Rook attacked again, he'd face a spell.

But the attack didn't come. I waited in fearful silence until I heard him whisper, "Nettie, what did I do?" Slowly, I got up and crawled around to face him. His eyes were their normal blue. His expression was one of horror. "Did I touch you?"

The men on the ground drew my attention. One of them sobbed and shivered, as though he were cold. The other lay flat on his back, staring blankly at the sky above.

"Get up," I said, trying to sound commanding. The crying fellow hastened to his feet, pointing at me in terror.

"Stay away!" he yelled, and helped his companion stand. The quiet man moved as he was bid but didn't seem terribly aware of his surroundings.

"What were you doing?" I held up my blade, though I wasn't so forceful. We were all too terrified for shows of bravado.

"Stay away!" the man cried again, and the two ran down the alley. Rook pulled me to the ground as I tried to go after them.

"Don't. It's what they want," Rook gasped, holding me back.

"But they attacked you."

"Wasn't me they were after. They grabbed me when they couldn't snatch their true mark. Anyone could see that."

"What?" And then I realized that Rook had been walking with *me*. Cellini himself had said others would attack. "Oh God."

"I don't think they'll be back." Rook rubbed his eyes. "I scared them off."

"Yes, thank you."

"No." He shuddered. "I hurt you. How could I have done that?"

"You didn't know it was me."

"Exactly. We couldn't tell you from the others."

Now I was truly afraid. *"We?"*

"The voice in the dark whispered . . ." He stopped. Horrified, he looked at the scars along his left arm. "I'm a freak."

"We have to speak with Fenswick about this."

"No. I don't want anyone else to know," Rook grunted. He pulled away and went to Blackwood, who was beginning to awaken. We couldn't argue now, so I bit my tongue and joined them. Rook helped the sorcerer sit up. Groaning, Blackwood rubbed the back of his head.

"What on earth happened?"

"I tried throwing force at the men but lost control and hit you instead. I'm so sorry." My apology was sincere, which lent credibility to my lie. "They got away."

"I thought I saw . . ." Blackwood paused as he studied Rook. He shook his head. "Probably hit my head too hard."

To change the topic, I said, "Thank God you sensed something. Who could they have been?"

"London's full of dangerous men," Blackwood muttered. "This is why you must never leave the ward again without a companion."

We helped him to his feet and let him lean on us both as we shuffled toward home.

Once we were inside, Agrippa and the housekeeper fussed over Blackwood. Rook seized the opportunity to slip away.

Soon as I could, I ran up the stairs to the servants' corridor and knocked on his door.

"Rook. Please let me in."

After my third round of knocking, he said, "I don't trust myself, Nettie. You must stay away." His voice sounded strained, as though he was lifting something. Or, perhaps, holding something at bay.

I pressed my palms against the wood. I wanted to claw my way through. "I'd feel so much better if I could see you."

"I want to let you in," he groaned. I heard him move farther away from the door. "But I can't."

"The ball's the day after tomorrow. All you need to do is hold on till then. All right?"

"Yes." His voice was so, so faint.

Only a few more days. Rook could hold on. He would.

He had to.

21

LILLY HELPED ME INTO A CRIMSON GOWN, AN OUTFIT I'd not yet worn. I was determined to enjoy this night. Rook was secure in his room, excused from work on account of the afternoon's attack. That was a comfort; my nerves were raw.

"First time at the theater." Lilly sighed. "You'll need something ever so special." She showed me a paper bundle. "For your hair, miss. From the garden." They were several red roses, the perfect color of my dress. We de-thorned the flowers and inserted them in my hair where they might stay. When I turned for her, Lilly clapped. "Beautiful!"

I went downstairs, following the sound of the boys' voices and laughter. When I appeared, everyone fell silent. Dee grinned. Even Lambe and Wolff gave me an appreciative nod. But I felt Magnus's eyes on me from the moment I came down.

"Shall we?" he murmured, offering his arm.

The carriages dropped us at the theater, directly into a cluster of fashionable people. We entered the red velvet foyer. High mirrors in gilded frames reflected the crowd, giving the impression of a churning sea alive with faces and conversation. Burnished candelabra illuminated murals of pink-and-white ladies seated atop fluffy clouds, playing lyres and surrounded by winged cherubs. We looked about until we found Blackwood and Eliza. The instant she spotted me, she kissed me on both cheeks and took my hands.

"I'm so glad you've come. I wanted to show you this particular cut of gown. Do you like it?" She did a full turn for my benefit, charming in an emerald-green dress with puffed sleeves. She fluttered her black lace fan.

"It's lovely."

"I told Madame Voltiana to make its style into an especial cut for your commendation, since it's so fashionable. Do you plan on drinking any champagne tonight? George won't even let me try it," she said, tapping her brother's arm with her fan. He shook his head and smiled. His sister was the only person on earth who could remove his stoic facade.

"I've never tasted it before, actually."

"There! You see, George? If Henrietta gets champagne tonight, then so do I, and don't tell me I can't," she said.

Magnus approached us. Eliza smiled and held out her gloved hand in a rather theatrical gesture. "Hello, Mr. Magnus. It's been so long since we last met." She batted her eyelashes.

"My dear," Magnus said, kissing her fingers. "You've grown even lovelier. I didn't think it was possible." He bowed deeply as she giggled and fluttered her fan. God, they deserved each other. Blackwood cleared his throat and drew Magnus away.

With the young men gone, Eliza turned to me. "I've had a delicious thought. Once you're commended, we can design a

Howel seal. No one's designed a new sorcerer's seal in ages, so it'll be marvelous! Are you partial to unicorns?"

"Not really," I said with a smile.

"Oh. Well, just a small one, then."

At some point, we were obliged to take our seats in Blackwood's box. We'd a good view of the stage. Men and women squinted through small pairs of opera glasses to better watch the play, and to better watch one another. I wondered, uncomfortably, if any eyes turned toward our box. I craned my neck to look up at the domed ceiling, at the crystal chandelier, at the red velvet drapes and the magnificent painted screen in front of the stage. I could never have imagined such a place, and I was so overwhelmed I scarcely read my program. As the lights dimmed, small, mothlike creatures fluttered down before us. I almost swatted them with Eliza's fan.

"Don't," she whispered, "they're usher faeries." Indeed, upon closer inspection I noticed the small human creatures attached to those wings. The one in front of me shook its silver-blond hair and giggled, a thin, almost inaudible sound. The faeries flew to the stage, and the play began.

I enjoyed every moment. The four lovers were hilarious, though I found Helena stupid with all her crying and screaming. Titania and Oberon, the faerie king and queen, were so beautiful it practically hurt. Titania's skin glowed even when she stood far away from the lights.

At some point in the play, an unfortunate man named Bottom was given the head of a donkey. The faeries actually turned the actor's head into an animal's. The audience shrieked as the donkey brayed at us, a bit hard to understand with his mulish lips. Puck, a boy with green skin and leaves for hair, appeared and disappeared in the laps of several audience members. He even materialized in our box, kissing Eliza's hand and swiping a rose from me. Magnus swung to get it back, but Puck vanished.

"It's all right," I said. Magnus had had too much to drink, and frankly so had I. What a delicious experience champagne was! What was I on, my third glass? Magnus put his lips to my ear.

"He should have kissed your hand. You're the most beautiful girl in London tonight," he whispered. My whole body felt warm, somehow heavier.

Puck, at the end of the play, appeared before us on the stage. "If we shadows have offended, think but this and all is mended." Magnus leveled his stave at the actor.

"What are you doing?" I snapped.

"Steal a rose from you, will he? I'll give him roses." He aimed at one of the candles, and the leaves on top of Puck's head caught fire. Everyone screamed. The little faerie squealed and beat at his hair to put them out. Once he'd done so, he pointed to our box.

"Sorcerers! You behave yourselves, you drunken reprobates!" The theater erupted in laughter and applause.

Pointing his stave toward the ceiling, Magnus yelled, "For Her Majesty!" The boys and I all joined him (except Blackwood, naturally). The audience cheered. I had never felt so alive or wonderful.

With the play ended, Blackwood ushered me aside, grabbing my arm when I stumbled. "You're drunk, Miss Howel."

"I am perfectly all right." Really, he shouldn't look at me with such horror. I only tripped because the carpet was uneven.

"I'm taking you home. If anyone saw, your reputation would be damaged."

"Don't need a reputation." I stared at his shoes. They were lovely shoes.

"I want to get smashed, too," Eliza whispered.

"Eliza, be quiet. Put your head down, Miss Howel, and we'll—"

"Keep your hair on, George. I'll take her home," Magnus said, settling my wrap around me. "I can hold my liquor. You've got your sister to see back."

Blackwood nodded. "Fine. Be careful, the both of you." He escorted Eliza away. She waved to me and flashed a look at Magnus.

"Thank you, Father," Magnus grumbled. Snickering, we stole off, tripping once on my skirt.

WE CLIMBED OUT OF THE CARRIAGE, singing funny songs about fish. The butler looked less than pleased as we stumbled inside. "Shall I send Lilly up, Miss Howel?"

"I'll ring her when I'm ready. Thank you." Magnus and I clomped up the stairs. I held out my hand to shake. "G'night. Sleep well."

He kissed my hand, never taking his eyes from mine. "Good night, Howel."

That warm, liquid feeling returned. I walked to my room, trying to clear my head. I'd just gotten to my door when I heard a noise and turned. Magnus was behind me.

"What is it?" My voice sounded hoarse.

"I forgot something," he said. His eyes had the strangest light.

"What?"

He put his hands to my waist. I gasped, but he held me. He brought his lips to the corner of my mouth and kissed me.

"Wait," I said. He pulled back.

"That wasn't so bad, was it? I'll leave, if you wish."

That was exactly what he needed to do. There was Rook upstairs, the commendation, the war.

"Stay." For a moment, I couldn't believe what I'd said. *Take it back. Now.* But his kiss . . .

He slid his arms around me, brought his lips to the other corner of my mouth. I groaned as I turned to catch him, but he cupped my face in his hand, holding me in place. Gently, he pressed his lips to mine, only for an instant. I leaned forward, burning for more.

"Please," I said, the world swimming before me. This was so wrong, so disastrously wrong, but at the moment all I could do was feel how warm he was against me, how soft his mouth was.

"Oh my darling," he whispered, and kissed me again, harder this time. I ran my fingers through his hair. He kissed my neck, breathed against the hollow of my throat, and nipped my bare shoulder. Every molecule inside me exploded with light and heat. Magnus kissed my eyelids and then returned to my mouth. "To hell with all this," he whispered.

The hall spun. I heard my bedroom door close, and he pressed me against his body so that we lined up perfectly with each other. "I've wanted this for so long," he whispered into my ear, sending small signals of fire running down my spine. "You've wanted it, haven't you?"

"Yes," I said. Now *I* kissed *him*, wrapping my arms around his neck. I couldn't seem to stop. It was like when I set myself on fire, the spark giving birth to a full blaze. I trailed kisses along his jaw. He groaned and pulled me closer.

"You're an adventurous creature, aren't you?" His voice was rough, his breathing harsh. He ran his hands down my back.

"I don't know," I whispered as he kissed my neck. It felt as if I were running down a steep hill, my heart pounding with exhilaration. I made him look at me, traced my fingertips over his face and through his hair. Touching him was overwhelming. Did all people find kissing this intoxicating?

"You *are* adventurous," he murmured. I felt the flicker of his tongue as our kiss deepened. He touched my hair, cried out, and brought his hand away with blood welling on the tip of a finger. "How the devil—?"

"The roses? We missed a thorn," I said, half afraid he would stop. He laughed as he pulled the flowers out of my hair and kissed me again. My feet left the ground. I was lying down now, the canopy above me whirling. Magnus pulled my skirt up inch by inch, revealing my leg—

"No!" I yelled. I pushed him away, rolled off the bed, and fell to my hands and knees. No amount of alcohol would make me forget myself that much. I staggered to my feet and hung on to the bedpost. Magnus sat up, his hair rumpled.

"What are you doing?" I asked. What was I doing? How had we got here so quickly?

"I thought—well, weren't we going to?"

"No, for God's sake." I could barely speak the words.

"But what else are we supposed to do?" He sounded confused.

"That is something you save for marriage."

"But, my darling," he said, as if I were slow, "you know I can't marry you."

"Excuse me?" The drunken effects vanished. I'd never been more aware of anything.

"You know I'm engaged to be married."

"You are what?" Images flashed through my mind of spearing Magnus with a bolt of lightning.

"I told you. Didn't I?" Now he seemed hesitant. "Miss Doris Winslow, I'm engaged to her. Wait. Didn't I tell you?"

"No." The floor spun beneath me. I wanted to fall onto my bed and wake to find this hadn't happened.

"Oh God. No wonder you were enthusiastic. I'm sorry." He shook his head and ran a hand through his hair. "It slipped my mind."

"You thought you'd"—I choked on the word—"with me and then leave me?"

"No! Henrietta, I'm only marrying her because my family's destitute. I don't know how to earn money, so I have to have an heiress. But she's very dull, you know. Not like you." He came to me, that roguish smile back on his face. "You're the most exciting girl I ever met."

"But you wouldn't marry me." My voice sounded distant. Had I even wanted to marry him? His presence was so intoxicating, and I sometimes couldn't keep myself from thinking about him. But was that love?

I didn't think he could treat me this way if he loved me.

"I can't have two wives, can I? Look, we keep it a secret. Once we're commended, you have your house, and I'll have mine. It'll be easy to meet for—"

"My reputation would be destroyed."

"But you're going to be a sorcerer! You're not like other girls. Even if they found out, no one would—"

"You don't understand a damn thing about the world, do you?" Mr. and Mrs. Magnus would be accepted by society. I would be an outcast because loose women must always know their place.

"I want you more than any other girl I've ever met," Magnus said, reaching for my waist. Want. Not love. "If I could, I'd marry you tomorrow. As is, let's make the best of this bad situation."

I slapped the smile off his face, hard as I could. Grabbing Porridge from my sheath, I held it to his chest. He put his hands in the air.

"Don't do anything foolish," he muttered.

"Get out, or I'll scream."

Magnus opened the door and left. I sat on my bed for ten minutes, stupefied, then rang for Lilly. She didn't ask why I'd waited so long to call for her, and I didn't tell.

I huddled in the darkness until I heard the boys come home, the shouts and jokes echoing through the halls. I thought about the day I'd dueled with Magnus in the library, when he'd praised my eyes. I'd imagined there was something special in that attention, but I was wrong. He wanted me, nothing more. I was the fool.

A bloody fool, I thought. Magnus had tossed one of my roses onto the bed. I picked it up and tore all the petals out in a fistful, squeezing them tightly.

I thought about Rook, the two of us sitting out on the moor, back in Yorkshire. Everything had been clear, everyone in their right place. Who had I become? What was I becoming?

I cried while I listened to the boys go up the stairs to bed. The harder I cried, the more I hated it. I set fire to the petals to calm myself, watching them crisp and blacken in my hand. It worked. The flush of heat on my skin evaporated the tears. The fire scorched my sadness. Only an ember of anger remained.

22

"ARE YOU WELL, HENRIETTA?" AGRIPPA ASKED AT breakfast. I stared bleary-eyed into my tea.

"Just tired, sir." Across the table, Magnus ate in silence. When Dee tried to make a joke, Magnus shot him a look so black he shut up at once. The whole room was quiet except for Lambe tapping his water glass with a fork. Blackwood read a letter over and over, lost in thought. We were quite a merry gathering.

"We'll practice creating the column of fire this morning. When you've finished your breakfast—"

"I'm finished now." I pushed the tea and untouched toast away.

"You haven't eaten a thing."

"I'm not hungry, sir."

"I daresay too much champagne," Blackwood said, putting his letter away at last. He looked from me to Magnus. I could see that he suspected something. Damn him. "Perhaps Miss Howel might benefit from private instruction," he said.

The blood rushed to my cheeks. "I'm fine working as usual." I pushed my chair back and left the room without another word.

I IMAGINED A CANDLE FLAME THAT grew into a pillar of light. My hands felt warm, but the column of fire did not appear.

"Henrietta, you're not trying," Agrippa said.

"My head hurts." That wasn't a lie.

"Well, it can't. Tomorrow you'll either be commended or dismissed. No second chances. Everything must be perfect," he said. Blackwood stood by a wall, while Magnus looked everywhere but at me.

"I've done well so far, haven't I?" Massaging my temples did nothing.

"The queen is young and unsure in her reign. Her nonmagical advisors don't like the idea of a woman sorcerer. If you fail in any way, they'll persuade the queen not to commend you."

Sparks shone upon my dress but died. Agrippa puffed out his cheeks in exasperation.

"Why on earth are you so tired this morning? You went to the theater last night; it wasn't a walk to Northumberland." He circled around me.

"I don't feel well." Memories of kissing Magnus returned, tinged with shame.

"How you feel doesn't matter," Agrippa said.

"What do you mean?" I dropped my hands from my head.

"These men want to see if you are a sorcerer. They've no time for anything else."

The chamber filled with a great wind that knocked Agrippa down. He struggled back to his feet, his hand raised as a signal to stop.

"As long as I do exactly what everyone wants," I said, "I'll be worth something?"

"That's not what I meant." He attempted to get up again, but this time I forced him back. My breath quickened.

"I'm tired of catering to everyone's demands, and I'm tired of pleasing and pleasing!" My voice rose into a scream, and the wind rose with me. Agrippa cried out. Blackwood ran to help him up and shouted for me to stop.

Magnus gripped me by the arms. "You're going to hurt the Master." His gray eyes burned into mine. He was right. I didn't want to hurt Agrippa. The wind died down, and Magnus sighed in relief, squeezing my arm. "Thank you."

I set fire to the exact spot where Magnus held me. Screaming, he recoiled and stared in horror at his blistered hands. My thoughts swung broken and wild. I wanted to burn. I dropped Porridge and turned from them, head in my hands. Rage pulsed through me, and as it did, the flames leaped higher.

"Stop it," Blackwood cried. "You're losing control."

The blue flames rippled on my skin and clothes, whirling in a column as they rose to the ceiling. "I can't stop," I shouted as the fire grew. I couldn't silence the pounding in my head, the fury. I pressed my palms to my forehead and shrieked.

Great scarlet waves of flame turned the obsidian walls into reflections of hellish red. I couldn't calm down. Magnus had made me *vulnerable*. Of course he could never marry me—couldn't I see that? I wasn't worthy of that great honor. Blackwood and

Magnus crouched beside Agrippa and warded themselves. But the wards couldn't hold forever.

For an instant, the chamber was full of fire. They screamed for mercy. *They.* Agrippa and Blackwood were innocent. Would I just murder them? Would I just murder anyone, even Magnus, even by accident?

No. I forced my thoughts to calm. The fire died. Agrippa huddled in a heap while Magnus and Blackwood pointed their staves at me with real fear in their eyes.

"Stay back, Howel," Magnus said. He winced, his grip on his stave loosening. Good Lord, I'd ruined his hands. What if he couldn't be commended now?

What had I done?

"I'm sorry," I whispered, crawling to my feet. "Master Agrippa, I'm so sorry."

His look undid me. He found the sight of me repulsive. I turned and ran, and didn't stop until I was out of the house.

I KNOCKED SEVEN TIMES AT HARGROVE'S door before I forced my way inside.

"Please, you need to help me," I gasped as I entered the room. "I've done something terrible."

My voice echoed in the bare space. The place was abandoned. The table and chairs, the curtain, the mattress before the stove, Hargrove's treasure chest, all had vanished as if into thin air. Hargrove and the children were gone. Set sail for America, most likely.

I knelt in the now-empty room and wept.

AGRIPPA'S STABLES WERE FULL OF THE pungent scent of manure and the sweetness of grain. When I was certain no one else was about, I walked over to the stalls. The horses nuzzled me, searching for a treat.

"What am I going to do?" I said. Perhaps I could transform myself into a horse and stay here. But I wasn't that kind of magician, and, of course, animals had problems of their own.

"Howel?" Damn. Magnus ran toward me. His hands were bandaged. "Where on earth did you go?"

"I don't think that's any of your business."

"For God's sake, I'm sorry. I'd had too much to drink. I didn't mean to insult you."

"So you're not responsible for your actions?"

"That's not what I'm saying," he snapped. "I'm trying to apologize. It shouldn't have happened."

"But it did, and you can't change it." I hoped he would disappear. He didn't.

"You might apologize for trying to murder me," he said.

"I'm sorry for trying to murder you. Happy?" I aggressively petted a horse.

"What I said about wishing I didn't have to marry Miss Winslow was true." He moved close enough that I could feel his breath on the back of my hair. I half hoped, even now, that he'd put his arms around my waist. I hated that. "Really, if I didn't have this infernal engagement—"

"You think so much of yourself, don't you?" I turned to

face him. "Suppose I had no great desire to marry *you*? Suppose I found you handsome and charming and wanted to kiss you, but nothing else? Can you imagine a situation where a young woman wouldn't want to give herself to you, body and soul?"

He flushed and leaned closer. "Nice young women don't run around trying to get fellows to kiss them."

"I didn't try to get you to do anything."

"Don't play hurt with me, Henrietta. You enjoyed what happened last night, and if you're the type who likes to be kissed and nothing else, there are plenty of men—"

Something clattered nearby, startling us. Rook appeared from around the corner, looking ashen. A wooden bucket lay fallen on the ground. Its water crept across the stones.

Magnus cleared his throat. "Rook. Let me explain."

A wild light came into Rook's eyes. He threw the mop aside and struck Magnus across the face. The sorcerer staggered backward. Now the boys were locked together and grappling, Magnus with superior strength but damaged hands, and Rook with greater fury. Magnus fought Rook off and held him down.

"Magnus, let go! Rook, stop it!" The harder they fought, the greater chance Rook's power would be unleashed. "Stop it, I said!" And then it happened.

Darkness rushed from the stables in a wave, a shadowed mass that poured over them. Rook tore himself away from Magnus and rose out of the gloom, letting the other boy scream as he vanished from sight.

"Let him go," I begged. Rook ignored me, fascinated by his

handiwork. I slapped his face in a desperate attempt to wake him. The direction of his anger shifted. Now I could feel darkness growing around me. A chilled sensation formed on my skin.

With a cry, I lit my hand on fire and shoved it toward his face. There was a horrible moment when I thought I'd have to burn him, but it worked. The shadows lifted from me and from Magnus. Rook was himself again.

No, not quite. His eyes had returned to their normal color, yet there was strangeness in the cool way he regarded the effects of his work. The sight of Magnus huddled in terror seemed to please him. Standing with his arms relaxed at his sides, he cocked his head to study the scene from different angles. I recalled the Familiar girl, when I'd fought her at the edge of the ward. She'd tilted her head in a similar way.

"I don't remember any of it," he said, his tone distant. "I was so angry."

"I know," I said. Slowly, I approached the person who was not really Rook and touched his hand. He crumpled to the ground.

"Don't," he cried, his voice thick with anguish. He moaned, clasping his hands around the back of his neck. "The whispering wanted me to tear you apart where you stood. If you hadn't frightened it off with that fire . . . What's happening to me?"

The Shadow's chosen. That's what the Familiar had called him on the road at Brimthorn.

"I don't know," I murmured. *He should never have come to London,* I thought. And then, *I made him come here.*

During all this, Magnus had come out of his defensive

crouch on the ground. His hair was wild with bits of straw. I'd never seen him so pale. "What was that?" he said. Then, pointing to Rook, "What in God's name are you?"

There was no hiding it now.

Footsteps echoed over the paving stones. The footmen grabbed Rook and forced him to his feet. He didn't protest. If anything, he seemed relieved.

"Stop!" I cried. Magnus held me back.

"Don't make this worse," he whispered. All I could do was stand helpless as Agrippa and Blackwood rushed into the yard.

"What on earth is going on?" Agrippa shouted.

"We heard screams, sir," the footman said. "We came out to find the young master on the ground."

The others hadn't seen Rook's power, but Magnus knew. One word from him and Rook would be in the worst kind of trouble.

"Magnus, how many people are going to try killing you before this day is out?" Blackwood snapped.

"Why, Rook?" Agrippa turned to my friend, now held between two footmen. "Why would you do such a thing?"

Rook shook his head. "I cannot tell you, sir."

"You had better tell me, or you'll be out of my household this minute."

"No!" I pressed forward. "It's all Magnus's fault." Everyone turned to me.

"How is that?" Agrippa said. There was no good way out of this. Even leaving aside Rook's shadowed attack, by confessing the reason for his violence I would forever damage my reputation. But Rook mattered more.

"Rook overheard Magnus and me talking—"

"Joking, really. On my part, at least," Magnus said, cutting in with ease. "That'll teach me, I suppose."

"Julian, what on earth is going on?" Agrippa said. I held my breath.

Magnus swept back his hair, his confident smile returning. "I was teasing Howel last night about, oh, something or other. She got cross, so I followed her out here, teasing her more. Rook overheard me say"—here he paused and laughed, as if he couldn't himself believe it—"that I wished I hadn't kissed her."

"You did what?" Agrippa said, shocked. I bit the inside of my cheek.

"No, I didn't actually do it, of course. How could I kiss anything so cold? My lips would get stuck to her. It was a tasteless joke, but poor Rook seemed to think I was being serious. He defended Howel's honor." He laughed like it was the world's greatest gag. Truly, he'd make a fine actor. "Please don't punish Rook for being gallant. He struck a blow for decent women everywhere." I realized Magnus wasn't going to mention Rook's powers and could hardly believe it.

"You teased her. That would explain . . ." Agrippa looked to me, undoubtedly remembering what had happened this morning. "You must be more careful with what you say, Julian. One day, there could be dire consequences."

"I see that now, sir."

"Very well. Rook, you're to be locked in your room until after the ball."

"What? Why?" I cried.

"Do not question me, Henrietta."

Rook let the men drag him away; he didn't look as if he could stand on his own. As the crowd headed indoors, Blackwood grabbed Magnus and pulled him beside the stables. I slipped away from the others, waited along the wall, and listened to their conversation. Really, I was getting far too good at eavesdropping.

"You bastard," Blackwood said, his voice pure venom.

"Nothing happened."

"What's this other girl's name?"

"Doris Winslow," Magnus said, surprised. "When the devil did you find out about her?"

"Just now. But I'd have to have been an idiot not to guess what happened when you came down to breakfast. You couldn't look at each other, and you were always so comfortable before." He said *comfortable* like it was a contagious disease. "I presumed there might be another young woman. You are the lowest kind of filth."

"I never, ever thought it would go so far." Magnus sounded disgusted, but I didn't think with me. "The champagne loosened me up. It's not an excuse."

"I should never have sent her home with you. It was like having a wolf nanny a lamb."

"Howel is surprisingly capable of looking after herself."

"You could have ruined her life."

"It won't happen again," Magnus said softly.

"And nearly getting that boy sacked."

"I saved the day there, thank you so much. He'll be fine."

"Understand this, Magnus. She is worth ten of you, in every respect, and I will destroy you if you harm her again." That surprised me.

"You've certainly changed your opinion. It's a waste of time, Blacky. She's no interest in you; she told me so." I winced with embarrassment. "Besides, it would be the talk of the town. The great Earl of Sorrow-Fell taking up with some low-blooded girl. *Low-blooded* was your own term, remember, not mine." Magnus's voice was warm with anger.

"Don't remind me of that," Blackwood snapped. "I'm not in love with her, but I can see her value."

"Always about value with you, isn't it? Why don't you grow a personality? You're like a shambling ghost, curdling everyone's blood whenever you walk into a room."

"At least I don't spend my time seducing innocent young women."

"Someone's been reading novels again. What's the title of this one? *The Poxy Lordling and the Aggressive Milkmaid?*" Magnus sighed. "I tried to leave her alone, but I can't help myself. She teases me in just the right way—"

Blackwood made a disgusted noise. "I don't care. Unless you want an enemy, Magnus, leave her alone."

"Like you did, when she attended that school of yours?" The

wall trembled, as if someone had been thrown against it. There was a flash of fire. An instant later Blackwood raced past me, slapping at the smoking sleeve of his coat. "Handing down orders like you were God Almighty," Magnus called, rubbing the back of his head while he came around the corner. "No wonder nobody likes you, Blackwood."

"I'm not here to be liked," Blackwood snapped, heading into the house. "I'm here to do what's needed." Magnus stood for a moment, watching him go.

"I know you're there, Howel." Blast. I shrank even further into the dark. "You needn't worry. I won't tell anyone what happened. I really think they'd kill Rook if they ever found out." He sounded frightened. "But for all our sakes, I hope you know what you're doing." With that, he followed Blackwood into the house.

The butler met me in the hall, instructing me to see Agrippa immediately. Entering the library, I found him in the worst possible mood. His face was bright red with anger, and the veins on his neck bulged as he shouted at me.

"How dare you attack a fellow sorcerer? How dare you leave my house under such circumstances without asking my permission." His rage almost sent me to the floor. "You ungrateful girl, if anyone knew half of what had occurred, they'd have you out of London by tonight!"

"I'm sorry," I said, my eyes cast down.

"You attacked me. Me, of all people. I brought you into my house. I fed you, looked after you as if you were my own. I treated you like you were my—" He paused, as if to swallow the unspoken word. "I have never in my life seen such selfish, wretched behavior."

"I'm so sorry," I whispered. "I didn't mean to—"

"Now you will go upstairs and stay in your room until I've decided what's to be done. Do you hear me? Set one foot outside before I return, and there'll be the devil to pay."

"It was an accident." My throat tightened. "My emotions got the better of me."

"Get upstairs now!" Agrippa threw open the door, and I ran. The boys called to me, but I wouldn't answer. Once inside my room, I sat on the bed and stared at the fire. Agrippa hadn't given Porridge back after I'd dropped it in the obsidian room.

When Cellini had attacked me, they'd taken his stave. The pain of losing Porridge, the mere idea of it, threatened to crush me.

This would be the end, for Rook and for me. Rook. I'd destroyed his hope of relief from the power that plagued him. I'd ruined his chance of security. Heavy with misery, I fell across the bed, closed my eyes, and slept.

R'HLEM HELD OUT HIS HAND. "IT'S been some time," he said. I'd neglected Fenswick's herbs on purpose. I had wanted this meeting. The mist grew so thick I couldn't see the room.

"You can't have a great deal to do," I muttered, heading to my window. "Popping into my head every so often."

"I can do many things at once. Why do you want me here?"

I pressed my forehead to the glass. "I don't know."

R'hlem ushered me aside and gently unlatched the window. Outside, the streets of London had disappeared. My bedroom perched on the edge of a cliff. The fall stretched before me, seemingly endless. This terrain was unfamiliar, a desert of pink-and-red rock, the earth barren and cracked. A crimson sun broiled above me. Great black creatures with leathery wings cavorted through the sky.

"I want to go home." I rubbed my eyes. This had been a mistake.

"There is no home for you, is there? I cannot read your mind, but I can guess your thoughts. You live at the mercy of other people." His voice was soothing and gentle, at complete odds with his appearance. I gazed out the window. In the valley below, the other Ancients walked.

Molochoron rolled, of course, a pulsing mass of moldy gray.

On-Tez, with that grotesque old woman's head upon a black vulture's body, soared through the fever-orange sky.

There was Callax. He was so large and bulky with muscle that it didn't surprise me when he crushed a thick ledge of rock with the effort one might use on an eggshell.

Zem slithered by with his long, sleek lizard's body. A giant frill fanned out about his head, and he breathed a stream of fire and noxious vapor.

Nemneris, the green-and-purple Water Spider, climbed the side of the cliff to fashion a giant, hideous web.

And there was Korozoth, the old Shadow and Fog.

"Poor child." R'hlem didn't sound like a hideous beast. "You need someone to look after you."

I realized why I'd wanted him to come. My time at Agrippa's house was over. Hargrove had gone to America. Who would help me now?

R'hlem offered his hand again. I finally understood what made ordinary humans flock to him, transform themselves into Familiars. There was safety in service and obedience. And R'hlem was a charismatic leader. . . .

No. My problems were my own. However hard the road ahead, I would walk it.

"Goodbye," I whispered, and tipped forward out the window, off the cliff.

THANK GOD FOR THE KNOCKING AT my door. Bleary-eyed, I stared out the window and found it pitch black. The knock came again. Agrippa stood at the threshold, still wearing his cloak and hat.

"I've thought a few things through," he said. My stomach lurched. Slowly, he brought his hand out from behind his back, holding my stave. "All's well, my dear. If you apologize to Magnus, I see no reason to drag this out." His eyes glistened with tears. He seemed as relieved as I.

I threw my arms around him, not caring how improper it might be. He clasped me back as I sobbed into his shoulder.

"I'm so sorry," I cried.

He petted my hair. "It was an accident. Accidents can be forgiven."

R'hlem was right. I did live at the mercy of others. But come tomorrow night, I'd have a true home in the sorcerers' fellowship. There was a path before me, and I would follow it.

 **23**

AGRIPPA AND I SAT BEFORE THE FIRE WHILE I ATE SUP-
per. It was only a little cold mutton, but it tasted heavenly. He
watched the flames, distant.

"Are you all right, sir?" I asked.

"Hmm?" He smiled. "Just distracted. Imagine, this time tomorrow night you'll be a commended sorcerer."

"I hope so." I gripped my teacup, savoring the warmth.

"It's impossible to be otherwise." He looked into the flames
again. "I would have had this talk with *her*, you know," He
sighed. "My Gwen."

"You must have been proud."

"More than words can say. She was my only child. There
should have been brothers and sisters for her, but when her
mother died, I couldn't bring myself to marry again. Everyone
thought I yearned for a son, but Gwen was enough for me." He
shook his head. "They told me I shouldn't train her. They even
told me to give her a stave, then take it back immediately and
bind it to leave her powerless."

What a monstrous idea.

"When I saw she could be a sorcerer," Agrippa said, "I

couldn't have been more pleased. And then that awful, terrible disease." He closed his eyes.

"I'm so sorry."

"Sometimes I go over and over that night—was there anything I could have done differently?"

"You can't alter the course of a fever, Master Agrippa." I stood, a bit awkward, and placed my hand on his shoulder. He gripped my fingers.

"Thank you, Henrietta. You've been such a comfort. It's wonderful to have a young woman in the house again."

"I never met my father, but I know that you've shown me as much kindness and care as he ever could have," I said.

Agrippa began to sob. His whole body shook as he leaned against an armrest, burying his face in his hands.

"I'm so sorry. Did I say something wrong?" Oh, what was I thinking? "I didn't mean to say I feel I'm your daughter. It was awkward and stupid of me." Was there no end to my idiocy today?

"Not at all, my dear." He wiped his eyes with a handkerchief and kissed my hand. "It will be so hard to let you go."

"Let me go?" My heart swelled. Was his concern that I would leave him once I had been commended? I wanted to tell him that I'd stay if he needed me, but before the words could pass my lips, he said, "Henrietta, perhaps you should go to bed. Rest for tomorrow. You'll need it."

"Of course. Good night, sir." I left him and moved up the stairs, feeling lighter than ever. What a difference a few hours make. Agrippa didn't want me to leave. I'd approach the subject after the commendation, but already I imagined him embracing me in joy.

And Rook? If the situation became more permanent, perhaps his status would change. Perhaps we could discuss his shadow powers with Agrippa. I kept calm, reminding myself that nothing was certain. But if I made it through tomorrow, all might be well.

I dreamed of Gwendolyn Agrippa lying in bed, her pale yellow hair arranged around her on the pillow. She looked peaceful and beautiful even in death. I was dressed in ragged boys' clothes, my hands and face dirty as a beggar's. I went to take a ring off her finger and put it on my own, but the mattress erupted in a fountain of blood.

I woke to a sharp knocking. Waiting for my heart to slow, I crept to the door and whispered, "Who is it?"

"Me," Blackwood said. I put on my wrap and opened the door a crack. His appearance shocked me. His black hair was wild and unruly. His shirt was undone at the throat, his white cravat rumpled under his chin. With his eyes rimmed in red, he looked as if he'd been drinking. "I need to speak with you. The library."

When I found him before the fire, he frightened me. Usually so composed and elegant, he clung to the marble ledge and leaned his head against it, his eyes closed tight. He muttered something to himself. All I could make out were the words *lost* and *time*.

"What on earth is the matter?"

"Please sit down." He ushered me into an armchair, then turned, a dark silhouette against the flames. "What I'm about to tell you I've never told another living soul. Not even my mother or sister knows this secret." I waited, hands clasped in my lap. "Before my father died, he told me something that he begged me never to repeat to anyone else."

"What on earth are you talking about?"

"My father had an open mind," Blackwood said, rubbing his chin. "He believed in making England stronger through harnessing forces beyond our natural understanding."

"Like magicians?"

"Yes. Magicians. Listen," Blackwood said, kneeling before me. "Do you know why I pay Jenkins Hargrove?"

"Out of charity."

"No. Not really. It's part charity, part . . . debt, I should say."

"I don't understand."

"I pay him because his real name isn't Jenkins Hargrove. It's Howard Mickelmas."

I almost jumped out of my seat. Howard Mickelmas? The evil magician who had worked with Mary Willoughby to bring our world to an end? *That* was the man who had trained me? If anyone ever knew, I'd die.

I couldn't reconcile the untidy, rather drunk fellow I knew with the insane monster he was supposed to be. No, they couldn't be the same person.

"How do you know he's Howard Mickelmas?" I gasped.

"Because my father told me who he was and to pay him."

"Why would he have done that?"

"Mary Willoughby and Howard Mickelmas brought ruin down on this country, yes, and they tore open the breach that allowed the monsters to cross over. But they needed a third to complete the trinity of power, and that third," he said, his face twisting in pain, "was my father. And no one," he snapped, noting my look of horror, "outside myself and those concerned has known about this. Not until tonight. Not until you." He moved away from me to the fire. "My father, once the Ancients had been unleashed, knew what word of it would do to the Blackwood family. He fixed it so that it would appear Willoughby and Mickelmas were to blame, not he."

My mind raced but settled on one detail. "You said no one knows but yourself and those concerned. Who else?"

"Mickelmas, obviously. And Master Palehook," he said. "I can't imagine how, but he knows what my father did."

"That's why he's so free to be rude to you?"

"Precisely. Father knew how unscrupulous Palehook was. I was instructed to obey him in all things. I did." He looked at me again, guilt written upon his face. "Until recently."

"What did you do?"

"He wanted something I'd no right to give."

Like a burst of light I saw the scene again: Blackwood coming into the magician's home, with Rook of all people . . . Blackwood hurrying me along, leaving Rook behind . . . his burst of insight, when he thought—no, when he knew—Rook would be in trouble. I leaped from my seat. He caught my wrists.

"How could you?" I cried.

"I couldn't. It's why we went back. Whatever he had planned, I knew I'd no right to sacrifice Rook to save myself."

"What does Palehook want with him?"

"I've no idea. I swear." He fell to his knees, his hands clasped together. He looked as if he were praying. "I'm so sorry."

Trying to breathe out the anger, I sat. "Why are you telling me this?"

"Master Palehook said that if I didn't give him Rook, he'd reveal my family's secret. I received a letter this morning. Every sorcerer in the city will know by breakfast tomorrow. I've failed."

"Why tell me now?"

"Because I wanted to give you a chance," he said, his eyes wild. "I called you low, pretended I was your born superior. Here." He gripped my wrists and put his face in my hands. "Strike me, burn me, do whatever you want. I deserve your punishment more than anyone else's." He looked half mad.

The younger, less complicated me would have gladly attacked him. But I knew how it felt to lie for my own survival. Tentatively, I stroked his hair.

"This must have been a terrible burden to bear alone."

Blackwood lowered his head onto my knee, almost as if he were melting in relief. I slid down to sit beside him. We looked into the fire together.

"I was wrong about you," he whispered. "At first I saw you

merely as a pain to be endured. But now you're the only per-son in this entire house who could understand me." He wasn't wrong. We were similar people, keeping vast and terrible secrets from the world. "For the first time in a long time, I've wanted someone to think well of me."

He'd shown me his soul. To be worthy of that, I had to be honest.

"I'm not a sorcerer," I said. "Mickelmas told me my father was a magician and had my fire abilities. I'm not special. I'm not your prophesied one."

It should have hurt. It should have been terrible. But all I felt was a sweet, calming relief in telling the truth.

He considered this. "The prophecy called for a girl-child of sorcerer stock. Magicians are descendants of sorcerers. Perhaps that's what it meant." A flare of desperation showed; he needed to be certain of my status.

"Mickelmas believes the Speakers wouldn't make such an error."

"You can use a stave."

"I'm a mix of both races, but I was born a magician. You have to know the truth." My heart pounded as I waited for his reply.

He was silent a moment. Then he said, "We need you. That's what's important. The rest is titles." Gently, he took my hand in his own. It wasn't a romantic gesture; it was deeper than that.

We sat side by side, our burdens eased, if not lifted.

———◈◈◈———

WE WERE SILENT AT BREAKFAST, BUT nothing happened. No letter arrived. Agrippa didn't leap out of his chair, point at Blackwood, and shout, *Off with his head!* All Agrippa did was ask for more marmalade. I thought Blackwood would faint by the end of the meal. I didn't feel much better myself.

I wanted to call on Palehook and find out what was happening, but the day's preparations made that impossible. Almost as soon as we were done eating, we went through a brief, final round of training, and then began the absorbing task of scrubbing and dressing.

The household was in a bustle of activity all day, with the boys looking for their hats or wondering if their boots were correctly polished or wishing they could grow a proper beard.

Lilly bathed and powdered and primped me until I felt I would run mad. She shoved pins into my hair, scratching my scalp so that my eyes watered. As dusk began to creep into the sky, there was a knock at the bedroom door. Eliza entered with a parcel.

"There. I threatened Madame Voltiana with ruin if she didn't have this ready by tonight," she said before flinging herself on my bed in a most dramatic fashion. "You'll have to relay every delicious detail to me afterward. I'm not allowed at the ball until next year, when I'm sixteen. Tonight I'm to sit home with Mamma and sigh before the fire."

I opened the package and uncovered the most beautiful gown, intricately stitched gold lace filigree over a white satin base, with a capelike train fastened at the shoulders. The skirt was voluminous, taking up the entirety of the bed. I shook my head, overcome. It was a work of art.

"Eliza, it's too beautiful."

"Of course it is. I chose it."

Lilly ran her hands over the fine work. "Oh, let's put it on now!" she cried, grabbing fistfuls of the gown.

"Aren't you a dear?" Eliza cooed, satisfied with such enthusiasm.

I'd one last thing to do. Leaving the girls alone with the cherished dress, I raced upstairs to the servants' quarters, down the long hallway to Rook's door. I tried to turn the handle, but of course it had been locked.

"Hello?" he said, his voice faint.

"Rook, it's me. How are you?"

A pause. "I'm well, Nettie. Resting. Are you on your way to the ball, then?"

"Yes, nearly. Next time we speak, I may be one of Her Majesty's sorcerers." I laid my hand on the door, imagining I could simply melt through the wood and into the room.

"You'll have the life you always should have had." It sounded as if he was describing that life without him.

"You'll come with me, Rook. We're going to get control of this."

"Yes." He didn't sound convinced. If only I could see him.

"I'm sorry for what happened."

"So am I. I didn't want to hurt anyone." He sounded afraid. "That's all I seem to do now." There was a moment so silent I thought he'd ended the conversation, but then he whispered, "Is anyone nearby?"

"No. What is it?"

"What Mr. Magnus said about . . . was he telling the truth?"

I closed my eyes and leaned my forehead against the door. I could just lie to him. "Yes," I whispered.

"Oh, I see," he murmured. I could almost sense that he'd put his own forehead against the door, much in the same way. I looked down and found his shadow stretching into the hall, reaching for me. With a gasp, I pushed away. "I'm sorry," he cried. The shadow slunk back under the door. There was a weak thump, as if he'd beat his fist against the wood. "I'm trying so hard."

"Rook."

"Be careful tonight. My scars hurt again." With that, I heard him move away.

24

THE CARRIAGES DREW UP THROUGH THE GATES AND into an enormous courtyard. They delivered us before the palace, white and elegant in appearance, like a wedding cake. Red-liveried guards stood at attention. A wigged footman ran to our carriage and lowered the step. I dropped to the ground and gazed up in wonder.

"Come along," Blackwood whispered.

They announced us into a ballroom shining with candles and chandeliers. I waited on Master Agrippa's arm, as frightened as I'd been the day we'd faced the Familiars on the hillside. They announced the Duke of Buckingham, Lady Evelyn Rochester, and then:

"Master Cornelius Agrippa and Miss Henrietta Howel."

As we descended the stairs, I heard whispers passing among hundreds of people, with so many eyes on me. The gold filigree caught the light and glowed as I moved through the crowd. *It looks like fire*, I realized. Eliza had been cunning in her choice of dress. I kept my face an indecipherable mask, just as Blackwood had instructed. Eventually, the rest of the boys joined us, and Agrippa excused himself to discuss something with the Earl of Southampton.

"You feel it, don't you?" Dee whispered while elegant men and women glided past, their eyes sweeping over us. "The whole of society is going to pay attention now, notice every little thing we do."

"I thought you'd be better adjusted to the idea." I wished I had a spell that turned me invisible.

"No, I don't really like London. If I had my way, I'd go back to my grandmother's estate in Lincolnshire and just worry over the cottages and the gardens. I'm not much for society. Not like Magnus."

Indeed, Magnus appeared completely comfortable with a glass of punch in his hand. He laughed and flirted with a young woman in a white dress—yet another conquest—and I looked away.

Eventually, Dee and I were dragged into conversation with Palehook.

"We expect the pleasure of your abilities soon, Miss Howel. I believe the war shall run smoothly with you officially on our side." Palehook didn't smile. I noticed that he appeared sallow and sweaty. He coughed a good deal, and his eyelids were swollen and rimmed in pink.

"Are you well, Master Palehook?"

"I've been unwell. Thank you for inquiring. I believe it may have something to do with how much energy I spend in maintaining the ward. Korozoth, you know, exhibits such a forceful attack."

"The ward is growing thinner, isn't it?"

He smiled thinly. "It's through no fault of mine, I assure you." Dee went to get some more punch. I seized my opportunity.

"Why haven't you informed all the Masters about Lord Blackwood?" I asked. That certainly surprised him.

"Has Lord Blackwood made mention of our disagreement?"

"He's told me everything. What are you planning?"

"Nothing." He held out his hands in a gesture of giving. "His secret is safe with me. I confess I nearly did tell, but it occurred to me that if his secret is known, he's out of my power. Now my power is greater than before." He smiled. "Don't you think?"

Hateful man. "What did you want with Rook?"

"I applaud it, my dear. Your devotion to one so disgustingly low." Before I could respond, he bowed and disappeared into the crowd. I had to breathe slowly to avoid going up in flames.

The dancing began. Magnus came to me as Dee and I stood on the sidelines, contented to remain observers for most of the ball. "Would you join me in the first waltz?" he said, bowing. I wanted to strike him. I wanted to tell him to leave me alone, but tonight I also wanted as little trouble as possible. There were too many watchful eyes in this ballroom. Besides, I couldn't give him the satisfaction of seeing me that upset.

"Better you than me," Dee said into his glass. "I'll surely be a laughingstock the moment I dance my first step."

So I took Magnus's hand, and we turned onto the floor. We orbited each other, our hands arched over our heads, and then we folded together and spun, the lights and the people a blur around us. His dancing was perfect. Of course it was.

"Are you ready?" he whispered.

"Yes." I made my voice as stiff as I could.

"For God's sake, I'm sorry. Can't you forgive me?"

"No," I said. If I counted to ten, I could avoid getting angry. He gripped me tighter about the waist and pressed me as close as he might dare while we danced.

We applauded the musicians when the waltz ended.

"I don't imagine that you want any refreshment," Magnus muttered.

"No."

"I must say, it's staggeringly mature of you to answer me with one word at all times. 'Do you agree, Miss Howel, with Plato's concept of knowledge as recollection?' Yes. 'And how would you go about describing it?' No. 'What is your favorite color?' Maybe."

"I'm more than ready for my commendation. It means my time with you will be coming to a merciful end." We were snapping at each other now, and a cluster of young girls with fluttering fans noticed and giggled.

"Where will you go once you're commended?" Magnus said in a low voice.

"I'm not sure yet, but I'll think of something. Rook will come with me."

"Yes, of course, mustn't forget dear old Rook. Also mustn't forget his powers of eternal night and nameless horror—that's a *very* good trick for parties." He paused, then said in a less angry tone, "You need to be careful around him. Something terrible might happen." As we neared Dee, he whispered, "Despite what you may think, I do care what happens to you." He swept back into the crowd in search of a new partner.

Blackwood and I took to the floor in a quadrille. He was a skilled dancer, elegant and nimble. The dance also gave us an excellent chance for conversation.

"What did you talk about with Palehook?" he asked as we made a turn.

"Your situation."

"And?" He had to wait for us to circle back to each other.

"You're safe," I whispered. "I think you'll have to do something about it one day, but for now you're safe." After a few more turns, the music ended. The dance was done.

"I didn't know how lonely I was," he said as we bowed, "until I had you on my side." We left the floor together, his hand on my back.

After that, we waited with Dee until Agrippa came out of the crowd. He clapped for the music and nodded to me.

"It's time, Henrietta. The queen will see you first."

"Shouldn't we all go in together?" Dee said, putting his glass down.

"Henrietta is a special case. Come, my dear."

"In fifteen minutes, it will all be done," Blackwood said.

I took Agrippa's arm and walked toward my destiny.

25

WE ENTERED A LONG RECEIVING CHAMBER. GENTLE-
men milled about, some in army uniform, others in fine dress.
I recognized Imperator Whitechurch, who watched me with an
unreadable expression. The men parted and formed an avenue
toward a great throne, where Queen Victoria sat.

Lord, she was only a girl, scarcely older than I. She was pale,
almost sickly, her dark hair curled in fashionable ringlets, her
tiny hands clasped in her lap. She wore a rich blue velvet gown
and a great diadem upon her brow. I took a card with my name
on it to a gentleman in a powdered wig waiting near the throne.
He handed it to the queen. When she nodded, I curtsied before
her. She extended her gloved hand, and I kissed it.

"Your Majesty. I am your humble servant. I seek your royal
commendation to take up arms against England's foes and to
defend Your Majesty's life with my own."

"Thank you, Miss Howel," she said, her voice soft and high.
"We are most pleased by your presence. They tell us you are to
be a weapon in the war against our aggressors. We dearly hope
this is true." She glanced at the army of men stationed around

her throne, as if checking that she had done right. How must she feel, receiving requests and demands from these much older gentlemen day after day? I felt a brief and bizarre kinship to the queen.

With her permission, I entered a circle of seven polished stones set on the floor. Agrippa came forward as a servant brought me my stave. I'd been forced to leave it with my cloak at the entrance.

The servant moved to a long table laid by the side of the room, took up a silver bowl filled with water, and placed it before me.

"Now is the time of judgment," Whitechurch said, his voice rising over the crowd. "This young woman comes to be commended in our most sacred and ancient arts. We shall see if she is worthy."

Agrippa whispered, "Water first."

With the correct stave movements, I brought the flowing circle up around my body and transformed it, from water to ice, to sleet, to snow, to rain, and then to the three different variations of attack. I delivered them all perfectly.

The queen leaned forward.

I took a large rock, broke it into sand, brought it back together, broke it again into sixteen pieces, arranged and rearranged those pieces into different orders, and then bound the rock into a neat little wall. I created the spinning vortex of flame, flew around the room five times before creating a column of wind to escort me slowly to the floor, and warded Her Majesty's spaniel so that no man could reach him (slightly to Her Majesty's terror). The queen seemed beside herself with delight. Once I'd freed the dog, she cuddled him like a schoolgirl, giving no thought to her regal appearance.

At last, the time had come for the column of fire. This was what the gentlemen and the queen most wanted to see, my singular ability to help defeat the Ancients. With a sweep of my stave I rose into the air, where I went up in a blaze of blue flame. The men gasped. The queen clapped her hands wildly. I unfolded my arms and hung there in pure triumph. With a thought, I brought myself to the ground, extinguished, and curtsied. My breathing was deep and my muscles ached, but I felt glorious.

The crowd went wild with excitement. Even the Imperator smiled, nodding slowly. The queen seemed eager to leap to her feet and applaud, checking about the room to see if anyone would mind. The air hummed with victory. I was a sorcerer. I had done it.

Then, from the back of the room, came a slow, deliberate clap. Palehook pressed forward through the collection of men.

"What an extraordinary talent Miss Howel possesses." He smiled.

"Thank you." I tensed. What was he doing?

"Shame, really. Such a shame." He shook his head.

"What is?"

"That you've lied to all of us."

The room broke out in murmurs. The queen looked confused.

"What are you talking about?" I said, attempting to keep panic out of my voice.

"Explain yourself, Master Palehook," the queen said.

"Our prophecy calls for a female *sorcerer*, Your Majesty, not a female *magician*."

"What?" I cried. God help me, I would not faint. The queen rose from her throne.

"How can she be a magician? She couldn't have been trained. Such a practice was expressly forbidden by my uncle, King George."

The Imperator signaled to Agrippa, his face white with shock. "Sir, explain this insane accusation."

Oh, thank heavens. Agrippa would sort this out. I was almost dizzy with relief.

"Every word is true, Majesty, Imperator," Agrippa said, without looking at me. "Her father was a Welsh solicitor named William Howel, a magician. He also possessed the ability to burn without harm to himself. He passed the talent to his daughter. She is a magician, nothing more."

It sounded as if the shouts and cries and questions around me came from deep underwater. I should have raised my voice along with the rest, but I couldn't breathe. When I called Agrippa's name, he turned his back. That was the gesture that almost broke me.

Keep the pain down, I thought, forcing myself not to wail. *Fight now, hurt later.*

"How can a sorcerer train a magician?" the queen said.

"That is not possible." The Imperator's stunned look turned to anger. "Our approach to magic is entirely separate and impossible to reconcile. You should not have been able to train her," he snapped at Agrippa.

"It was deceit, sir. She let me believe she benefited from my teaching, but she sought out a magician who could help her perfect her abilities in an effort to pass as one of our kind."

Then I understood what was coming. The guards placed along the walls rushed me when I took a step out of the circle. I thought of fighting my way out, but if I got past the men, there were always Agrippa, Whitechurch, and Palehook to deal with. I was trapped.

"Who on earth trained her?" the queen said, her frustration apparent. As if on cue, a door at the far end of the room opened. Two guards entered, and between them, they half dragged a ragged, stumbling man.

"Howard Mickelmas," Agrippa whispered. Men shouted in fear. The queen shrieked. The Imperator stood before Her Majesty, his stave in hand in case a battle broke out.

"You bring that *thing* into our sovereign's presence?" he cried.

"You have nothing to fear from me, Majesty," Mickelmas said. His right eye was swollen, and there was a long, ugly cut on his forehead. "I've come to confess."

"Confess what?" the queen said.

He took a deep breath. "That Mary Willoughby and myself were responsible, solely responsible, for the arrival of the Seven Ancients. That I've hidden for many years when I should have accepted punishment for my crimes. And," he added, looking at me, "that I have trained this young woman to be a servant of darkness. I've trained her to use her powers to fool you, gain commendation, and destroy the royal sorcerers from the inside, all in the service of the Seven Ancients, my true masters, long may they reign in chaos and in blood."

"He's lying!" I screamed, my voice ringing off the walls. The guards caught me. Stretching out my hands to him, I cried, "Master Agrippa, tell these gentlemen the truth."

Agrippa turned away from me again.

"Your true master has confessed, girl," Palehook said. "It's cowardice not to admit your treason."

This worm wanted to lecture me on cowardice?

"Bastard!" I pulled away from the guards and thrust Porridge forward in some vain attempt at a spell. Palehook had his stave, though. He struck me with warded force, and I collapsed. A guard ripped Porridge out of my hands.

"She attacked," someone murmured. Two of the queen's guards seized me and pulled me to my feet. Another guard stood before me, saber in hand.

"If you even think of putting yourself on fire," he said, pointing the saber at my chest, "I will run you through."

Agrippa came out of the crowd. His eyes glinted with tears.

"She is not a sorcerer. I've been training a magician all this time," he said. Shamed, I sought out Mickelmas. He was only standing because the guards held him upright. They'd tortured him into saying this.

"Your Majesty, my lord Imperator, they're all lying to you!" I cried. Everyone in the room regarded me with a cold, unfriendly eye. Five minutes before, they'd been delighted. The shame was unbearable.

"God help her," Agrippa said.

"What I don't understand," the queen said, shaken, "is why you brought two *magicians* before me in such a way. How dare you risk my—*our*—safety."

"Indeed," the Imperator said, his voice icy.

"The fault is mine, Majesty, Imperator." Palehook bowed to both of them. "We only discovered this yesterday. Miss Howel is a cunning creature and had kept herself from detection for so long. Poor Cornelius went along with my suggestion. He could think of nothing else on such short notice."

The queen sighed. "In the future, Master Palehook, you will not raise our hopes before deliberately dashing them. Guards, take Miss Howel down and confine her. We shall decide what's to be done."

26

I WAS TRAPPED IN A WINDOWLESS CARRIAGE. THEY'D
chained me in manacles. Two guards sat across from me. One of
them held Porridge. The other had a hand on the hilt of his saber,
ready to kill me should I make this journey difficult.

"Where are we going?" I asked several times before I gave up.

The carriage took a sharp left and jolted to a halt. They
hauled me out and dragged me across a stone courtyard. Soon
I was led down several flights of steps, all the way to a long corridor of seven sectioned-off cells with iron bars. They set me inside one of the cells, swinging the door shut and locking it. This
was a dank, windowless room, furnished with only a stool and a
meager cot. I rattled my chained wrists, unable to believe any of
it. I wouldn't cry. I refused.

Footsteps and voices sounded down the staircase, and
Agrippa stepped into view. The guard unlocked the door and
allowed him to enter. He stood before me with a mournful expression.

Something almost amusing occurred to me. "Do you remember the last time you came to see me in a cell? You said I

was a sorcerer. You were going to take me to London to see the queen. And look where we ended up. Funny, that."

"Yes," he said. His voice wavered.

"Why?" I didn't cry or beg, I didn't shout. None of that would help me now.

"To save you," he whispered.

"Save me?" I'd felt numb for the entire carriage ride, but now I sensed the first stirrings of anger. "From royal commendation and a place in society, oh yes, you've saved me entirely. Now I'm imprisoned and might be—"

"You will be executed tomorrow. They break your stave at dawn."

Of course this was how it all ended. More than anything else, I felt tired.

"Yes, I'm a magician. But Mickelmas and I had no plan to harm any of you. I didn't even know he was Mickelmas—" I stopped. I couldn't betray Blackwood's secret. "Until recently."

"I believe you," he said.

"Then why did you do this?"

"Because I recognized the signs. I ignored them once, and it ended in disaster."

"I don't understand. Were you planning this from the beginning?"

"No. I thought you were a sorcerer until our lesson yesterday morning." He shook his head. "You lost control of your emotions, and your power almost destroyed us. Only magicians manipulate their abilities in such a way." Apparently

Mickelmas had underestimated how much sorcerers knew of our kind. "After you attacked Julian, I went to speak with Palehook. He'd wanted to speak with me. He'd found Mickelmas and had forced him to talk of knowing you and your father." Of course Palehook had "found" Mickelmas. He'd known where he was all along, no doubt. Had his own men recognized me leaving the magician's home when they had gone to kidnap Rook?

"What signs did you recognize? When?" I leaned forward.

"Gwendolyn. If I'd heeded the signs, she might not be in such a terrible place now."

"You speak as if she were alive."

To my amazement, he said, "She is."

"She died of scarlet fever. Everybody knows."

"Everybody knows as much as I've told them." Agrippa went to the cell door and leaned against the bars, looking into the hall "Gwen was the brightest, most brilliant girl. From the moment of her baptism, I knew she was a miracle. God help me, I indulged her in every possible way. After we found that tapestry, I thought she was the prophesied one.

"But the Ancients called to her. I don't know how or why, but in her the pull was extraordinary. I noticed her short temper, her sullenness, her questing interest in them. From where had they come? Why? What did they want with us? She grew violent and hot-tempered, read every book on the Ancients she could find. She used her powers to damage objects. She hurt people. She complained of terrible dreams."

"Dreams?" I sat up straight. "What kind of dreams?"

"Dreams of fog. That's all she'd tell me," he said. Dreams of fog, indeed. Dreams of a Skinless Man with an offer, more likely. "It got to the point where I had to lock her in her room. Then, one night, she disappeared.

"For an entire week, I feared the worst. I searched every corner of London, until the day she materialized on my doorstep. She looked feverish and strange, and I put her to bed. Later in the night, I heard a noise—I'd been patrolling her hallway, making sure she did not run again—and I entered her room. It was full of a hellish light, and voices whispered in the corners. The language they spoke wasn't human.

"She stood with her back to me, facing the window. The mirror shook; the combs and brushes on her vanity jumped. She turned to me. 'I see now, Daddy,' she told me, holding out her hands. 'Daddy, I can see so well now.'

"She held her eyes in her hands. She'd torn them out. Blood ran down her cheeks like tears, and the laughter." Agrippa paused, cleared his throat, and continued. "At that moment, there came a sound at the window. An enormous black beast, like a stag, pawed to be let in. I fainted. When I woke, the window was open and Gwen had vanished."

That Familiar with the threaded eyes. It couldn't be.

"You think I'm on the same path?" My voice was hoarse. Wasn't I? I had the dreams. I'd used my power against my friends. I was unpredictable. I had felt the temptation to submit to R'hlem. I . . .

I had refused R'hlem's hand. I would never give in to him.

"I don't believe that women should do magic now," Agrippa said, his tone mournful. "Whether witch, sorcerer, or magician, they cannot be trusted to control their abilities. The dark powers call to them too strongly."

"I'm not Gwendolyn." I had made mistakes, but I would never be Gwendolyn.

"Women are ruled by emotion, and when they receive power, they warp themselves to fit it. You can't help yourself. I'm not doing this because I hate you." Tears spilled down his cheeks. "I'm trying to save your soul. I cannot allow such a terrible thing to happen to another girl I love." Love? My throat tightened, my eyes burned. He didn't love me if he wanted to kill me. "I would rather that you died tomorrow, innocent and pure, than be called into the service of the Ancients."

"Do the others know?" I couldn't bear to think of Blackwood smiling at me as he led me off the dance floor to my death.

He shook his head. "They think you've been escorted elsewhere for the evening. When it's over tomorrow, I'll tell them."

"And what of Rook?" I clenched my jaw.

"Rook will be fine. I'll see to it." But I trembled to think of what might happen to him once his own abilities were discovered. Agrippa tried to take my hands. "Henrietta, I know you can't understand now, but one day—"

"One day when I am dead?"

"When you are in God's own kingdom, safe and secure, you will thank me."

A thought occurred. "Last night when you cried by the fire and said it will be so hard to let me go, you meant to my death. Didn't you? I thought, stupidly, that you would miss having me in your home."

"From the moment I met you at Brimthorn, I felt so much affection for you. You're as dear to me now as any child of my own flesh." He took my face into his hands and wiped tears from my eyes that I didn't know had appeared.

"Don't let them kill me," I whispered.

He visibly struggled with himself. "One day you'll under-stand."

"I never will." I pulled back, stifling a sob. "Get out. I can't talk to you anymore."

"Listen to me—"

There was commotion upstairs. We jumped at the echoed sounds of shouting through the corridors, of running to and fro. Cursing, the guard unlocked the door and let Agrippa out.

"What's happening?" I said.

"Hush up," the guard snapped as he locked the door. He spoke with Agrippa as they moved for the stairs. Agrippa looked back one last time and vanished. I listened to the shouts and shrieks, running, and what sounded like pots and pans clattering to the floor. Mystified, I clutched the bars and waited. Twenty minutes later, my guard returned. He mopped the sweat from his brow and took up his post again.

"What was it?" I said.

"Why don't you be quiet like a good girl. It's nothing that concerns you."

THEY HAD PORRIDGE, AND WITHOUT IT I was lost. I twisted my wrists about in the manacles over and over again, but there was no way I could work a hand free.

"You all right, miss? I mean, you don't need water or nothing?" the guard said, peering at me through the bars as though I were some exotic animal on display. My golden ball gown was perhaps not the normal prison fashion. He smiled as he looked at me in my cage. Something about the expression on his face struck me as being overly friendly.

"No water, thank you."

"You're polite. Poor little thing." He was a young blond man with a bit of a second chin. He leaned against the bars. "You know, they got different ways of treatin' sorcerers and magicians. Sorcerers, they take the stave and chain 'em, and that's that. With magicians, they chain the neck to the feet, so that they can't stand up, and chain the hands behind the back. Gag 'em, too, so they can't speak. Back in the old days, they'd even cut out the tongue. Master Agrippa ordered you was to be treated like a sorcerer. Very good of him."

"Yes." I tried to conceal my revulsion. Why was he looking at me in so familiar a way? "Can you tell me where I am?"

"The Tower of London. This is the magic wing. They built these cells for troublesome magic users hundreds of years ago."

Another guard in uniform came down the stairs. "It's my turn," said a young man with a rough voice.

"No it ain't. She's mine for the night. They already told me," my guard said, sounding annoyed. "Go on."

"You're due for a break."

"Come back in an hour. I'm busy." After some more hushed words, he sent the young man back up the stairs. The blond guard leaned against the bars. He smiled at me. "You got nothin' to worry about from me," he said. "Them others might mistreat you, bein' a dangerous magician and all. I won't hurt you."

"Thank you," I muttered. His gaze was unsettling.

"Lockin' up a pretty little thing like you." He sighed. "What's the world comin' to?"

I turned to the wall, considering. He thought I was only a weak, pretty little girl. What had Magnus said about acting? Show them what they want to see, and they'll believe anything.

Concentrating, I set fire to the bottom of my gown and screamed. The guard threw open the door and helped me beat the flames out. Much to my distaste, I pretended to faint.

"Careful!" the guard said, catching me as I collapsed. He touched my cheek. "Poor, scared little thing, ain't ya?"

"My powers are so temperamental," I whimpered.

"How could they harm a sweet little thing like you?" he said, sounding cross. I gave a weary sigh. He lifted me up in his arms, set me down on my cot, and left. I forced myself to lie there for ten minutes, waiting for the right opportunity. "They taught you all this fancy magic stuff?" the guard said, returning to the door.

"Yes. I can't control my power." I sat up, shyly playing with a tendril of my hair. "It got so bad they had to teach me to give somebody else temporary access to my abilities."

"Why would they do that?"

"In case I burst into flame and couldn't put myself out. It was helpful to have a man who could take control."

"Why would you give a sorcerer your power? Don't they have their own?"

"No, this transferred my power to a normal person. The best magic to help me is my own. Anyone could do it, and the footmen in Master Agrippa's house helped me practice. It was great fun for them, to be allowed to have a sorcerer's powers even for a short time." He mercifully took the bait.

"How would I receive your powers?" He said it casually, but his look was interested.

"Simple. You need to fetch my stave."

He paused, then shuffled off and retrieved Porridge from somewhere out of sight. Good.

"Take some blood from me and rub it on your bottom lip."

"That's disgustin'."

"I know, but it's the only way."

He opened the door while I sat there, chained and ever so proper. Winking, he rubbed his thumb across my cut lip, the result of Palehook's attack. I forced myself not to shudder when he lingered. He painted the blood onto his own mouth.

"Now?"

"I confer the power upon you." I touched my thumb to my

- 341 -

blood and traced the image of a five-point star on his forehead. "Let's see if it worked. Take the stave, place it to the ground, and say its name: Porridge."

He did, and Porridge glowed blue. I gave as much of a girlish clap as I could, wearing those manacles. I knew that men loved being praised beyond life itself. Indeed, the guard looked as if he'd been appointed prime minister. "That it? I can use your power?"

"Absolutely. There's one more thing you need to do to have complete control. Hold the end toward yourself—that's right—and now twist it in your hands two times to the left." I kept my breathing steady. If he heard the slightest waver, the barest hint of excitement . . .

"Why?" Did he sound suspicious? Was that my imagination?

"Because it conveys my power to you. Imagine that the power is rushing out of the stave to meet you." I kept my hands in my lap and a smile on my face. I was the image of sweetness.

Pleased, he did as I'd asked. Warded force struck him in the face and chest, and he collapsed to the floor. A quick examination showed me he was still breathing. Relieved, I took up Porridge and got to work on my manacles. I adjusted Mickelmas's teapot-to-rodent spell, and within seconds had transformed the shackles into white mice. They scampered down my dress and raced across the cell floor. I was free. Stepping over the fallen guard, I took his key ring and was in the process of locking him in the cell when I heard footsteps coming down the stairs.

"Enough, Joe. It really is your break," the young guard said as he returned, and stopped dead. "What the blazes—"

"Stay back!" I cried, thrusting Porridge at him. The guard took off his hat and stepped out of the shadows, revealing a familiar shock of auburn hair. "Magnus? What in God's name are you doing here?"

"Saving you. How the devil did you get free? And knock out the guard?" Eyes wide, he took the keys from me and locked the door. Voices shouted and echoed above us. There was the sound of many feet running in unison down the stairs. He winced. "Smollett and Fisher must've spoken to each other and realized I shouldn't be here. Come on!" He took my wrist and led me down the long corridor of cells.

"How did you know where I was?" I couldn't believe it.

"That's something we really should discuss when we're not running for our lives," he said, looking up and down at the rows of cells and counting on his fingers. Now the guards spilled into the corridor from the stairwell. "Would you care to unlock number six?" he said, handing me the keys. "I'll distract them."

Magnus strode back down the hall. With an expert move, he slammed his stave into the floor. The stones beneath the men's feet turned into soft mounds of sand, and the guards fell on their faces. With another movement, Magnus created a blast of wind that rocked the corridor, coughing up a cloud of dust that blinded the men.

I found the key and opened the door. We ran inside, locking it after ourselves.

"I just escaped from one cell, you've put me in another one?" I said, bewildered.

"Try to have some faith," he muttered, looking around.

"It was a brilliant escape!"

"Hush!" He started touching the walls, the bars, a puzzled look on his face.

"What?"

"There's something we can use to flee."

Frustrated, I searched the cell for a trapdoor, only to discover a circle of carvings. They looked amazingly odd, like squiggles and backward letters. "A porter's circle!"

"Yes, that. Get us out of here. As the resident magician, you'll have to figure it out."

"You know?" I felt naked before him. Yet Magnus had still attempted a rescue, knowing full well what I was.

"Never mind that now. Get us out of here." He pushed me into the circle, and as the guards came, he blasted them with a shock of energy, mangling the door in the process.

I knew what to do, but there was room for only one. "Magnus, how will we both fit?"

"Don't worry about me. I'm doing splendidly." He called the moisture from the stones in the ceiling and drooled brackish water onto the men below.

"I won't leave you here."

"Stop the heroics and go, Howel," he snapped. Well, that decided it for me. I leaped onto his back, wrapping my legs and arms about him as best I could in my gown. Magnus teetered backward into the circle.

"Let's ask it nicely to take us home," I said.

As the now-soaked guards pulled the cell door down, the image of the house in Hyde Park Corner sprang into my mind. The world disappeared, and we fell into blackness.

"THAT WAS A STRANGE SENSATION," MAGNUS grunted as we tried to reorient ourselves. He took a few steps forward and stopped. "Howel, you're a lovely girl and not terribly heavy, but I think we'll make better time if you get off my back." He set me down. We'd landed in a wooded area, the mud squishing beneath our feet. "It's Hyde Park. Never mind, I know where we are. Follow to the right, we'll make the rendezvous in five minutes." We set off through the trees.

"Rendezvous? The others know?"

"Every one of them." And apparently none of them cared. The relief was sweet. We walked for a bit, and then he stopped. "Howel, are you all right? They didn't hurt you, did they?" He touched my chin, studying my cut lip. "Because if they did, I can always turn around and go back. Stuff them into a kettle and make tea, see how they like it." He tried to keep his tone light, but I heard the anger underneath. I stood on tiptoe and kissed his cheek, without thinking. He touched his face in surprise.

"Thank you for coming to help me," I said.

"We had to. You're one of us. The boys would do the same for me, after all."

One of us. The thought made me smile. "So would I."

"Well, then the rescue would be guaranteed to go well. Er, Howel?" Even in the moonlight, I could see he was blushing.

"What I said in the stables, about you being awful for wanting to be kissed? I didn't mean it. Really, you can kiss anybody you like. You can kiss the whole lot of us. Good old Dee could use a kiss, really. Kisses. Wonderful things. I'm babbling. I'm sorry for what happened."

"You snuck into the bloody tower to save me. That wipes your debt away. There's no need to apologize."

"Then I take it all back."

I gave him a playful shove and we moved ahead. I bunched my skirt in one hand, a bit sad, even now, to think of the gold back trailing away in the muddy ground. Eliza had been so proud of it. "What will they do when they find out you helped me?"

"What matters is you'll be safe and far away from here by then."

I hooked my arm through his. "You're a true friend."

His face lit up. "I am your friend, aren't I?"

"Of course." I squealed as he picked me up in his arms and carried me.

"To hell with this. I won't have you sully your dress on the ground."

"I can walk. Please put me down." I laughed. He did, reluctantly.

Within a moment we saw the house ahead of us, lit like a beacon in the night. The boys stood at the park's edge, all newly commended and wearing the black silk sorcerers' cloaks. Snatching up my skirts, I ran for them. We were reunited within moments. Dee caught me up in a tearful hug. Wolff and Lambe patted my back.

"Come," Blackwood said, looking about. "We have to move quickly. Before they—"

There was a great booming noise. The ground trembled, and overhead there came a piercing scream. Black shapes skirted the top of the dome. The Familiars had arrived, dozens of them, maybe even a hundred.

The bells began to toll. "He's come back," Blackwood whispered. "And he's brought an army."

Korozoth had made my escape far more difficult.

27

WE RAN DOWN THE STEPS TO THE SERVANTS' EN-
trance, seeing no one as we moved through the kitchen and
toward the stairs. We had to find Rook. Blackwood and I ran to
the attic.

Rook's door was unlocked and open. Inside, we found the
bed had been flipped, the pillow torn. These were signs of struggle, and Rook was nowhere to be seen.

"Where is he?" I said. My voice sounded small.

"Howel!" Dee thundered up the stairs, the floorboards trembling as he arrived in the corridor. "Lilly's in your room. She's
crying."

We found Lilly curled up in a corner, her cheeks marked
with tears. She burst into fresh sobbing when she saw me.

"What happened?" I said.

"It's R-Rook. Th-they snatched him." She couldn't get
enough breath.

"Who?"

"Master Palehook and his young gentlemen. Master Agrippa
let 'em in about an hour ago—"

"Master Agrippa's here?" I said, my blood running cold. I'd hoped he'd still be at the ball.

"Yes. Soon after he came home the men arrived. He let 'em in and they went up to the servants' rooms. Master Palehook waited in the hall while his men went inside the room. Rook fought them off. I tried to help, but it all got so strange. The room went dark. They were screaming, like they couldn't get out of it. Then Master Palehook put a knife to me." She began to sob, her chest heaving. "Said he'd kill me if Rook didn't go with them. The darkness vanished, and then they knocked him sense-less and took him away. I wanted to help, but they were rough with me." She covered her face with her small hand. Her wrist bore a patterned bruise, like finger marks.

"Where were they going?" My head was buzzing.

"I don't know," she wailed.

"Where's Agrippa?" God, I would make him sorry for this.

"In the library, I think."

Dee helped Lilly off the floor and set her in a chair while the rest of us stormed downstairs. I entered the room first. We found Agrippa slumped in a chair before his fire, lost in thought. When he saw me, he leaped to his feet. We all five stood together in a half circle, blocking his exit. I pointed Porridge at his chest.

"What have you done with Rook?" I struggled to keep from shouting.

"What in God's name are you doing here?" He didn't seem angry so much as bewildered. "What is all this?"

"I ought to knock you straight into your own fireplace," Magnus growled. He stood beside me.

"You don't know what she is."

"A magician?" Wolff scoffed. "You think we care about that?"

"She's one of us," Lambe said. He and Wolff went to Agrippa's other side; we were all circling him now.

"Where is Rook?" I shouted.

"He told me it was the only way," Agrippa muttered, the expression on his face torn between grief and terror.

"What does Palehook want with him?" Blackwood said.

Agrippa collapsed into his armchair. "I don't know."

"You must have some idea," I said.

"I was trying to remedy my mistakes. Was that such a terrible crime?"

"It is if it harms the innocent," Blackwood said.

"I'm trying to keep her innocent! That's what's most important!" Agrippa looked like a caged animal. The doors boomed open, and Dee strode into the library, the tips of his ears flushed pink. We all scattered before him. He loomed over Agrippa, who shrank further into his seat.

"Did you let them hurt Lilly?" Dee's face turned crimson. I'd never seen him this angry.

Agrippa winced, his shame evident. Dee balled his fist and walloped Agrippa across the jaw, knocking the man over the arm of his chair. Lambe instinctively moved to tend to our Master, but Wolff held him back.

"Where have they taken him?" I said, tucking Porridge

just beneath Agrippa's chin. He brought his hand to the already swelling right side of his face.

"I have no idea."

"We trusted you," I said.

Agrippa closed his eyes. "I wanted you to trust me. I never dreamed any of this might happen."

The sincerity of his tone nearly undid me. "This *has* happened. Now help us find him."

The library doors opened and the butler entered, holding a letter. He didn't seem to notice anything amiss as he threaded his way through one bewildered, heartbroken boy after another, nor did he seem to observe that I was in the act of threatening the master of the house. He approached Agrippa's chair.

"This just came for you," he said. Agrippa reached for the letter, but the butler handed it to me and left.

"What is it?" I said, bewildered. The envelope bore my name, and nothing else. Agrippa moved, and I pointed my stave at him again. "I won't let you up until you help me," I snapped.

"How am I supposed to tell you what I don't know myself?"

"God save us, if he's hurt, I'll—"

"Er, Howel, maybe you should read your letter," Magnus said. He reached over to take the envelope.

"In a minute. Don't move!" I cried as Agrippa again tried to rise.

"It's rude not to read a letter addressed to you. Here, I'll open it."

"Well, it's my letter, isn't it?" I clutched it to my chest.

"Just open the letter," Blackwood said, struggling with a sense of urgency.

"Why is everyone so bloody interested in my letter?" I cried, half crumpling the thing in my fist. All the boys responded with gasps and pained expressions. Wolff pulled at his hair, and Lambe reached as if to snatch it from my hands. Mystified, I tore open the envelope. "This had better be something miraculous."

I screamed as Mickelmas exploded out like a malicious jack-in-the-box. He rolled across the floor, sprang up, and hobbled close to the fire. Groaning, he rubbed his back and straightened his legs, composing a symphony of cracks and pops as he did so.

"Oh, my poor bones. Poor back. And you," he said, whirling to face me. "The next time you get a letter, *open it*! Were you raised in a barn, you uncivilized snipe? It's rude!" I cried out in joy and hugged him, which softened his anger. "Well then, there's a good apprentice," he said, patting my back. "I forgot how compressed one feels traveling by post."

"That is ever so much better than coming through the front door," Magnus said, watching our reunion with an amused expression.

"*You.*" Mickelmas noticed Agrippa and walked toward the sorcerer. "I want my cloak and I want my chest, and I want them now."

"I don't have them." Agrippa stood and backed behind the chair.

"Come, a magician's rune cloak and an enchanted box? Those are priceless artifacts for a collector. This room holds books and paintings and tapestries enough to put the National Gallery to shame. Now, give me my things."

"Palehook took them when he came to collect the boy."

"Have you hidden them in the servants' quarters? Shall we turn each room upside down in a merry investigation?" With a few muttered words, Mickelmas exploded the armchair in splintering wood and fluff. Agrippa stumbled aside.

"I tell you, Palehook has them!"

"Mr. Hargrove. I mean, Mr. Mickelmas," I said, gripping his arm. "They kidnapped Rook. If you help us get him back, we can find your things."

"How on earth did you escape?" Agrippa said, staring at the magician with horror.

"That tower is not exactly a challenge for one as skilled as I, particularly when the guards are tired or drunk. In this case, they were both. The thrill of the chase injected some excitement into their otherwise excruciatingly dull lives. Sadly for them, I was uncatchable." He studied his fingernails with smug satisfaction.

So that had been the shouting and running I'd heard.

"I wanted to swoop in and rescue Miss Howel," he continued, "but without a runic cloak, my methods of transportation were limited. Fortunately, your young charges," he said, bowing to the boys, "are far more open-minded than I'd come to believe sorcerers could be."

And this explained how the boys knew what I was.

"You remembered the porter's circle," I said.

"And told your young friends, who sent a disguised Mr. Magnus in to save you, which I thought brave and ridiculous."

"Well, I'm wonderful like that," said Magnus.

"Just so we're clear as to what happened," Mickelmas said to me, "Palehook rounded up my children. He told me that if I didn't give myself up and say those horrid things at the commendation ball, he'd kill the whole lot of the little darlings. I wasn't about to see my charges murdered. Do you understand?"

"Of course."

"Now, my cherub, let's move on to more important things. My cloak and box and, yes, your young friend Rook. How are they to be rescued from the vile Palehook?" He tugged at his beard and scanned the crowd of young men. He caught sight of Blackwood and bowed. The young sorcerer nodded in return but looked uneasy.

"Why did they take Rook?" I said.

"My Lord Blackwood," Mickelmas said, moving toward the boy, "your father was not a nice man."

"I'm aware of that," Blackwood said, and we both held our breath. Mickelmas couldn't reveal his secret here.

"Many years ago, when the war was young, Palehook was charged with discovering a way to create a ward to protect London from attacks. Everything he did failed, and Charles Blackwood, well—" I shook my head, begging him to be discreet. "He knew of my reputation. He knew I couldn't afford to be handed over to the Order, and so he captured me and forced me to help devise a system. Palehook made me do the most unspeakable things, reach across the farthest boundaries of the spirit world to find an answer."

"But you found a way to do it," Wolff said. As the warding expert, this had to intrigue him.

"Oh yes. Purely by chance, we discovered the only force strong enough to protect the city. The Unclean."

"How?" I said.

"There is a spell, a powerful and very black spell, that allows a magic user to drain a person's life force, and use that power to increase their own. We tried draining the souls, for lack of a better word, of many people without success. We hunted the gutters, the poorhouses, searching for the lowest citizens to sacrifice. We left them lying in the alleys, certain the great machinery of London would swallow them whole." Mickelmas stopped for a moment, struggling with the pain of the memories. "No matter how many we killed, there was not enough power. And then one night, while wandering along the river, we came across an Unclean man begging for food and drink. He'd been touched by Molochoron—it was obvious; his skin was bloated and rotted, beginning to fall off his bones—"

"I don't think we need any descriptions," Wolff said, wincing.

"Palehook was the one who came up with the idea of using his soul. Why not? He was better off dead anyway. When the Unclean were murdered and their souls sucked dry, that was the only force powerful enough to allow Palehook to create the ward he needed. Something to do with the strength of the Ancients, I shouldn't wonder. Funny that their poison should prove the most effective block against them."

I remembered the Unclean man I had seen sitting outside Mickelmas's flat, and how he'd disappeared. "They're going to steal Rook's soul to fortify the city?" I recalled how flimsy the ward had seemed recently, how paper-thin and rotten. Palehook had been running out of support.

"Yes. Charles Blackwood's colony in Brighton provided ready victims. He knew they would need a steady supply to refresh the ward from time to time. Wonderful man, really." Blackwood turned to the fireplace, looking ill. "Rook's strength must have made him a tempting morsel."

"Where are they now?" I said, tightening my grip on Porridge.

"There will have to be some obsidian present, but it won't be in an obsidian room. Black arts strip the power from a holy place. I haven't worked with him in over ten years, so I don't know where he's been going." He spoke to Blackwood as he moved toward the fireplace. Lambe touched my arm.

"I can help," he whispered, his pale eyes shining with a hazy light. "I need something precious to Rook to make a connection, but I could see where he is."

"Oh, Lambe, could you? We should go to his room and look for something to use." I'd no idea what, of course. They'd destroyed everything.

"It needs to be precious to him. If you don't mind, Howel,

I have to do this." He gripped my hand in both of his, bowed his head, and closed his eyes. I flushed, but before I could object, something tugged at the edge of my consciousness. It felt as though I were falling backward.

Rook lay on something cold, shivering, with his hands bound on his stomach. He was disoriented, almost sick. They had given him something. A black gate was to his left, separating him from the rest of the crypt. Palehook smiled, lighting candles while he spoke to someone. They'd tied rosemary in the ropes around Rook's wrists, and Palehook dipped his thumb into a small bowl and touched Rook on the forehead. It was cold, and when some of the liquid dripped onto Rook's stomach, he saw that it was blood.

"Where is the moon? I tell you, if I can't perform it quickly, the split will occur—"

Lambe released me. We sank to the floor, and the others hovered around us.

"Howel, are you hurt?" Magnus said, helping me to my feet.

"I know where they are," I said. Lambe lay back in Wolff's arms. Wolff stroked the boy's pale hair with a surprising amount of affection.

"Where?" Magnus said.

Lambe raised his hand like we were in the schoolroom. "St. Paul's Cathedral, on Christopher Wren's grave."

"Perfect." Mickelmas looked surprised. "Why didn't I think of it? It's an obsidian slab in the center of town and underneath a dome, which gives the energy something to mold itself after. Well done, my dear boy. Finally, a sorcerer with a useful power."

He clapped Lambe on the shoulder. "We've one advantage. The moon's hidden behind the clouds, probably because of Korozoth. They can't kill Rook until the sky is clear, or the power won't take. So to save your boy, we must fly. It may not be too late."

Agrippa stepped forward. He'd been so silent I'd nearly forgotten he was present. "If you do this," he cried as the boys ran from the room, "the ward may snap. Korozoth could destroy us all."

"I might as well add," Mickelmas said, "that Palehook can easily ward the entire city. He's chosen not to in order to provide his sacrificial slab with victims." At this, Agrippa sank to his knees, all his power to persuade gone.

"Thank you," I said to Agrippa as Mickelmas followed the boys out the door.

"For what?"

"I believed that sorcerers were England's great hope against her enemies. I believed that you were better and kinder than other men." There was no emotion in my voice. I was beyond feeling. "Thank you for teaching me not to believe in anything."

I turned my back on him and went to rescue Rook.

28

WE DROPPED OUT OF THE SKY BEFORE THE STEPS TO St. Paul's. The enormous entrance was, of course, locked.

"Damn," Magnus said as the moon appeared from behind the clouds. Above us, dark shapes skimmed the dome, leaving bright yellow streaks.

"What are they doing?" Wolff said, turning in a circle as he watched them.

"The ward is thin, my young friends. They're looking for a way in, but they won't find one yet." Mickelmas cleared his throat.

"What is it?" I asked.

"Agrippa had a point. You realize that if we save Rook, the ward will likely fall. If you do this, you could be executed for treason." Murmurs passed among the boys. They hadn't considered that.

"I don't care," I said.

"Of course not. You're attached to the boy. For my part, I'm willing to do it as a way of atonement. But the young gentlemen must understand." He turned to them. "This isn't a game. Are you prepared for what you may unleash tonight?"

The boys looked at each other, wide-eyed. Even knowing what Agrippa had said, they'd not thought about this in their zeal to help Rook. Truth be told, I hadn't really thought it through myself. The idea of all those creatures descending on the people asleep in their beds left me cold.

Blackwood broke the silence. "The outside's lain vulnerable for years. People have been murdered." He caught my eye and nodded. "No one innocent life is worth more than another. Ever." We all murmured our agreement. Every one of us felt the weight of the moment on our backs.

Magnus blasted the wooden door, which opened with a splintering crack. We raced down the echoing nave toward the crypt. I slowed to run alongside a wheezing Mickelmas.

"Are you all right?"

"I'm not in the great condition I once was. Come to think of it, I was never in the great condition I once was."

"Thank you for coming back for me."

"I had to. It was the only way to find my cloak and chest."

"Oh."

"I suppose I didn't want you to die, either. There's something I still must tell you about—"

Blackwood hushed us as we entered the crypt and paced between the pillars. Voices rose and fell ahead of us. We found them by Christopher Wren's tomb.

Four boys, all wearing their new sorcerers' robes, stood guard outside the gate. Hemphill was among them. They had their staves out, prepared to defend what was going on within.

Inside the tomb, Palehook stood before Rook, who lay bound and gagged on the obsidian slab. He convulsed while Palehook murmured, *"The moon rounds in her virgin glow, the blood is on the stone, both separate the body's soul from body's flesh and bone."* A white mist rose out of Rook and hovered in the air. He arched his back, caught in a torturous fit as the mist grew. Palehook leaned forward, a gleeful smile on his face.

"His life force," Mickelmas whispered.

"Stop!" I ran forward.

Hemphill whistled softly as I entered the room, my friends at my back. "They're here, Master. First visitors we've ever had." The guards laughed.

Palehook snarled and leaned over Rook, like a perverted version of a mother protecting her child. "Keep them away. They have no idea what has to happen tonight."

"Let Rook go." I understood what I had seen. Palehook had used words in his magic. "You can perform magician's work. You're like me, aren't you? A hybrid."

Palehook's face twisted in fury. "I'm nothing like you, girl," he growled, every word soaked in self-loathing. "I'd only pollute myself with magician trickery to save this city. Do you want to sacrifice the whole of London to save your worthless little friend?"

"You mean the chosen parts of London," I said.

"My wife and children live in those chosen parts. If you think I'll let you open them up to slaughter, you're mistaken. Stay back," he said as I took a step forward. At Palehook's command, the four guards readied themselves for an attack. "You've received commendation, haven't you? You can't kill a fellow sorcerer now, not unless you want to join him in death."

Palehook was right. Behind me, the boys whispered to each other. They sounded concerned.

"I'm not commended," I said, refusing to back away.

"Nor I. I'm not even a sorcerer." Mickelmas moved out of the shadows. Palehook shrank back. "Hello, Augustus. You've only gotten balder and uglier over the years. It suits you." Palehook muttered something I couldn't make out. Mickelmas laughed. "Speak up, old fellow. Granted, you must be tired. Black magic does rather deplete one's energy." Mickelmas rubbed his hands together and, with a flick of his wrist, sent a ball of white light sailing at the tomb.

But none of us anticipated how fast Palehook could be. With a swift movement of his stave, he bent one of the iron bars and severed it, sending the pointed tip through the ball of light and directly into Mickelmas's side.

"Damn, damn!" Mickelmas fell, his blood pooling on the floor. He waved off the boys' attempts to help.

Palehook turned to the mist hovering over Rook and inhaled deeply, smacking his lips like some grotesque vampire. His skin glowed as he took more and more.

"Come on, then," Hemphill called as I frantically sought a way to the gate. "If you're not commended, Miss Howel, then nothing can stop my putting a blade through your heart. I missed the last time, but I won't tonight."

Magnus roared and slammed his stave to the floor. The ground shook, throwing our opponents off balance. The battle had begun.

Around me, the sorcerers dueled furiously. They summoned winds that whipped along the corridor, and the bricks beneath our feet rattled and bucked. Lambe and Wolff ran side by side, their wards activated, and smashed into one of the guards. Blackwood collected the fire from a torch and exploded it in someone's face. Dee pulled stones out of the floor and threw them. Magnus, teeth bared, dueled Hemphill with warded blades.

There was a path open to the tomb.

I took the opportunity and ran, setting myself on fire to keep the guards away. Palehook slammed the door in my face, but I blasted it open and entered, the blue flames rising around me as I reached for him.

"Get out!" He struck me with wind. A tendril of Rook's life curled out of his open mouth like smoke.

Rook lay motionless on the stone. He looked terrifyingly flat. Please, God, I couldn't be too late.

"Get away from him." I struggled to keep my fire from touching Rook. Palehook leaned against the wall, beads of sweat dotting his forehead. He really had weakened, and I used it to my advantage. When he tried to move in any direction, I was there. His only way out was through fire.

"Stop!" he cried. But he was afraid; I could see it.

"If you yield, throw down your weapon."

Palehook was still a moment, deciding. Then, slowly, he

dropped his stave. It clattered to the floor, and he put his hands up. I stopped burning, created a warded blade, and held it to his throat. Palehook kept his chin up. He swallowed, wincing as the blade cut him slightly.

Behind me, the fighting ceased. Glancing quickly over my shoulder, I saw that both sides had paused, watching us, waiting to see who would win.

"Don't be foolish," Palehook said. Life force puffed from his lips with each word he spoke. "Think of what you're doing. You're condemning all of London to death."

I cut him along the cheek. He hissed in pain. "Release what you stole from Rook," I said.

"Let me finish, and I'll convince Her Majesty I was wrong about you." Even defeated, he still tried to manipulate me. "You'll be a sorcerer. You'll have everything you ever wanted."

"I want Rook." I slashed his other cheek, deeper than before. This time, he howled.

"You'll be the death of us all!" Blood ran down both sides of his face, like tears.

"Do you want to die?" I didn't know if I had the heart to murder a defenseless man, even if that man was Palehook, but my threat did the trick. Glancing at my blade, Palehook shook his head. Slowly, he moved over to Rook. He gave a few huffs of breath, and the vapor spilled out of him. He guided it so that it descended back into Rook's body. Rook didn't move.

No. It couldn't be.

"Wake up," I cried, shaking him.

"Howel!" Magnus yelled.

I shouldn't have taken my eyes off Palehook. Stave in hand, he slashed at me. In my hurry to get out of the way, I slipped and dropped Porridge. With that, Palehook prepared for a killing blow.

The tomb's shadows pulled him into their depths. Rook had raised himself up onto one elbow. He slowly brought his extended hand into a fist. Palehook screamed as the blackness bubbled and began to spread. It might take over the entire tomb, drawing us all in. I grabbed Porridge and braced myself for an attack on the encroaching gloom.

And then it stopped.

"Are you hurt?" Rook whispered. He gazed at me with concern. His eyes were black but not wicked. The power was not in control this time; *he* was.

"No," I gasped.

Palehook started screaming inside the darkness, screaming fit to wake the dead. To my right, there was a stampede as his followers bolted out of the crypt, dragging Hemphill with them. It was all too much for them. That was the loyalty Palehook deserved.

My friends came over to the gate to peer in at Rook. They all looked afraid.

"Never seen anything like it," Dee murmured.

"Let him out." Blackwood winced. Palehook's screams were growing more ragged and insane. "You can't leave him there."

With a sigh, Rook closed his eyes and collapsed on the stone.

The shadows dissipated, revealing Palehook, swatting wildly at the air. He shrieked before realizing that he was out of the darkness. Stumbling twice, he got to his feet. His breathing was erratic.

"Do you yield?" I asked. But Palehook was staring at Rook.

"The darkness is alive," he muttered, shaking his head. "It speaks to you. It tells you the most horrific things."

Magnus made a sound of recognition. But he otherwise kept silent.

"Do you yield?" I said again, growing increasingly nervous. Palehook's eyes flickered to me. He grew eerily calm.

"He's a monster," he whispered. "He must be destroyed."

"Yield now, or I'll—"

Palehook whipped his stave, knocking me aside with a sudden blast of wind. My head struck the floor, and the world spun. There was no time to stop the sorcerer as he raised his blade, aiming for Rook.

Something sliced through the gate and into Palehook, knocking him against the wall and to the floor. He didn't get up. Slowly, my head still ringing, I crawled over to him. He was dead, an iron spike lodged deep inside his neck. Blood spurted from the wound as his sightless eyes gazed at the ceiling. Through the gate, I saw Mickelmas propped up on his elbows, his arm still outstretched from sending the spike. He nodded.

"What," he gasped, "the bloody hell was that shadow business?" He collapsed.

Rook coughed. I forgot everything else and went to touch his face, smooth his hair. He smiled.

"You came," he said.

"I couldn't do otherwise." I laid my head on his chest to listen to his heartbeat. "You took control."

"I had something to protect," he whispered. His voice was not strong, his breathing thin. Damn. I helped him sit up, and we faced our audience. The boys regarded us blankly. Oh God.

They all knew.

"Is it," Lambe said, patting his chest by way of illustration, "because of the scars?"

"Yes," Rook said. His voice was so weak.

"The Order must be told," Blackwood said. Trembling, I clutched Rook against me. He was dodging in and out of consciousness.

"He's been getting better. He controlled the darkness this time," I said.

"How often has this happened?" Dee asked. Magnus caught my eye and shook his head. He wouldn't tell them.

"Not often," I said. My voice was shaking. "He's going to master it. They'll kill him. Please." I buried my face in Rook's hair. "Say nothing. It's the greatest favor I'll ever ask."

If Rook lives. If any of us survives the night.

No one moved or spoke until Magnus stepped into the tomb with me. He saw what this meant to me, what Rook meant to me. His nostrils flared, and he drew his stave. He was going to finish what Palehook had started.

"No," I gasped, but Magnus nodded and presented his stave. A sorcerer's bow.

"I swear to keep it secret." He motioned to the others. One by one, they bowed in agreement. Blackwood was the last one. He pressed his mouth in a thin line, but he finally nodded as well.

"For your sake," he said.

I could have cried in relief.

There was a great boom. For a moment it seemed as if everywhere was illuminated with hot white light. My ears popped. When the light cleared, there was an instant of silence, which gave way to shouting in the streets outside. "What happened?" I said, pressing a hand to my ear.

"The ward has fallen." Blackwood sounded grim as he looked to the ceiling. "We have to go. Korozoth will be heading for the heart of the city."

Feeling sick, I helped Rook off the obsidian slab. As he left it, the slab trembled and, with a great splitting crack, broke in half down the middle.

"Huh," Lambe said, smiling. "It did break."

"What?" Wolff said. His confusion gave way to delight. "Oh! The slab."

"I suppose I'll be staying in London," Lambe said. He ran with Wolff, Blackwood, and Dee up the stairs. Magnus helped Rook stay on his feet while I knelt beside Mickelmas.

"There's nothing we can do for him," Magnus said. "Howel, we have to get you away from here."

I grasped the magician's cold hand. His dark skin had taken on a sallow, grayish hue, and sweat beaded at his temples.

"We need to get you to a doctor," I said.

"Now? That's impossible, silly creature. Besides, Palehook is dead. That's enough for me." He shivered. "God, I'm cold."

"They wrapped me in a blanket to keep me from struggling," Rook murmured. He moved to get it but fell back to his knees. Magnus set him down gently and ran to the tomb. He returned with something crumpled in a ball. I unfurled it and wrapped it about Mickelmas. It was garish, red and orange and purple—

"Your cloak!"

Mickelmas buried himself in the thing. "That's one accounted for, at least." He slid his arms into the sleeves and wrapped himself up tight. "Time to seek out a safe place for healing." He was silent for a moment and then nodded. "It'll take a tick, what with my weakened state. Oh, blast!" He grabbed me. "There's the thing I wanted to tell you. No time, no time, I'm such a fool."

"What?"

He pulled me down closer to him. "Your father didn't drown."

"Excuse me?" I gripped him by the front of his coat. "Say that again."

"Listen to me. He didn't drown. He—" Mickelmas disappeared. I was left holding the empty air, stunned.

"What?" I whispered. My father hadn't drowned? Was he alive? Imprisoned? Had he been executed for murder or anything else that would force my aunt to lie to me? What was so important about it that Mickelmas needed to mention it right now? *What on earth did it mean?*

"Does he think that was fair?" Magnus said, astonished. His voice brought me out of my stupor.

"We can't think of that now." This wasn't the time for distraction.

"Howel, you must want to know."

"I'll see Mickelmas again, and he'll explain. Right now, we have to run." I forced myself up, feeling half mad. Together we raced up the stairs and through the cathedral. At the entrance, we stood agog at the sea of pandemonium.

Korozoth had brought every Familiar he could. The gray fog shapes of his riders, the black ravens of On-Tez, even the skinless warriors of R'hlem—they all descended out of the sky. We were at the mercy of the Ancients.

29

PEOPLE HAD COME OUTSIDE THEIR HOUSES TO VIEW the commotion. Now they raced back inside, only to have the monsters follow them, smashing windows and bashing down doors. The creatures flew through the air carrying lit torches, chattering as they set fire to building after building. Familiars snatched people from the ground. A woman in a nightdress rushed past us just as a raven swooped down, gripped her, and soared up into the air. The beast's talons ripped through the flimsy cloth, and the woman fell thirty feet. Her end was horrible.

Saving Rook had been just, but these people were dying because of what I'd done. I hated myself. I hated Palehook for engineering this hideous situation. In a small, guilty part of my soul, I hated Mickelmas, too.

"Get ready to run," Magnus said, clapping Rook on the shoulder as he coughed. There was no sign of the others. We had no time to search for them. "Don't look back." We pushed forward on our own.

Sorcerers descended out of thin air in a flurry of black silk.

Some staggered about, still drunk from the ball. They made formations and created a wall of wind that drove the Familiars back.

Flames licked up the sides of walls; smoke poured out of windows. People collapsed into the street and were butchered. We stopped to send streams of water toward the fire, but the job was beyond us.

"This is my fault," I whispered. Magnus grabbed my hand and squeezed it tight.

We hadn't gotten far from St. Paul's when Gwen descended out of the air before us and leaped from her mount. She rolled back her smoke hood and slithered toward us on a carpet of fog.

"He wants you," she said, focusing her sewn eyes upon me. "It is the greatest honor. He has chosen you specifically."

"Stay back," Magnus grunted. Rook groaned and fell to his knees. The rider gestured to her stag.

"You're to come with me."

Now that I knew who she was, I couldn't attack her. I held up my hand, and she stilled.

"I know your name," I said. "Please, I don't want to fight you." I brought Porridge down slowly. Her nostrils flared. "You can turn away from all this."

"Um, Howel?" Magnus said, pulling Rook to his feet. "What are you doing?"

Gwen kept listening. Desperate, I pushed on.

"It's so lonely for me, being the only one," I said. She tilted her head to the side. She appeared to understand what I meant. "Maybe it was that way for you, too. We're alike. I can help you, if you'll let me. We can help each other."

She licked her lips. It was a slow, thoughtful movement. Finally, she said, her voice low and normal, "We can be alike." She held out her hand, smiling. "You must come with me before the bloody king. He will make us alike."

There was no hope. I blasted at her with the wind, knocking her down. When I tried to rush by, she leaped to her feet.

"Little lady sorcerer," she rasped, snaking toward me. "He wants you alive. He said alive, not intact." She swung at me. I dodged and called fire into my stave, slashing it through the air. Snarling, she leaped toward me with a raised dagger.

A blast of wind caught her off balance. Master Agrippa strode into view, his stave held out before him.

"Let her go." He stopped a few feet from the Familiar, his face broken in sadness. "Gwen, just let them go."

"Gwen?" Magnus said, eyes wide. "Gwendolyn Agrippa?"

"Run, all of you," Agrippa said as he blocked his daughter's thrust and forced her backward. Gwendolyn mounted her stag, hissing. "Gwen, please stop. Even now, it may not be too late," Agrippa cried. "You remember me. I know that you do. Please, my love. Don't leave me again."

She relaxed her dagger and murmured, "Father?"

Crying out in joy, Agrippa walked toward his child. In a move as fast and deadly as a snake striking, Gwendolyn grabbed for Agrippa's arm. He stumbled to the ground, breaking her grip. Undeterred, she dug her long fingernails into his leg, rising with her mount into the air.

"Stop!" I shouted, grabbing on to Agrippa, firing at Gwendolyn as she rose higher into the sky. Agrippa's hand began to slip from mine. "Hold on," I said as Magnus tried to ward him out of her grasp. Despite our efforts, we were losing.

"Henrietta, let go," Agrippa said.

"No." Frantic, I placed Porridge at our joined hands and murmured a quick spell I'd learned from Mickelmas. Our grip fused; it would be near impossible to break now.

"Why?" he shouted, bewildered. "Why help me?"

Because despite his betrayal, I could never really turn my back on him. My heels lifted off the ground. I struggled not to panic.

Agrippa shut his eyes and created a warded blade. "Please forgive me," he cried. I realized what he was about to do.

"No!" I screamed. He brought the blade down and was gone, moaning as Gwendolyn flew away with him. I fell to the ground, landing on my back. He'd cut himself off at the wrist, the quickest way he could see to relinquish me.

I broke the spell, dropped his hand, and stood as Magnus stared into the sky. "We could have saved him," he said, looking pale and sick. "Why would he do that?"

"To protect us." Agrippa was gone. He was my betrayer, the man who'd saved my life, who'd conspired with Palehook to discredit me, who'd played chess with me before the fire. My last real words to him had been hateful ones, and my vision blurred with tears. *Please forgive me,* he'd said. Why hadn't I done it?

"Howel!" Lambe and Wolff ran out of the fog. Swallowing my grief, we gathered by the side of a building and warded ourselves. Lambe inspected Rook, who was still falling in and out of consciousness. "He's not going to last much longer. Palehook took too much of his energy."

"What can we do?"

"Fenswick's at the house. Go there." Three of the ravens came out of the sky and dove for us. They slammed against the warded walls and screeched as they flew back up.

"I've never seen an attack like this. There aren't enough sorcerers in the city for the Familiars *and* Korozoth. Wolff, can you get the ward back up?" Magnus said.

"Impossible. Palehook is dead. We don't know the spell he used to consume Rook's life force, and even if we had it, we probably couldn't use it. And even if we could, we wouldn't," Wolff muttered. "The only thing I can think of at this point is to kill Korozoth." We waited for Magnus to stop laughing. "Most of the Familiars are his. Without him, they'd be like a colony of ants without a queen."

"It's impossible," Magnus said.

I had an idea, a wild and stupid one. "There might be a way to destroy him. Get the rest of the boys and find us. Do you know where Korozoth is?"

"He's coming from the west," Wolff said. "He should be leaving the river by now."

"First we need to deliver Rook to Fenswick back at the house. Then we'll all go off to face him together."

"Yes, but what will we do?" Lambe said.

"Something you've tried before. It failed, but with me it might work."

"You should leave," Magnus said as Lambe and Wolff ran to get the others. He placed his hand on my back. "This is the perfect time to escape."

"I can't leave, not now." Ahead of us, we spied an empty wagon with a horse harnessed in, the beast struggling to loose itself from the post where it had been tied. Magnus freed the creature while Rook and I settled into the back. Magnus jumped into the driver's seat and took the reins, and we were off, fighting our way through the chaos. We continued into a cleared area, away from the attacks.

But people started running in the opposite direction from where we were headed. To the left of us, the streetlamps all guttered out. The blackness and silence became oppressive. . . .

"Turn right!" I screamed as Korozoth swept into the square, quiet as shadow and fog when it wanted to be. The horse sensed the monster's approach and reared, pawing at the air before falling over in terror. The wagon snapped and the bottom fell, throwing Rook and me to the ground.

Rook screamed and turned his face up to the monstrous thing. Korozoth stopped, perhaps sensing one of its "children" crying out to it.

I pulled Rook to the ground, wrestling him into submission.

It wasn't difficult. He gasped and wheezed. He couldn't continue like this much longer. Magnus leaped from the driver's seat and flew into the air.

"Howel, get out of here," he called. Where could I go? It wouldn't be possible for Rook to drag himself much farther. Footsteps sounded and Blackwood appeared out of the night, the rest of the boys behind him. He pulled me to my feet and checked to see if I was hurt, then examined Rook. While the others assembled, he activated his stave.

"What's your plan?" Blackwood asked.

"I have to get Rook home first."

"There's no time for that now. We have to attack here, or we'll all die."

"Make a formation, me at the center. We can manage with six. Using my fire, build a net and bind him. It may be strong enough. Magnus, come back down!"

"I'm a touch busy at the moment," he shouted. Blackwood organized the boys while Magnus returned to earth, dodging Korozoth. We stepped into formation.

The fire rippled on my skin. The others spun their staves together, weaving a great net. I felt the energy flowing from me and into them. It was a strange sensation, like someone stealing the air from my lungs. Once everyone had a light, we spread out. Porridge grew warmer in my hand the faster I spun. Finally, we ran forward and propelled our great net of flame. It arched upward, so impossibly high that it went over Korozoth's head and pinned him to the earth. The enormous fiend bellowed and thrashed, tentacles straining against the fire. We all ran to different sides, keeping the beast down.

"I think we've got him," Dee yelled, waving to me.

But with the sound of snapping wood, the monster burst through the net, its tentacles waving and its hideous shadow mouth open in a triumphant call. We rushed to regroup.

"It's too strong," Blackwood said grimly. "It can't be stopped."

A tentacle came out of the darkness and nearly slammed on top of me. Magnus pulled us to the side.

"Are you all right?" he shouted.

"Yes. We have to turn back." We tried to protect one another as we moved down the street.

"I'm not running," Magnus said, warding a blade as the tentacle began to slither away. With a great cry, he leaped into the air and brought the blade down, severing the thing. Half of it went flopping along the street like a landed eel. Korozoth screamed as foul black fluid erupted out of its stump, coating Magnus, who, blinded, tried to get away. Another tentacle walloped him off to one side. He rolled a few times and lay there.

"Let me go," I shouted as Blackwood wrapped an arm around my waist. Korozoth moved toward Magnus, prepared to absorb him.

Rook appeared beside me. He bled and sweated so badly that his clothes clung to his body. His eyes were black, but I could see that he was in control.

Cupping my face in his hand, he whispered, "All will be well, Nettie." His breathing was a slow wheeze.

"Stay here," I gasped, clutching at him. He stumbled toward the monster with his arms above his head, calling in that terrible, screeching voice. Korozoth stopped a mere foot from Magnus and paused, as if determining the best course of action.

Rook called the shadow to him.

Korozoth bellowed in surprise as Rook began to summon wisps and tendrils of its own body. Cloaked in the monster's darkness, he yanked at the beast. Korozoth turned away from us, inch by inch. Rook was actually pulling it after him. He dodged the tentacles twice. His luck couldn't last, though. With a grumbling cry, the monster finally struck him down and held him while he thrashed and screamed. Blackwood put a hand to my mouth to stop my shrieking; I bit at him in an attempt to free myself.

Finally, the monster released Rook. He lay on the ground like a broken toy, his arms and legs at strange angles. He wasn't moving. I screamed as Korozoth inched toward him, fighting free from Blackwood.

I grabbed Wolff's arm. "If I give you a light, can you manage the rest of the net?"

"What? Yes, of course."

I ran, my heartbeat loud in my ears. I had to turn the monster, keep it from consuming Rook and Magnus. I created a column of wind and rose high into the air in front of Korozoth. With a shot of blue flame at eye level, the beast noticed me. I brought myself back to the ground as fast as possible. A tentacle landed beside me as I touched down. Frantic, I summoned up

Mickelmas's duplication spell, and a moment later, there were *four* of me stationed around Korozoth, every one of them—of me—brandishing a stave. As I moved, my copies moved.

Mystified, Korozoth struck down a duplicate, and I saw my chance. Taking a deep breath, I forced myself to race toward the thing. It rose above me, a wall of black smoke. I warded myself as I ran. If this didn't work, I would die.

I didn't even think. I just screamed.

Blackwood shouted my name, and his voice was the last sound I heard as I ran straight into Korozoth and blackness overtook me.

30

THE DARKNESS WAS ABSOLUTE. I PICKED MY WAY down the stairs slowly, trying to keep the candle flame from guttering. "Hello?" I whispered, shivering. My nightgown wouldn't keep out the chill. I might have a cold tomorrow, and Mr. Colegrind would never allow me a day in bed. I frowned as I came down the final step. The darkness felt closer than usual.

"Who is it?" a little voice whispered. A small blond boy squatted at the back of the cellar, among the bags of potatoes for tomorrow's peeling. He sat wrapped in an old shirt, his hair damp and his black eyes bright with fever.

"What's your name?" I put the candle down, tucked my hair behind my ear, and crouched beside the boy.

"I don't know."

"You must have some idea."

He shook his head. "Can't remember nothing." He trembled in pain, rubbing his left arm.

"I'm Nettie Howel. They say you got scars all over. Can I see?" The boy pulled at the neck and sleeves of his shirt to let me glimpse the horror of the pulsing sores. Mr. Colegrind said girls shouldn't take an interest in such gruesome sights, but I couldn't help my curiosity. The boy whimpered as something moved inside the cellar. "Don't be scared. It's probably a mouse, or maybe a rook. They get trapped down here all the time. I got something for you."

"What?" He hugged his knees. Feeling sorry for him, I held out a small cup.

"Miss Morris said this would be good. It's black pepper, mustard seed, and mint leaf, to cool the fever. Mr. Colegrind told her she should let God do what he must. I snuck into the kitchen to get it." Proud as only an eight-year-old could be, I gave it to the boy and coaxed him past the spice and bitterness. As he drank and sighed in relief, the darkness around us seemed to become less oppressive. When he opened his eyes, I could see I'd been wrong. His eyes weren't black, but blue.

"Thank you, Miss Howel."

"You don't have to call me that. Just Nettie." I rocked back on my heels, studying him. "You sure you don't have a name?"

"No. Maybe you could give me one, Nettie." We talked for two hours, trying to imagine a proper name. I wanted Edgar or Fitzwilliam or Nebuchadnezzar. He wanted something else. But I stayed with the boy in the darkness until his fever lessened.

I STOOD IN THE BLACKNESS AND listened to my ragged breathing. I wasn't dead. Not yet. I blinked the remnants of the vision away. Korozoth had such a skill with illusion that apparently entering him allowed the victim a perfect re-creation of a past memory. I wasn't sure why I'd glimpsed that childhood moment with

Rook. Perhaps it was down to chance, nothing more. Perhaps Korozoth sensed which memories were most precious to me.

There was a sharp pain in my heart. Rook couldn't be dead.

Voices swirled around me. I lit myself on fire and looked about. Now inside the monster, I could dimly see that it was a great funnel of a cloud, not solid fog all the way through. Forcing myself to be calm, I constructed another column of wind.

I rose higher and higher, my fire illuminating the undersides of tentacles. All the while, faces appeared and disappeared within the shadowy folds of the monster, mournful, pale faces that morphed in and out of existence. There was a man with a gray beard, who cried and vanished. Here was a young woman, weeping and wailing. Charley sobbed until her image was pulled back into the shadow. The higher I climbed, the more I could hear the whimpers and the cries of those who had been absorbed. If my ward failed, I would join them.

Master Agrippa appeared before me in the blackness.

"Henrietta, why did you let it take me?" he groaned.

He reached out to me with two perfect hands. This was a trick, one of Korozoth's illusions. Still, seeing his image brought tears to my eyes.

"I'm sorry," I whispered, and continued on. Mr. Colegrind came out of the darkness, trying to touch me with spidery fingers.

"How dare you escape me?" he hissed. I passed him. Mickelmas appeared this time, swirling his coat and pulling at his beard.

"You made a bad choice," I called to Korozoth, my voice almost lost in the torrent of wind. "He doesn't frighten me." As if acknowledging the mistake, Mickelmas disappeared and was replaced by Aunt Agnes. I knew that long face, that pale brown hair, and those darkly accusing eyes the moment I saw them.

"You were a horrid child," she said, her voice a hollow whisper. "That's why I sent you away. No one in their right mind could love you." It felt like a hot needle pierced straight into my heart.

"That's not true," I whispered, inching backward in fear. "I have friends."

"The magician who lied to you? The sorcerer who wanted you dead? The boy who saw you only as a plaything?" I felt myself weaken as I was sucked deeper into the black cloud. She stretched out her hands to touch me . . . and why not? Wasn't she correct?

No. Hargrove had helped me, Magnus had come back for me, and there was Rook. There had always been Rook.

"You're a liar!" I shouted. I scanned my surroundings, searching for the perfect opportunity to put my plan into action. How strange that this hadn't been more difficult. No tentacles attempted to grab me. It felt almost as if Korozoth were granting me safe passage. I found that unsettling as I flew higher and higher. . . .

I stood in a blindingly white room. There were no windows, no furniture. Where in God's name was I? I was no longer inside Korozoth. When I turned around, I came face to face with R'hlem the Skinless Man.

He was as hideous as he had been in my dreams, the pulsing blue veins and arteries strung along his arms, the taut stretches of bloodied muscle that bunched or released with his movement, and that burning, ugly yellow eye at the center of his forehead.

I shied away, pressing my back against the wall. The monster moved toward me.

"My dear child," R'hlem said, his voice disturbingly human, "how tired you must be of all this fighting." He stroked his bloody chin with his raw fingers.

"Where am I?" I whispered.

"My faithful Korozoth's finest illusion, stronger than any dream. It gives us space to talk." He reached out a hand and stroked my cheek. Retching, I pulled away from him and wiped at my face. "I want you to come with me, my dear. Your abilities are interesting, particularly the fire. Where did you learn such a skill?"

"I won't go anywhere with you." I touched the walls, pressed against them. R'hlem laughed at me.

"You've a fine inner strength. Falling out of that window to escape me was impressive. You show far greater resilience than the last girl the sorcerers honored. She gave in to my dreams so quickly. Embarrassing, really." I stopped and stared at him. Gwen. He'd destroyed her body and her soul, and now he dared to be contemptuous of her. "I'd hoped she'd be a trophy for me, but in the end I unloaded her onto Korozoth. But you."

"Stay away from me."

"After careful evaluation, I've decided to offer you a place by my side. I want to assign you to my elite service of Familiars." His voice was soothing, despite his hideous appearance. "I want to train you for great power."

They said R'hlem kept only a few personal servants. They also said he tore off their skin to make them like him.

"No." I tried to run, but he blocked me.

"You must accept. You won't survive this without agreeing to my offer." He reached out that bloody hand to me.

"Nothing could compel me to join you." He herded me into a corner of the room. I was trapped.

"The ward has shattered." He smiled, a particularly hideous sight. "Korozoth has you now, secure inside himself. He can take you back to me this instant. He can leave your city in peace. If you surrender, he will go. If you do not, he will level every building, every home. He will devour as many people as he can stomach, and his appetite is tremendous. His Familiars shall decimate the sorcerers. If you do not surrender, everyone you know will die." He took me by the neck and choked me. I gasped, tried to pull his arm away. He studied me with his great, lidless eye. "Does that compel you?"

"No." I got some pleasure out of the look of irritation that crossed his face.

"The city will be gone by morning."

"They won't let that happen." I barely got the words out, wincing as his grip tightened.

"Your sorcerers? A collection of boys playing with wind and rain?" He saw that I wouldn't give in. "What's your name, child? Before I end your life, I'd like to know." He squeezed tighter and tighter, and dark spots exploded in my vision.

I was going to die. Part of me wanted to give in to him, to let it end quickly.

The logical part noted that if R'hlem could touch and harm me, perhaps I could do the same to him.

"What is your name?" he said again. I motioned that I could not speak. He loosened his hold.

I drew a ragged breath and said, "Henrietta Howel." With a thought, Porridge sprouted a blade. "Goodbye."

I struck for his heart, but I hit empty air. I was back inside Korozoth, and falling. Screaming, I grabbed for Porridge with both hands. There was an instant where I could feel the stave hurtling just out of my grasp, which would end with my death on the ground. But I snatched Porridge, and the wind returned, buoying me upward.

Why had R'hlem let me go? Perhaps he couldn't truly kill me in an illusion and had returned me abruptly to Korozoth to let me fall to my death.

Never mind. It was time to put my plan into action. I hung in the void, my breath coming fast. What if this didn't work?

All I could think of was Rook, Rook striking Magnus when he thought I'd been insulted. Rook sitting with me on the moor, the wind blowing his fair hair, a smile on his face to be out of Brimthorn. Rook leaning toward me in the kitchen, our lips almost touching. Rook lying there, dead. If I failed, his sacrifice would be for nothing.

Moving fast, I un-warded the protective shield about myself. With a sob, I exploded into flame, catching the fog around me on fire. Flames rippled on my skin, whirled about me, and turned scarlet. As I moved within Korozoth, up and down, the fire spread. The beast roared as it transformed into a flaming vortex. I could hear the groaning and whirling of a great wind, and realized with horror that we must be taking off.

The monster returned to the earth with an unceremonious thump. My friends had done it, used the fire to fashion a net and bind him, burning, to the ground.

The flames billowed and rose to such a scorching degree that the world became consumed in brilliant white. I burned so hot that I believed I was beginning to die. I felt Korozoth's death release and heard the cries of thousands of voices, the ghosts freed at last. When the monster disappeared and the flames vanished, I could see the stars above me.

I dropped headfirst for the ground, too tired to fly. Arms caught me, and Magnus eased us both to the street on a cushion of air. He laid me across his lap and cradled my face.

"Howel? It's done. He's dead. He's actually dead. Sweetheart, it's done." He stroked my cheek.

"Where is he?" I croaked. I broke from Magnus's grasp and crawled to Rook, who lay still on the ground. He wasn't breathing. "Rook," I whispered. His image was blurred. The smoke from the fire had damaged my eyes.

"You did it! Howel, you did it! Look, my God, it's wonderful," Dee called, his face stained with soot. People began to rush into the square and gape at the ash and embers floating out of the sky, all that remained of Korozoth. I bent my head, clutched Rook against my chest, and cried.

31

"YOU'VE SAVED US, HENRIETTA." FENSWICK STOOD ON my bedside table and saw to a cut above my eye. The little hobgoblin spoke with affection. "Your queen will be pleased. They tell me she survived." I winced as Fenswick pressed a stinging, wet cloth to my head. It didn't much matter, of course. Rook was dead. I wanted to go to sleep and stay asleep.

"The gossip among the servants has it that your queen will want to put the sorcerers more on the front lines now. What a difference that will make." Fenswick made an irritated sound when I didn't respond. "There's no need to lie there like a fish, you know. You're not *that* badly hurt."

"I will be once the soldiers come to take me back to the tower. The queen ordered my execution."

Fenswick huffed. "Not this again. Do you really think you'd have been in this bed the past two hours if the queen thought you dangerous? Her Majesty took advice from the wrong people." He dried my face. "No one will hurt you now."

My vision blurred with tears. "They might as well kill me. I let Rook die."

"What?" Fenswick's right ear twitched and bobbed. "No, he's alive. I've told you already."

"What?" I grabbed the unfortunate hobgoblin by the shoulders and lifted him from the table. "How? Where is he?"

"Unhand me! I suppose I can't blame you, you were half blind and raving when Magnus carried you back here. Hopefully, this time you'll remember what I've said. Ow! Stop squeezing!"

"How could he be alive?" I gasped.

"Rook teetered on the edge between life and death. I merely saw to it that he tipped over the correct way." Fenswick proudly flapped his ears.

"Where is he?"

"Resting in Blackwood's room. Do you think you can remember all this information? If you give me a moment to put my kit away, I can take you there."

I tossed Fenswick onto the bed, threw the blanket off my legs, and stumbled for the door while he yelled at me to come back and carry him. Tripping twice, I checked every door along the boys' corridor until I found a room with a fire in the hearth and Rook propped up in a canopied bed, his arms and chest bandaged. Lilly dozed in a chair. When I said Rook's name, his eyes opened. Oh God, he was alive.

"Don't crush me, Nettie." He laughed as I crossed the room and fell onto the bed beside him. "I'm not beyond the reach of death."

"Are you all right?" I touched his hand. His breathing sounded shallow and strained, but at least he *was* breathing.

"I've some new scars."

I buried my face in his shoulder. He stroked my hair.

"I'm so glad you're all right, miss," Lilly said when I'd composed myself enough to sit up. She grasped my hand. When she let go, her fingers were all sooty. "Oh dear. I'll get the young gentlemen." She wiped her hand on her apron as she left the room.

"You saved me," I said.

"We saved each other. Always have." He smiled. It was him, just as he'd always been. No, not quite. The more I looked, the more I realized something was different, though I could not tell . . .

The boys entered to embrace me and gather around the bed. Magnus and Blackwood stood by Rook's side, talking with him. Wolff and Dee each shook my hand before moving to pay their respects to Rook as well. They were all smiles and acceptance. I sat down, my knees weak with relief.

"Very well done," Lambe said. He stood before me and placed his hand on my hair, almost like a blessing. "You were brave."

"Thank you."

"Just take care about the woman." His eyes got that glazed, half-asleep look. "She got out of the fire. You must keep her away from the wood." He patted my head and went to join the group.

Another vision. Sighing, I rubbed my eyes. It could wait till tomorrow.

I felt a pull at my skirt. Fenswick, huffing and puffing, motioned me out the door. Embarrassed for having forgotten him, I carried him into the hallway.

"Henrietta, I need to tell you something," he said when we were alone. "It's about Rook's scars."

"Yes, he has new ones from the battle."

"Well, that's just it. They seem to be overpowering him." The hobgoblin stroked one of his ears and stared down at it, not meeting my eyes.

"How do you mean?" I asked, careful.

Fenswick sighed. "I've known what his powers are for some time. For both your sakes, I've held my tongue, but now they're getting worse."

"You're wrong. Rook was in control. He battled Korozoth, for heaven's sake!"

"Rook taking control doesn't mean what you wish it did, not according to my examinations. He's learned to master a certain amount of power. Additional scars will mean additional strength. The more he takes control, the more he changes."

"Changes?" My voice sounded hollow.

"There are subtle differences now, in the eyes, in the ears. So long as he was safe in Yorkshire and his powers lay dormant, he was mostly a normal boy. He is in a state of transformation now, becoming less human."

"No." I put my hand on the wall to steady myself. I hadn't come so far, pulled both of us through so much, for this. "Korozoth's dead. He can't hurt Rook anymore."

"Hmm." Fenswick tucked all four of his hands behind his back. "We know that sorcerers may bestow powers upon their chosen human servants. Who's to say the Ancients can't do the same?"

Was that the purpose of the Unclean? If they were receptacles of power . . . *His abilities lay dormant. He's transforming. I brought him here. I forced him to come.* "We're going to help him." I clenched my jaw.

"It's beyond all my medicine," Fenswick said. He patted my hand. "I think it would be kindness to, well . . ."

"End it?" As though Rook were some rabid animal to be taken into the yard and shot. I grabbed hold of his paw. "You and I will work together. I don't care what it takes, we're going to stop this transformation. No one else can know."

"You're asking me to put us all in danger."

"I'm asking you not to give up on him so soon," I said, my voice shaking with desperation.

Fenswick considered this, removing himself from my grasp. "He's a good boy. I would hate to destroy him. But if he cannot be brought back," he warned, "if his suffering grows too great, I'll tell the Order, and they will end his pain."

"Agreed," I whispered. "But first we try." I wanted to fall to my knees. Not this. Not more pain, and not now. "I wonder if you might clear the boys out, doctor. I'd like to stay with him awhile."

"Naturally." Fenswick waddled in, yelling, and a moment later shepherded everyone from the room. Lambe carried him out, petting his right ear.

Rook seemed so small in the bed. Alone, I sat beside him again.

"Are you well, Nettie?" He smiled. He didn't know. He wouldn't know.

"Yes." I sounded strange, even to myself.

Rook said, in a more subdued tone, "When I'm healed, I plan to leave this place."

I startled. "What? Why?"

"You don't need me. You've great new work to do, and . . . new friends. I'll hold you back. I can find work—"

"You have to stay with me, Rook. Please." Tears spilled down my cheeks.

"It's not proper."

"Who's to say what is proper? I already live outside of society's good opinion. How much more damage can this possibly do?"

He laughed. It looked as if he wanted to agree, but then he said, "You have Mr. Magnus—"

"Magnus means nothing to me, not in that way." My voice almost failed. "You are the most important person in my life, and you've always been. Please don't ever leave." He placed my hand over his chest, so that I could feel his heart, a soft and steady beat against my palm.

"I won't go if you don't want me to."

Not tonight, not tomorrow, not a year or twenty or fifty years from now. My shoulders shook. Why should love be so painful?

"You know I'd hate to ever leave your side," I said.

"As you wish, Henrietta," he murmured. I leaned my forehead against his. His breath caught, and we drew nearer . . . until the darkness at the corners of the room began to close in around us. Instinctively, I flinched. The shadows vanished. "I'm sorry," he sighed. "It always seems to get in the way."

"Yes." I wore a false smile. In his eyes, I recognized the change I'd noted before. The irises were pure black. No blue at all. *There are subtle differences now, in the eyes. . . .*

Someone cleared his throat. Magnus watched from the doorway. "They sent me to tell you there's a messenger. The queen has summoned you. It doesn't look dangerous." He appeared to have heard everything. I didn't care about that. At least, I couldn't. Not anymore.

"Thank you. I'd like to wash up, but afterward I'll go directly." I squeezed Rook's hand and left the room, brushing past Magnus on my way out the door. A moment later, I heard his footsteps behind me. He looked determined.

"What is it?"

"Howel, you don't understand—"

"Yes, I do. You came back for me when most others would have left me to rot. You're my dear friend, as you'll always be." I emphasized the word *friend*. I held out my hand to him, praying it remained steady. "I hope you'll invite me to your wedding. I want you to be the brother I never had."

I already regretted this. That didn't make it any less right.

He stared at my hand for a moment, as if he didn't know what on earth it was. Slowly, he took and kissed it. "I'd be honored to be that close to you, Howel."

"Thank you," I said. He held on for too long. Then he kissed my hand again. That tingling warmth spread throughout my body. I wanted . . .

No. This had to stop. I tried to politely slip away, but he held on. There was a determined look in his eyes.

"I can't," he whispered. "I can't let you go."

"You will." I yanked out of his grasp. "Or we won't see each other again." I walked off, feeling sick to the core of my being. If he felt half as awful as I in that moment, he was sorry enough.

THERE WAS NO FANFARE, ONLY A servant who led me down dark halls to a large room. My heart was pounding despite my best efforts to remain calm. After all, if the queen wanted me dead, she wouldn't have allowed me to have Blackwood and Fenswick as escorts, though they'd been instructed to remain in the front parlor. I just hoped I'd got all the soot off me.

I was shown into a small receiving chamber. On the far side of the room, Queen Victoria sat in a chair before the fireplace, her dog in her lap. She looked very small and young now that she had removed her jewels. She smiled when I entered.

"Sit, Miss Howel." I did. "We . . . that is, I know what you've done tonight."

"I'm glad that I was able to stop Korozoth, Your Majesty."

"Lord Blackwood came to see me straight after the fighting and explained how the ward happened to fall." Would she now blame me for the trouble in the first place? "It grieves me that Master Palehook could have abused my people and my trust so shamefully." She stroked her little dog's head. "Even if I could replenish the ward, I would not."

"So Your Majesty isn't angry?" I twisted my hands in my lap.

"No. I'm pleased, both with the destruction of one of the great Seven, and what I've learned of your people."

"My people?" The sorcerers? The magicians? I felt no surge of belonging to either.

"The sorcerers have been left to their own devices long enough. They behave as if they are sorcerers first and Englishmen second."

"They're not my people, Majesty. My father was a magician with a talent for fire. Howard Mickelmas did teach me how to pass for a sorcerer. I was prepared to accept your commendation and lie to everyone."

"Your confession is good to hear, Miss Howel." Now the guards would arrest me. "Your honesty makes a strong case for your integrity. I need that on the front lines."

"Even if I'm not the prophesied one?"

"I'm not sure I ever had tremendous faith in that idea," she said, raising an eyebrow.

"But I'm not a sorcerer."

"You use a stave. You employed many sorcerers' techniques in Korozoth's destruction, so they tell me."

"Hargrove—that is, Mickelmas—told me that I was a cross between the two races. Magicians are descended from sorcerers, after all. I belong nowhere."

"Then it seems you may choose your own path," the queen

said. What a strange and heavenly idea. "But I warn you that you have an irrevocable decision to make. I recognize you were born a magician and may need to control those aspects of yourself, but if you become a sorcerer, you must turn your back on a magician's label and life."

My mouth went dry. "You'll commend me as a sorcerer, Majesty?"

"If you wish. It will come with the privileges of that rank, but the responsibilities as well." She drew herself up by every royal inch. "I mean to send us on the attack. We will retake Canterbury from the Vulture Lady, we will destroy Nemneris and preserve our coasts, and we will march through the midlands and the north until we come to R'hlem himself. And we will finish him, before this war drags on further into its second decade." I could hardly contain my astonishment—or delight—at her words. "You will be a part of my plans, should you choose this path."

"Are you certain this is a wise decision?" God, what was I saying, challenging the queen? She smiled.

"My advisors are against it, but they were led astray by Master Palehook, and even old Agrippa." Sadness tinged his name; she could believe it no more than I. "They tend to look suspiciously on any woman who dares to challenge their authority." The edge in her voice couldn't be mistaken. Perhaps she understood my situation better than I imagined. "I feel we must try what has not yet been attempted, and you have given us the first clear hope of defeating these monsters in eleven years. Now, Miss Howel, have you made your decision?"

What did I want for myself?

As a magician, there would be the possibility of learning more about my past, about my father. But my work would be outlawed, and my influence in this war would be less. As a sorcerer, I would be on the front lines, but I would look behind every step of the way, in case an enemy from my own camp planted a knife in my back.

But I had friends now. And above all, I had to help Rook. There was only one path that would allow me to stop his transformation.

"I choose to become a sorcerer, if Your Majesty wills it."

"Kneel."

I did as commanded. "Your Majesty. I am your humble servant. I seek your royal commendation to take up arms against England's foes, and to defend Your Majesty's life with my own."

She placed a delicate hand on my hair. "I grant my commendation, Henrietta Howel, that you will take up arms in my defense, that you will live and die for my country and my person, and that your magic shall find its greatest purpose in the service of others. Rise and be known." I stood again and towered over the queen. Tiny as she was, I bowed my head to her as my leader.

"Thank you, Your Majesty."

She smiled. "In time, I believe I will have you to thank, Miss Howel. We will all have you to thank."

32

TEN DAYS LATER, NOT TOO LONG AFTER MY MORE public commendation before the court and the Order, I wandered Agrippa's garden, trying to grab a moment's peace. There had been many parties and celebrations lately, what with Korozoth's destruction, but I couldn't enjoy any of them. The Queen was taking more of an interest in sorcerer affairs. And I was responsible. People who had claimed to be my allies snubbed me. I often felt alone when I went out in public.

There was one friend, however, I could always rely upon. "Howel, wait," Blackwood called as he came over to me. I smiled to hear my plain surname from his lips at last.

"So I am a sorcerer now, my lord?"

"Yes. You may as well start calling me Blackwood. No need to stand on ceremony." He proceeded with me about the grounds, stopping to admire the red roses in bloom. He plucked one and handed it to me. "Your seal, sorcerer Howel."

"It would have to be on fire to be truly mine." I laughed. My official house sigil was a burning rose. I liked it, though Eliza had been upset by the lack of unicorns.

"Have you any plans for where you'll go now?" Blackwood asked. "Master Agrippa's house will be closed soon."

"I had planned on receiving my orders and going from there."

"You can take orders while living with me. If that suits you?" he asked, with a quick glance. "I know you don't have any money of your own. Eliza would love another lady in the house. Rook would come, too, of course."

"Thank you for keeping silent about him," I said. "I swear you won't regret it."

"I protect my friends."

I smiled and took his arm. My dear friend, Lord Blackwood. Two months ago those words would have been impossible. "I accept. Where will the others go?" I thought of Magnus for a moment and hastened to quash the thought.

"Most of them will stay with their families. Wolff will rent rooms. Still, no one should get too comfortable. They say we'll be deployed to Cornwall before the month is out. Nemneris is our primary concern now that Korozoth is dead."

"I hope I prove equal to the task."

"Do you think you won't?" He stopped, surprised.

"Blackwood." It felt strange to say his name. "I was born a magician. I'm still a woman doing men's work. Suppose it is too much for me? Suppose I do go mad, like Gwendolyn Agrippa?"

"Women aren't the only ones who can be swayed by dark choices," he said. "You are stronger than you can imagine. I see it. In time, you'll see it, too."

We would have continued our walk, but Lilly stopped us as she ran out into the garden.

"Miss Howel! There's something you ought to see!" She half dragged me into the house. "It's in your room. I was packing up odds and ends, and there it was. Oh, miss, I daren't go near it."

There on my bed sat Mickelmas's wooden chest. "How did it get here?" I whispered.

"I'm sure I don't know, miss. It appeared right out of thin air. It started—ah, there it is again!" Lilly cried as the chest rocked back and forth on its own, bouncing atop the bed.

Blackwood tried to open it but couldn't. "I should blast the thing," he muttered, removing his stave.

"Wait." I brushed him aside and laid my hand on the chest. It stilled beneath my touch. I knocked once, just to see what would happen, and the lid swung open. Inside, we found a single plain, folded piece of paper.

"What on earth does it say?" Blackwood asked as I took up the note. Written in an elegant, spidery hand were these words:

Never what you want,
ever what you need.
Until we meet again.
—M.

"It's from Mickelmas." So he was alive. I sighed in relief. "But it's a magician's box. I can't keep it." I threw the note into the chest and slammed the lid.

"Perhaps you should," Blackwood murmured. "Normally I'd say caution is a virtue, but we need to know why it's come to you."

"What if someone sees?"

"No one has to know about it except the three of us." Blackwood turned to Lilly. "What if I asked you to come into service at my house as Miss Howel's lady's maid?"

He wanted to keep her near. For my part, I would be glad of another friend.

"Yes, m'lord. I'd like that ever so," Lilly said.

"You won't speak of this to anyone?"

"Speak of what?" She batted her eyelashes in innocence.

"Nothing." Blackwood smiled. "You can pack Miss Howel's things later." Lilly left, and we returned to staring at the chest. "We'll keep it with us until we decide what's to be done." It was odd and touching to hear him so involved in my affairs.

"You're putting yourself in danger, you know."

"These are dangerous times. Speaking of, I need you to help me choose a new headmaster for Brimthorn. I hear the old one is untrustworthy."

"I might have one or two recommendations." I laughed. He helped me slide the chest beneath the bed. "Thank you for everything you've done."

"I told you that I would always give my allegiance to the prophesied one," Blackwood said as we left the room.

"I'm not the one." There was still relief in saying it. "You know that."

"Well, as I said, we need you. The rest is titles. How important is a title, really?"

"Not important at all," I said.

We turned back out to the garden, to enjoy the last of the July afternoon's sun. We would have to hurry. Night was coming, and there were traces of a storm on the wind.

ACKNOWLEDGMENTS

This is the single most daunting task I've faced during this process. Not only do I have to be short and succinct, which won't happen, but I have to adequately thank all the incredible people who've made this possible.

Chelsea Eberly, for believing in this book, and for making it the best that it could be. Your suggestions challenge me to do better, and your questions lead me to the most exciting ideas. It's sometimes embarrassing to think you understand these characters better than I do, but it's always thrilling.

Brooks Sherman, for being an extraordinary agent and the first to see potential in this story. Thank you for guiding me through the insanity, and for not hanging up on our first phone call when I made weird noises and had no questions. You're a gentleman and a scholar, and sometimes Batman.

Thank you to the wonderful people at Random House, including Mary McCue, Hannah Black, Melissa Zar, and Mallory Matney, for so much hard work and energy. Massive thanks to Nicole de las Heras, Hilts, and Tracy Heydweiller for the sensational cover design and packaging. Setting things on fire never looked so good.

Thank you to Jenny Bent, Molly Ker Hawn, and the incredible team at the Bent Agency for all your help and insight.

Brandie Coonis, yin to my yang, Spock to my Kirk, Pike to my Cole. The best friendships are a perfect balancing act. Thank you for your sharp eyes and sharper wit. More wine, Doris.

Alyssa Wong, for your creativity, your courage, your compassion, and Catbug. We'll always have the Skinny Emo Space Lords. Yes, that's in print now.

Isabel Yap, for writerly wisdom, grace, and sending me pictures of sad anime boys.

My cohorts from the Clarion Writers' Workshop, who have become my second family. Team Rocketship Spatula forever. Thank you to Shelley Streeby, Karen Joy Fowler, and Kelly Link, who opened the door for me.

Thank you to Victoria Aveyard, Tamara Pierce, Sarah Rees Brennan, and Kelly Link (again) for being so gererous with your time and mad blurb skills.

Josh Ropiequet, for night drives, fancy dinners, and ten years of friendship. Ten more, please.

Jack Sullivan, who coined the phrase *Victorian Cthulu Harry Potter* to describe this book.

Ronen Kohn, Zev Valancy, Jessica Puller, Emily Crockett: Thank you for being in my life.

The Forbes-Karols (Robby, Terra, JoJo, Cory) and the Rosenblums (Mike, Alison, Jordan), for love and support.

The Sweet Sixteens and Class of 2K16, thank you for your community. Traci Chee, for bonding over scavenger hunts. Tara

Sim, for the transparent heads. Audrey Coulthurst, for crashing that party with me. Gretchen Schreiber, for singing along and bringing me ARCs.

Barnes & Noble at the Grove, for not minding that I was the world's worst barista. Special thanks to Amanda Santos, who read my query letter in the break room.

Patricia McGahan and Claire Hackett, for giving guidance and teaching lessons.

My parents, Joyce and Chris, and my sister, Meredith: Thank you for loving me, putting up with me, and encouraging me. It means more than you know. The rest of my family, Blanche, Margo, Angelo, Janet. Finally, for Mike Ozarchuk, who didn't get to see this, but who would have enjoyed the hell out of it. Love you more.

ABOUT THE AUTHOR

JESSICA CLUESS is a writer, a graduate of Northwestern University, and an unapologetic nerd. After college, she moved to Los Angeles, where she served coffee to the rich and famous while working on her first novel. When she's not writing books, she's an instructor at Writopia Lab, helping kids and teens tell their own stories. Visit her at jessicacluess.com and follow her on Twitter at @JessCluess.